DANNY ALLSUP

Danny Allsup

By
D. Dean Carroll

© Copyright 2023 by D. Dean Carroll – All rights reserved. It is not legal to reproduce, duplicate, or transmit any part of this document in either electronic means or printed format.

Danny Allsup

Chapter 1

"By gosh, I like it!" the hawk-nosed man exclaimed, gazing at his reflection in the mercantile window. He was admiring the coat, called a Duster, just purchased from the store. It was a loose-fitting, full-length coat with a short cape over the shoulders. It fit his slim frame long, almost down to his ankles and passed his wrists, but he didn't mind. He liked the way it looked and how the coat's tan color matched well with his newly acquired Stetson hat; its chinstrap dangled loosely around his chest. His cow-skin boots, which he was told would keep his feet dry, would take some breaking in. However, they pinched his toes and rubbed the back of his heels raw. He should have bought them earlier, but hadn't, and now he would have to endure their discomfort until his feet, or the boots, adapt to the new change. But he liked what he saw in the store window and imagined he looked the part of a traveler out west.

"Mr. Allsup? Is that you?" A heavy-set man walking towards him in a full gray suit called out as he approached.

"Why, yes, it is, Mr. Welch. It's me." He extended his hand in greeting.

"Why, what is this coat?" Mr. Welch inquired, examining the garment as he raised the cape off one shoulder.

"It's called a Duster."

"A Duster? Why, I ever heard of such a coat. Do you know that it appears unfinished in the back?" He was referring to a slit running up the back to the waist.

"Yes, yes, that's not an oversight, Mr. Welch, but an intended cut. It allows your legs to stay dry when mounted upon a horse. See?" He turned his side to show his meaning, then he continued, "each flap covers your legs, keeping them dry in the rain and protects your pants from being torn by thistles and shrubs when riding."

"I've never seen one," Mr. Welch admitted.

"Neither have I until this morning when I purchased it from Reynolds' Mercantile." He gestured towards the store with his head.

"I like that unusual hat, too. Did it come with the coat?" asked Welch.

"No, I acquired it several days ago from this same establishment."

"Well, most unusual, I must say, but I like the look."

"Thank you, so do I." Allsup was back admiring his ghost-like image in the window.

"If I may ask, Mr. Allsup, why did you decide upon such unusual apparel?"

"I'm leaving, Mr. Welch. I'm leaving Lebanon."

"Leaving! Why? Where do you plan to go?"

"I'm going off to see the Pacific."

"The…the ocean?"

"I know of nothing else that bears the name; one and the same, Mr. Welch, one and the same."

"But you were born here in Lebanon, Pennsylvania. You've lived here all your life."

"I know, I know, but with Nancy gone…" Allsup looked off in the distance before continuing, "we lost our two boys down south in the war, as you know, and well, I don't want to farm anymore, not without Nancy and the boys."

"I'd heard you sold the farm to McKinney if I'm right."

"Yes, Albert McKinney offered me a fair price, so I took it."

"So, you're off to see the ocean, are you?" Welch asked, his thumbs hanging from the small pockets of his vest.

"Yes, sir, I've always wanted to."

"Well, you do know there's one a lot closer, I trust." Welch pointed out jovially.

Allsup laughed and said, "I've seen that one. But it's not just the Pacific I want to see. That's just the destination. I'm curious to see everything between here and there."

"Well, that's quite an undertaking, Mr. Allsup; I admire your courage for taking it, especially at your age. To start all over in a distant land, knowing no one, well, I find it disconcerting, frightening even.

"How will you travel?" Welch inquired. I dare say, if you'd hold off your intent for a year or two, they may get that blasted railroad done! You could travel all the way by rail.

"I believe the connections have already been made. It's completed."

"Well, there you go then. Ride out on the rails."

"No, sir, I've got my mind made up on going by horse."

"Really? And have you selected an animal?"

"Yes, I have. See that chestnut stallion hitched across the way, standing solo?"

"I do, yes."

"I picked him up early this morning from Chub Johnson at the stables. A three-year-old mix that just wants to run and run, according to Chub."

"A handsome animal. You're not worried about it being difficult?"

"No, he'll have no reason to be. If he wants to run, I'm going to let him. I plan on his company for the duration of the trip; I want us to get along."

"Well, I'm sure I don't know about that," Welch commented. "It is just a horse."

"Well, that's just my outlook on things," Allsup explained, pausing from admiring his reflection to look at Welch. He thoughtfully added, "I find if you give respect, you'll get it back in turn; it applies to people, animals…most all living things."

"Well, I'm sure I don't know about that," Welch repeated, unconvinced. After a minute, he asked, "When will you be leaving, Mr. Allsup?"

"As soon as we say our goodbyes here and now."

"Oh, already?"

"Yes, I've got a bedroll strapped to the back of the saddle and two saddlebags containing a coffee pot, cup, pan, a fork and a couple of sharp knives, with enough hardtack and jerky to last about a week. I've got a Winchester Yellow Boy repeating rifle, a six-shot pistol and bullets for both, and I got me a horse over there that's as eager as I am to be on our way."

"Then I will keep you no longer. Will you ever be back this way again?"

"I like to think that I will someday, Mr. Welch, but realistically, no. I'll probably not make it to the Mississippi!"

"You'll be fine, I'm sure of it. Well, God protect you, Daniel Allsup," Welch said as they shook hands, "I hope you see the Pacific."

"God bless you and your family, Mr. Welch. Goodbye."

Chapter 2

"Does this road go west?" He received no response as the two passing riders chose to ignore his inquiry.

He'd traveled to the far western part of Lebanon where town merged into country and foot and cart traffic dwindled. There were still a few people in sight, a man walking ahead and a horse-drawn wagon following behind. Earlier, upon occasion, he'd pass someone going in the same direction and they'd converse. He would tell them of his mission as casually as possible so as not to appear a novice traveler, but eventually, his enthusiasm would get the better of him, and he would conclude his discourse excitedly. Most had their own stories to share, and after civil pleasantries and "Safe travels" or "God speed," they would move on.

"Does this road go west?" he asked again.

Eventually, he came to this fork in the road. It occurred to him that he could just randomly make a choice and let fate take him where it may, but he only had a week's worth of provisions, and it would probably be safer traveling with others, especially at night.

Why not follow the path of many? he reasoned. Surely there will be a benefit to my movement westward by following the same route as others.

"Does this road go west?"

He decided to give experience and knowledge a chance by asking the travelers who had made the choice before him. It confounded him that none chose to respond.

"Excuse me, sir." He rode up alongside a man on a buckboard wagon. "Excuse me! Can you tell me if this road goes west?" He did not successfully conceal his irritation.

The man on the buckboard pulled off to the side and stopped having noted the rudeness and curtness of tone from the stranger on horseback. A heavy-set man with suspenders wrapped around a protruding stomach, he turned sideways on the bench seat of the wagon, allowing his left leg the pleasure of resting stretched out. Hoisting a large clay jug from beneath the seat, he pulled out the cork and took several long swallows. Holding it out, he offered it to the rider.

"Water?" He sloshed the jug's contents.

"Thank you, no, I just want to—well, actually, I will have a swallow if the offer still stands." He rode up close to the wagon.

"Offer still stands, have your fill." The man passed the jug over to Allsup. "Don't have but a couple of hours before home."

The water from the jug was cool. Allsup thought it might possibly be the best water he'd ever had. Water from the well on the farm was refreshing, but this had something more, something better. It tasted better. Maybe it was the clay jug. He filled his mouth with water and held it just for a second before swallowing. He could feel the coolness making its way down into a grateful stomach.

After his third mouthful, he passed the water jug back, saying, "I thank you for your generosity."

"Glad to be able to offer," the wagon driver responded as he re-corked the jug and slid it back under his seat. Then he asked, "Now, what was it ya be wantin' to know?"

"I'm heading west and wanted to know which fork of the road would best get me there."

"Oh." The driver studied him, scratching his chin. "Which way is that?" He pointed westward.

"West," answered Allsup, his chestnut getting anxious to move on.

"Yep, and which direction are both'a those roads headin'?"

Allsup looked at the man on the wagon, trying to figure out his game. He looked over at the two roads and then back at the man before answering, "West."

"So, don't it seem reasonable to conclude that either road

will take ya west?"

"I'm trying to find the one that will take me *farthest* west. Do you catch my meaning?"

"I do indeed. Afraid I won't be of much use to ya there. I know the south fork runs 'bout three miles west, but that's 'bout all I know. I only know that cause my farm is 'bout three miles down that south fork."

"You've never been past your farm?"

"No reason to go further."

"What about the north fork? Any idea how far it goes?"

"Never been down the north fork, got no idea how far it runs."

"Oh."

"You're just gonna have to pick one, traveler. Put your faith in Providence," advised the driver, who, with a flick of the reins, started his wagon moving.

"I guess you're right," Allsup said to the departing wagon before immediately asking, "Hey! One more thing! How long have you lived around here?"

"All my life," the driver called over his shoulder.

"Hmm..." Allsup watched the wagon disappear down the south fork.

I think I'll take the north. I don't want to get stuck riding with him for three miles.

"All right, Chestnut," he said as they trotted down the north branch. "You been wanting to run, here ya go! Hee-ahh!" He gave the horse the slightest nudge with his heels, loosened the reins, and like a bullet, the horse was barreling down the road.

Allsup was frightened at first and attempted to steer the horse around the other travelers. They wove between carts and horseback riders; along the side of the road passing a line of four wagons hauling someone's belongings and got into a short race with three young riders looking for a story. The chestnut gave them one.

It didn't take long for him to grasp the fact that the horse was not responding to his directions; without knowing, they had been agreeing on common routes. Allsup realized the horse was choosing where it wanted to go, running fast and hard, and racing whom it wanted to race. He was just along for the ride. He could feel the horse stretch out taunt, muscles exploding with energy. The wind blew his hat off but was saved from lost by its chinstrap. He decided to just hang on and enjoy the ride to the sound of hooves rapidly pounding the hard ground.

So, they continued, swerving in and out and along the sides for miles. Allsup rode low over the horse's neck, hands clutching the saddle horn, trying to anticipate where the horse would go next. Where Allsup would have guided them was not usually the chestnut's choice, often resulting in a sudden move, jerking to one side or the other almost throwing him off. The horse's hooves against the hard-packed road and the occasional shouts. "Be careful!" or "Watch where you're going!" from those they sped past were all that Allsup could hear. The ride was frightening and exhilarating at the same time.

Gradually, the horse slowed to a canter, then a trot, and finally a walk. Lathered in sweat and breathing heavily, it now accepted his rider's guidance as various roads branching off to new directions offered choices and diminished traffic. Allsup and his chestnut kept to the main road as, one by one, their fellow travelers turned off and headed to locations elsewhere.

The day was getting long, and looking around, Allsup found that he was now the sole traveler on the road. He decided that it was time they found a place to stop. He had hoped to find a village or inn, but that appeared unlikely now. Trees surrounded them with branches forming canopies overhead leaving no clearing above, so as the afternoon grew later, their route grew darker.

Another rider approached from the opposite direction. Allsup called out a greeting,

"Afternoon, fellow traveler!"

"Howdy," the rider replied.

"How are you on this fine afternoon?"

"Fair-to-middlin'," answered the man without slowing his ride.

"By chance, is there a town or inn on the road ahead?" asked Allsup.

"If ya travel far enough, there be."

"How far would you hazard I'd have to go to find one?"

"Next town up ahead would be Hummelstown, where you'd find both."

"I know that town. Never been, but back in Lebanon, people have spoken of it."

"Lebanon, huh?" the stranger commented, before adding, "Never been."

"Hummelstown, how far is it?" They were side by side and while Allsup had stopped the chestnut to converse, the other rider had not, so while Allsup was pursuing his inquiry, the other man continued, "How far up ahead would Hummelstown be?"

"Two maybe three miles," the rider replied as he passed. Allsup twisted in his saddle, trying to maintain contact. The man rode up the dirt road without further comment; there were no cordial "goodbyes" or "safe travels," just the back of the man and horse disappearing around a bend.

"Don't know if I want to ride another two or three miles," Allsup said to his horse. He patted the chestnut as he said, "I'm not used to sitting astride a horse this long; I'm starting to feel a bit chafed."

He dismounted and led the horse into the woods, looking for a place to rest for the night. His long wool underwear stung the tender, irritated skin on his thighs with every step. A small distance in, he found a good size clearing, almost a field, and decided that was as good a place as any for their first night on the road.

He hobbled the horse's front legs with a rope before

removing the saddle, blanket and bridle. Once the horse was free of its tack, it was left to graze in the field.

Allsup had ventured into the woods in search of firewood when the sound of a creek caught his attention. He discovered that it wasn't more than fifty feet from their camp, so he went back, un-hobbled the horse, and brought it to the creek where both welcomed and drank their fill of the fresh, clear water. Allsup walked along the bank and found a small pool formed by a depression in the creek bed. He looked around and after assuring himself he was alone, took off his pants and cotton shirt and tucked his socks into his boots before wading out into the crisp cold water in his long underwear, sitting down in the pool.

"Whoa! That's cold!" he exclaimed as the water ran over his legs and up around his chest. "My balls may have disappeared, but my thighs are rejoicing!"

The chestnut watched for several minutes. After a time, the horse decided to try it as well and waded into the water. There the two remained, enjoying the cool creek, relaxing after their first day's travel. Allsup listened to the lapping water flowing along the creek, which served as an accompaniment to the songs of the different forest creatures sharing the same home. The early evening sunlight peeked through the leaves of the trees giving it at times an almost biblical likeness; the sun's rays illuminated different features of the forest before fading.

All was right with the world, Allsup pondered, the back of his head resting in the water, his eyes closed. He must have slept because upon opening his eyes, he realized dusk had set. His legs felt numb; he was shivering cold and had yet to start a fire!

Clumsily jumping to his waterlogged feet, he sloshed across the creek to the bank where he'd left his clothes. The horse remained standing in the water watching the man frantically pull his boots onto his wet feet. Grabbing his shirt, pants, and socks, he headed through the woods toward the campsite. Midway, he stopped, looked over his shoulder and turned back to the creek.

"Come on, horse!" he called out to the stallion standing in the creek, looking somberly at the man. "Come on!" he beckoned with his sock-filled hand. He once more commanded, "Come on!"

The horse didn't budge.

"All right, I'll come get you!" Irritated, he threw his clothes to the ground, pulled his boots off and waded into the creek. Taking him by the chin, Allsup led the horse, which followed obediently, to the creek bank. "Why'd I have to come get you if you were going to come anyway? You contrary animal!"

As soon as they made their way back through the woods and were at camp, he hobbled the horse and started a fire. It didn't take him long to dry, but his clothes took time. He was, however, dressed by dinner. Stretched out alongside the fire lying on his linseed-oiled canvass ground tarp, with stars high overhead and the sound of his chestnut stallion grazing not too far off, he dined on jerky, hardtack, and coffee that left considerable room for improvement.

He felt contented. He was finally on his way to see the Pacific. It wasn't just a thought this time to occupy his mind while plowing. He was really on his way. He slid down on the tarp, his head resting against his saddle, and let out a sigh as he relaxed. If this is how the rest of the trip was going to go, it was going to be a great experience.

D. Dean Carroll

Chapter 3

The morning dew was heavier than usual; small drops fell from the brim of his hat onto his nose and chin. He threw off the duster he'd used as a cover sending little pools of collected dew out onto the already drying ground. He sat up, his hat falling, and with his elbows resting on his raised knees, wiped the sleep from his eyes with the palms of his hands. He slowly rose to his feet and, with a loud, "Ahh!" stretched out as far as his arms and legs would go only to discover that his inner thighs and bottom were about as sore as he'd ever known. Sitting astride the horse all day yesterday reminded him of how little he traveled in that manner; he was used to a buckboard wagon to get from place to place. Taking baby steps, he tried to walk off the pain but realized his body needed to become acclimated to horseback riding, and until then, he was going to have to endure the discomfort.

Still, it was a beautiful day. He stood enjoying the break of morning just as the sun's rays streaked across the sky. A light fog still hung over the tree-tops whose inhabitants announced their greetings in their own way. A wisp of smoke still rose from the embers of last night's fire, and the coffee pot still sat at its side. He was about to pour a cup when he noted something amiss. He looked around the clearing but could see nothing, nothing!

"Where's the horse?" he wondered aloud as he painfully walked towards the clearing's center, looking for any indication of where it may have gone.

"Hey! Chestnut! Come here, horse!"

Seeing nothing, he stood at a loss, worrying about what he would do if he lost the horse; sure, he had enough to purchase another, but that would cut into his reserve. There will certainly be emergencies ahead that the money could help alleviate. Using a good portion of it now to replace a lost horse, on only his second day out, was not a thing he desired to do.

Taking small steps with the intention of causing as little pain as possible, he headed toward that part of the woods that led to the creek. Maybe the horse became thirsty during the night and went where it knew water could be found. About halfway into the woods, he saw chestnut. His hobble rope snagged on a broken, exposed root of a big oak tree. The horse calmly looked back at the approaching man, waiting as if he knew he'd eventually be rescued.

"You see the trouble you get yourself into when you wander off on your own?" Allsup scolded as he approached. He tried to free the horse from entanglement, but the rope was pulled taut and the knots around its ankles had become so tight that Allsup feared he might have to cut the rope to free the animal. He tried to coax the horse backward, possibly freeing the tether from the tree root, but the horse refused to comply. Out of frustration, Allsup pulled out his knife to cut the restraint. When the horse saw the knife, his eyes widened. He jerked his head away and took a step back which resulted in the desired effect: freeing the tether from the restraining root.

"There you go, boy! Did you think I was going to use the knife on you? You don't know me yet, do you, boy? Well, we don't know each other yet, do we?"

Now that the rope was free, Allsup was able to untie the tether and release the horse, which immediately headed for the creek and the desired water. Allsup followed, sitting down on the bank and waiting patiently as the chestnut waded through the water drinking its fill.

After a short time, the horse slowly made his way back to the bank and stood before the man.

"Did you get enough?" he asked as the animal lowered its head for attention. Allsup reached out and scratched behind its ears. "Did you get enough? Ready to get going?"

D. Dean Carroll

He rose from the creek's edge and began walking back to their camp. He didn't look to check on the horse this time; he just walked on through the woods. The horse watched and looked back at the creek before following.

Chapter 4

He took his time packing. After returning to the campsite with his horse, he sat and drank the remains of the lukewarm coffee. He forced himself to clean the coffee pot and cup at the creek while chewing on a bite of jerky. He moved slow and painfully, the muscles in his haunches cried out in agony with every step, yet the Pacific called, and he was determined to continue his quest.

When everything was secure and ready, when the chestnut stood still and waited, Allsup forced his leg up and his foot into the stirrup. Crying out in pain, he threw his leg over the saddle as gently as possible, lowering himself onto it.

"All right, horse, let's at least try for Hummelstown," he said as he gently prodded its sides with the heel of his boots. The chestnut, eager to be on its way again, lunged forward causing a sharp pain to shoot throughout Allsup's lower body.

"Ahh! whoa, whoa, whoa!" He reined the horse to an abrupt stop. "All right, all right," he whispered harshly, sitting astride the animal. Sighing, he declared, "You know what, Chestnut? The Pacific Ocean isn't going anywhere today, and neither are we; no point in being fanatical about it. It'll be there when we get there, and I'm thinking maybe we'll start tomorrow."

They returned to the campsite where the ashes still radiated heat. He pulled his bedroll down and freed the horse of its burden and restraints before collapsing down by the ashes to rest and falling into a deep sleep.

The bewildered horse looked at the resting man before turning and slowly walking towards the center of the clearing, grazing on the tall grass. A rabbit scurried away from the approaching animal while a mother quail followed by her covey used the same path to escape. Insects buzzed and chirped as the morning sun rose higher into the sky; birds flying overhead and in the surrounding trees sang their songs, argued and talked.

Daniel Allsup opened his eyes to the glare of the overhead sun. He sat up and noted his lower half didn't feel as painful as before. The chestnut, he saw, was standing at the edge of the clearing in the shade of nearby trees; he appeared to be sleeping. With a bit of awkwardness, Allsup managed to get to his feet and stretched. He decided he wanted more than jerky for lunch and would try to walk off his pain and hunt at the same time.

He crossed the clearing through the tall grass, a light breeze giving it the appearance of waves as the blades bent and swirled in unison with each gust. He found a path of flattened grass, indicating a larger animal had passed through recently, maybe a boar or deer. Encouraged, he followed the path to the north end of the clearing and into the woods where he lost the trail. While searching the general area for tracks, he came upon an apple tree with fully ripe fruits losing their hold on the branches and falling to the ground.

The apples weren't pretty, yellowish-green with patches of brown blemish. They didn't look particularly appetizing, but being as hungry as he was, he bit into one just plucked from the tree. Juice trickled down the sides of his mouth and dripped from his chin. He knew he was hungry, but he swore, hungry or not, he'd never tasted anything so sweet and delicious as that apple. He consumed it in a matter of minutes and eagerly started on a second.

It occurred to him that horses like apples and maybe Chestnut might like a treat, so he leaned his rifle against the tree and began gathering up fruit. He put one in each pocket, several in his hat and returned to the clearing where the horse was still standing at the other end of the field.

"Hey! Horse! Come here! I have something for you!

Danny Allsup

Come here, boy!"

The horse didn't move.

"Hey! Chestnut! Come here, boy!"

Allsup thought he saw the horse's head turn slightly in his direction but wasn't sure. This got him thinking: a horse should come if called. A well-trained horse should know a few commands just in case of an emergency. He ought to at least come when called and stop when told to do so. This appeared as good a time as any to educate the animal.

Allsup walked across the clearing toward the horse, who turned his head to acknowledge the approaching man. As he walked, Allsup cut an apple into four wedges and popped one into his mouth.

"Hey, Chestnut, look what I've got here for you." He offered a wedge on his hand held out flat. With a swish of his tail, the horse sniffed the apple slice before eating it. Obviously finding the apple as good as the man had, the horse took a step toward him, anxious for another.

"No, no, no," Allsup said, taking a step back while hiding the apple slices behind his back. The horse stood, confused.

Allsup took several more steps back, then extended his hand offering another wedge, and whistled, a sharp whistle quickly rising in pitch. The horse looked at the man, saw the apple, and sauntered over to consume it. When he'd finished that piece, Allsup walked back further and repeated the routine. Each time, he walked further and further away, and each time the horse would cover the distance to obtain the treat. Finally, Allsup walked to the opposite side of the clearing leaving the horse standing alone. He whistled without offering the incentive; immediately, the horse crossed the field to him. The reward this time was a stroke on the forehead and softly offered words of praise.

Allsup walked back to the campsite and sat down next to his saddle. He was pleased with how quickly the horse had learned the command. That was one smart animal, he marveled. Next, they'd work on stopping. He wasn't sure how he'd go about doing that but confident he would think of something.

He leaned back against the saddle, happy, as he started on his third apple. Yes, sir, he was feeling better; he'd almost forgotten about his sore backside. He'd be on his way again tomorrow. The fruit had appeased his appetite, so all in all, he was feeling quite content.

Something was nagging him, though. There was something he was forgetting, something he was supposed to do, but...He slid down to take a nap using the saddle as a pillow and smiled as he closed his eyes. He could hear the passing traffic from the road on the other side of the stand of trees closest to the campsite. Someone was herding cattle; they were whooping and whistling them along. Two people called out greetings as they passed and stopped to talk for a while; Allsup could hear their voices but couldn't make out what was said. It sounded like a lone rider was on the road; he sounded angry, loudly shouting profanities. If he was with another, they were never heard to respond. A rifle fired off in the distance; a hunter getting dinner, he imagined.

Dinner. What was he going to do about dinner? Allsup contemplated this as he tried to sleep. He didn't want jerky. He decided later he'd get the rifle and try to find something to eat.

Then it hit him: The Rifle!

He was up and running across the field as fast as his sore legs would take him. He ran into the woods and found the apple tree but no rifle. He searched the area; it was nowhere to be found. He had left it leaning against the apple tree, but it wasn't there. There was no other place he could have left it. Someone had taken it.

With a great deal of disappointment, he emerged from the trees into the clearing and walked back towards the campsite. The idea that someone had his gun and could be watching him was troubling. He stopped in the middle of the field and looked around its perimeter, not expecting to see anything, but maybe...

Retrieving his pistol from the campsite, he ventured into the woods, looking for food.

Chapter 5

The squirrel looked smaller, impaled on the stick suspended over the fire. Allsup had hoped for a rabbit, but he was no good with a pistol on a moving target. As it was, he felt lucky it only took four shots to hit the squirrel. He could hear the fire searing the meat and the smell of it cooking played with his hunger. He reclined against his saddle and slowly turned the stick holding his dinner.

Losing the rifle spoiled his mood. It wasn't so much that now he'd have to purchase another, but that someone else had his weapon, someone that could be watching him at that very minute.

What a coincidence, he thought, that a person would pass by that spot at that time and find my rifle. What a coincidence! Well, I hope it serves them well and betters their lives; possibly good would come from the theft.

A squirrel leg pulled free easily from the charred carcass indicating his meat was ready. As he sat eating the leg, careful not to burn himself as it was still hot, he considered his options and decided he basically had two: he could stay in the clearing for another night or move on at least as far as Hummelstown. He felt sure he could ride again, and only a couple of miles would help break him in.

Also, he wasn't sure he'd be able to rest easy staying here knowing that someone had his rifle and might be waiting for the opportunity to use it resulting in several possible outcomes, none ending to Allsup's benefit. He glanced around at the thought of someone coming up on him, but only the horse standing in the shadow of the trees could be seen. He wondered how many eyes amongst those trees were watching him. That settled it; they'd be moving on, at least as far as Hummelstown.

Chapter 6

Mounted on his horse, Daniel Allsup rode into the borough of Hummelstown in the late afternoon. He noted two church steeples rising higher than the few surrounding buildings, a couple of saloons, a mercantile, a livery stable with a smithy outside working his forge, and a small building with a sign attached to its front facial boards identifying it as a hotel. It was to this plain-faced building with a window on either side of the door that he turned his horse.

Entering the hotel, he found himself alone in what appeared to be a parlor. He stood waiting, looking at the two pictures hanging on a wall. One illustrated Jesus on the cross; the other was a ghastly picture of a man forcibly having a tooth extracted as he was held in a chair by three men while a fourth held him down with a knee on his chest and pliers in his mouth. He walked over for a closer look when he heard an approach from another room.

"May I help you, sir?" a woman asked. A gray-haired woman who looked as if she'd led a hard life. Her face was wrinkled and weathered to brown leather, and she walked stooped and tired.

"Yes, please. I'm looking for a room for the night."

"I am Mrs. Jansen. I will be glad to assist you with that. How many people?" She asked as she walked to a small table along a wall.

"It will just be me."

"Just one…Well, we currently have all three rooms available at this time. Do you have a preference as to your room's location?"

"Location?"

"Yes, sir. Would you prefer a room with morning sun, afternoon sun, or perhaps one that is completely enclosed?"

"Oh, I see. Completely enclosed, does that mean there

are no windows?"

"Yes, sir, some prefer complete darkness regardless of the time of day."

"I see. So, the only access to the room is through the door."

"Yes, sir."

"I don't think I like that. I think I'd like the Morning Room, please."

"Certainly, if you'll just sign our registry, I'll show you to your room."

"How much will that be?" he inquired.

"It's fifty cents per night for the room with the morning sun."

"Does that include meals?"

"No, sir, but the Hummelstown Tavern right down the street serves five-cent meals with their beers."

"Oh, all right. If I may ask, how much is the room with the afternoon sun?"

"The Afternoon Room is fifty cents per night."

"And the room with no windows?"

"Fifty cents."

"I'll stay with the Morning Room, if you please."

"Certainly, Mr..." She looked at his signature in the registry then said, "Mr. Allsup. That's payment in advance."

Allsup counted out fifty cents and handed it to the proprietor, who pocketed the coins and handed him a room key.

"If you'd like to get your belongings. I'll show you to your room."

"I just have a couple of small bags. I'll bring them in later. If you'll show me to my room now, I will be grateful."

"As you wish." She led him down a short hallway and stopped at the first door on their left. "This will be your room." She motioned with her hand towards the door.

Using the key, he unlocked the door and stepped inside, followed by the woman. There was a single bed along one wall, with a washstand and a chair along the other. Opposite the door, and at the end of the room, was a window facing the side of another building not three feet away.

"This is the morning sun room?" he asked skeptically.

"Yes, sir, it faces east."

"How does morning sunlight get past the building?"

"Oh, at this time of year, usually around eleven, when the sun's elevation allows the morning light to shine between the two buildings. If your head is resting upon the pillow at its corner there, it'll shine directly on you, and I guarantee it'll wake you from your slumber."

"Ah, I see." He looked around the room and noted two oil lamps, one mounted on the wall by the washbasin and the other on the wall by the head of the bed. There was a single picture hanging on the wall by the washstand. Upon closer scrutiny, he discovered it was of a man having his leg amputated with a crowd of spectators observing the procedure.

"Quite unusual pictures you have hanging on your walls." He noted.

"I find them fascinating," she answered flatly.

"Where does one obtain such pictures?"

"I found them in a medical book left in a room. I removed the more interesting ones and had them framed."

"You have a framer here in Hummelstown?"

"No, no, I had Mr. Baker, the undertaker, construct them for me. He's very good with wood."

"Ah, I see."

"Will there be anything else?"

"No, no, thank you. I think I'll bring in my belongings and tend to my horse. I noticed a stable just down the street; would you recommend I quarter him there?"

"As it's the only one in town, I would. Pete's a good man. He'll take good care of your animal."

The general store was just a vacant lot down from the hotel; on his walk from depositing his horse at the livery

D. Dean Carroll

Allsup stepped in and bought a new rifle, another Winchester Yellow Boy, the only one in stock.

"It's quite the coincidence that you would have the rifle I desire," he happily told the store clerk.

"The only rifle in stock!" the clerk cheerfully noted. Happy to have made the sale."

"I can take it out back and try it?"

"You can, but I gotta warn you they have a strict policy about firing weapons in the town."

"I leave town tomorrow. I'm reluctant to go with a weapon I've not fired."

"Well, sir, I'd say it's your call." The clerk stood with his arms crossed.

"May I have a shell?"

"You may, sir." The clerk pulled out a half-filled box of bullets and handed two to his customer.

Taking the bullets, Allsup loaded one into the rifle chamber and retained the other in his hand.

"Would you be kind enough to inform me when there's a break in the traffic?" he asked.

"I will," the clerk responded and walked to the storefront to look out the window.

Allsup quickly walked to the back of the store, vacated the building through the back door, leaving it open, and waited.

"Well?" he shouted.

"Now!" cried the clerk, and Allsup raised the rifle, targeted a thin pine and fired.

A flock of blackbirds rose from the tree, loudly voicing their anger at being disturbed. Allsup blew out the barrel as he returned to the store.

"Well?" asked the clerk.

"I'm pleased. Thank you, sir." Allsup walked out the front door. As he stepped out onto the packed-dirt street, two men with badges pinned to their coats came running up.

"Sir!" said one as they stopped to catch their breath with

hands resting on their knees. "Did you hear gunshots?"

"I did, but it came from down there." Allsup pointed toward a church. "I'm sure of it."

"Right, let's go!" One officer said to the other and off they went while Allsup sought out the Hummelstown Tavern.

The tavern's outside appearance was almost identical to the hotel, but inside it was completely different. A long bar ran along one wall while the rest of the room was filled with tables and chairs. In the back was an upright piano not being played.

Allsup took a chair at a table towards the back of the room and sat down. As he waited, he looked over the other patrons in the tavern, of which there were five. A couple sat together towards the entrance, an elderly-looking man with a full gray beard sat solo at a table nearby, and two men stood at different ends of the bar drinking. The elderly man nodded a greeting; Allsup returned the gesture.

The bartender came in through a door from the back carrying a heavy box. Upon seeing Allsup, he called out, "Hey, Dory! Ya got someone out front!" When Dory failed to materialize, he called out again, "Dory! Ya got a customer out front!"

"All right! All right! For sweet Jesus' sake! Gimme a minute, would ya?" Dory came in from a side door, wiping his hands on a dirty white apron. He wore no shirt. A carpet of curly hair ran down his chest and covered a large protruding belly. The only thing covering his upper body was the suspenders holding his pants up high around his waist. He had short brown hair and a matching mustache; his body was dripping with sweat from his head down to the waist of his damp-stained pants. He used the bottom of his apron to wipe his forehead as he approached Allsup.

"Afternoon," he said as he reached the table.

"Hello," answered Allsup.

"What can I get you?"

"Well, I'd like a beer, first off, please, and then something for dinner."

"All right."

"What do you have to offer in the way of a meal?"

"We got beef steak with tators 'n what I call wild game stew."

"Wild game stew? What does that consist of?"

"Well, ya got your basic stew ingredients: tators, onions, carrots, salt 'n pepper, 'n wild game a'course."

"What sort of wild game?"

"Whatever they could git this mornin'; probably rabbit, squirrel, some snake maybe. I don't know. They throw anythin' they kill into the pot. It ain't bad! It's fresher than the beef steak. I can tell ya that."

"The beef steak isn't fresh?"

"Hell, mister, I ain't even sure its beef," Dory confessed. Sometimes an old horse will turn up missin' 'n we're servin' beef steak again. Sometimes they put it into the stew, 'n I don't call it wild game stew no more."

"I'll have the wild game stew, please."

"Be back in a jiffy with the beer." Dory wiped his face again on the hem of his apron as he walked away.

"New rifle, I see," said the elderly man sitting nearby. He was referring to Allsup's gun lying across the table.

"Yes, sir, I've just acquired it from the nearby store not ten minutes ago."

"I thought I heard'a gunshot. Well, Johnny's gonna have to order another, I'll warrant," the man noted.

"Yes, sir, he said it was the last of his inventory."

"Haven't seen ya round here before."

"No, sir, I'm just passing through."

"Where ya from?" the elderly man asked as Dory delivered a dripping glass of beer to Allsup's table.

Allsup thanked the waiter with a nod of his head before answering, "Over Lebanon way."

"Lebanon? I ain't been to Lebanon before. How far away

Danny Allsup

is Lebanon?"

"A little more than a day's ride, I'd say."

"They don't sell rifles in Lebanon?"

"They do. As a matter of fact, I'd just purchased one yesterday before leaving. It was stolen."

"Stolen? Between here and there ya lost your rifle?"

"I did. I spent the night in a clearing just a mile or two from here. I found an apple tree with the best-tasting apples on it, and I rested the gun against the tree while I gathered up about a dozen. My thoughts were distracted, and I forgot it for a spell. When I returned to retrieve it, it was gone."

"No chance ya just forgot what tree ya leaned it on?"

"No."

"Ah, times is changin', that's all I gotta say, times is changin'. I can remember when I was a boy and there was almost nobody livin' in these parts. Hummelstown was 'bout half this size. Hell, there was still a few natives living round here. You'd see one upon occasion."

"Really?"

"Yes, sir. I remember a time. I was mebbe fourteen or so. I kilt a small boar amongst the trees over yonder by Swatara Creek. It was'a pretty good size hog and I strung it up to drain and gut before tryin' to haul it back, lighten the load if ya catch my meanin'."

"I do."

"While I was a'waitin' for it to empty out, I hap to look up and there was two natives, one with arrow and bow, the other with a spear; they was out huntin' too, 'I 'spect. Anyways, they skeered me, I can tell ya that. I stepped away from the hog and indicated they could have it if that's what they be wantin', but no, the one with the spear shook his head and made a sign with his hands they wanted to pass by. I sort'a bowed my head and waved my hand that they was free to do so. That was somethin' alright. Could be natives that took your gun, but not likely."

Allsup sat drinking his beer; the old man sat quietly,

perhaps remembering earlier times.

"What brings ya to Hummelstown?" the man asked.

"I'm traveling through."

"Where ya bound for?"

"My mind is set on seeing the Pacific Ocean. That's my intention."

"Ya tryin' to sell me a lame horse?" the man skeptically asked.

"No, sir, I'm not. It's been on my mind for some time."

"Huh…and so you're doin' it."

"Yes, that is my intention."

"Ya travelin' alone?"

"I am, yes."

"And ya like it?"

"Well, you do encounter others on the road and sometimes we talk, but usually it's just me and Chestnut, my horse. I don't mind."

"Seems to me it'd be profoundly more enjoyable with somebody else; to share the experience is my meanin'."

"I see your point, and perhaps if I make a return journey, I'll have companionship, but alas, this trip I make alone."

The waiter returned with the ordered bowl of wild game stew and a long loaf of bread carried under one sweaty arm. Allsup noticed a drop of sweat dangling at the end of the loaf and grimaced. The waiter set the bowl down before his customer, grabbed the loaf of bread and wiped it off on his pants before placing it alongside the bowl.

"Anything else?" he asked Allsup.

"Another beer if you would, please."

"Another beer."

The older man at the other table said, "I'll leave ya in peace to enjoy your meal. Pleasure talkin' with ya."

"Thank you, sir. I enjoyed the conversation; a good night to you."

Allsup wasn't sure he liked the looks of any of the ingredients in the stew; the color was bad, more greyish than beef and all the ingredients looked the same. He glanced around the tavern to see if anyone else was dining, but no one was eating. He looked over and noticed the old man at the other table watching him. Allsup smiled, nodded to the man, and pushed what he suspected to be a potato around in the bowl.

"It looks like shit, I know," the old man acknowledged with a grin, but it don't taste like it looks. It ain't bad. I had some a bit earlier and I'm still here

Again, Allsup smiled before lifting a spoonful of stew and emptying the contents into his apprehensive mouth. To his surprise, it was incredibly tasty! Maybe because he was hungry, but he was sopping up the bottom of the bowl with a chunk of bread and requesting seconds by the time the waiter returned with his beer.

D. Dean Carroll

Chapter 7

Chestnut ambled along the dirt road amongst a stream of others, all heading for Harrisburg, the state capital. He was restrained from dashing off again by Allsup, who held him in check. For his part, Allsup was in no mood to be jostled about by the horse; he'd awakened in the early morning hours with a bad case of diarrhea that continued to inconvenience him every twenty or thirty minutes. It was the stew, he knew it was the stew, but he partially blamed himself for consuming three bowls. Gluttony is a sin, and he was now paying for his.

He almost convinced himself to stay over in Hummelstown one more night, but his state of progress to the west coast was so minimal that it depressed him to consider not moving on that day. Putting the miles, and that stew, behind him, already made him feel better, even as he continued pulling off the road to answer nature's call.

He was told it was twenty miles to Harrisburg, so he'd be spending the night along the road. As he considered it, he shuddered at the thought of sleeping under the stars again. It wasn't that he was frightened or afraid. He was just uncomfortable with the idea of sleeping outside when there were so many other people traveling in the area. He decided as he walked out from the bushes, having taken care of bodily requirements, that there would be many more nights of sleeping out in the open; the sooner he accustomed himself to it, the better.

In the early afternoon, he became acquainted with a family also traveling west, but only as far as St. Louis. A man and his wife were riding upon an open buckboard wagon transporting all their worldly possessions. Their two young daughters sat at the back of the wagon with small thin legs dangling over the end, swinging with the motion of the wagon.

They were from Doylestown, the father informed Allsup, located in the eastern part of the state. Mrs. Marsha Robbins, wife to himself, Aaron, has a sister outside of St. Louis whose husband has a thriving business and urged them to come out and join them and take advantage of the opportunity. When Allsup inquired about the nature of her brother-in-law's business, Mrs. Robbins answered, "Dairy farming."

"He's got about twenty-five head of good dairy cattle on a farm just outside St. Louis," Aaron Robbins added. "Every drop of milk from those cows goes into the city. I declare he says they can't milk them fast enough! They are, if you'll excuse my pun." Mr. Robbin's eyes twinkled with merriment as he finished, "lapping it up! Ha ha! Do you get my jest?"

"He understands your pun, dear," amused, his wife informed him.

"Will you get your own farm?" Allsup asked.

"No, no, we plan on working with Marsha's family," Mr. Robbins answered. "The more people, the more cows can be milked, the more milk, the more money."

"I, myself, farmed in Lebanon," Allsup told them. "I had about twelve acres where I had a few head of cattle and grew corn, wheat, and tobacco."

"Couldn't make it work?" Mr. Robbins asked.

"No, no, for a while, it was profitable, but then I lost my two sons in the war, and last year my wife died from consumption, so...I lost interest and thought more and more about heading west."

The Robbins expressed their sympathies and for a time, they traveled in silence. The two girls were playing in the back, taking turns jumping off the moving wagon and climbing back onboard at the risk of falling and being left behind. Their laughter caused all three adults to turn and smile at their gaiety.

"What was your employment back in Doylestown?"

Allsup asked Robbins.

"I clerked at the mercantile and occasionally at the Downtown Tavern."

"Have you farmed before?"

"My father had a farm; grew corn and wheat. We had a couple of dairy cows, so I am familiar with the milking process."

"Didn't stay with your father, huh?"

"No, he passed. Got shot walking by the Downtown one afternoon."

"I'm sorry to hear that."

"Thanks. He was just walking by. Two men inside got into a quarrel and one pulled his pistol to make a point; the gun fired and struck my father in the side of his head, right above his ear."

"My goodness." Allsup shook his head.

"So, Momma sold the farm. I was eight and an only child; what else could she do? We moved into Doylestown, and she started sewing. Eventually, she remarried Jim Dover; they decided to move back to join his family in Binghamton, New York. I was sixteen and already working at the mercantile. I decided to stay."

"He was already trying to woo me by then," added his wife, smiling. "I might have had an influence on his decision."

One of the two girls fell while trying to climb back on the wagon and started crying.

"If either one of you falls and break'a leg, we're leaving you behind," Robbins shouted over his shoulder. "You hear?"

"Yes, Papa," they answered, even the one sniffling, tending to her scrapped knee.

Allsup looked back at the girls and smiled, remembering his own two sons at that age. Did they play like that? They must have, but he couldn't remember a time. Joshua was the eldest by just over a year, but George grew into the taller of the two. His memory of his sons consisted of their working the farm together and walking through the fields. Maybe it was because he learned of their loss at the same time they remained together in his mind.

They were taken at different engagements, at different locations far from home. By unforeseeable events, the notices of their deaths arrived the same day. If the letters had been delivered a month apart, weeks, or even a single day, perhaps Nancy could have handled it better, perhaps the light of life that burned within her would not have diminished so, but the soldier hand delivered both at the same time. It was not his fault. He must have realized on his ride to their farm that he carried tragic news made worse because it was doubled. As he rode up to their house on a red bay, searching for someone to help with his ominous task, Allsup watched him from the barn.

At first, he thought maybe it was one of the boys coming home, but as he became more certain that he did not know the man, his hopefulness turned to panic and he rushed to greet him before his wife, who'd just come out the front door wondering about the soldier who remained sitting on his mount. By the time he reached the two, Nancy clutched the two unopened envelopes tightly to her breast as if her refusal to read their contents would somehow deny their purpose.

Allsup turned his thoughts back to the road and his travels. Aaron Robbins was speaking, but his remembrance had prevented his hearing.

"What? Come again? I'm sorry, my mind was adrift." Allsup apologized.

"I was mentioning that I thought we'd soon find a place for the night. You're more than welcome to join us if you like."

Relieved that he wouldn't have to spend the night alone, he answered, "Thank you, I think I will."

D. Dean Carroll

Chapter 8

They stopped at the top of a rise located on the side of a much taller hill. They were overlooking a valley that stretched far between rolling tree-covered mountains. They could see for miles off in the distance; it was the view alone that convinced them to stay for the night.

A farm could be seen on the valley floor, a little cleared patch sliced from within the surrounding trees. There were no other signs of habitation: no roads, railroad tracks, or waterways.

"How do they make it?" Wondered Marsha Robbins before adding, "I'd be scared to be out like that all alone."

They were standing together admiring the valley. Mr and Mrs Robbins with their two daughters at their sides and Allsup with his unsaddled horse. Even after Allsup had removed the bridle, the horse continued to stay and look, seemingly appreciating the view as much as the humans.

The Robbins's two horses were hobbled and grazing on what they could find on the hillside. Allsup had assisted with unloading the necessities from their wagon and found himself a spot on the other side of what would become the campfire.

"Suppose I go look for firewood and maybe a couple of rabbits for dinner," Allsup suggested.

"Give me a second to get them settled in and we'll go together," answered Robbins.

While the father helped his wife with the necessary utensils and bedding for the evening, Allsup, followed by Chestnut, waded through the woods collecting firewood. When he returned with his load of kindling, he inquired if they'd like him to start the fire.

"That's kind of you," Mrs. Robbins told him sincerely, "but thank you, no. I've been buildin' and keepin' fires all my life; it's second nature to me now, like threadin' a needle or bakin' a pie. I'll get the fire goin'; you bring me back somethin' to cook on it."

"I'll do my best," Allsup said with a tip of his hat as he joined Aaron Robbins and headed toward the woods.

"What should I bring back for dinner, dear wife?" Robbins asked as they walked away.

"Don't be prideful!" she scolded, smiling. "Just bring somethin' back!"

The two men disappeared into the woods happily keeping a sharp eye for food. Allsup carried his rifle with the butt tucked under his shoulder and hanging loosely over his forearm while Robbins carried his military style, resting against his shoulder.

"How accurate is your rifle?" Robbins inquired as they entered a clearing.

"I don't know; haven't aimed at anything yet."

"No? You really should find its perks before you need it."

"I know, I know, but it was just purchased yesterday. I haven't had the opportunity."

"Want to try it now?"

"You don't think that might scare away our dinner?"

"It's your call," Robbins told him. "If you miss by a mile on your first attempt, it won't be much of a difference than taking a practice shot."

"If I miss by a mile," Allsup responded with a grin, "it'll probably be because I'm a poor shot."

"Hold it!" whispered Robbins, his hand held up. He pointed off in the distance towards a stand of sycamores. There were two rabbits crouched together, nibbling on green clover.

"See them?" he softly asked.

"I do," answered Allsup placing his rifle firmly against his shoulder.

"You taking the shot?"

"I was thinking of it, but maybe you should. If we collect three or four, then I can give it a try. No point in losing dinner because of my incompetence."

"How 'bout you take the first shot, and I'll be ready in case you miss and they try to scatter?"

"Sounds good," Allsup agreed, lining the rifle's sight on the rabbit. "I'm aiming for the one this side of us."

"All right, give me a countdown when you're ready."

The two stood side by side, rifles raised and ready. A breeze rustled the leaves in the nearby trees and surrounding grass. Allsup wiped sweat from his eyes. The chatter of birds and the buzz of insects filled the air.

"Well?" Robbins asked.

"Here we go, one…two…three." Both men fired. Robbins immediately after Allsup. Two rabbits went down; one still and lifeless, the other kicking its hind legs attempting to flee.

"Bully!" cried Robbins. "That was boss!"

"We got them both!" Allsup declared, slapping his companion on the back.

"Let's go collect them and try for at least one more on the way back," Robbins suggested.

"Right! At least we won't go hungry tonight."

"No, sir, we will not, but truth be told, I feel as if I could eat one by myself."

"Then we best find two more because I feel the same!"

"Two more it is, then," Robbins agreed as he stooped and picked up a hare by its ears.

Chapter 9

The two men walked through the underbrush, making their way back to camp. Each man carried his rifle in one hand and two rabbits by the ears in the other.

"Marsha's going to be proud of—" He was stopped mid-sentence by the screams of his two daughters. He dropped his rabbits and took off, tearing through the woods. Allsup scooped up the rest of their dinner and ran hard to catch up. He entered the clearing just after Robbins, who had stopped and was frantically searching for his family. He found them standing on the opposite side of their wagon.

What the two men saw, what the rest of the family had been watching, was Chestnut attempting to mount one of the Robbins's hobbled mares. The stallion nipped at the mare whose aversions to its advances were inhibited by the rope binding her front legs. When she tried to move away, he followed, making every effort to get behind her. His intentions were clearly displayed on a rather impressive scale.

"Oh, my!" Allsup exclaimed, embarrassed.

"What do we do?" inquired a befuddled Robbins.

"On the farm I let 'em finish; seemed wrong to interrupt."

"But what about my daughters?"

"Might be educational, Mr. Robbins. I'd suggest you take advantage of it. I propose the truth will be a lot less frightening than what their imaginations can come up with if it's not discussed."

"Maybe you're right," Robbins said gravely before an enlightened look crossed his face. With a happy expression, he declared, "I'll get Marsha to do it!"

Chapter 10

As night slowly pushed the light of day over the horizon, the Robbins family sat around the campfire with their guest, Danny Allsup, devouring three of the four rabbits acquired earlier that afternoon. The fourth remained on the spit over the fire. Mrs. Robbins had supplemented the meal with boiled potatoes and onions, and she still had half a loaf of bread she purchased while passing through Hummelstown.

"Help yourself to that last one if you've a mind to." Aaron Robbins gestured towards the cooking rabbit.

"If it was rabbit alone we were eating, I'd have no trouble, but the rest of the meal was outstanding, and I believe I've reached my capacity. Excellent vegetables, Mrs. Robbins, my compliments and gratitude."

"Well, I'm sure you are welcome, Mr. Allsup. It's amazing what a little salt and pepper can do."

"Tell me, sir," Robbins asked as he poured himself another cup of coffee, "are you bound to a schedule of any kind?"

"Schedule?"

"Yes, sir, I mean to ask, is there anywhere you have to be by a certain time?"

"No, no, my time is my own. I stop when I want, move on when inclined to."

"Well, then, if you will hear my proposal. Mrs. Robbins and I were talking and thought it might be nice and beneficial to us all if we travelled the rest of the way to St. Louis together. What do you think?"

"Your proposal has merit and sounds attractive. It was my intention to travel on my own, but as we would be parting in St. Louis, I can still do that. Allow me to consider it if you will."

"Aaron failed to mention that we will be staying in

Danny Allsup

Harrisburg for three or four days," Mrs. Robbins added. "I have a brother there that has asked us to spend time with him. Lord only knows when I might see him again."

"I see. Well, I will factor that information into my consideration and let you know."

"My goodness, it's dark already!" Mrs. Robbins exclaimed, rising. "Girls, it's time for bed! Say good night to your—"

Off in the distance, a gunshot sounded. Everyone grew quiet, listening.

"That was nothing, darlings," Robbins told his daughters reassuringly. "It was—"

Another shot interrupted his fatherly opinion. One of the daughters began crying against the leg of her mother who gently stroked her head.

"What do you think that is?" he asked Allsup, growing concerned.

"I think it's someone trying to scare off a bear or bobcat."

"You think so?" Mrs. Robbins asked.

"Sure, sure, and we have nothing to worry about because we have a fire!" Allsup pointed out a bit animatedly for the benefit of the two young girls.

"That's right!" added their father. "We're in the safest place we can be! Now you two get to bed. Mr. Allsup and I will sit right here to make sure everything's okay."

The two girls gave their father a hug and kissed him goodnight and bid the same to Allsup, who returned the sentiments. Their mother tucked them into their bedrolls under the wagon and then busied herself cleaning up after the meal.

"What do you think it was?" Aaron Robbins asked softly when just the two men were sitting by the fire.

"I don't know," Allsup answered while wondering, could it be my rifle?

D. Dean Carroll

Chapter 11

They had a short distance to travel from the campsite to Harrisburg, only four or five miles. The girls riding on the back of the wagon chatted, laughed, and teased each other for most of the distance. Allsup liked to listen to their banter. He didn't know if his sons played so when they were of the same age, but he thought probably not.

The Allsup home was a quiet home; there wasn't much laughing that he could recall, and he wondered why? Nancy and both the boys had liked to laugh. There was time a big bug dropped atop his birthday cake that Nancy baked just before the boys left, and when it landed on top of the cake, which she was carrying, she screamed and dropped it with a splat! Icing and cake scattered everywhere, and all three of her men waited to see her reaction. She couldn't help breaking into laughter, saying, "Cakes served, boys, have at it!" They laughed for the longest time over that cake, but he couldn't remember another time.

There was too much work to be done on the farm, he rationalized, and at the end of the day, they were all too tired to do anything but go to bed.

Ours was not a joyful home, he told himself, but it was a good home. He missed it now as he remembered the past; he missed those loved ones that were gone that made it a good home. He wondered if he'd ever feel that way again. His chest felt heavy as the realization came crawling up. He would not witness it again, ever. The faces, the smiles, the tears, the gentle memories, nothing.

The closer they came to the state capital, the more congested the road became. People like themselves just passing through, on their way to a place beyond the city ahead, people going in for business. They passed a man leading a cow towards town and many carts and wagons filled with vegetables, fruit, and other products to sell. A man with the biggest wagon Allsup had ever seen, pulled by a team of huge Clydesdales, lumbered towards their common destination stacked with cages filled with resigned chickens.

As they crested a hill, they could see the capital spread out before them. Church steeples rose above surrounding structures, and the capitol building itself pulled the eye to its domed façade supported by pillars. Amongst its archipelago of islands, the Susquehanna River was busy with traffic of its own: barges and steamboats carrying commerce and people up and down, back and forth; piers and docks lined the riverbanks on both sides.

The late morning sun illuminated, like a spotlight, all the activity within the city; people busy going to appointments and shopping; carts and wagons, some empty, some full, travelled up and down the streets. A long, enclosed wagon with windows pulled by two horses rolled down a street, stopping at every other corner. People waiting at the corners would board the wagon through its front while people having reached their destination emptied out through a door in the back.

"Look at that." Allsup pointed to the wagon. "What sort of wagon is that?"

"It's called a trolley," Mrs. Robbins informed him. They use it to carry people around the city, so they won't have to walk or tether a horse."

"What a clever idea! Has the idea spread to other cities?"

"Oh, yes," answered Mrs. Robbins. "I'm told all the major cities have them."

"Is Harrisburg a major city?" Mr. Robbins inquired.

"Well...I don't know," admitted his wife.

"It looks like a major city to me!" exclaimed Allsup. "They have trolleys!"

They paused like many others cresting the hill and seeing the state capital for the first time, but now they fell in with the sporadic line of travellers entering the city. The two young girls had been sitting up front with their parents taking in the view, but once they continued, they returned to the back where they could play without the scrutiny of their parents.

"Is this the first city you've seen?" Mrs. Robbins asked Allsup as he rode beside their wagon.

"Technically, no," he answered with a smile, remembering. "When I was a boy not much older than the two girls, my parents took our family to visit my uncle in Toms River, New Jersey. We had to pass through Philadelphia."

"What do you remember about it?" inquired Mr. Robbins.

"Mostly just its size," he answered. "We saw Independence Hall. I remember that. My father insisted that we see where the birth of our nation began. But what really made an impression on my young mind was all the people, it seemed so busy! I recall I worried that if my parents lost me there, they'd never be able to find me again. My parents couldn't figure out why I suddenly became clingy; if they weren't holding my hand, I was clutching my mother's dress or my father's coat."

They rode on in relative silence, except for the two girls riding in the back of the wagon talking and giggling and the occasional reprimand by Mr. Robbins scolding his team of horses.

"Did it appear this big?" Robbins asked, gesturing towards Harrisburg spread out before them.

"In my young mind, it was as big as the ocean!"

The talking subsided again as they concentrated on keeping with the flow of traffic that became more and more crowded as they neared their destination. People angrily shouted at one another as impatience grew the closer they came to the capital. Animals became more fidgety and short-tempered as they were clustered more together in the slow-moving traffic.

Allsup's mount, Chestnut, was becoming difficult and agitated for reasons at first unexplainable, resisting the commands of the reins and heel prodding.

"This confounded animal definitely has a poor attitude today," Allsup complained as he struggled to keep the animal abreast of the wagon. "I don't know what's gotten into him."

"Looks to me like he's behaving similar to yesterday with our mare," observed Robbins.

"I don't get your meaning."

"I'm suggesting that there's a good chance amongst all these animals there's a mare in heat."

"Oh…"

"What's in heat mean, mommy?" one of the girls inquired from the back of the wagon. The two parents looked at each other questioningly; the father smiled and said quietly to his wife, "She asked you."

"Mommy?" The little girl pursued.

"Well, dear, you know when you've been outside in the sun working too long and you can almost not stand how hot you are? That's being in heat." Mrs. Robbins looked at her husband hopefully.

"Oh," responded the daughter, evidently satisfied, and they continued without mentioning the topic again.

As they rode through Harrisburg's streets, they marveled at the people, the congestion, and the different shops and offices offering services. They passed a bakery with a huge, three-layered, ornamented cake in the window which caused the girls to squeal with delight that such wonderful things could exist in the world. Allsup made no comment, but the confectionery in the window enamored him as well.

"My lord, look at all the people," exclaimed Mrs. Robbins. "How do they feed them all?"

"The capitol building ahead is where we want to be heading," Mr. Robbins announced. "Marsha's brother said we should take State Street north from the building. It'll take us to Wren Street, which leads out to their farm."

As they came into the proximity of the state building, Mr. Robbins said, "Should be coming up anytime now."

"This is it." Allsup pointed out as they reached the intersection. "State Street."

"We'll turn here, then," instructed Mr. Robbins.

"Not me, I think," Allsup announced. Robbins pulled his team to a halt.

"You're not coming with us?" His voice betrayed his disappointment.

"No, I believe I'll continue on." He smiled regretfully. "I just feel I need to cover ground, let Chestnut here run a spell. I've got a sense of urgency, makes me inclined to want to keep moving."

After a pause, he added, "I've enjoyed making your acquaintance and having the Robbins family as travelling companions." He looked back at the girls and said, "and I mean that sincerely. I wish you all the best with your future plans."

"Thank you, sir," Mr. Robbins replied, extending his hand in farewell.

"God bless you, Mr. Allsup," Mrs. Robbins said with a wave of her hand.

"If you come back by way of St. Louis," her husband continued, "we'd appreciate it if you'd look us up if you have the time."

"If I do, I will," Allsup responded with a fingertip to his hat.

"Momma, I'm thirsty!" the little girl with the skinned knee called from the wagon as it turned the corner onto State Street, parting ways with the rider watching their departure. "It's hot. I think I'm going in heat back here!"

Chapter 12

He found a tavern west of the Pennsylvania state capital and, desiring a break from riding and to appease his appetite, decided to stop and partake of their offerings. The bar was deserted, but the seven tables were all occupied.

"It'll be a minute," a waiter advised as he passed with a tray laden with plates of food. On his return with the tray hanging by his side, he said, "Unless ya don't mind sharin' a table, that is. I got one over there that two are sharin' at this time and seem to be gettin' along well. I can't see how addin' one more would make a difference."

"I have no objection," Allsup told him. "In fact, I'd welcome the company."

"Come ahead, then." As he led Allsup through the tables, he asked, "What's your name, sir?"

"Allsup, Daniel Allsup."

"Gentlemen," the waiter said as he approached the two at the table. "This here is Danny Allsup, a lone diner like yourselves in search of good food and company. Might he join you?"

"He's welcome as far as I'm concerned," answered one holding a full cup of coffee.

"Can't guarantee the food or the company," replied the other. "It's a gamble for us all, but you are welcome to join us."

"Thank you both," Allsup said as he pulled out a chair. "It's actually, Daniel Allsup."

"Ain't nobody want to sit with a Daniel," the waiter whispered as he wiped off the tabletop before him. "What'll it be, Danny? We've got steak, bacon, and ham, and we'll throw in as many eggs as ya want. Course coffee's always available; milk is extra."

"Gentlemen, any recommendations?" asked Allsup.

"We're still waiting to determine that," answered the first man with a chuckle. "I ordered the steak."

"I selected the ham," added the other diner. "Always been partial towards a good cut'a ham."

"Then I'll try the bacon along with three eggs—fried, coffee and we'll see what's what," Allsup told the waiter who nodded as he left to turn in the order.

"Can't say I'd prefer ham over bacon or steak," commented the first diner. He was a rugged-looking man with long brown hair falling around his shoulders and a walrus-type mustache that completely concealed his mouth. His eyes twinkled, betraying his gruff appearance. A gentler, good-natured demeanor sat behind the facial façade.

The other guest at the table was a long, lean man dressed in a dark suit that was made lighter in appearance by accumulated dust. His ears were unusually small for a head his size and his short haircut emphasized that fact.

"I've always been partial to ham," he told the others. "It was the meat served on holidays and special occasions in my home as a boy growing up. I guess I order it now for sentimental reasons."

"There ain't no better reason that I can think of," replied the longhaired man. "Name's Holtman, John Holtman," he extended his hand to Allsup, "and our eatin' companion here," he indicated the man sitting across from him in the suit, "is Marcus Hill."

"I am grateful to you both for allowing me to join."

"Do you reside here in Harrisburg?" Hill inquired.

"No, I do not."

"Well, if I may ask for conversation's sake," he pursued, "and not to appear too forward or rude, but what brings you to our table, Danny?"

"It's Daniel, actually, and I welcome the opportunity to converse. I'm passing through."

"And where are ya headed?" Mr. Holtman joined in.

"West, to the Pacific." He once again felt a surge of pride

Danny Allsup

acknowledging his great endeavor.

"My word!" exclaimed Mr. Hill. "What prompts such an undertaking, and at your age?"

This only amused Allsup, and he happily explained the circumstances that led to where he was. They probed him with questions and made exclamations of amazement to many of his answers. They marveled mostly about his courage to take on such an enterprise—at his age.

During this exchange, the waiter arrived with their food placing each order correctly before each man.

"Are you two citizens of Harrisburg?" Allsup inquired as he cut into an egg.

"Not I," answered Holtman.

"Nor I," Hill told him.

There was general silence around the table as the three men began to consume their meals. After taking a sip of coffee, Allsup asked, "What brings you here?"

"I been sent down from Scranton," Holtman informed him. "I work at the steel mill there. The company's trying to get us to work more hours per shift and six full days. They won't negotiate. Hell, they won't discuss it! I been sent down to try to get the government to intervene."

"How's that going for you?" Hill inquired.

"Don't know yet. Today's my first day to make an attempt. I got an appointment to meet with a couple of representatives later. Hopefully, they'll lend a sympathetic ear."

"Who are you meeting with?" Hill asked before taking a bite of ham.

"Let me see," answered Holtman, digging into his pant's pocket and extracting a crumpled sheet of paper. "I got them wrote down right here: a Senator Stevens and Representative Hill."

Allsup looked up and over at their other table guest, who was looking at Holtman with a grin.

"Hill?" Holtman said questioningly before looking at the

smiling Representative and, with the realization, said, "Why, that be your name."

"Is that you?" Allsup asked.

"It is," Hill answered, laughing.

"You're a representative in government?" he asked.

"I am. I am a member of the Commonwealth of Pennsylvania's House of Representatives. I'm currently serving my third term."

"Well, you're the man I need to speak to then!" exclaimed Holtman.

"And I will be glad to listen to all that you have to say, sir, but not while we're eating. I prefer to separate business and pleasure, and I do consider my meals a pleasure, usually."

"I understand," Holtman told him. "We'll talk later. How is the ham, sir?"

"Quite good, thank you, and your steak?"

"Very good, sir, flavorful and tender. And you, sir?" he turned to Allsup. "How do you find the bacon?"

"It is bacon, Mr. Holtman," replied Allsup, smiling. "Unless it's burnt to a crisp, it's hard to do it harm."

His two dining companions laughed and heartily agreed before lapsing into another period of silence as they diminished their meals.

"I have a proposal," Allsup announced, wiping his mouth with a napkin.

"And what would that be?" asked Representative Hill as Mr. Holtman looked up from his food attentively.

"I propose we each share a sample of our meats so that we might fairly judge which of the three is superior. I'll share my bacon with the two of you if you'll obligingly share a taste of your meat with me."

"That's a splendid idea!" exclaimed Hill. "I've been eyeing that bacon for some time now."

"That's an ace-high idea, all right!" declared Holtman. "Allow me to cut a piece of my steak for you both."

Danny Allsup

The three men divvied the meat on each of their plates and passed them to the other while collecting a sample. They sat cutting, chewing, and nodding their heads with each different test. After several minutes and sips of coffee, they leaned back in their chairs contented.

"That was mighty good ham," Holtman announced, chewing. "I may have to withdraw my previous opinion."

"So was the steak," replied Hill. "I believe if I dine here again, that will be my choice."

"I found them both delicious!" declared Allsup. "But I have no regrets about selecting the bacon."

"No, no, the bacon was good," Hill affirmed.

"I must confess," noted the man from Scranton, "I prefer my bacon cooked longer. I like it more crispy than chewy, but it is bacon, so it's good."

There was no further discussion at the table until the last plate was pushed away and the crumpled cloth napkins were tossed aside. Holtman and Allsup scooted their chairs back from the table and stretched out their legs, relaxing. Representative Hill leaned back in his chair with a coffee cup in hand and his legs crossed under the table. Presently, he set the cup down and removed a pipe from his side coat pocket along with a tobacco pouch. He loaded the pipe bowl and struck a stick match along the side of its container. Soon, he had the tobacco burning to his liking and sat puffing out plumes of smoke.

"Mr. Allsup," Hill spoke in between puffs.

"He said to call him Danny," interrupted Holtman.

"Well, no, actually—" Allsup attempted to correct their misunderstanding, but—

"Danny," Hill broke in, "I've a thought I'd like to share with you regarding your travels, if I may?"

"My preference is Daniel, and yes, please, favor me with your thoughts."

"Well, sir," his pipe clenched firmly between his teeth, "have you given any thought to travel by water? Or is your heart set on riding that horse of yours?"

"No, no, I've nothing set in my mind regarding my means of travel. I have my horse that I intend to keep, but a boat, train or wagon; I am open-minded in that regard. My sole purpose is to end up with my feet in the Pacific."

Mr. Holtman rolled a cigarette during this exchange and, after lighting it, leaned back in his chair to comfortably follow the dialog.

"What I'm suggesting is that you take a boat of some kind, steamboat or flatboat, from Pittsburgh on the Ohio all the way to the Mississippi. It's my understanding that you can go all the way by water to Missouri."

"But wouldn't that require I cross the mountains to get to Pittsburgh?"

"Danny—"

"Daniel," he once again corrected.

"Daniel, I'm not an expert on the terrain of this great land of ours, but it is my understanding that to go anywhere west of here requires that you cross mountains. If you're going west to the Pacific, you'll be crossing many mountains, I warrant."

"Yes, I'm sure you're right," Allsup noted. "I really never thought about that. Upon consideration, there are probably many different types of terrain I'll encounter that I hadn't considered."

"Rivers," Holtman pointed out.

"Yes, well, of course, rivers," Allsup answered, sounding a bit condescending.

"Deserts, I would imagine," added Hill.

"Really? Deserts?"

"Yes, yes, I'm sure of it. And gorges and canyons, probably."

"My word…" Allsup said thoughtfully.

"I don't want to be a croaker, but ya might just want to reconsider your goal," Holtman suggested tossing the remains of his cigarette to the wood floor and grinding it to mash with the toe of his boot.

Allsup did not immediately respond but continued to stare contemplatively off into the distance.

"No, no, I will not be deterred," he finally said with a smile as if happy with his resolve. "I will see the Pacific. I will undertake this adventure just as those explorers had before me. They didn't know what to expect, yet they persevered; there is more known now about the unknown into that which I will be venturing because of their courage and determination. I will be no less brave and no less determined."

"I see your mind is set on this issue," Representative Hill said, rising from his chair. "Consider my suggestion, sir. It is a viable alternative to what you are about to embark, and I believe it will hasten your progress." He extended his hand in goodwill and said, "I wish you all the success, Danny, Godspeed." They shook hands firmly as Hill concluded, "Now I must take my leave as I have an appointment with a gentleman from the great city of Scranton."

"That'd be me," Holtman said hastily, getting up from his chair and shaking Allsup's hand. "Good luck to you, sir. I hope your ocean does not disappoint." He left quickly to catch up with the congressman already at the door, saying, "Our meal is done, sir. I reckon we can discuss it now."

As he rode on, Daniel Allsup continued to consider that seed planted by his dining companion regarding his means of transportation; that is, catching a ride in Pittsburgh on the Ohio River and taking it around the states rather than passing through them. There's much country he would not see, he acknowledged, but the view from the river must be unique and memorable in its own way. He decided to make Pittsburg his next destination and would then determine how to proceed. But first, he must cross the mountains.

D. Dean Carroll

Chapter 13

A water route up the Susquehanna and branching off westward on the Juniata River was one route he considered in traversing the Appalachians, but eventually, he would have to switch to horseback or train. There was always the Penn Canal that followed those same rivers, but he was told that while the canal was quicker traveling, it was more expensive. The Penn Central Railroad would take him all the way to Pittsburgh, easily taking him through and over the mountains, but transporting the horse added considerably more to the cost. He had several options, and each had its own value, but he ultimately decided to continue on horseback and try his hand at self-sufficiency like those original explorers that came before him.

Traveling by water so early in the trip prior to the Ohio, in his mind, diminished the value of this leg of the journey. In the retelling of his adventures later in life, he believed that too much traveling by water would bore the listener. Besides, he eventually would have to switch to horse or train at some point, and he was still east of the Mississippi! No, he reasoned, a water route at this early point in his travels would not do. But he did decide to catch the Ohio River and take it to the Mississippi.

He would cross the Appalachians and try for a direct route to Pittsburgh, direct, as they say, as the crow flies. A route as straight as possible over those tree-covered, round-topped mountains from one city to the other.

He headed westward out of Harrisburg on a dusty dirt road along with others trying to get an early start; the morning sun shone on his back and the excitement of adventure filled the air.

After an hour or so, the road took a turn to the north. Allsup moved his horse off to the side and stopped, allowing those behind him to pass. There he stood as a steady stream of travelers proceeded by, but he was paying no attention to the wagons, pedestrians, and riders as they moved on. His eyes were on the large rolling mountains that loomed ahead. They were just forests covering big hills, he reasoned. He'd made his way through virgin forests many times in his life, and he'd stood atop many large hills. Perhaps none as large as those that spread before him now, he conceded, but what was one dense forest or one giant hill but something to be passed through and crossed.

A gentle prodding coaxed the stallion on. They crossed the road through the traffic and headed onward, through shrubs and scattered trees into the forest; he let Chestnut have his rein straight towards the Appalachians.

Chapter 14

The horse ran for the longest time and quickly found his rhythm. Horse, rider, and supply bags attached to the back of the saddle were no longer bouncing around haphazardly, threatening to break free but fell into synch with the movement of the animal. They were making tremendous time and covering considerable ground as the mountains that at first appeared small and at a considerable distance now loomed ahead and presented a formable obstruction to their journey.

Eventually, the horse grew tired and breathless and slowed his pace to a well-determined walk. They were reaching the toes of the mountain's foothills and the gradual incline became noticeable. Allsup often found himself leaning forward to compensate for the angle of their climb; at one point, he was leaning so far forward that when the horse abruptly raised its head, he knocked Allsup's hat off.

They reached a new rise, which led into a dense forest that covered the mountain like a blanket and Chestnut came to a stop. Horse and rider stared ahead at the trees so thick they melted into darkness. The horse looked to its left, then right, and then back in the direction from which they came as if trying to decide if he really wanted to continue. Allsup dismounted.

"You ran a long way for a long time there, fella," he said brushing the horse's forehead with his hand. It came away wet from sweat and covered in hair. "I was hoping to make it a bit further along, but you've done enough for today and it doesn't look like the climb is going to get any easier. We'll rest here for tonight and make the top tomorrow."

Allsup unburdened the horse of saddle, blanket, and bags. He pulled a withered-looking apple from a bag and offered it to the horse, which it accepted eagerly and consumed with enthusiasm. He poured water from a water skin into his hat and allowed the horse several large swallows. Searching through another bag, Allsup found the bristle-hair currycomb he'd purchased back in Lebanon and began to brush down the weary animal. As he tended to his horse, he talked softly, complementing the animal on the distance covered and how lucky he was to have such a fine horse. Chestnut grazed on the various bushes and grasses surrounding them, every once in a while glancing back at his groom.

While he was scouring for firewood, Allsup came upon a small stream trickling between the rocks down the mountain. It wasn't more than 8 or 10 inches across, but it afforded the man and horse cool fresh water, and both drank their fill.

Forgoing the search for fresh food, he dined on salted beef jerky and hardtack. Reclining back against his saddle by the fire, he gazed up at the stars, sang a couple of songs quietly to himself, and then settled in for the night. He lay with his hat over his eyes, blocking the firelight, and thought, about his plans to travel west.

The issue of traveling the Ohio by flatboat or steamboat was on his mind as he drifted to the cusp of sleep when a shot sounded off in the distance. He immediately rose to a sitting position and listened; his hat pushed back atop his head. He heard it two more times. Pulling his own rifle from its scabbard, he jumped to his feet and moved out of the firelight's perimeter. Crouched low in the darkness, he waited and watched, not knowing what to expect or to expect anything at all. After a time, he decided all was safe and returned to his bedding by the fire. He needed rest to tackle the long climb up the mountain.

Chapter 15

The incline was much more than he imagined; earlier, he'd dismounted from fear of toppling over. Together Chestnut and he zigzagged through the thickest forest he'd ever encountered, always walking at an angle upwards, first up to the northeast, then up towards the northwest. Sometimes he would take the lead and use the reins of the bridle to pull the horse after him; sometimes, the horse would lead, and he held onto a stirrup to be pulled along. The sun rose high into the sky and soon, the forest floor became hot and humid from the dripping condensation falling from the canopy of trees overhead. They walked for hours and never felt as if they were making progress.

Occasionally, they would stop to rest and catch their breath, both panting from their efforts.

"What am I doing?" Daniel Allsup asked himself aloud at one such break, frustrated with their progress. His horse looked back at him, watching to see what he was going to do next.

"Chestnut, look at how high up this mountain goes!" Allsup stood facing the upward side, looking straight up; his hat fell from his head and dangled by the chinstrap.

"We've got to find a level place, just a little level, to stop for the night. My God, what am I doing?" he was filled with despair at his failure to realistically consider the possibilities. He looked up at a sky concealed by foliage; streams of sunlight found holes to highlight patches on the ground. Allsup looked down at the different shapes of brightness. He walked up to the saddle and retrieved his water bag. After taking three long pulls, he filled his hat and allowed the horse to have the same.

"Alright," he said as he returned the water bag to the saddle. "You want to take the lead, or should I?"

Without command, the horse lumbered upward, with the man following close behind.

It was dusk and the sound of the forest was changing; different life awoke while others retired for the night. It added a sense of urgency as he scaled the mountainside, searching for a place to stop. He had the lead and had just led them around a small cluster of trees and there was an opening, an almost flat room-size area created by a rockslide thousands of years ago.

"This will do nicely, won't it, Chestnut?" Allsup was happy to have a place where they could stop and rest and stop leaning. He unsaddled the horse and removed its bridle giving him his freedom. He unrolled his bedding atop the most level area, satisfied he would not roll off in his sleep.

"I'm going after firewood," Allsup told the horse as he slid the rifle out of its scabbard. "Don't roam far."

Chapter 16

The rising morning sun found the two already in motion, single file, up the mountainside. Anxious to be over the top of this obstacle, Allsup skipped coffee and breakfast to get underway. He took the lead at their start. The horse followed behind with its neck stretched out, urged on by the man pulling the bridle reins. They continued in this manner, taking turns in the lead throughout the day.

As the sun rose, so again did the heat and humidity. At one point in the early afternoon, Allsup decided to remove his shirt in an effort to find relief, as his coat was already laying across the back of the saddle. It was only a momentary refuge as a swarm of deerflies discovered his exposed skin and began to take nourishment at every opportunity.

Concerned as they climbed that they would be stuck for another night on the upward side of the mountain, Allsup pressed harder to reach its summit. At one point in the late afternoon, Chestnut came to a stop and refused to move another step. Regardless of Allsup's urging, the horse remained where it stood, with its tail swatting at the flies and shaking his head to disperse them from his face. With each shake, the insects would take flight only to immediately return to cause more aggravation to the animal.

"Let's be moving on," Allsup said as he tried to coax the horse onward. "These flies are going to stay with us, I warrant until we get off this mountain. The sooner you decide to start walking, the sooner we'll accomplish that task."

Still, the horse refused to move. Allsup checked him for injuries; no lost shoes or rocks wedged in his hooves. He found nothing to impede the horse's progress. It looked as if Chestnut had decided he'd had enough for the day, but there was still a considerable amount of daylight left. The flies

Danny Allsup

continued to annoy and Allsup was losing his patience.

"So, you're done for the day, is that it?" he shouted at the horse, who failed to acknowledge his outburst. "You want to spend another day on this side of the mountain? We're almost to the top! I'm at sea as to why you don't want to get away from these flies, over the top and off this thing! I'm almost certain that the top is just a short distance ahead, and I, for one, am ready to reach it! If you're not coming with me, I'm going on. I'll wait for you up there!"

Angrily, Allsup dropped the reins and set out for the summit leaving the horse behind. The horse watched the man struggle on, slipping at times on the wet leaves. After he had climbed a short way ahead, the horse shook his head and decided to continue, soon catching up and passing the man and taking the lead once more. As he passed, Allsup gratefully grabbed a stirrup and allowed himself to be pulled along.

It was in this manner, as they climbed, that it became clear they were about to reach the top. Trees and Earth no longer appeared ahead, only the sky. Thrilled at the prospect, Allsup rushed to the front, grabbed the reins, and urged the horse on.

"There it is, boy!" he declared, pointing to the top. "We're almost there! It's going to be easy going from now on—all downhill! Come on, Chestnut! Come on!"

They reached the top. Still concealed under the canopy of the trees, they could see nothing but familiar terrain, but it no longer inclined. The ground began to level off until they were no longer climbing but walking on relatively flat land.

Allsup filled his hat with water from his water bag and allowed the horse several swallows as a reward for his effort. The man drank from the bag, wiping his chin with his shirt sleeve. He sat down on the damp ground next to where the horse stood, using his hat to swish the flies away from his face.

When the horse would lower its head to nudge him

affectionately, the man would chase them away before rubbing its nose or scratching behind its ears.

"We did it," he said softly. "Tomorrow, we'll get off this mountain and hopefully find the Ohio. We'll travel by water for a while instead of walking. How's that sound?"

The horse gave no response; he stood tired, staring ahead, listening to the sound of water droplets falling from the leaves overhead until he fell asleep.

Allsup watched his horse drift off. He found it both amusing and comforting. This relationship he had with his horse was the first he'd had since his wife's passing. There was contact with other people, but that was cordial and business-like; no evening dinners, no card games, no hitting the bars or hanging out at the livery.

It was just him on his farm. He did the work; he farmed, and he tended to the fields and the livestock. He kept the house clean and cooked his meals and made sure everything was presentable like his wife had, like she would have wanted it, just at the happen-chance a visitor might stop by. They never did.

Now, when the boys were…at the farm. Then they'd have other young ones over so they could play, accompanied by their parents. It was nice and social; his wife enjoyed it. But after the boys were gone, all of that stopped. Still, she was ready just in case, and so had he been.

For almost two full years, he lived on the farm alone. His human contact was the occasional times he'd go into Lebanon for "necessities," as his wife had called them. He'd talk with Mr. Jackson, the mercantile clerk. Mr. Jackson was also the town reporter; nothing happened in Lebanon that Mr. Jackson didn't know about, so Allsup would catch up on the news during those visits. He'd talk with Chub Johnson down at the livery when purchasing feed and seed. Chub liked to talk, but his vocabulary was limited and most of it consisted of profanity.

Allsup was no puritan, but after a time, he'd get tired of

listening to it and make his excuses to be on his way. If a traveling tin man came by, they'd talk for a bit, usually at the well over a ladle of cool water. That was the extent of his social life.

They had no dogs. Plenty of cats, but if they wanted to eat, they had to provide for themselves. There were few rats on their farm. Horses were for work and transportation. Cows and pigs were food and more; they were given no names, and there were no sentimental attachments.

Therefore, the relationship with this horse this bonding was new to him. It made him feel comfortable.

He awoke in the middle of the night wet. It was raining. Chestnut stood nearby, looking as soaked as if he'd just emerged from a river.

"My God," Allsup exclaimed as he stood, chilled, in his drenched clothes. He found his slicker and covered his head and as much of his body as he could. He wasn't using it to keep dry. He hoped it would keep him warm.

The rain was loud. It had twice an impact: first with the broad leaves and conifer needles in the canopy above, then again when it fell from the canopy and hit the ground; it sounded loud, like the continuous musket fire of armies in battle.

It was dark in the forest at night in the rain without a moon or stars to provide light. He could barely make out the horse, which appeared to be a shadow.

Allsup was angry with himself. He was caught completely unprepared. He'd neglected his horse, his supplies, and himself.

This is a lesson learned; he told himself through gritted teeth as he shivered from the cold. He sat on the ground with his knees up to his chest, wrapped in the slicker. The brim from his rain-soaked hat hung limp around his head; water pouring from it fell onto the slicker and down to the ground forming puddles where he sat. After so much time, he could take no more.

Rising to his feet, he shouted over the noisy din, "Chestnut! I don't know about you, but I'm wet and cold and see no possibility of sleep in the immediate future; I say we move on!"

The horse gave no indication of having heard him. Allsup wondered if the animal might still be sleeping.

"Chestnut, are you awake?" he asked. "I know we won't have much of a clue as to where we're walking, but we know what direction to go. We'll just take it slow and careful, but we'll be covering ground and getting off this mountain. Then it's easy traveling for a spell. We'll rest up on the Ohio. How 'bout that?"

At first, the horse made no acknowledgment, and again, Allsup wondered if he was sleeping, but just as he was about to approach the animal, Chestnut turned his head and looked at him. With a snort, he shook his head, spraying water from his mane, before slowly walking over as if to indicate he was prepared to proceed.

Allsup saddled the horse, loaded their supplies and his soaked bedroll onto Chestnut's back and in the darkness, in the deluge of rain, the two made their way slowly across the mountaintop. After a time, Allsup noticed that they were heading downward on a slight gradient, and he felt satisfied that they might be off the mountain by the end of the day.

Dawn began to break, and the rain stopped.

They were on the wrong side of the mountain to appreciate the rising sun's morning rays, but its illumination allowed them to see and that eliminated the hindrance to travel due to lack of vision.

As the sun rose higher, so did the temperature along with the humidity, but these were barely concerning as the horse and man made their way down the mountainside. Allsup was searching for a break in the overhead growth that would allow them to see what lay ahead. He had visions of the Ohio winding its way through the countryside far below, flowing through fields and farms and forests, busy with boats, rafts, and barges carrying commerce and people up and down the river.

Pittsburg should be visible somewhere below and it excited him to imagine that this arduous passage over the mountain would soon come to an end.

Toward late morning, their descending incline became much greater and he dismounted so the two could safely continue in a single file. Ahead, Allsup could see a bright stream of sunlight penetrate the overhead foliage where the ground was brightly illuminated. Eager to look down at their destination from this elevation, Allsup encouraged Chestnut to hasten his pace as they meandered their way through the thick forest.

As they closed in on the clearing, Allsup could see that a fire must have caused its occurrence. Tree stumps and undergrowth were charred black, creating quite a contrast with the surrounding green. A few of the burnt trees had toppled over while others remained defiantly standing, but no leaves adorned their branches.

Anxious to see what lay past the mountain, he released his grip on Chestnut's reins and ran ahead, slipping and sliding down the sharp slope. The bright sunlight caused Allsup to shield his eyes after being so long on the dark forest floor. Through squinting eyes, he searched through the opening in the forest, searching for the winding river, for farms and villages, or Pittsburg down below. What he saw caused him to moan aloud and drop to the ground with a thud. His unimpeded view revealed another mountain, larger than the one they were now descending.

He reclined on his back with a sigh, his arm shielding his eyes and felt the warmth of the direct sunlight upon him for the first time in a while. Chestnut joined him and nudged the man's arm with its muzzle. As he reached over to scratch its nose, Allsup said, "This is going to be a lot harder than I thought."

D. Dean Carroll

Chapter 17

They made it down the mountain by the end of the day and camped in the valley. There was a small stream at the base of the mountain and Allsup decided to stop by it for the night. There was still a considerable amount of foliage overhead covering most of the area, but the river's floodplain was open and grassy and appeared an ideal place to stop.

Chestnut enjoyed the fresh grass, and Allsup caught two large trout from the stream by trapping them in a pool with his shirt. He fried both in a pan over the campfire. While he dined on the trout and watched Chestnut wading through the stream, he thought that this is what must make some people cease their travels to choose not to continue on.

This valley appeared perfect to Allsup. It was all virgin land, untouched by human hands, at least white hands. It had a water supply and the ability to sustain plant life, which meant the land could be farmed and support livestock. In addition, it was nuzzled between two large mountains that served as walls to keep out intrusions. The thought occurred to him that maybe he was the first white man to see this land, and it could stay that way for years to come. The only disadvantage to staying that he could conceive was that he'd be completely on his own.

A person would have to be self-sufficient; do everything themselves if they were to stay, and at his age, he didn't think he wanted to take on that big of a challenge. He smiled to himself as he thought that he wouldn't want to take on that challenge at any age. Farming was difficult and lonely, but Lebanon was close enough to get needed supplies and neighbors all joined together to lend a hand. Those were all luxuries he'd have to do without settling in a valley like this. He did not intend to travel for the rest of his life; one day, when he did decide to settle down again, those extras would help determine where.

He did not continue the next day. One more day would do no harm; the rest, water, and food would be beneficial. He was not on a schedule, he reminded himself. There was no place he had to be; no one was expecting him. So, he lingered in the valley for another day.

It was while he was crossing to the other side of the valley, across the small stream and on the long, arduous climb up the next mountain that Chestnut began to act up. The horse stopped several times abruptly and seemed inclined to change their westward direction to one more northerly.

Allsup corrected the horse several times before it decided that was enough and bucked with the intention of throwing his rider. Allsup quickly decided that the horse could have its way; it was better to accompany the animal than to chase after him. The next time Chestnut tried to veer to the right, Allsup didn't stop him. At first, the horse walked on at the pace they'd been traveling all morning, but once it realized that it had free rein, it broke into a trot, then canter, and proceeded to accelerate into a hard gallop.

Again, they were traveling at an incredible speed. It was exciting how fast they were going and fascinating how the horse picked its route. It whipped around trees and jumped bushes as nimbly as an antelope. In open areas, closer to the stream, it would let loose and run hard, building a sweat that darkened the leather reins brushing its neck. Suddenly, the horse came to an abrupt stop, panting deeply, his head turning left and right as if searching for something.

"What is it, boy?" Allsup asked the horse. "What are you looking for?"

Chestnut pawed the ground with his right hoof and whinnied aggressively, throwing up his head.

"What is it, boy?" Then, in the distance, Allsup heard a horse reply, and like a bullet leaving the barrel, they were running again. He tried to rein the horse in, but to no avail, so he hung on tight and hoped he wouldn't be thrown rounding a tree or jumping a bush.

Soon, a horse and rider became visible, tiny figures at this distance but growing quickly. As they drew closer, he could see the horse ahead was acting agitated and its rider was having a difficult time managing it. Then Allsup realized the situation.

"Get off your mount!" he shouted to the rider. "Get off your mount!"

The rider looked up surprised when he heard Allsup and must have feared a robbery because he tried to urge his animal on by kicking its sides and whipping its rump with a strap. The horse reared up. The man fell back and off. As soon as he could, Allsup dismounted.

The two horses played their courtship game: the filly acting hard to get and Chestnut strutting his studliness. They danced in circles, intertwining their necks one minute, Chestnut nipping at her neck and rump the next as she scooted out of his way to avoid his advances.

Allsup looked over at the man recently thrown, sitting as he landed. He was dressed in a white shirt and tan jacket; his pants were held in place by a large, buckled leather belt and suspenders. Looking considerably older than Allsup, he wore a bushy gray beard and had a full head of matching hair. He looked over at Allsup, caught him watching and grinned while raising his hat in greeting.

As Chestnut mounted the man's horse, the man got to his feet and, brushing the dirt from the seat of his pants, walked over to Allsup.

"Guess ya cain't stop'em once their mind's set," he observed as he approached. "Jist like people. Delbert Cross, sir," he extended his hand. "That's my horse yours is taking advantage of."

"Daniel Allsup." Shaking his hand. "I apologize for the lack of control over my horse, Mr. Cross."

"Nah, no need. Truth be told," he admitted chuckling, "I

know how the stud feels and envy the animal."

"What? No!" Allsup burst into laughter. Delbert Cross could not contain himself; surprised by Allsup's amusement, he broke into laughter as well. Together it became contagious, and they found themselves in a situation where they could not stop. When one's laughter would begin to subside, they only had to look at the other and would find themselves starting again.

"I hope he's not harming your saddle," a gasping Allsup said, attempting to change the subject and put an end to their merriment.

"Not to worry." Cross struggled to respond calmly but convulsed into laughter as he said, "I bought it harmed!"

Allsup dropped to his knees, overwhelmed again with waves of laughter. In between spasms, he cried out, "Oh, dear! Oh, dear, I've got to stop. I'm going to embarrass myself!"

"I fear the only response I got for that is," Cross said, wiping tears from his eyes. "Please don't!"

Cross was on his way east to the state capital while Allsup was making slow progress in the opposite direction, so traveling together was not an option. Allsup immediately took to the man, so quick to laugh. It brought to his attention how little amusement he'd experienced in life; he wondered how much had been there and he just failed to see it. Cross was just happy to have a receptive audience. It was agreed they would make camp together.

They decided to forgo any hunting expeditions and settled with what they possessed. Allsup had beef jerky and hard tack along with coffee, a pot, and water to brew it. Cross contributed a can of beans along with smoked ham and corn bread wrapped in a woman's white embroidered hankie, all compiled by his wife that morning before his departure. He also brought a bottle of whiskey, of which his wife had no knowledge.

They sat around the campfire and shared histories and

stories as they dined on their potpourri meal. Cross, a farmer of moderate success, was on his way to appear before the state supreme court regarding a land dispute with a neighboring farmer. The land was clearly Cross's, but the disputing farmer had built on the property, lived on it for a number of years, and now claimed squatter's rights. Cross only knew the land by map and was under the impression it was forested. He was in the process of expanding his productivity when he discovered it was inhabited. He refused to sell; the squatter refused to pay rent. The case had been appealed from one court to the other through the pyramid of courts until it reached the pinnacle of the state judicial system, where Cross was certain the issue would finally be resolved in his favor. Right was right, he reasoned, and he had the papers to prove it.

Cross was intrigued by Allsup's adventure and perhaps a little envious as well, but he, like the others, shook his head, doubting the benefit of what he would gain if successful, as opposed to what he'd given up. It was not a topic of dispute; Cross respected Allsup's courage and determination. It was just not an enterprise, he believed, a man should be undertaking at this stage in his life.

"Delbert, you never long for the excitement of adventure?" Allsup asked.

"At my age, my excitement comes from my children and grandchildren," he explained. "A good harvest or the birth of a cow, or the success of an investment's return. I put some money in Avery Miller's livery stable back home; he had a well-thought-out plan for expandin' his place but lacked the funds to do so. That's where I came in. I purchased twenty-five percent of his business and got my first return just a week ago past. We'll start a new house with that money. Talk about excitin', travelin' somewhere 'cause I've never seen it don't even come close."

"Delbert, you never mentioned a wife," Allsup pointed out.

Danny Allsup

"I'm sorry, I thought we was talkin' about excitement," he responded smiling. "My wife is not excitin'. She was once, a long time ago when I could still see my...feet. We been together too long, the sharp edge of excitement has been worn away by time, forty-seven years, as a matter of fact. My wife is no longer excitin' to me, Danny, but she *is* the definition of comfort and home. She has been with me forever. She's my friend and my wife. She knows what I like: my favorite foods, how I like my clothes, what bothers me and what don't, when I'm bothered and when I'm not. She knows me. Because of her, I sleep at night. She is my definition of comfort and home."

Allsup sat quietly, thinking and remembering.

After the meal, Cross uncorked his whiskey, and the two travelers passed the bottle back and forth. They talked and laughed, becoming more animated with each round. The evening drew on, the fire burned low, and as the bottle continued its rotation, the talking diminished and finally came to a stop.

Allsup shook the bottle, determined it empty, and set it down on the ground between himself and Cross, who had fallen asleep on his side with his head resting on his saddle. Allsup reclined upon his ground tarp, flat on his back, and lay relaxed, looking up at the stars. Thinking, as he drifted off to sleep, that if he were Cross, he'd not make the journey either.

They departed early without pausing for food or drink. They shook hands, wished the other well, and with a tip of their hats, were on their way in opposite directions.

D. Dean Carroll

Chapter 18

He crossed many more mountains before reaching a clearing that allowed him a view of their destination, the city of Pittsburg, on the Ohio River. The crossings were uneventful except for the night after his parting with Delbert Cross when he heard a gunshot again in the early evening. He knew it could not be his stolen rifle left leaning against a tree in a forest. He knew it couldn't be…but in his mind, he thought that it was.

When he entered the clearing on the west side of the last mountain, Chestnut stopped. Allsup had been watching for the city as they drew closer, but he'd long since given up ever escaping this endless mountainous terrain, so his expectation was to see more of the same.

The late morning sun had just crested the mountaintop casting a bright yellowish light on all that lay before him. Down below in the distance was their destination, the city located on the convergence of the Monongahela and Allegheny Rivers forming the mighty Ohio. There was a great deal going on far below: tiny wagons, like toys from this distance, entering and leaving on roads leading to different routes in different directions; all manner of vessels were traversing along the city's waterfront, from small skiffs to multi-storied paddle boats with plumbs of black smoke rising from tall smokestacks.

Allsup and the horse stood in the clearing, looking below skeptically. That the city was finally before them, was difficult for him to grasp.

"Well, I'll be," he said, removing his hat and wiping his brow on his shirt sleeve. "Looks like we made it, Chestnut. We're done with mountains from here on out. No more mountains." And with a gentle prod, he encouraged the horse on, saying, "Let's get off of this one!"

Chapter 19

Finding lodgings in Pittsburg was difficult compared to Harrisburg. In the end, he settled on a room with a bed and chair over a saloon. It was late in the day when they reached the city. Gray clouds hinting rain obscured the setting sun, so estimating time was difficult, but he placed it more early evening rather than late afternoon. He was tired, and so was the horse. He just wanted to find somewhere to bed them both down.

The first five hotels he tried had full occupancy; a clerk at the last suggested he take the alley down to the end of the block, where he'd find a bar. There the bartender could set him up with a room and have someone see to his horse. With a great deal of apprehension, he went down the alley and to the bar, and as advised, the bartender set him up in the room he now found himself in. He saw to the stabling of Chestnut himself; a livery just down what they called a block.

The room was the dingiest he'd ever found himself in; the walls were gray from unfinished plaster, there was a curtainless window overlooking the street, a straight-backed wooden chair, and a bed with a single stained blanket lying across an uncovered mildewed mattress. Nevertheless, it looked good to Allsup and after removing his hat, coat, and boots, he collapsed onto the bed and fell into a deep sleep.

After several hours, a light knock sounded on his door. He tried to ignore it, but the knocker was persistent, so Allsup stumbled off the bed and opened the door.

"Hey, cowboy," A scantily clad woman of about fifty years of age greeted him. "Thought ya might like some company if ya know what I mean." She smiled a toothless smile and gave him a knowing wink.

"No, no, thank you; not interested." He closed the door and returned to the bed.

D. Dean Carroll

Someone's shouting woke him a second time; it came from the bar below. A voice loudly responded, and a gunshot followed. Frightened, Allsup lay on his side on the bed, his back pressed against the wall. He decided during this time that he wouldn't be spending another night in this establishment or any in this area! It might be time to move on. Eventually, the voices diminished and soon, all was quiet. Without realizing it, Allsup slipped into slumber again.

There was no way of measuring how much time had passed between when he'd fallen asleep and another knock sounded at his door; it seemed to Allsup just minutes. He didn't wait for them to repeat but was up and had the door open before they could rap again.

"Yes?" he curtly asked.

"Papa?" asked a woman dressed in a bonnet, a diaper, and wrapped in a blanket with a thumb in her mouth.

"What?" Allsup was trying to clear his head of sleep.

"Papa, Baby's scared!" The unusually dressed woman sounded childishly frightened. "Want to sleep with you!" She tried to push her way past him, but he stood his ground and wouldn't let her enter.

"No, no, no! Go away!" he ordered as he pushed the door closed. Then suddenly pulled it open again and shouted into the hall, "Not interested!... Guy in this room is not interested!... Just wants to sleep!... Please do not bother! Thank you!"

He heard her approach. He couldn't get back to sleep and was trying to make plans for what must be today when he heard the boards creak lightly. He raised himself up on his elbows and watched the light shining in through the gap at the bottom of the door, and soon it was shaded. Before she could announce herself at the door, he was up and had it open.

"If that don't take the rag off it all!" he shouted as he opened the door. "But you whores are a determined bunch!"

Danny Allsup

There before him stood a boy, no more than five or six. "Want your clothes washed, mister?" he asked without reserve or hesitation. "Have'em back by mornin'."

"No, no," Allsup stammered and closed the door. He wasn't going to give his clothes to a boy he didn't know. Anyway, his clothes were still good for a few more days. He sniffed at the armpit of his shirt and cringed; clean clothes might be nice. Abruptly, he opened the door and called out to the boy walking down the hall. "No, wait! I've changed my mind! Come back!"

The youngster, just taller than a tabletop, turned and sighed wearily before returning.

"How does this work?" he asked the boy. "What do I do?"

"Ya got anythin' else to put on?" the boy inquired.

"I do, but not with me, so no."

"Here's a towel." He tossed a bath towel up to the man, who caught it on his shoulder. "Take'em off, hand'em to me, and I be back with'em b'fore checkout."

Allsup closed the door and quickly undressed. Hiding behind the door, he offered his pants, socks, and shirt to the waiting boy.

"Where's the johns?" he asked, looking through the clothes. "Ya gotta wash the johns or might jus'as well not wash anythin'. Johns is the dirtiest part. Ya gotta wash the johns."

Allsup closed the door again and, with a great deal of reluctance, removed his long underwear. Again, hiding behind the door, he handed the boy his johns.

"See ya soon with'em washed 'n cleaned," the boy said as he headed down the hall to the next room.

Allsup stood behind the closed door of his room looking down at himself. He was in a room without any clothing available, just a towel. He began to question the wisdom of what he had just done. What if there was a fire? What if there was a fight and it escalated and grew with more and more people until nowhere in the bar was a person safe, and he was stuck up in this room naked? With only a towel!

He self-consciously wrapped the towel around his waist and went over to the bed, where he wearily sat down. He was tired, he reminded himself, and not making wise decisions. People are generally good, he reasoned. Chestnut was fine at the stable. He'd get his clothes back before checkout as promised, and he'd be out of this place; either looking for new accommodations or passage out of the city.

He lay back onto the bed with a sigh and re-examined, again, the wisdom of his decision to travel. He was a farmer and not cut from the same cloth as a man of adventure. Thinking back, the lure of traveling, of having a quest seemed so exciting, but the reality was hard; much harder than he'd imagined. And they were still in Pennsylvania.

The rap, rap, rapping on the door jarred him awake yet again. It was morning. The sun was up and shining. Apparently, he was able to get a little sleep, for he felt rested and ready to be on his way. He went to the door, as the repetitive knocking sounded once more, and opened it. There stood the young lad with Allsup's folded clothes. He reached out an extended hand, palm up and open, waiting expectantly.

"That's two bits, mister," he announced.

"Yes, right, just a minute," Allsup said behind the partially opened door as he went through his saddlebag for the money.

"Here it is, here it is." He placed the two bits in the boy's opened hand and went to reach for the pile of folded clothes when the boy moved them out of reach.

"And the towel, mister," he reminded.

"Oh, yes, right." Stepping behind the door, he removed the towel and handed it through the opened door to the boy, who grabbed the towel and shoved the stack of clothes into the awaiting hand.

"Hey!" Allsup exclaimed, "These are still wet!"

Danny Allsup

"Washed and cleaned is all we promised!" called out the boy with a laugh as he ran down the hall. "Didn't say nothin' 'bout 'em bein' dry!"

D. Dean Carroll

Chapter 20

After checking on the horse, Allsup made his way down to the riverfront, searching for passage on some type of water transport. He walked along the docks with the hopes of finding someone able to educate him regarding the best means of travel on the river. There were various types of boats engaged: steamers and barges being loaded and unloaded, families mooring and departing on flatboats and skiffs; animals crated and carried; other, larger hoofed animals were forced to cross a plank to board for passage. There were people everywhere; the din was so loud thinking was near impossible.

Allsup, walked, taking it all in, and wondered how he would find someone to ask. He expected activity, but organized activity, with a person clearly in charge. Here, there was no way to tell from what he could see, the dock workers carried bundles and boxes on and off the docks, yelling and hollering profanities at each other as if all were the same, but he could see no one with paper in hand making sure the job was done correctly; nothing to indicate authority.

At a loss, he decided to enter a riverfront business and ask for assistance, or at least direct him to one who could be. He was standing in front of a building with a sign advertising, 'Caldwell Freights, By Land and Water, Daily Departures,' and entered the building.

"Good morning," greeted a neatly dressed clerk behind the counter. "How can I be of assistance?"

Allsup noted the question and decided he had made the correct decision.

"I'm on my way to see the Pacific," Allsup responded. "And want to know the best way to go west from here by river."

Danny Allsup

"You mean the manner of vessel?" the clerk clarified.

"Exactly."

"Well, I suppose." the clerk looked around to see if the other two men in the office were listening; satisfied they were not, he continued, "first, what are we shipping?"

"A man and a horse."

"A horse? That makes things more…"

"Difficult?" Allsup suggested.

"No, I was thinking, interesting. Okay, so we have a man with a horse that wants to travel; how far?"

"All the way to the end."

"The Mississippi?"

"Yes, I'll be traveling by land from there."

"Okay, so how are we set financially? What's the budget?"

"The budget is open, but I don't want to spend money senselessly on extravagance or the like. I'm more interested in saving as much as I can for future necessities, and I'd like to take in the countryside as much as possible. So…"

"Taking into consideration these different variables," the clerk explained. "The fact that there's a horse to consider, and while money's no object—"

"I didn't say that," Allsup pointed out.

"You know what I mean…and the desire to see, if not explore, the countryside upon occasion, I would suggest, perhaps… a flatboat."

Just as he finished speaking, the door to the business opened and two men entered, talking boisterously. They continued speaking loudly as they approached the counter, where one of the two held open a swinging door for the other.

"Thomas, how goes it here?" the man who first walked through the swinging door inquired of the clerk. "Eh? How goes it here?

"Well, Mr. Caldwell. I was just assisting Mr.…"

"Allsup," he quickly answered, approaching Mr. Caldwell with an extended hand. "Daniel Allsup, sir."

Caldwell was a man that appeared to be affluent and comfortable with his affluence. He was round in girth, with dark curls escaping from beneath his stiff white hat with a yellow-stained headband.

"Very good to meet you, sir," Caldwell replied. "How is Thomas assisting you today?"

"Well, I was just explaining to Mr. Thomas that I wanted to…"

"Ship some cargo!" put in Thomas.

"Cargo, eh? What sort of cargo?" Caldwell further inquired.

"He's sending livestock down to a relative east of Cincinnati."

"Didn't want to take them myself," Allsup informed the man. "Too far away, and I don't like my cousin."

"Yes, well, if I can be of any assistance, you ask for me personally, Mr. Allsup." They shook hands as the man who had held the swinging door stood waiting outside another.

"Aaron Caldwell at your service."

"Thank you, Mr. Caldwell, but I believe Mr. Thomas has everything well in hand. A capable clerk, too, I might add."

"Point taken, Mr. Allsup. A good day to you, sir."

"Thank you, Mr. Allsup," clerk Thomas said as soon as the two men were behind closed doors. "I haven't been doing too much right as of late from his point of view. 'Course, his is the only view that matters, and I need the job, so what you said, well, that had to have helped. Thank you."

"It was nothing, Mr. Thomas, nothing. I meant what I said. Now, let's get back to what you were saying."

"Yes, well, where were we? Oh, yes! I was suggesting you consider a flatboat as your conveyance."

"A flatboat?"

"Yes, a flatboat. You're familiar with them, yes?"

"Well, I…"

"Look out the window there, Mr. Allsup. Those long, snub-nosed barges with the buildings on them out there cluttering up the river, those are flatboats."

Allsup studied them silently for several minutes before asking, "Why a flatboat?"

"First, they can accommodate the horse; most are already carrying livestock of some kind, so it won't require anything special."

"Second?"

"Second, they occasionally stop along the way; tie up for a night or two. It will give you the chance to see the countryside. Third, you'll get a place to sleep, and they'll feed you. I'm told the foods not bad, it's the same that they eat, so it's usually palatable. And finally, it's not expensive; a lot cheaper than a steamer which would require a lot more inconvenience and provide greater limitations."

"Sounds like you don't like steamers?" Allsup observed.

"I got nothing against them. They're dirty on the outside from all that ash but relatively clean on the inside."

"So, you'd recommend a flatboat?"

"From what you've said, if I were you, I do."

"Alright, then book me a passage," Allsup said as he pulled a pouch of coins out of his pants pocket.

"Oh, I can't do that, Mr. Allsup." Thomas had an embarrassed smile on his face. "We're a freight company. We don't ship people."

"I knew that," Allsup grinned sheepishly as he returned the pouch. "I was so engrossed in the conversation. You sounded like it was your occupation. You had it so logically figured out."

"No, sorry, just boxes and crates and whatever, but not people."

"Well, where do I go?"

"They have message boards all along the riverfront with notices of people announcing their departures, how many vacancies they have for one like you wanting to hitch a ride. Some are businesses needing crews, most are families heading west, looking to settle somewhere new, make a new start. If it's just a couple of families traveling together and sharing the expense, they might want an extra hand or two to share the work and the watch. Those poster boards, that's where I'd start if I was you. Get a couple of names, and go check if they're still here and still looking for hands. Compare a couple, look them over. One may be more comfortable than the others. Keep the horse in mind. You're going to do fine; I can tell. Good luck, Mr. Allsup." They respectfully shook hands.

"Thank you, Mr. Thomas, and may I say, you shouldn't be working here with freight. You should be working somewhere with people; you're very personable. I'm impressed and grateful for your knowledge and advice. Good luck to you, Mr. Thomas."

He found a board at the end of the block covered with slips of secured paper rising and falling with the breeze as if waving. The first he examined advised that a man was heading down the Ohio with various bags of produce and was looking for someone heading that way with goods of their own to share the expense of a skiff or flatboat.

Many of the slips of paper displayed the effects of weather indicating they'd been up on the board for some time. One, yellowed and frayed, the writing faded to almost illegible, noted three men were traveling to Owensboro, Kentucky and had a vacancy available for those interested. Those that were should contact Daryl O'Reilly at the Resting Oar Tavern to discuss arrangements.

They must surely be gone by now, Allsup thought as he glanced at several others. One advertised that Miller Shipping was willing to buy goods at reasonable prices for those that had to choose between staying and going. Another stated that two families with children, possessions, and livestock were seeking one or two other individuals to share the cost and labor. Interested persons should contact Williams or Arnett at Bigsbee's Boat Works on the riverfront. That didn't sound bad, Allsup considered, depending on how much cost and labor. The paper looked new, crisp and stiff, and the writing was dark enough it could have been written that morning.

It seemed worth checking out, so Allsup began walking up along the riverfront, weaving between the hustle and bustle of people determinedly engaged with purpose. He stopped several times for the passing horse and wagon, usually a flatbed with no sides to accommodate various sized cargo.

Eventually, the shops and offices began to thin out and only the occasional bar or tavern could be found among the hotels and apartment buildings where most of the labor resided. In front of one bar, two men were having a disagreement that had become so heated their shirts had been discarded and hands were clenched in tight fists ready to pummel the other. A third man was standing between them, attempting to keep the two apart while urging calm and reason, but to no avail. One man quickly threw a punch that landed square to the head of the other, knocking him stumbling backward directly into Allsup, who was trying to pass un-noticed. Allsup and the fighter fell on their backs, the fighter on top of Allsup.

"Let go'a me, damn you!" the fighter shouted as he struggled to his feet. Allsup remained on his back, trying to catch his breath. Two men helped him up as he gasped for air.

"There now, you'll be all right, mister," one man was saying as he brushed off Allsup's coat.

"Adams is a big man to have fall on ya, I can assure ya of that!" the other said through an almost toothless grin while supporting his arm. "He's a big fella!"

Coughing, Allsup held up his hands, waving the two men away. They each stepped back.

"Fine…" he wheezed. "I'm—fine!"

Another man approached carrying a beer-filled mug; the white froth capping the dark brew sloshed over the side as he walked.

"Here ya go, mister," he said as he extended the mug towards Allsup, bbent over, trying to regulate his breathing. "I thought this might help, so I ordered it up and paid for it outta my own pocket. No, no, no thanks needed, no, sir. I did it outta generosity towards my fellow man, to make things better in this world. I see a man in distress, and I wonder what can I do to help? Get that man a mug a beer, I answers, and so I did. No thanks needed."

Finally standing upright, Allsup took the mug and emptied it, never stopping, chugging it straight down, foam and all. With a loud "Ahh!" of satisfaction, he returned the empty mug and looked around at the small crowd of people who'd stopped to watch the altercation and its aftermath.

"Better now, mister?" one of the two men inquired.

"Yes, thank you," Allsup answered, wiping the beer from his mouth on his coat.

"Used my own money," the man holding the empty mug repeated. "With no thought of thanks or compensation."

"Thank you," Allsup said as he straightened his coat.

"Think nothin' 'bout it at all," the man said loudly. "I might not be able to afford a drink for myself, but what I have, I give it up gladly outta compassion."

"Perhaps I can reimburse you," Allsup suggested reaching into his pocket.

"No, sir, no," the man adamantly declined, turning away. "I don't need food nor drink. I place myself in God's hands. His will be done."

"No, really, I insist." Allsup offered him several coins. "As a gesture of appreciation for your kindness."

"Well, if ya insist, I guess...."

"I do, I do insist. Here my good man." He placed the coins in the man's hands. "Take this along with my gratitude."

"Well, God's will be done," answered the man. "If you'd throw in another bit, I could get somethin' to eat 'long with

Danny Allsup

the drink."

"Of course," handing him another coin.

"God's will be done!" shouted the man, his hand pointing skyward as he headed quickly down the street.

With the distraction over, people began to disperse, resume their conversations and conducting enterprise. A man stepped off the front porch of the tavern in which Allsup was standing and approached him.

"Excuse me, mister," he hesitantly said, nervously wringing his hands.

"Yes?" Allsup turned to the man, who was dressed in brown pants, a stained tan shirt, and a dark green checkered vest.

"That man you were just speaking with, your friend...."

"He's not my friend," Allsup corrected. "I've never seen him before today, just now. Nice enough, fellow, though."

"Well, sir, he said you and he was friends, and he...."

"He said we were friends?"

"Yes, sir, and...."

"Why would he do that?"

"Well, I think that's what I'm leading up to," the man said a little impatiently.

"Please continue."

"Well, when that ruckus commenced out here," the plaid-vested man explained. "That guy who's not your friend...

"Nor acquaintance," Allsup added.

"Nor acquaintance...came into the bar and tells me you sent him in to buy two beers: one for him and one for you. I hand him the poured mugs, which he takes and heads for the door. 'Hey! That beer ain't free, ya know!' I holler at him, but he keeps walking. At the door, he drains his mug and turns and tells me that you'll be right in to cover the tab. By that time, I hears the commotion and follow him to the door, where I see you flat on your back and big Tim Adams lying atop ya. I saw him hand ya the beer; I saw ya drink it."

"The scoundrel," said Allsup bitterly.

"That don't solve my problem, sir," the bartender replied. "I'm out the cost'a two beers."

"I sympathize with your dilemma, sir," Allsup told him. "But how does that pertain to me?"

"It's my opinion ya owe me for the beer."

"I ordered no beer. The beer I drank was a gift from the man who is no longer here."

"My point, exactly!" rebutted the bartender. "Your friend is gone leaving ya holding the proverbial empty mugs!"

"He is not my friend; I will not pay."

"Mister, I don't care a continental! Ya drank the beer!"

"It was a...oh, enough! I will offer a compromise: I will pay for *my* beer, the one that I consumed, presented to me as a gift, but not for his. Not one penny more."

"Agreed!"

Allsup handed him a five-cent piece, advising, "I want the change. I don't believe your behavior warrants a tip."

"That's fine, that's fine," replied the bartender as he turned to go back into the bar. "Have to come inside to get it, though. I gotta business to run, already spent too much time out here."

"I will gladly come in." Allsup followed.

"Come in and bend an elbow on the house," the bartender said as he disappeared inside.

Allsup stayed for the free beer and then consumed two more at his own expense, having struck up a friendship with the bartender, whose name was Charley Smith. Charley had served in the war, fought for ol' Abe and the Union, and lost the last two toes on his left foot to infection. He stepped on a spike and it didn't heal right. Lost the pinky toe first. He was limping barefoot cause his foot was too swollen for his boot. He lost it somewhere along the way; he never missed it until Nathan Taggert pointed out it was gone.

The toe next to the pinky came off in his fingers.

Danny Allsup

As was the natural course of the conversation, it branched off into Allsup's adventure, and when Charley Smith heard Allsup's intention to obtain transportation on a flatboat, he looked perplexed and flustered until he could no longer hold his tongue.

"Danny, my friend, if it's your intention to gain passage on'a flatboat, don't do it here."

"Why's that, Charley?"

"Ya ever been on a flatboat?" Charley asked.

"No."

"Well, neither has any'a them palookas that's buildin' 'em out there! They're all as shave-tailed as yourself! You say ya got yourself a fine horse?"

"I do."

"Then keep on ridin' straight across to Steubenville on the Ohio side. By the time these folks reach Steubenville, they'll realize how hard it's really goin' to be; the difficulties lyin' ahead of 'em! They'll see two or three men to maneuver those boxes just ain't enough. They'll be lookin' for help; they'll be glad to have ya along."

"You know, you just may have something there," Allsup acknowledged pondering the information. "I see your point."

"You're a smart man," Charley told him with a wink. "I knew you'd catch on. Mark my words, you be in Steubenville when they come 'round and they'll be beggin' ya to come join 'em."

"Thank you, Charley Smith." Allsup gratefully shook his hand. "I believe that's sound advice, and I believe I'll get started right away. I thank you for your hospitality and enlightening conversation."

"Safe travels, Danny Allsup. Safe travels."

D. Dean Carroll

Chapter 21

One and a half hours later, Allsup and his chestnut left the western perimeter of Pittsburg, the last vestiges of habitation. When they could no longer see the last farm, and no farm appeared before them, he let the horse go with a hoop and a holler. The horse ran unrestrained down the hard-trodden road passing the occasional traveler. To each that he passed, Allsup would raise his hat in greeting and receive hardy salutations in return, though a few would call out reprimands for his recklessness or the dust raised and his lack of consideration. They failed to perceive that it was the horse that determined how fast and where they would go. He was merely the rider.

The horse could run for hours, it seemed.

He would dash around carriages, carts and wagons as if the road was an obstacle course and the goal was to get through it as quickly as possible. If two wagons were passing in the opposite direction, the horse would leave the road and run along the side or angled on a grassy hillside to avoid slowing its pace. Allsup couldn't steer the horse in the direction he desired nor stop the animal if he chose to do so, but in truth, Allsup felt a type of freedom giving the horse its rein. The animal seemed to know to follow the road, to swerve this way or dart that to avoid a collision, and he would continue in that manner until he was lathered and breathless or his rider encouraged him to slow and stop.

It was approximately forty miles from Pittsburgh to Steubenville, and at this pace, they would have been able to reach the border between the two states within the day if he hadn't dawdled with Charley Smith. Their banter cost him the morning and so he found himself on a schedule that would have them reaching their destination late into the evening. Chestnut slowed to a canter as they headed directly into the late afternoon setting sun. Allsup resigned himself to the fact that they'd be sleeping off the road and under the stars once again.

He didn't build a fire; they were too close to the road and he didn't want it to be a welcome beacon. But that was all right. He dined on hardtack and jerky and washed it down with water. He unsaddled Chestnut and gave him a good brushing after the day's run before sending him off to graze on whatever desirable grass might be growing in the area.

Allsup lay back on his canvass tarp, his head resting upon his saddle, looking up at the stars. It was at times like this he would start reflecting on life, its meaning, its purpose, and what happens after.

It was at times like this he would start sorting through his memory's images, recalling different times in his life: images of his wife on that gray winter day when he took her in the clearing on the hilltop in the snow; images of his oldest son, when just a baby, squealing with delight when squirted with milk from their dairy cow's teat; images of his youngest son coming to him, crying because he'd hit his thumb with the hammer again before going back and trying one more time; images that brought on melancholy and sadness.

These thoughts and memories would run like an endless loop through his mind, denying any possibility of rest or sleep.

Then he saw three shooting stars, one after the other, streaking westward. He sat up, keeping his eyes on the night sky perforated with tiny pinholes of light in different sizes and intensities, waiting for something more.

Daniel Allsup did not consider himself a religious man. He attended church when his family did. But his convictions regarding religion were shaky. He believed he was a good judge of character; he thought he had a relatively good understanding of the nature of man. With this understanding in mind, he was skeptical about acts of God being distorted, exaggerated, and magnified by man to benefit himself. His belief in God was strong, rock-solid; he just blocked out most of everything else espoused by humans. In his life, too much good, despite all the sorrow he had experienced, too much good had happened for sorrow to overwhelm it.

He knew why he'd lost his sons; they were the price paid for the rights and freedom of others, freedom to decide; like abandoning everything for this adventure; for everyone to do as they choose. But what a blessing they both were. What a pleasure to have watched them grow into fine young men and to nurture them and share their happy times and bad.

Allsup stood smiling, looking up at the night sky. He didn't know if those shooting stars were a sign from his family or a sign from God; it was probably just a coincidence. Nonetheless, there were three shooting stars, all going west. It had to mean something…It meant he was going west.

Chapter 22

The sun felt warm on his face as he drifted along with the slow current of the river. A light breeze rustled his dark hair as he lay back on the cabin roof of the fourteen-by-twenty-five-foot flatboat. After all the difficulties he'd previously experienced traveling over the Appalachians, he could not believe how easy traveling was on the river. He was traveling westward, actually moving, while lying on his back in the sunshine doing absolutely nothing.

"This is the life," he murmured as he heard a call from a passing skiff.

The flatboat on which he reclined was owned by two families. The husbands were brothers Thomas and Kenneth Holcomb from Kellysburg, Pennsylvania. They were the youngest of five children. Their father had made it clear that the small farm on which they were raised would be going to their elder brother and his family. Their two older sisters had moved in with their husband's families leaving nothing but a fresh start for the two at the bottom of the hierarchy. Resenting that their father basically cast them off, advised they were on their own, and left to their own devices, the two decided to head west, maybe to Arkansas or Missouri. Rumor had it both states were a bit mountainous and not that different from Pennsylvania. They would throw their lot together, get some land and start a farm of their own.

Thomas Holcomb was the father of two, a son and a daughter. The older of the two, the boy, was named Thomas after his father; he was called Tommy. At five, he was sure he knew how things worked in life and took it upon himself to impart his worldly knowledge to his three-year-old sister, Greta, three-and-a-half if asked.

Greta was all girl. She liked dressing up and playing with her doll. She didn't mind helping when told to do so while inside. She hated working outside where it was either too cold or too hot and where it was always dusty and dirty. She did not like to get dirty, just like her mama.

Savannah Holcomb was a devoted wife. Her family was in Kellysburg. She grew up there just like Thomas. It was hard for her to leave the family home when she married her husband. At twenty, she'd only been away from her family three previous times.

First, when she spent the night with Sally Hall. She was twelve at the time and excited about being away from home for the first time and spending the night with her friend. Sally, who was two years older, convinced Savannah to sneak out of the house with her so she could meet her boyfriend, Cage Douglas. Savannah knew it was wrong but didn't want to disappoint her friend, so late into the night, the two crawled out the bedroom window and ran across fields to the Douglas farm about two miles away.

When they came out of the cornfield into the clearing at the farm, there wasn't a soul to be found. Sally decided Cage must have forgotten or fallen asleep, so she tapped on his bedroom window, only it wasn't his bedroom window. It was his parent's bedroom window. It was Mr. Douglas that opened the window and helped the two girls in. Because of the dark, it wasn't immediately evident he was not Cage and it took just seconds before they realized their error. Mr. Douglas hitched up the surrey and delivered each girl back to her own home. The whole ride, he never said a word, which frightened the two girls along with their anticipation regarding their fates when they reached home, neither spoke.

They reached Sally's farm first. Mr. Douglas climbed down from the surrey's bench seat and lifted Sally gently down. They walked together to the farmhouse door where Mr. Douglas rapidly knocked several times. Eventually, a light appeared within. Sally's daddy answered the door and Mr. Douglas explained the intrusion.

The two men shook hands, and as Mr. Douglas returned

to the buggy, Sally was abruptly pulled inside, followed by the sound of a slamming door. This gave Savannah even greater cause for concern. They proceeded on to her home, where the initial events followed closely to those at Sally's. Only her father didn't jerk her into the house but held the door open for her to enter, and he didn't slam it after she'd stepped inside.

"You should get some sleep," he said as he headed up the stairs to return to bed.

She tried to but worried about what the morning might bring. She was so angry with herself for allowing another to lead her into doing something she knew to be wrong, and now she had to suffer the consequences: feeling terrible, racked with guilt and fear, and worrying over the repercussions from her parents.

There were no repercussions. Nothing was said at the breakfast table that morning. Everyone ate in silence, knowing a terrible wrong had been committed and justice must be served—but nothing was said. As she and her mother cleaned up after breakfast, when her daddy and brothers were out in the fields and she and her mother were alone, her mother said without a single glance in her daughter's direction, "Never again."

The second time that Savannah Holcomb left her family home was with her mother. Her mother's sister in Greenville, Aunt Peg, had taken ill and needed assistance, so the two of them went together without male accompaniment. It was an exciting day on the old road, two parallel paths worn bare from usage and a strip of scrub grass growing along in between. They stayed for almost a week before her Aunt Peg claimed she was well enough to resume her wifely duties.

Moving in with her husband's family, the Holcomb's, was the third time she left. They were nice, decent people and made her feel welcome and part of their family. Her mother-in-law allowed her time to watch and observe how things were done in the Holcomb house, and eventually, Savannah saw little gaps where she could step in and help. It was appreciated, and gradually, more and more gaps appeared until she had her own everyday routines to fulfill. She ground and made coffee each morning. She checked on the yeast starter to be used later for bread. Morning biscuits also became her responsibility as all the Holcombs claimed her's to be the best. Another factor that added to the ease of adjustment, she was close enough to her own family to visit regularly—and did.

When Thomas told her about the plans Kenneth and he had made to move west, her heart stopped; her stomach surged into her throat forcing her to swallow. He was so excited; she felt extremely anxious. When she asked if they'd ever return, he smiled sadly, understanding, and told her maybe, someday, but she knew.

Now she found herself on a boat, a box really, floating down a river with her two children, brother-in-law and his wife, and two strangers who both looked as if they might be criminals—killers maybe. This floating box had a large windowless cabin that contained their living quarters, a stove, and two sleeping areas made up of bunks; they slept in shifts.

The back was shared by two oxen and four horses, and because of them, the smell made her feel like she was living in a barn and found it repugnant. She worried about how it may affect the children, whom she had to acknowledge seemed to be having a wonderful time.

Daniel Allsup rose up onto his elbows from reclining on his back and surveyed their surroundings and progress. As they lazily meandered around turns and bends on the river, he looked at the passing farms, fields, and forests too thick to see into, waving to the occasional people on the bank.

The man at the rudder would call out an approaching turn or traffic and the men would prepare for it by grabbing the side paddles and attempting to thrust them away, pushing the

Danny Allsup

paddles back and forth. There were times when they were busy, passing larger towns or large farms equipped with their own docks. All they could do was float past and hope if they bumped into something it wouldn't cause damage.

They were on a particularly wide area of the river one day, Theodore was at the rudder and doing an excellent job of keeping them in the mid-portion of the river, and Allsup wondered again if life could get any better. He could smell food cooking on the stove within the cabin and it reminded him that he'd skipped lunch. Mrs. Holcomb was having her children recite their letters while she cooked, and then they sang a counting song several times. It was a catchy tune that caused Allsup to smile.

Kenneth Holcomb came walking across the cabin's roof towards Allsup.

"Danny," he called out as he neared.

"Daniel, actually," Allsup corrected.

"Yeah, okay. Thomas and I thought we'd start looking for a place to tie off," he advised. "I know it's early, but we wanted to give the livestock a chance to roam a little, and frankly, I wouldn't mind the opportunity myself. I'm getting' antsy on this thing. What'd you think?"

"That's fine, that's fine," Allsup told him. "Whatever you gentlemen decide. I appreciate the opportunity of riding with you."

"Alright then…well, be ready cause once we find a site, we'll have to get busy to get us there."

"Just give out a call. I'll be ready."

"Alright then, Danny." Satisfied, Holcomb started back across the roof.

Kenneth Holcomb was the youngest in the family. He arrived later in Mr. and Mrs. Holcomb's life and was unexpected. A fact his parents never let him forget, usually pointed out in jest but too frequently for it to be long past humorous anymore. Kenneth welcomed the chance to take off with Thomas even though he thought his sister-in-law a pain. She carried a dark cloud with her all the time and sometimes, it blocked out the sunlight of others.

Kenneth's wife, Rachel, was just the opposite. She always smiled and was quick to laugh. She was as excited as him to go on this adventure and start a new life, especially when she discovered she was with child. She was glad that her baby would be born in a new state and a new start. She had not revealed the news to anyone, not even Kenneth, but believed her sister-in-law, Savannah, had her suspicions. It was her hope that they reach their new home before making the announcement.

"Ho! Thomas!" called out Kenneth. "Up ahead! Yea or nay?"

"Nay!" Thomas answered while operating the rudder. "Not on a bend! People be bumping into us all night!"

"Right, right," agreed Kenneth, frustrated. Thomas always saw the right of things, and his brother begrudged him because of it.

"Watch for an area along a length of the river, so people won't run against us," Thomas advised.

"Yeah, yeah, I know," Kenneth muttered under his breath.

"Doesn't have to be too long, mind you," Thomas continued as he pulled the rudder back, trying to keep the flatboat center of the river. "Long enough to unload the animals, is all!"

"I know, I know…."

The children playing on the deck at the forward part of the flatboat had overheard the exchange between their father and uncle, so during their play, they kept a lookout for a landing, too. They were as eager as the animals for space and legroom to feel the ground beneath their feet and the grass between their toes. In the midst of their play, young Tommy happened to glance up and eyed a clearing a considerable distance down the river where it stretched straight and true.

"Papa!" he called out. "Up ahead! See!"

"I do! I do!" his father cheerfully responded. "That's what we're looking for! See it, Kenneth?"

"Yeah, I do."

"Good work, Tommy. Mr. Allsup! Mr. Tunny! Will you lend us a hand?" asked Thomas. "We've found a spot for the night!"

Danny leaped to his feet and walked back towards Thomas, who stopped him in mid-stride. "If you man the right paddle, there, Mr. Allsup and push it forward, it should help turn us in towards shore. You see the clearing we're aiming for?"

"I do," answered Allsup. "I've got the right paddle."

"Thank you, sir. Have you seen Mr. Tunny?"

"I have not."

"Tommy! Are you up there?" he called out to his son.

"Yes, Papa?"

"Check and see if Mr. Tunny is asleep in the cabin."

"Who?"

"Mr. Tunny. One of the men who's traveling with us."

"Is he the one with the pretty horse?"

"No, that would be Mr. Allsup. He's here with me now. Tunny is the other one."

"Does he have a horse, Papa?"

"Tommy! Just go see if there's a man asleep in the cabin! If there is, wake him and ask him to come up. Tell him I need his assistance."

"Yes, Papa!"

Thomas Holcomb smiled as he looked at Allsup, also amused standing at the paddle. Holcomb shook his head and asked, "Have any kids, Mr. Allsup?"

After a moment's pause, Allsup answered, "Yes."

"How old?"

"Both grown."

"So, you have some experience with this."

"I do."

"Does this period of inquiry last long?"

"Not long enough, sir, not long enough."

Tommy entered the darkness of the cabin, passing his mother and aunt sitting on stools by the door using its light for their knitting.

"Where are you going, Tommy?" his mother softly inquired.

"Papa told me to fetch that man, Mr. Tummy. I'm off to wake him."

"That's Tunny, Tommy," his Aunt Rachel corrected. "Mr. Tunny!"

"Yes, Aunt Rachel."

"What's his name?" his mother asked.

"Mr. Tunny, Mamma."

"That's right. You're a good boy, Tommy," she told him with a mother's loving look. "Now run along and do what your father asked."

Tommy entered the darkened cabin. There were several hanging lanterns, turned down, providing just enough illumination to see. Inside the cabin, to the left, was a large cast iron stove his Papa was bringing with them for their new house. "We'll have the fireplace on one end and the potbelly on the other," his Papa had declared. His Mamma and Aunt Rachel used it now for cooking, so it was always real hot in the cabin. He brushed aside the curtains of one section serving as walls between the sleeping areas and the rest of the room and found no one sleeping on any of the beds stacked three high along the wall. The neighboring curtain concealed Mr. Tunny, a heavy-set man occupying the second bunk, on his left side facing the wall, his back to Tommy.

The young boy stared with wide eyes at the large back covered in red flannel crisscrossed by wide, black suspender straps. He stepped back into the main cabin allowing the curtain to fall. Looking to his left and right, a perplexed expression revealed a mind perplexed.

The boy pulled the curtain open again and peered inside. There was a low guttural sound coming from the man that added to his reluctance to proceed. He stepped inside; the curtain closed behind him. Less than a foot away, all that was necessary was for him to poke the man's shoulder once or twice and call his name.

The man snorted and coughed and moved as if he might turn onto his back, but with a throaty rattle, he snuggled back down and settled again onto his side.

He had to do it and do it quick before Mamma came in wondering about the delay and woke the man herself. He reached out and stayed his hand; finger pointed, suspended in mid-air, then lightly prodded the man on his shoulder.

"Mr. Tummy," he softly said.

Another poke with the finger, a little firmer this time, still nothing.

"Mr. Tummy."

The poke, this time, actually caused the man's shoulder to push forward, and when he called the man's name, it was almost a holler. "Mr. Tummy!"

The sleeping man's breathing stopped momentarily, then resumed as a light snore. Tommy wondered what more could he do? . He could not strike the man. That would surely result in a butt-warming. He thought of pouring water on the man's head but knew that to be rude, another cause for a butt-warming.

Then the wide suspenders caught his eye. He pulled in the middle where the two straps crossed and found that they stretched with a firm inclination to snap back. He pulled, stretching it out, then slowly allowed it to return. After practicing this exercise several times, he pulled it back as far as he could and let it go with a sharp 'Crack!' against the man's back while at the same moment shouting the man's name, "Mr. Tummy!"

"Aaaugh!" cried the startled man, jumping upright on his bunk.

"Aaaugh!" screamed little Tommy running out of the cabin. After just a second, his head popped back inside and he loudly announced, "They want you up on the cabin, sir!" before disappearing elsewhere on the vessel.

"Mr. Tunny! I am glad to see you're able to join us!" Thomas Holcomb exclaimed.

"That imp of yours!" growled Tunny.

"Sir?"

"I said that imp of yours needs to be taught some manners and respect!" fumed Tunny.

"Yes, I'm sure you're right," Holcomb genially agreed. "But what brought it to your attention?"

"Landing!" Kenneth called out.

All eyes turned to the approaching white shore in the middle of a tree-lined riverbank; amidst fallen trees and limbs dangling out over the water, the clearing they were striving for drew quickly nearer.

"Grab that side sweep there, Mr. Tunny!" Thomas ordered. "Mr. Allsup! Backstroke it hard and let's see if we can land this thing in that hole!"

All three men on the cabin were busy working the oars, pushing and pulling the side sweeps, with Kenneth on the deck staffing the small forward paddle. His brother Thomas shouted out instructions and encouragement while attempting to steer with the flatboat's rudder. What at first seemed slow progress down the river now seemed to be moving rather quickly as they made their approach to the almost barren patch of riverbank.

The heavy flatboat came to an abrupt halt as it collided with land. Everyone lunged forward and then before falling back from the impact. Kenneth jumped ashore with a rope and tied it off to a large oak a few feet from the water's edge.

"Mr. Allsup!" Thomas called out. "Jump down and toss the line out from the back."

Allsup did as requested; Kenneth caught the rope and secured it to a tall Evergreen with a cluster of long-needled pines growing at its top. They were secure and as close to the bank as the river would allow about two feet. The two wives, Savannah and Rachel, struggled with the plank made of three heavy boards nailed together. They were trying to lay it across the open water from flatboat to land, but its size and weight were proving to be too much. Mr. Tunny, seeing their dilemma, rushed to their aid and together, the three managed to lay it across.

The first ashore were the two oxen, each tethered by ropes to large, wooden beams of four feet in length to prevent their wandering too far, too quickly. Next came the four horses whose front legs were hobbled together to keep them from dashing off. The two children were assigned the responsibility of watching the hens and roosters, who seemed to appreciate dirt beneath their feet for a change rather than wood.

The women laid out blankets higher up on a level portion of the riverbank and enjoyed the solidness of the Earth upon which they sat. After all was settled, the adults sat or reclined upon the blankets while the children chased the chickens in their efforts to confine the fowl to a specific area. Allsup joined the group with a rifle in hand.

"It's early yet." he pointed out, glancing up at the sky. "I thought maybe I'd go out and see if I can bring back something for dinner."

"It's not necessary," the elder brother advised. "We have enough food."

"Truth be told, I've a craving for fresh meat, and I want to let my horse run a spell. He's a runner, and I'm sure after being cooped up for the last four days, he's ready to stretch his legs. Do you object to my going?"

"No, no, you're certainly free to go—and now that I consider it, fresh meat does sound inviting. Just know we won't starve if you find the game sparse."

"Wish me luck then. I'll be back shortly."

As he passed the basket of food, he picked out an apple and tossed it into the air.

It returned to Earth and smacked into the palm of his

hand.

"Mrs. Holcomb!" he called out.

"Yes?" the two Mrs. Holcomb's answered simultaneously, causing all to smile.

"I'd like to take this apple, please."

"I think that would be alright," answered Mrs. Kenneth Holcomb, smiling.

"It's for my horse."

"Still, all the same," she replied before turning to Mrs. Thomas Holcomb and asking, "What do you think, Mrs. Holcomb?"

"As long as it's not wasted," declared Mrs. Thomas Holcomb.

Allsup bounded up the hill tossing the apple repeatedly into the air. He found the stallion grazing on the grassy hillside up from the river on the opposite side of a well-used path.

He gave out a short whistle that quickly rose in pitch. The horse raised its head, its ears perked and watched as Allsup approached. Seeing the apple, the horse, with his front legs tethered, clumsily crossed the field to greet him.

"How are you, Chestnut?" he asked as the horse took the apple. Allsup stroked its forehead, gently whispering compliments while it devoured the fruit. Nudging its nose against Allsup's shoulder, it expressed its appreciation.

"Ready for a run?" Allsup asked. "Eh? Let's go saddle up."

He reached down and un-hobbled the horse before leading it by the chin down the hillside, across the path, and back to the moored flatboat where he retrieved his saddle and bridle.

"You've not left yet?" Kenneth called, reclining under the shade of a large Elm.

"Just getting started," Allsup replied as he swung onto the saddle.

Danny Allsup

"We might be eating before long," Savannah informed him.

"Don't let me hold you up." Having said that, by a clenching of his knees, he informed the horse that he was ready to go; the chestnut reared up on his hind legs, impressing the others, and with a leap, bounded up the hillside disappearing down the path.

The horse's hooves pounded on the hardened, rarely used road the width of a cart. It ran free of hindrance from its rider; legs stretched out before and behind; there were times when it felt airborne rather than restricted by gravity, offering a smooth ride for Allsup, who sat at ease upon the saddle. The south side of the path, the riverside, was relatively free of obstacles, such as bushes growing along the trail and leaf-covered branches hanging low from nearby trees, so Allsup kept the horse to that side as much as possible. Even then, they often swerved or leaped over obstacles in their way while Allsup ducked low when an unavoidable branch overhead would present itself.

"By God, but this is something!" he cried out as the horse opened up, galloping as hard as it was able on the path that followed along the river. The wind blew his hat from his head and streamed behind, like a kite by its chinstrap.

"Hee-ah!" he yelled, his head down low, one hand clutching the reins and saddle horn while the other rest gently against the horse's neck. "Hee-ah!"

The sun was beginning its descent, and the horse was lathered with sweat when Allsup pulled the reins gently back. He wondered how long Chestnut would have, *could* have, continued at that almost break-neck speed. They slowed to a trot as Allsup turned the horse around toward the direction from which they came. It would be dark by the time he made it back to camp if he returned directly. Allsup still wanted fresh meat and was determined to obtain some before his return.

After a time of trotting, Allsup slowed the horse to a walk

and began to examine the countryside for clearings in the woods or open areas filled with tall grass, anywhere a rabbit might find it habitable.

As they continued, the horse tended to turn south towards the river. Allsup returned him time and again to the middle of the path, but Chestnut seemed determined and veered back toward the river.

"What the heck, boy," he chastised the animal, turning him away from his desired direction. "What's down there you want so bad?"

After giving it a minute's consideration, he said, "Oh! You thirsty after all that running? You need to quench your thirst? You've cooled down enough. Let's head down so you can drink; then we can go where *I* want to."

Chestnut found his way down the steep embankment and stepped just slightly hoof-deep in the river before lowering his head and drinking deeply; he breathed loudly through his nose as his mouth slurped the water. Occasionally, it raised its head with water dripping from its chin as it looked across the wide river to the distant shore. Allsup waited patiently, his arms folded, and his left leg crossed around the saddle horn.

"It's going to be dark by the time we get back whether I hunt or not," he told the horse. Chestnut, having drunk his fill, turned slowly in the water and, under its own volition, started back up the embankment. Allsup quickly uncrossed his leg, and his foot found the stirrup as he sought to maintain his balance up the steep incline.

They were almost to the top when they heard a rustling in the leaves a short distance away. Allsup brought the horse to a stop and slowly pulled his rifle from its scabbard. There were two rabbits playing around a bush; one would hop around it and stop on the opposite side, soon followed by the other. Sometimes they would bounce around two or three times before stopping.

Allsup raised his rifle and sighted it on the larger of the

Danny Allsup

two. Waiting patiently, he held his aim as he slowly pulled the trigger. The rifle sounded loud, ricocheting back and forth across the river between its high banks, startling Chestnut, who bolted up the embankment and headed back down the trail the wrong way at full gallop. Allsup had no chance to check his success.

"Wait!" shouted Allsup trying to rein in the frightened animal with one hand while holding his rifle in the other. "Whoa! Whoa! Stop, horse!" he angrily exclaimed. He may have missed his shot. It didn't matter. He had no idea where he'd made the attempt. Chestnut slowed, breathing heavily, and allowed himself to be turned around and once again head back to the flatboat.

They rode along the path in darkness; were it not for the semi-full moon and a cloudless night, he'd not be able to see enough to follow their route. They rode in silence for a while. Only the clomping of Chestnut's hoofs broke the quiet.

Soon, Allsup chuckled softly and said, "You know, Chestnut, it never occurred to me what it must be like to have a rifle fired unexpectedly over the top of your head for the first time. I think it would give me quite a scare as well. Sorry I barked at you back there."

He saw the campfire from the road. The children were playing at something they shouldn't because they were being severely reprimanded by their father.

"Tommy, you're the oldest and should know better!" admonished the father.

"But Pa..." he began to protest before wisely deciding against it. "Yes, sir."

"If the two of you—Well, Mr. Allsup has returned!" he announced. "Any luck, sir?"

"No, no luck at all," Allsup answered, swinging down from his horse.

"We heard a shot earlier," Kenneth Holcomb advised as he joined the two men. "It sounded a good distance off. I guess it wasn't you."

D. Dean Carroll

"It was me, all right," Allsup revealed, grinning. "I forgot I'd never shot around my horse, and it spooked him. He took off like a fox caught in the hen house. If I did hit anything, it's someone else's dinner tonight."

"Would you like a plate of dinner yourself?" Thomas asked.

"I would, thanks."

"Come join us," he suggested with a wave of his hand towards the fire, where a large metal pot hung suspended above it. "The ladies have made an excellent vegetable stew."

The three men approached the fire, joining the others, as Savannah Holcomb ladled the stew onto a tin plate. Soon all were sitting serenely around the fire, talking about their past, their future, and what a pleasant evening it turned out to be—even without fresh meat.

Their travels continued, stopping as often as possible at the end of each day for a respite from their labors down the river. Occasionally, when no breaks along the river's banks were available, they'd continue through the night with the men monitoring their progress in two-man shifts.

Mr. Tunny and little Tommy were becoming fast friends. The days now found them together, sitting at the back of the flatboat fishing. Tommy's father had taught him how to bait a hook and remove a fish, so it involved nothing more from Mr. Tunny but to throw out a line, sit back and relax. They would engage in humorous conversations, often eliciting cackling laughter from the boy. Thomas frequently joined them; often, his brother would as well, but not Daniel Allsup.

He never took to fishing; it never hooked him; he liked to jest.

His life and interest had been totally absorbed with the land, how to farm it and use it most efficiently. Water was for drinking, not just for himself and his family, but for the crops and livestock as well. Until his travels on the flatboat, he'd not eaten fish two times in his life. Now they had it regularly, nightly it seemed, and while he'd come to enjoy the mild flavor and unusual flakey texture, he still preferred meat.

He spent his time at the side sweeps and steering oar. He liked being busy, doing something constructive or beneficial. The steering oar usually required considerable effort. Allsup liked to work it to see if he could get it to respond to his will. Move the flatboat to the side of the river as if preparing to allow passage of traffic; then move it back to the center again to ride the current and go with its flow.

It wasn't long before his ability with steerage was noticed, and Thomas suggested that it be his charge for the duration of the trip. Allsup accepted, glad to have the responsibility; it gave him purpose, something he'd not felt for a while. He enjoyed his travels, but other than heading west, there was no direction to his life. The wood handle of the steering oar felt good in his hands. He would guide them safely. He would get them there.

They entered a long stretch of straight river with no turns and few protrusions, the longest they'd encountered to date on their trip. Thomas speculated that it must go on for miles, maybe five or six. It gave them a chance to view the river, wide open, without the obstructions of twists and turns that gave the impression the river was ending abruptly ahead when in fact, it was a wall of forest on the backside of a sharp turn.

A man rowing a small boat informed them they were under Ohio, the state and on the Ohio, the river. This information brought about a pleasant feeling of good cheer; their efforts rewarded by their progress. As the afternoon turned into early evening, they noticed that the river traffic had all but disappeared. There were still other flatboats and barges making their way on the river, but most had found mooring for the night; they regretted not having done so sooner.

"Well, it looks like we'll have to run through the night,"

Thomas informed the men gathered on the roof of the cabin. "All the clearings appear taken, so we're forced to continue on."

And continue they did, down the river as dusk turned to night. Except for the occasional steamboat passing in the night, their massive paddle wheels churning up the river creating wakes that gently rocked the flatboat, the river was free of other traffic.

Allsup enjoyed watching the paddleboats, whose different levels were illuminated by oil lamps attached at intervals along the walls. They looked like floating circus wagons, he thought, gaily decorated, exciting in appearance. He had heard about the various forms of food and entertainment within and made the decision to one day travel on a riverboat.

With only a lopsided crescent smile of a moon to light their way, the men on duty had to stay alert. Bumping into a floating tree or log did not present an immediate danger; not clearing the debris from the flat front of their boat in a timely manner could result in their becoming tangled with other similar debris floating freely. That could impede their already difficult ability to steer.

Thomas Holcomb and Allsup got along well and usually paired up for late-night traveling. They had the first watch. With Allsup at the rudder, Holcomb stood at the front of the boat, with an oil lamp suspended from a long pole extending out before them, providing the possibility to foresee upcoming obstacles.

"Tree down on the right," Thomas called out even though they were well towards the center of the river with considerable distance between themselves and the fallen tree.

"I see it," Allsup responded.

"Gotta a turn coming up!"

"Which way?"

"Left turn!"

"Okay."

"Should I come up?" Holcomb asked.

"Yes, I think so."

Holcomb climbed up on the cabin roof and went to a side sweep. Together they maneuvered the flatboat to the best position to change directions. With the help of an almost too-quick current, they easily made the turn and positioned themselves back toward the river's center.

Holcomb saw them first, being on that side of the cabin roof, three canoe-shaped shadows coming from the shore. There were two or three inhabitants in each, all paddling to intercept their passage.

"Kenneth! Savannah! Wake up!" Thomas shouted, stomping on the cabin rooftop. "Mr. Tunny! Wake up!"

Allsup jumped down from the front of the cabin's roof and stuck his head inside the cabin door. "Hey! Everyone! Wake up!"

Thomas jumped down and joined him as they watched the dark silhouettes floating on the river before them—waiting. Kenneth, followed by Tunny, the women, and the two children, rushed from the cabin in near panic.

"What?" asked Kenneth, "What is it?"

"Looks like we're in for some trouble," Thomas said, pointing to the floating party still a bit ahead.

"Who are they?" Tunny asked.

"I don't know," admitted Thomas. "Robbers, I guess."

"What do we do?" Savannah looked to her husband for assurance. The distance between them slowly diminished as the flatboat drifted with the river's current.

"I—" Thomas began to respond when a loud 'Crack!' sounded in the corner of the boat's cabin sending a small explosion of splinters into the air, followed by the loud report of rifle fire from the riverbank echoing across the previously silent river.

"Everybody into the cabin!" shouted Allsup, and they rushed inside for protection.

"They want us in here," Allsup pointed out. "Makes it easier for them to board us."

"We're in a tight spot!" exclaimed Tunny.

"The man on shore is the problem," Thomas advised. "What can we do about him?

"I'm going up on the roof," Allsup declared. "I'll lay flat and try to pick off the boarders."

"You're sure to get yourself shot!" Thomas pointed out.

"Maybe not—I'll be lying flat. I'm not a big man," Allsup said with a chuckle. "Hopefully, I'll be hard to hit."

"I'll go up too," Kenneth offered. "I'll watch for rifle fire from shore and try to return it to some effect. Maybe I can get close enough to cause concern."

"You can't go up there!" protested his wife, Rachel. "You can't risk getting shot!"

"But, Rachel—"

"I'll go up." Tunny interrupted. "I'm a pretty good shot."

"You're a pretty good target, too!" Thomas replied, not in jest. "You *will* get shot."

"Well, I'll not be as flat as Mr. Allsup here, I'll grant you that, but I got good eyes." he said earnestly. "And there's sure to be a flash when he fires that rifle this dark'a night. I'll watch for the flash and fire right back at it. I think I'll be okay."

"That's all well and good, Mr. Tunny," Kenneth admitted. "But, it's our flatboat. We bear the responsibility for protecting it."

"Well, you're both married men with families and children to bring up; Mr. Allsup and me, well, we got nothing so important as that."

"I couldn't agree more," Allsup frankly told them. "Very well said, I might add." Then to Thomas and Kenneth, he said, "You two keep watch. If any gets passed us, you'll have to deal with them—Well, I'm going up!"

He exited through the door and quickly climbed onto the cabin's roof. Lying prostrate, as flat as possible on his stomach with his legs outstretched and spread eagle to make for slimmer targets, he set himself at the front edge of the cabin where he could see the boats and their occupant's now just yards ahead.

When he felt Tunny join him in a similar fashion but facing the shore, Allsup said, "Well, shall we begin, Mr. Tunny?"

"Yes, sir, let's do it—What do we do?"

"I believe I'll start firing on those boats and you shoot the shooter on shore."

"Right!"

Aided by the illumination from the extended light-pole lantern, Allsup's visibility was much better than those in the canoes. He fired a missed shot at the closest approaching boat containing two occupants. Another shot caused the forward man pain, and he dropped to the boat's hull. As the second man stood to return fire, he lost his balance and fell into the river.

"That's one down!" Allsup called out just as a piece of rooftop wood splintered and a bullet burrowed its way toward him, eventually coming to a stop.

"Did you see that?" he asked Tunny.

"I saw it."

"Why didn't you fire?"

"Cause I got 'im—I got 'im."

"Okay," a skeptical Allsup replied.

One of the remaining two boats started firing at the flatboat with no success; whether it was because of poor marksmanship or the unsteadiness of their craft, the result was the same.

Allsup returned fire and, after three attempts, was able to conclude another's work for the day. A shot sounded next to him causing him to jump before he realized Tunny had fired just as a bullet ripped into the wood inches from Tunny's left side.

Tunny looked at the tunnel created by the bullet and the

spot at which it came to rest still beneath the wood. He looked at Allsup, watching and conveyed a smile of relief.

No sooner had the bullet made its appearance known when a shrill followed by a stream of profanity filled the night and the sound of a rifle fired from shore was heard.

"He got me boys!" the voice on shore cried out, dismal in sound and amplified by the water so that it carried well. "I donno how, but the bastard got me!"

His cohorts on the water, hearing his announcement, and noting the reduction of their own number, deemed it wise to turn back and put an end to their endeavors.

"They're turning back!" Allsup called out. "It's safe! You can come out now."

Everyone filed out through the cabin door and excitedly inquired about the gun battle, going on the rooftop to see the embedded bullets and requesting they retell the events over and over. The women and children all gushed about how brave the two men were while Thomas and Kenneth looked on, appearing envious.

"Gentlemen, we're lucky to have you traveling with us," Thomas stated, shaking each man's hand. "Maybe you would like to get some rest now after all that excitement."

"Not me," Tunny advised. "My heart's racing too fast to sleep. You can go on if you want to," he told Allsup. "But I'm staying on top."

"I think I will too, actually," Allsup informed them. "The rest of you can return to your rest. Mr. Tunny and I will watch the river."

"You're sure?" Thomas asked. Both men agreed, so he said, "Well, we can all rest easy knowing we have the two of you guarding us."

The families returned to the cabin as Allsup and Tunny climbed to its roof again. Allsup resumed his place at the steering sweep, and his fellow river bandit fighter took his station at the front, watching for debris.

Chapter 23

The flatboat drifted down the river without additional interference, other than river traffic becoming more congested with each passing day. Where before it was not uncommon to see one or two steamboats a day running up river or down, now they were passing one or two an hour. Steamboats traveling one after another; steamboats passing in opposite directions.

One steamboat passing another going in the same direction often resulted in a race between the two. They would pass the flatboats at incredible speeds, the fast-turning rear or side wheels throwing water high into the air, leaving a wake that would cause the flatboats to bob like fishing bobbers on the water.

Those on flatboats would stop their activity and watch the steamboats race until no longer in view; then, the men would quickly rush to the sweeps to control their craft and return them to their place on the river.

They were getting closer to Cincinnati, a thriving river port on the Ohio, where the Licking River and the Ohio merge. Cincinnati is located on the north side of the river. Goods coming up the Mississippi stopped there to send and receive from the northern part of the state via the Miami Canal, the man-made waterway that meandered all the way to Toledo.

The narrower the distance between the Holcomb flatboat and the "American" city, the busier the river traffic became. Rafts, flatboats, and rowboats came out onto the Ohio from large streams and smaller rivers, joining the rest to ply their trade in the big city.

The landscape began to change the further west they traveled, with the river valley becoming more prominent, with steeper sides on wider valleys. They passed by towns and villages like Hanging Rock, Portsmouth, and Manchester stopping for a day or two in order to stretch their legs and socialize with someone new. Allsup would take Chestnut out to release pent-up energy. It made the time on the water more than tolerable and more enjoyable.

The newness of traveling by flatboat had long worn off for all those aboard. Everyone tried to remain cheerful and civil, but it was becoming difficult in such close quarters. You could find no place on the flatboat to be alone; everywhere you turned, someone was there. People were becoming irritable and easily agitated, and often it was not the words spoken but rather *how* the words were spoken that caused that sharp prick allowing some of the resentment, some of the animosity, some slight or misconception from the past, a little pinhole that allowed these emotions to seep out and drip exposed.

Mr. Tunny made a comment about the evening meal Mrs. Rachel Holcomb had prepared and she took offense. In her description of the offense to Savannah Holcomb, she wasn't sure what he said, exactly; he'd used words she was unfamiliar with, but the way that he said it, the sound of his voice and his lackadaisical demeanor, it had to be offensive.

Regardless of Mrs. Savannah Holcomb's effort to apply reason and logic, Mrs. Rachel Holcomb wouldn't see it. Mr. Tunny was an insensitive and unappreciative man, she declared. She didn't think she wanted him eating her cooking any longer. How could she serve him after such a slight? The wound had been inflicted. Only the absence of one from the other would allow it to heal.

Problems arose amongst the small ones on board. Little Tommy had grown so tired of the company of his little sister, Greta, that it appeared he had taken it upon himself to bring an end to the problem. Now, no one seriously thought that he would intentionally harm his sister, but little things done made one wonder.

There was the time Greta asked for a knife to spread jam

on her biscuit and Tommy threw the sharp knife used for carving meat at her. To her, Tommy claimed. Harder than necessary all agreed, but he *was* just a boy. He was sternly lectured by both parents about the dangers of throwing things, sharp knives especially, and warned it should not happen again.

Or the time they were fishing off the stern of the flatboat, Tommy, Greta, and Mr. Tunny, and a school of large fish came swimming close to the surface. Tommy and Greta were pointing out different fish by their size or color, or shape. Tommy pointed to one fish with unusual markings that Greta couldn't see. He pointed toward the side of the boat where she should look. As she leaned further and further out, Tommy appeared to reach out and push her arm, causing her to almost slip into the river. Mr. Tunny anticipated her going overboard when he saw her extended out too far and grabbed her by the back of her dress as Tommy reached out.

Greta, crying in her mother's lap, claimed that Tommy pushed her. Tommy said he was only trying to grab her arm before she fell. Mr. Tunny said it appeared that Tommy's arm went out before she started falling, but he couldn't be sure, so he accepted the boy's explanation having no reason to believe he would lie or, for that matter, want to harm his sister.

There were other little incidents, but the Holcomb brothers decided for the sanity and safety of all, they would stop every night as often as possible to vent the cabin of animosity and allow those on board to breathe the fresh air of terra-firma.

They were drifting toward Mayville in Kentucky when the wind began to pick up. The day started out overcast, but the clouds grew darker and more ominous through the morning. Around noon, it became obvious that many of those traveling on the river were tying off along the riverbanks in anticipation of bad weather.

"What do you want to do?" Kenneth called out to his

brother just as the wind attempted to carry away his hat.

"Let's get past the bend coming up and we'll secure it on the other side!" his brother answered.

The river became increasingly choppy as the wind grew stronger. Allsup was manning the steering sweep while Tunny was on the port sweep. Both were finding it difficult to maintain any control over the heavy floating box. Thunder sounded in the distance as the women herded the protesting children inside the cabin; lightning flashed over land not far away.

They had experienced thunderstorms before, but nothing severe. The storm that was brewing now had them worried; it threatened to be severe. The temperature was dropping, the thunder sounding closer, and the lightning appeared more frequently.

Allsup asked that someone fetch his duster. Rain started falling in big, cold droplets as Kenneth handed him his coat. He struggled to put it on while still working the steering sweep. The rain fell hard into the river causing splashes as high as the flatboat's side. The speed and size of the raindrops, along with the wind blowing over the open water made visibility difficult and for those staying exposed to the weather, painful.

Try as they might, they could not prevent the wind from pushing the flatboat across the river, threatening to run it into the southern shore. Tunny worked the side sweep back and forth to keep the flatboat right of the river's center, but gradually they found themselves in the middle and edging closer to the left bank.

Thomas Holcomb carefully crossed the cabin rooftop and stood beside Allsup.

"I can't see a thing in this weather. How about you?" he loudly asked.

"Barely!" Allsup yelled back. "I think maybe I'd see what's floating ahead of us, but a clearing for landing—I can't make anything out!"

Allsup had no sooner finished speaking when they saw a steamboat rounding the bend ahead, traveling full speed to counter the force of the wind. With smoke billowing from its two towering smokestacks on either side of the pilot's house, it was approaching amazingly fast.

"Does he see us?" shouted Thomas.

"Don't know," answered Allsup. "It doesn't look like it!"

"What do we do?" asked Thomas.

"No use fighting the wind and risk colliding with that paddleboat! Let's go on across the river and hope we can get out of its way!"

With a nod of agreement, Thomas said, "I'll go tell Mr. Tunny to switch to the other sweep! Hopefully, we'll make it!"

Allsup began working the rudder to move them across the river. Lightning flashed overhead, followed by deafening claps of thunder. The rain grew colder and colder as the sound of it slapping against the wooden boat grew louder.

He was the first to notice that the large, cold raindrops were bouncing on the cabin roof and floating little balls in the river. The raindrops no longer streamed across the cabin roof but rolled.

"Hail!" Allsup loudly announced, and before he had finished speaking, the falling water completely turned into various-sized balls of ice. They bounced against the wooden structure at times as high as Allsup's head, occasionally striking him. The sound was now so loud that you could hear nothing else but drumming on the cabin's roof and pelting water.

"Get below!" shouted Thomas to those working on the roof. Kenneth and Tunny jumped down and entered the cabin as quickly as possible to escape the painful hail. Allsup pulled his duster protectively up over his head and continued to work the sweep back and forth.

Thomas attempted to run across the roof to Allsup, but the balls of hail worked like marbles under his feet, and they soon flew out from under him. With a loud 'Thump!' he painfully landed on his backside atop the roof and cried out in pain. Allsup was about to offer his assistance, but Thomas waved him back.

The steamboat continued barreling towards them, getting closer by the minute. Thomas, on his hands and knees, crawled over to Allsup, who helped him to his feet.

"Ouch!" Allsup cried out, having been struck on the shoulder.

"We can do no more here," Thomas shouted into Allsup's ear. "We need to go below and trust in Providence!"

"We're almost out of its path!" Allsup countered. "I'm staying here. I think we can make it!"

"You won't go below?" Thomas incredulously asked, to which Allsup shook his head. "Then, I'll stay with you!" he carefully made his way to the side sweep and began working it with all his might.

Allsup removed his hat to wipe the trickling streams of water from his forehead before they entered his eyes when he was struck on his hawk-like nose by a piece of hail the size of a large grape. He staggered backward, almost falling off the cabin's roof; were it not for the tiller tucked under his arm he'd have surely fallen either onto the hard deck or into the water.

"Danny!" Thomas cried out as he observed the strike before rushing to Allsup's aid, but again his feet flew out from under him, and he fell onto the roof with an 'Oomph!'

"Don't you roll off!" shouted Allsup hanging onto the rudder, his hat barely protecting him from the falling hailstones and blood running in rivulets from his nose. The hail gradually turned back into a cold rain that almost obscured the opposite side of the river. As Thomas struggled to regain his footing, he glanced up at Allsup still at the sweep, and the expression on his face caused Thomas's heart to stop. Standing upon the cabin roof in the pouring rain, he looked over his shoulder to see what had alarmed Allsup just as the steamboat rammed into their front right corner.

The flatboat bounced off the paddleboat like a thrown rock bouncing off the side of a barn knocking Thomas off his feet and sending Allsup off the rooftop, landing on his back on the deck below. The flatboat, heavy and cumbersome, began swirling in circles towards the riverbank; dusk, along with the storm-darkened sky and pouring rain made it impossible to get any sense of direction. Thomas grabbed the steering sweep and attempted to regain control of the spinning craft; just as he managed to push the sweep's arm, the flatboat slammed into the river bank and with a loud 'crack!' a stump extending out over the water broke through its side. It held the flatboat tightly in place so that neither the wind nor river could free it.

With rain falling in curtains, Thomas looked down from the roof at Allsup on his back.

"How are you?" he shouted through hands forming a cone. Allsup raised his hand and gave a thumbs up but made no other effort to move.

"Should I come down?" Thomas asked. "I'm coming down! Don't move!"

Thomas ran to the front of the cabin, climbed down, and ran through to the back, checking on everyone as he went; they were rattled, of course, but there were no injuries. He ran between the livestock and out the back door to find Allsup still on his back. He picked Allsup's hat up from the deck and held it over the injured man's face. Allsup attempted to speak, but Thomas couldn't make it out, so he leaned in.

With his ear close, he heard Allsup say, "I can't move."

Chapter 24

Allsup did not move; he could not move. The muscles in his back had seized up, locked tight. Any effort caused excruciating pain, so he remained on his back on the rear deck of the damaged flatboat.

As soon as the storm ended and they determined the extent of Allsup's injuries, they constructed a shelter to protect him from the elements. Kenneth used Chestnut to search for a farm where they might be advised of the whereabouts of a doctor. Late in the day he returned with one from Mayville, which was just a few miles ahead.

The doctor, Andrew Kelly, examined the patient, who related the events that led to his current incapacitation. He hadn't hit anything on his fall from the roof and landed flat on his back just as he saw him.

"He hadn't hit his face in the fall?" the doctor asked. When Allsup assured him that he had not, the doctor asked about his nose, how did it get so bent?

"Got 'it by a 'ailstone," Allsup explained, his voice sounding as if he had a severe head cold, stuffed, clogged up and congested.

He could move his arms and legs to limited degrees, but anything more was painful. After several pokes and prods, which elicited cries of pain from the patient, Dr. Kelly concluded that his back had suffered severe trauma.

"Nothin' can be done for it," he advised. "Just have to let him rest, make him as comfortable as possible, 'n hope he gits better sooner'n later, but I believe he will get better. Let's take care'a that nose 'fore I go." He leaned over and placed an index finger on each side of Allsup's nose.

"Now, lemme warn ya that this is probably gonna hurt a lot," the doctor said just as he snapped the broken nose back into place, causing Allsup to shriek in pain.

"There." He examined his work. "Not much improvement, but that's the way God gave ya to us, I suppose."

Thomas and Kenneth escorted Dr. Kelly back to his horse grazing at the top of the riverbank, leaving Allsup in the care of the others: the two Mrs. Holcombs, the children, and Mr. Tunny.

"We ab a problem," Allsup advised.

"What?"

"I, uh, I ab a need of growing urgency."

"What?" they wondered again, looking confused. It was little Greta who diagnosed the problem. "He has to go to the bathroom." Allsup, with difficulty, nodded his head.

"Oh!" they began discussing how to best remedy the situation.

"Let me ask, Mr. Allsup, sir," Mr. Tunny discreetly inquired. "Would it be solid or liquid that we're, uh, discussing here?"

"Children, let's go inside," Mrs. Savannah Holcomb said, herding the protesting children into the cabin; they wanted to know what was going to be done, too.

Once they had privacy, Mr. Tunny asked again, only differently this time, "You have to pee or shit?"

"Pee."

"Okay, so what do we do? Any ideas?"

"Yeah, let's get my pants off," Allsup answered as he began unbuckling his belt. "Then you can cover me with my bedroll."

"All right, I'm going to pull your boots off."

"Okay —work quickly because I'm feeling desperate – Ow!"

"Sorry," Tunny responded, working on the second boot. When the boots were off, Tunny walked up over Allsup one leg on each side. until he reached Allsup's waist,

"Now, this is probably going to hurt," he advised as he unbuckled Allsup's belt. "You want to do it fast and get it over with or slow and maybe lessen the pain?"

"Fast and hurry!"

"Hips up on the count of three, one—two—three!" Tunny grabbed the waist of Allsup's pants and pulled them down with a single hard yank causing Allsup to cry out.

"One more and they're off! One—Two—Three!"

"Aaugh!" Allsup grimaced in pain before announcing, "Look out!"

Tunny jumped back quickly, bumping into the cabin wall. Allsup's relief made a perfect arch up and over the side of the flatboat. It continued for several minutes, with Allsup releasing 'Ahhs' of relief until completion.

"If you would get me a bucket of water, I'd be grateful," Allsup told Tunny, who was standing off to the side looking across the river at the Ohio shore.

"Bucket of water—right." And he disappeared within the cabin, receiving a barrage of queries regarding Allsup's wellbeing from those within. What did he need? how were they to manage?

Little Tommy asked, point blank, "How did he pee?"

They provided Tunny with a bucket for water and a blanket. He returned to find Allsup as he had left him.

"Mr. Allsup?" he said as he tossed the bucket over the side and, by rope, pulled it up filled with water.

Danny Allsup lifted his head with a grimace before dropping it with a thud back onto the deck.

"I have a bucket of water, Mr. Allsup."

"Set it down beside me, by my hand," he instructed, raising the fingers on his right hand. Tunny followed the directions setting the bucket down before backing away.

Allsup attempted to pick up the bucket with his right hand, but it hurt his back too much. He dropped his hand back down and asked, "Would you wash me off? I thought I could manage myself, but I cannot."

"Sure, what do you want me to do?" Tunny stepped forward.

"Just pick up the bucket and wash me off."

"Wash you off?"

"Yes, please, just wash me off."

"With my hands?"

"What? No! I want you to slosh that bucket of water over me! Just pour it on! Direct it primarily at my—at my, uh…"

"I got the idea. Ready?" He picked up the bucket. "Prepare to get sloshed!" With a grunt; Tunny sent the contents of the bucket out over Allsup, soaking the reclining man from chest to toe.

"Yeow!" exclaimed Allsup as the water hit him. "Geez, that's cold!"

"Yep," agreed Tunny as he flung a blanket over the exposed Allsup.

"I appreciate your assistance with all this, Mr. Tunny," Allsup told him as he adjusted the blankets.

"Glad I could help," answered the heavyset man.

"I will repay you one day," the injured man promised. "I don't know when or how, but I won't forget your kindness."

"Bah, think nothing of it. I'll tell ya what ya could do though if you've a mind to repay kindness with the same."

"Yes! Certainly! Tell me what?"

"You could call me by my given name, ya know—like we was friends or the like."

"What? Most certainly. What is your name?"

"Noah—my family calls me Noah."

"Noah," Allsup repeated as he dropped his head back with a grimace that morphed into a smile. "I'd take pride to be amongst those privileged to address you by that name and would be honored to call you my friend. I'd raise my hand to shake yours, but by gosh, it hurts."

Tunny squatted down and took the hand of the injured man; holding it loosely, he gently shook it before saying, "Get better, Mr. Allsup."

"Daniel," Allsup corrected him. "My friends call me Daniel."

"I thought the Holcomb's call you, Danny."

"Yeah, they do, but…"

"I like Danny better. I got errands to tend to. I'll see you later." Noah Tunny disappeared within the cabin.

"…they're not really friends."

Chapter 25

New routines developed after the storm and their attachment to the Kentucky riverbank along the Ohio. The animals were free to graze along the grassy hills above the river. It was the responsibility of the Holcomb children to monitor the animal's movements and report any wanderings. Tommy was also responsible for maintaining a full bucket of water beside the injured Daniel Allsup so that he could cleanse himself after taking care of his necessities while on his back debilitated.

The Holcomb brothers continued to take daily excursions to Mayville. Either Thomas or Kenneth would ride Chestnut at Allsup's request. Upon their return, they'd sit at the front of the flatboat with their wives and have private conversations.

Savannah and Rachel Holcomb would check on Allsup, providing him with food and making sure he and the area around him was clean.

They would often sit and talk to alleviate his loneliness and provide clean clothes when necessary. The wives avoided any of his attempts to discover their plans for the future or when repairs on the damaged craft would begin by abruptly changing the subject or pleading ignorance.

Noah Tunny visited Allsup throughout the day. He made it a point to have lunch with him and most dinners as well. They discussed different things, but always the conversation would turn to when they'd be able to be back on their way. While the Holcomb's insisted they were biding their time for Allsup's recovery, the two men were mystified why they made no effort to work on the flatboat, free it from the impaled tree stump and repair the damage. Tunny was becoming impatient; he had a job lined up with a logging company in Arkansas and worried the extended delay might jeopardize his employment.

Five days after the storm, Allsup was able to move without intense pain; he described it now as more of an intense discomfort. His arms and legs moved freely, but his back was stiff as a board. Everyone gathered to watch him stand and attempt to walk for the first time, and he received a round of applause for the first step, the second caused his lower back to scream and the third brought him to his knees.

"Too soon!" he exclaimed as he dropped. "Too soon!"

A week after the storm, he was able to sit in an upright position for short periods. He usually did so at dinner so he could join the others, and it was at dinner on the ninth day that Thomas Holcomb announced that they'd decided to stay and settle outside of Mayville. There was thirty acres of good farmland south of the town, a lot of it hilly and forested that needed to be cleared, but the owner was asking a fair price and what timber they didn't use, they could possibly ship and sell down river. They would use the wood from the flatboat to build a temporary shelter. Once they signed the papers, they could start as soon as within a couple of days.

"We know you both to be good men," he told Allsup and Tunny. "You're both welcome to stay and join us. We'd hire you on and eventually help you build places of your own. Whatever you decide, you're both welcome to stay as long as you need to." He looked at Allsup to emphasize this last point.

"I appreciate your offer and your kindness," Tunny told them. "But I got a job lined up in Arkansas I need to be getting to."

"It's with a timber company, isn't it?" Kenneth inquired.

"Yeah."

"Well, you could be cutting trees here with us!" he pointed out. "Eventually, you'll have your own land, a farm of your own."

"Well, sir, farming is not in my future plans," Tunny explained. "And I doubt you could pay what the logging company's promising."

"What are your future plans?" asked Allsup.

"I've got my mind set on finding a small, growing town and building a rooming house; a rooming house with a kitchen open to the public."

"Criminy, that's ambitious!" Allsup exclaimed with a laugh.

"Maybe you could do that here," Thomas suggested.

"Maybe, but I think I'll move on."

"Well, stay as long as you need to," Savannah Holcomb told him with a sincere smile.

"I'll stick around until Danny here," a nod to Allsup, "can mount his horse under his own power again. Then be on my way. I'll be glad to help out with what I can until then."

It was decided that Thomas and Kenneth would ride into Mayville the following day and acquire the land. Then the three able men would head into the forest and begin clearing. Everyone was excited about this change in plans; their new beginnings in north Kentucky and talked with enthusiasm about their future.

Danny Allsup vowed to himself he'd be riding Chestnut again within the next seven days.

D. Dean Carroll

Chapter 26

The two men rode together side by side, one on an old sway-back yellow mare, the other on a fine chestnut-colored stallion whose friskiness betrayed its youth; his rider had to keep him in check to travel alongside their companions. The north Kentucky road, or rather the trail, twisted and turned as it followed the river westward; furrows of bare earth, wagon wheels apart and made from years of use marked their route. Each man rode on his own side of the parallel paths falling one behind the other when necessary or off to the side completely to allow passage of opposing traffic.

"Are you stopping in Cincinnati?" the rather large man atop the yellow mare inquired.

"I was thinking I would," answered the slim man riding the chestnut. "You?"

"I don't know…was thinking of maybe heading on."

"Ready to get to work, eh? Make some money?"

"Yeah, sure," the larger man sheepishly answered. "But it's not all about the work or the money."

"No?"

"My cousin, there in Arkansas, says there's this widow who owns her own house. Well, she's looking for a husband."

"You're going to try to marry the widow?"

"Yeah, sure, why not? My cousin, Wilcox, says she's old and mean and not close to being pretty. Wilcox says it was her meanness that led her to becoming a widow."

"You can handle meanness, can you?"

"Sure, I'm pretty easygoing, you might'a noticed; it takes a lot to get me riled. Eventually, though, I do reach a boiling point and I go off! Boom! Like a bomb! It sort'a sets everything back to normal, and I start over again. I can handle old and ugly; I can handle mean if there's a house in it for me. I always wanted my own house, a place to stay forever; maybe let out a room or two and open a kitchen."

"That does sound nice."

They rode in silence, conversation-wise, for the birds still sang on that pretty, sunny day, and bugs still flew independently and in swarms buzzing from this flower or stem to that. Rabbits still scurried through the tall grass and foxes slept on ledges basking in the warmth of the late morning sun. The human intrusion into their habitat had little effect on the immediate community.

"You ever have a house, Danny?" Noah asked.

"I did. I had a farm once."

"A farm—was it big?"

"Pretty big; big enough to support a family and market some."

"Why'd you let it go?"

Danny Allsup looked at the man riding at his side and smiled.

"Sometimes I do wonder about that, Noah," he answered. "How wise was that decision?"

"Well?"

"Well...well, after a while, I was all that was left of family, and it seemed to have no point to it anymore. Why bother? And—I want to see the Pacific Ocean."

"That's sad," Noah observed.

"Yeah, well, it *is* sad, but you know what? right now, I'm a happy man! I'm riding with a friend on a warm sunny day on a horse that's had enough of me talking and wants to run! We'll meet you up ahead! Hee-yaw!"

With no more encouragement, the chestnut bolted like a rabbit chased by a fox and left the old yellow mare and her large rider behind, appearing stationary.

"Still," said Noah, urging the mare on with a gentle prod to her sides, "it's sad."

Chapter 27

Cincinnati was busier than Pittsburgh. The waterfront was more active than a beehive, with boats, barges, flatboats and skiffs making their way to the first available openings at the docks and piers. Smoke from the steamboats, factories, and homes drifted across the Ohio like clouds.

On the Kentucky side, just east of Covington, Noah Tunny and Danny Allsup sat upon their mounts gazing down from a high hillside at the chaotic activity below them and across the river.

"I'll be," Tunny exclaimed. "Don't think I've seen a busier place then down there. I'd bet there's over ten thousand people!"

"Looks busy, all right," agreed Allsup.

"Are you crossing that bridge?" Tunny gestured toward the massive suspension bridge connecting the two states. Constructed with stone, cement, wood, steel and cables, it towered over the river and dominated the city's riverfront. Scores of people were crossing it, using various forms of transportation. Wagons and carts laden with goods or empty pulled by oxen and ass. They streamed across the bridge in two directions. Many were on horseback or riding in buggies; others traveled on foot.

"I don't know. It looks intimidating."

"What's that mean?" Tunny asked.

"Scary."

"Yeah, it's intimidating."

They sat astride their mounts staring up at the expanse.

"What's this, 'Are *you* crossing the bridge?'" Allsup turned in his saddle, grimacing from a twinge in his back to address his friend. "Don't you mean, 'Are *we* crossing the bridge?'"

"No, Danny," Tunny solemnly answered. "I'll be riding

on."

"You don't want to cross with me just so you can say you've been in Ohio?"

"Bah, that kind'a thing don't mean much to me. I can say I saw it; that's good enough."

"Well...would you ride with me to the bottom of this hill and check the rates of that ferryman down there?" inquired Allsup. "If he's reasonable, I'm going to hire him. If you get a mind to come along, I'll pay your crossing, too. If you still want to head on, we'll say our goodbyes from there."

"No, Danny," Tunny squirmed in his saddle, looking out across the river. "I'm ready to say so-long here."

"Well..."

"You been a good friend to me, Danny Allsup. We haven't known each other that long, yet I feel as if you are my good friend. Criminy, we hadn't known each other long at all when you accepted me as your friend. What does that say about a man? What does that say about a man who'd blindly accept another as a friend like that? A man who'd reach out and take the hand of another out of friendship by request? Who does that kind'a thing? I don't know a lot of people, Danny, but I don't think anyone of them would be that—that—"

"Friendly?"

"No."

"Compassionate?"

"Compassionate. What's that mean?"

"You have feelings; care for others."

"Yeah, compassionate! That's the word I was looking for. Compassionate. That's a blessing from above if you ask me. A rare quality found in a man when sincere. It's nice when displayed for the impression of others, but when it's sincere? Well, it's a blessing. We'll probably never see each other again after this, Danny Allsup. I will always remember you with fondness." Noah Tunny extended his hand.

"You travel safely, Noah Tunny. It has been my pleasure.

I hope that your future holds all you desire—and that the widow be neither too ugly nor too mean."

They shook hands affectionately before Tunny urged his old yellow mare on with prodding heels. The horse reluctantly responded and slowly ambled along the trail. Allsup remained seated atop his stallion and watched his friend ride away.

After several minutes, Tunny called out over his shoulder, "If I were riding that fine chestnut, you would no longer be able to hear me speak!" With a final wave of his hand, he said, "Git on, mare!"

Chapter 28

Seven hills rose high, forming a crescent shape behind the city. Because its riverfront attracted more and more business, Cincinnati was growing quickly. Church steeples pierced the sky from one end to the other, each designed to illustrate the religious worthiness of its parishioners. Surrounding the churches were two, three, and occasionally four-story buildings; each building, each floor, and each room was a center of economic enterprise or creative endeavor. Furthermore, if the mere appearance of the city wasn't evidence enough that it was a living entity, the sound, smell, and smoke served as additional proof this growing metropolis was brimming with life.

Danny Allsup thought that the toll for the ferry a bit high and was reluctant to commit to its use as a one-horse surrey with a resistive filly made its way onto the vessel. He stood off to the side and stared at the mammoth bridge suspended across the river.

"It's this or the bridge," the ferry owner advised. "There's others that will take ya over, but you'll pay more."

When Allsup gave no response, the ferry owner asked, "Ya thinkin' of takin' the bridge? Cause if ya are, I'm gonna go on and take that buggy across before its horse jumps into the river and takes everythin' with it, including my fare."

"No, wait—I'm going with you," Allsup advised, repeatedly glancing up at the bridge.

"It's safe. I guarantee it." The ferryman referred to the bridge with a jerk of his head. "Look at it. Have ya ever seen anythin' so massive?"

"Maybe when I leave," Allsup replied as he led his horse to the ferry.

The crossing went without incident. When Allsup asked if they'd be let off on the city's waterfront, the ferryman answered, "Maybe."

"Where else would we get off?"

"Somewhere around there."

"In the city?"

"Look." The ferryman turned and faced Allsup directly. "We're gonna get ya to the other side, all right? We'll get ya to a city dock or pier if we can. If not we'll get ya as close as we're able. That's all we can do."

"Yes, I see. I understand." Allsup returned to his horse at the back of the ferry.

The ferryman watched him. He shook his head and returned his attention back to getting them across the river.

Chapter 29

The warmth of the afternoon sun, intensified with the inclusion of heat generated from the large gathering of life in motion, caused his brow to perspire. Man and animal milling through crowded streets, shouting and braying, calling out to others between buildings rising four stories high. It unsettled Allsup and caused him to ride warily down streets, around carts, wagons, and vendors clogging the traffic. The stallion was skittish, too, sensing its rider's apprehension.

As he rode northward away from the riverfront into the midst of the city crossing the Miami Canal, the traffic began to thin, and the pace and activity slowed. Men were sitting on benches in front of storefronts that lined the street, talking and waving away flies.

Women with young children casually strolled on wooden walkways stopping to shop or socialize. The general tone of the city changed with the diminishing population as the general atmosphere became more small-town, neighborhood-oriented, and relaxed. Allsup calmed under the new setting, his horse did too.

As he rode along the store-lined street, with restaurants, bars, and offices, he approached a sign advertising '*Mother's Eats*' and decided he would. The restaurant consisted of a large open room with a number of white cloth-covered tables scattered throughout, several of which were in use. He stood just inside the doorway with hat in hand, waiting for guidance. Should he seat himself or wait for a guide to a specific table?

"Doesn't matter," advised a man sitting alone at a table. "They don't care where."

"All right, thanks."

"You're welcome to join me if you've a mind for

company," the man offered, adding, "I don't relish eating alone."

"You're sure?"

"Absolutely," answered the man as he pushed a chair out with his foot.

Allsup took the chair, and the man offered his hand while introducing himself, "John F. Torrance, sir."

"Daniel Allsup. I appreciate the hospitality."

"Not at all, not at all...Here for the Exposition?"

"Exposition?"

A waitress approached their table requesting Allsup's order.

"What's he having?" he indicated his table companion.

"I've got fried ham, eggs, and tators with toast and coffee," Torrance answered. "I like breakfast for dinner occasionally."

"That sounds good. I'll have the same. And you can't get the coffee here quick enough," he added with a grin.

"How do you want your eggs?" the waitress inquired; she looked as if she'd been waitressing a good many years.

"Sunny side up and in fat, if you have it," he answered.

"Oh, we have it. I'll get your coffee."

"Sunny side up and fried in fat," exclaimed Torrance with a chuckle. "Is there any other way?"

"Not in my book," Allsup answered just as his coffee was placed on the table.

John F. Torrance's breakfast was at the midpoint of consumption as he tore a piece of toast from a slice and dragged it through a puddle of grease and yoke that accumulated at the center of his plate. He was an elderly man, well to do by his dress and demeanor. His suit fit well, and he sat straight with an air of authority.

"What's the exposition?" Allsup asked again after sampling his coffee.

"Oh, it's an idea the city's cooked up. Give the citizens a chance to do a thing together, show the city off a bit, like looking into a mirror, see how we look."

"Really? I'm not sure I know what you mean."

"Well, there will be exhibits presented by the local industry and businesses. Food vendors and artisans are available for those that get hungry or appreciate skilled work. Arts, flowers, you name it, if it's in Cincinnati, you can see it at the exposition."

"And it's open to everyone?"

"Yeah, sure! And it's all free—except for food and the like."

"That sounds like a big undertaking."

"It has been a challenge, but it's the city's first. It's hoped to become an annual event."

"I'm sure it'll be interesting." Allsup's meal was served, and he eagerly cut into a slice of ham.

"Go see for yourself," suggested Torrance. "It's here for the week."

"Yes, well, first, I have to find lodging for my horse and myself."

"The horse is no problem; Bucky's Livery is just down the street and around the corner. He's a good man and will take good care of your horse. But for you—that's a different story."

"Oh?"

"With the exposition just opening, and it being the first, people are curious. They're coming from all around. Lodging is at near capacity."

"Oh."

"Excuse me," a man sitting two tables away interrupted. "I couldn't help overhearing your conversation. If I may, I'm checking out of the Coffin Boarding House on the southwest corner of Broadway and Franklin, just down the street. I'm catching the 5:40 train this afternoon, so my room will be vacant and available."

"Really?" Allsup asked with an air of disbelief at his good fortune.

"Yes," answered the man. "No one knows of my departure as of yet, so you should have no trouble acquiring the room."

"That's great!" Allsup exclaimed. "That's wonderful!"

"When you go there," Torrance added as he finished his meal. "Tell them I sent you. I know the people there; they'll be sure to give you the room and maybe a discount."

"Really? Thank you! Thank you both!"

"Well, I'm going to finish this cup of Arbuckle's and be on my way." Torrance drained the remains of his coffee. As he stood, he told Allsup, "It's been a pleasure dining with you, Mr. Allsup. I hope you get the chance to visit the exposition. I think you'll be impressed."

Allsup wiped his mouth with his napkin and stood to say goodbye. "I plan on doing just that, Mr. Torrance. Now that I have the needed lodgings, I believe I'll stick around a day or two."

"Good! You won't regret it. You'll be able to boast one day to your grandchildren that you were at the first Cincinnati Industrial Exposition." Torrance slid his chair up to the table, shook Allsup's hand, and tipped his hat to the gentleman sitting nearby, saying, "Good day to you, sir."

It was while Allsup was checking in to the Levi Coffin Boarding House and mentioned John Torrance's name that the boarding house desk clerk quickly changed his room assignment.

"You know the mayor, do you, Mr. Allsup?" the clerk inquired without looking up from his ledger.

"What? The mayor? No sir, I do not."

"But you just told me that he sent you!"

"No, no, that was Mr. Torr..." Allsup's face appeared enlightened, like an adolescent on the brink of discovery.

"Torrance," finished the desk clerk. "Our mayor."

"Really? He never said a thing about being mayor."

"Well, that's who he is."

Danny Allsup

Chapter 30

The following day Allsup breakfasted at Mother's Eats, hoping to encounter the mayor again, but all he found was breakfast, hotcakes with dark corn syrup and bacon, cooked crisp, and coffee as dark as the syrup.

After breakfast, he freed Chestnut from the confines of the livery stable and informed the liveryman, as he had the boarding house desk clerk, that he intended to stay for at least another night. Having done so, he rode down the street at an easy trot, out of the city, and as soon as they were able, he let Chestnut run all the way to the top of the middle of the Seven Hills. From this vantage point, he could see the city from the north and all the activity surrounding the Exhibition as hundreds of people flowed in and out of its doors.

Allsup coaxed his horse back down the hill towards the Exhibition and decided to take it in as promised. He left Chestnut with a nearby livery with an outside corral containing about ten other animals and followed the flow of people down two city blocks, where they merged to enter the event.

Covering seven acres, the Cincinnati Industrial Exposition was the talk of the Midwest and beyond. The city's Music Hall serving as the centerpiece. There were halls filled with paintings, architectural models and drawings, and horticultural specimens, along with steam-powered machinery demonstrating the latest in manufacturing technology. There were halls devoted to specific products and art. Scattered throughout were ensembles of different musical configurations performing old and recently composed music.

Danny Allsup, filled with awe and wonder, strolled through the exposition fascinated by all that man had created without his awareness.

D. Dean Carroll

When did all this take place, he asked himself.

Was he so cut off from the outside world back on the farm that these achievements could occur unnoticed? evidently so, he'd lived in his own little world in the Pennsylvania countryside that expanded briefly during the war but mostly disappeared at its conclusion. After the passing of his wife, Allsup lived in almost total isolation on his farm.

The exposition was similar to being submerged in cool lake water for the first time, both shocking and exhilarating. He spent the entire day there like many others, not even stopping for lunch. He did have the finest beer he'd ever tasted, brewed by a local German brewery, and was encouraged to sample several varieties before moving on. There was a general feeling of revelry and pride throughout the exhibit. 'The feelings were stronger in the bars and taverns. The feelings were stronger in the bars and taverns. When Allsup finished his last glass of fine German lager, his new friends in the bar cheered him on and shouted tokens of goodwill as he left.

As he walked out of the Exposition, he came to the realization of two things. One, he had drunk much more than he was accustomed to; in fact, he was sure he was drunk. And two, he could not recall where he'd left his horse. He remembered the livery was just a couple of blocks away but in which couple of blocks, he could not recall. Awkwardly, he walked over to a city park bench and sat down with the intention of figuring things out and hopefully allow time for the Earth to become more stationary.

His head rested back against the bench and he closed his eyes to stop the spinning. With a sigh, he thought it would be better if he just rested for a minute and give his mind a chance to clear up.

How long he rested, he had no idea, but a tugging on his coat caused him to open one eye through which he observed that dusk was falling, and a woman was trying to extract his money pouch from the inner pocket of his coat. Reaching up quickly, he grabbed the wrist of her hand holding the bag.

"What's going on here?" he asked, sitting up, still clutching her wrist.

"Nothin'!" She tried to pull away. "I weren't doin' nothin'!"

Refusing to release her, he asked, "What are you doing with my money?"

She was a raggedy-looking woman, probably in her late twenties or early thirties, but she appeared older because of the harsh life she'd been living. Her dull brown hair was in disarray, and her skin appeared dry and leathery with lines caused by hardness around her eyes and mouth that indicated she'd led this life for a considerable time.

"Nothin'! Let go'a my hand!" she insisted as she tried to break free from his grasp.

"Let go of my money," he demanded.

"All right! All right, here!" She dropped his pouch onto his lap. "Now let go!"

"I should get the police," he told her. "You taking advantage of a man in an inebriated state."

"I weren't!" she argued, trying to yank free. "I don't even know what that means!"

"You were trying to rob a man passed out from drink!"

"I weren't!"

"What do you call it? You had my money bag in your hand!"

"I just wanna get somethin' to eat. I weren't gonna take all of it."

"You probably loiter out here and prey upon unsuspecting victims coming out like myself."

"Mister, I don't get most'a what you're sayin'!"

"I'm saying I'm probably not the first you've tried to rob during the Exposition."

"Oh." She looked sheepishly away before back at him with a crooked smile. "You'd be wrong to think that."

"How so?" he asked as he released her wrist and rubbed

his eyes with his hands.

"You'd be the first I *tried* to rob," she said, grinning. "All the others I *did* rob!" She broke into childish laughter that caused him to look at her again. It was contagious and he found himself smiling.

As he studied her face, it seemed to have changed, now fair of complexion made ruddy from exposure to the elements, soft grey eyes, and a pleasant smile that she was bestowing upon him at that moment.

"I'm sorry." Embarrassed, he looked away.

"For what?" she innocently asked.

"For staring—it was rude."

"Is that what ya call it? Staring?"

"Yes."

Laughing, she told him, "I stare a lot then!"

After a moment, he asked, "Were you impressed by the exhibition?"

"No."

"No? I found it pretty impressive myself."

"I ain't seen it."

"No?" he sounded surprised. "How can you not have seen it? It's in your city, and it's free!"

"They ain't gonna let the likes of me in there. They'd be worried I'd rob everyone."

"Why? Why would they think that?"

"Cause I'd probably rob everybody!" she replied, exasperated by the obvious.

"Aren't you curious?"

"Yeah, course I am."

"Well, why don't you go in and satisfy your curiosity."

"I done told ya, they'd kick me out!"

"They won't kick me out," he said defiantly. "I'll go in with you. They'll let you stay. Come on."

He rose and stood waiting for her to join him.

"Can we get somethin' to eat first?"

"Inside—they have lots of swell food inside. Come on."

He held out his hand. She took it and allowed him to pull her to her feet before letting go and walking by his side.

As they walked to the entrance, Allsup said, "There's something bothering me. I can't quite remember what it is, but it seems like I'm forgetting something."

She made no response as they walked together into the main exhibition hall. As they strolled down the aisles between exhibits, he constantly had to stop to allow her time to catch up. She was amazed by everything.

"I feel like everyone's staring at me," she whispered, looking at all the people.

"No one is looking at you. Why would they pay attention to you with so much else to look at?" He took her arm and guided her down a row between tables piled with different bolts of material woven there at the exposition.

"Yeah—you're right. Why'd anybody pay attention to me when there's all this stuff to see."

When they approached a food vendor, she would stop and sample their goods. Just the aroma of cooked food would result in a change of direction to locate its source. He marveled over the quantity of food she consumed, and she told him, with a mouthful, that she'd 'never tasted food like this before.'

Around eight-thirty that evening, as they were leaving the exhibition and she was finishing a cup of ice cream produced by a steam-powered churn, they were discussing his journey west when she asked his means of travel.

"How ya getting' there?"

"By horse—I have a stal—Chestnut!"

"Huh?"

"I'm sorry, but I have to go!" he exclaimed while digging in a pocket.

"Here." he handed her several crumpled dollars. "I've left my horse with a livery and must retrieve him before it's too late."

"Too late for what?" she asked.

"Too late for—I don't know. I just feel compelled to fetch him."

"Okay, but I can't take all'a this money."
"Sure you can!" He took a couple of steps back to begin his departure. "I had a good time."
"Yeah, but…"
"Take it!" The distance widened between them.
"How do ya know I won't spend it on drink or somethin'?"
"It's your money now. It's your choice! Best of luck to you!" He waved, turned, and began to quickly walk towards where he remembered the livery and his horse were located.
"Hey, mister!" she called after him. "What's your name?"
"Dan—Danny Allsup! What's yours?"
"Abby! They say I'm named after a president's wife!"
"It fits you good, Abby!" he called out. "Best of luck!"
"Be careful, Danny Allsup!" She waved as he disappeared into the night.

Chapter 31

He followed a road westward out of Cincinnati that ran parallel with the Miami Railroad that tracked along the banks of the Ohio River. Danny Allsup on his chestnut stallion, striking out once more towards the Pacific. As he took custody of his horse, a livery hand informed him that the land westward through Indiana and Illinois was about as nice a country as you could find anywhere in America.

It was mostly farmland now on rolling hills, some areas fenced in, most not. The forests were being cleared out to make way for more farming, so his travels wouldn't be impeded by much in that regard. From what he heard, the hand further advised the same geography extended even farther west into Missouri and Kansas. But, he discreetly cautioned, those two states were not friendly, still harboring past grudges, and he personally would recommend avoiding them if at all possible.

"If it was up to me, that's what I would do. Avoid those states," the stable hand repeated, concluding his testimony.

Allsup thanked him for the advice, and as he traveled out of the city, he reflected on the man's comments and decided that they would travel overland through the states and see all that farmland.

With sweating palms, a stomach clenched tight like a fist, and a great desire to change his mind, Allsup, leading Chestnut, joined those departing the city via the huge suspension bridge crossing over the Ohio to the Blue Grass state.

Don't look down, he reminded himself as he walked stiffly, taking one measured step after another, don't look down. His eyes fixed on the hills rising on the opposite side or glancing above at the many birds flying overhead. He did all that to avoid casting his eyes downward.

D. Dean Carroll

How people could traverse the bridge without a thought mystified him.

Didn't they know that at any moment, this man-made monstrosity could collapse and send them all to their peril? Hecould see the water flowing directly below. Don't look down—don't look down!

"First time on the bridge, I take it?"

Allsup, with a start, looked to his right to see a bearded man about his own age leading a donkey pulling a wagon. His brownish beard and hair were neatly trimmed, and he wore a dusty brown suit over a dull-white cotton shirt with a frayed black tie. He gave all appearances of a man who conducted business in an office, but the wagon was carrying a number of caged chickens, two piglets tethered by leg to the side of the wagon, and one full grown milking cow whose teats needed attention.

"What?" asked Allsup.

"I said it appears to be your first crossin' over the bridge."

"Yes, yes," responded Allsup with a nervous laugh. "It is. Is it that obvious?"

"You can always tell a first-timer," the man answered good-naturedly. "They don't know where to look. They only know they shouldn't look down. So, they're lookin' all over the place! But do ya know where their eyes always go?"

"Down," Allsup answered, grinning.

"That's right! Down! A unique characteristic of man—we always wanna do what we know we ain't supposed to. Am I right?"

"Yes, I believe you are."

"What'd ya do?" the man inquired.

"Well, actually, nothing." Allsup had to smile again. This was the first time he had to answer that question since leaving Pennsylvania. "I travel."

"Travel?" the bearded man sounded astounded. "You can get paid to travel?"

"Not paid, no. I sold my property, and I'm using the money from the sale to finance a trip westward."

"No family?"

"No."

"I think there was one, but ain't no more."

After a pause, "That'd be correct."

"That's too bad. Where ya from?"

"Pennsylvania."

"Ah, an eastern man. Never been there—never been anywhere to speak of. What did ya do back in Pennsylvania?"

"Farmed."

"Ah, a peer in the profession!"

"Mostly just able to be self-sufficient," Allsup admitted before adding, "barely."

"Same here, that's really the way'a life for grangers, ain't it? All we want is to be able to get through the year without goin' under. Am I right?"

"That's the truth of it."

"Wasn't so bad now, was it?" Smiled the man who stopped and stood looking at Allsup.

"What?"

"Ya crossed the bridge. We're on the Kentuck side."

"I'll be darned." Allsup looked back to see the length of the bridge behind him and the seven hills of Cincinnati in the distance.

"Just needed somethin' else to think about is all. I wish ya well on your travels, Pennsylvania." The man climbed up onto the wagon seat and clucked his mule onward. Without a glance back or a fare-thee-well, he turned the wagon eastward and, followed by two stumbling piglets and a floppy-teat cow, merged in with other like-minded travelers.

Allsup abandoned the road, train, and river routes after entering Indiana and decided on heading due west straight across the state. Following roads as much as possible. At times, he was compelled to ride the rows between growing crops or across pastures under the watchful eyes of curious grazing cattle. Chestnut required little coaxing to jump the confining fences. The horse seemed to derive a curious pleasure in jumping and would take every opportunity to do so; on more than one occasion, he turned on his own volition and jumped the fence back and forth just for the enjoyment.

They traveled past Lawrenceburg and were almost to Versailles when he decided to look for a place to spend the night. Sleeping out in the open farm country gave him a sense of comfort; he felt no threat from farmers and supposed there would be no bad blood roaming in this part of the country. Therefore, he decided to settle down for the remainder of the day and found a small grassy area between three wide trunk trees whose thick reddish canopy obscured the sky. The little stand was a few feet from the road on which he'd traveled that day, having encountered only one other traveler; a farmer with a wagon load of vegetables passed on the way to Lawrenceburg.

Allsup relieved Chestnut of his gear, and the horse immediately began grazing upon the shaded green grass. He no longer needed tethering; he never wandered far and would faithfully return when Allsup whistled. Leaning the saddle against the middle tree, Allsup unrolled his ground tarp and blanket atop the thick grass. Gathering firewood should have been a priority, but Allsup's back was bothering him. He thought it would feel better if he just stretched out for a spell and relaxed in a horizontal position. There would be time enough to gather firewood later.

He lay back with a sigh, stretched out and content, his hands folded across his chest and his head resting on his saddle. There was a light breeze rustling the leaves above that cooled him. He looked up at the thick shield of leaves high above and watched them sway with the wind, like arms reaching upward, allowing little bright rays of sunlight to break through.

Gradually, his eyes began to close for longer periods

until they did not re-open. He felt something crawling on his cheek and was about to swat it off when he opened his eyes and saw a bumblebee flying just in front of his face. It hovered directly before him, first over his eyes and then his nose, back and forth, back and forth, before flying away.

He raised his head and looked around; Chestnut was grazing in a meadow a few yards away, and a bee was crawling on his pant leg. He brushed it off with the back of his hand and watched it fly away before noticing one more on his ground tarp as another attempted to land on his nose.

Quickly scooting away from the campsite, he noticed a number of the honey-gatherers flying between the trio of trees. It didn't take long for him to discover the cause and source of the flying armed insect invasion. High up in the branches of the left tree was a bucket-size beehive. Dusk was falling and the swarm was returning home for the night. The darker it became, the more settled they would become. Allsup decided to gather his firewood with the thought that when he would be done, so might the bees be.

A campfire burned bright yellow-red a distance from the three trees with the intention of not disturbing the hive. Allsup, however, sat amongst the three Red Oaks studying the bee's lair. Long forgotten memories of his youth when his father came home one night with a dozen bee stings and chunks of honeycomb swimming in golden liquid filling the crown of his hat; this remembrance came flooding back. His recollection of that night was pure joy—the wonderful pleasure of dipping his finger repeatedly into the pool of honey and promptly placing the sweet nectar into his mouth was indescribable. As he stared at the beehive, his memories prompted him to consider a plan for reliving that youthful pleasure.

Darkness had fallen. Allsup could hear Chestnut grazing nearby. Occasionally, he would get up to toss a branch onto the fire, but he returned to the three trees where the liquid treasure hung high above his reach.

D. Dean Carroll

Eating a strip of jerky, he considered alternative plans for obtaining his new obsession. He was sipping water to wash down the dried meat when he heard horse hooves fall unhurriedly down the nearby road.

A single horse-drawn black buggy appeared at the perimeter of the campfire and came to a halt. The horse snorted either of weariness or impatience and pawed at the ground.

"Hello," a man's voice came from the dark carriage.

"Hello," responded Allsup.

"We come in friendship," returned the voice. "With no malice intended."

"Come ahead, then."

The horse brought the buggy into the firelight and came to a stop on its opposite side. A short, round man carefully climbed down.

"Come on, baby," Allsup heard the man say. "It's okay. Now you be good and obey grandpa."

The man lifted a little girl down. He took her hand and led her towards the campfire as Allsup stood to greet them.

"My name is Andrews," the man said as he extended his hand. "This is my granddaughter, Tammy."

"I'm Danny Allsup. You are both welcome. I have nothing more than jerky and hardtack, but you're welcome to both."

"Thank you, Mr. Allsup; anything edible will be appreciated." Taking a strip of jerky and handing it to his granddaughter, he kept the hardtack for himself.

Allsup laid out his blanket so the two would not have to sit on the bare ground, and Andrews, an older white-haired man dressed in a worn black suit, instructed his granddaughter to sit down. Tammy wore a yellow dress with white frills around its hem and sleeves; a tight braid of brown hair hung down her back. She looked from her grandfather to Allsup with innocent brown eyes.

"We're on our way home to Versailles from

Lawrenceburg," Andrews explained. "I admit I got to jawing with folks, which caused our departure to be later than intended. I believed we had enough daylight left to reach home before dark. Unfortunately, I was wrong."

"Well, this is no roadside inn," Allsup said with a smile. "But you're welcome to rest here if you like."

"We thank you. Little Tammy here is just about beat. It's been a long day for us both. She's particularly worried about not being home, but we'll be alright, won't we, darlin'?"

Tammy stared up at him, chewing the dried meat, but said nothing.

"She doesn't say much." Andrews observed as he rubbed the top of her head. "But that's a good thing—keeps you out of trouble, don't it, baby girl."

She continued to stare and chew.

"What took you to Lawrenceburg?" Allsup settled back against the saddle and glanced upwards. "If I may ask."

"I went to see a banker concerning financing. I plan to open a granary in Wilmington, about halfway between Lawrenceburg and Versailles, and I require money to get started."

"Just "business" would have sufficed," Allsup quickly informed him. "I didn't mean to pry into your personal affairs."

"No, no, I'm not ashamed—seeking assistance. If I get this loan, I will be a rich man one day. I'm not ashamed asking for help if it gets me ahead, no sir."

"I commend your determination." Allsup bowed his head before shooting another glance at the hive.

"I declare, Mr. Allsup, sir, you have me curious!" exclaimed Andrews with a chuckle. "What in tarnation, tugs at your attention up there?" The elderly man looked upward, as did the little girl.

"There's a beehive up in the branches of that tree, a rather large one, and I desire to sample its contents."

"Oh, I think I see it!" Andrews pointed up into the tree. "It looks like a shadow, but I believe that's it."

"That's it, alright," confirmed Allsup.

"See it, Tammy?" The grandfather pointed to its general location.

She nodded and softly said, "Yes, Grandpa."

Andrews addressed Allsup, "And you know it's a working hive?"

"Yes, I watched the swarm come home at dusk."

"It's been a long time since I've tasted honey," Andrews admitted. "I doubt Tammy ever has. When I was young, I spent a summer on my Uncle Samuel's farm. He had hives."

"Looks inviting, doesn't it?" Allsup looked up at the subject of their discussion, grinning.

"It does! See here, I propose we keep this fire burning through the night; we'll have plenty of hot coals in the morning when we'll need them. A time after sunrise, we'll throw those hot coals in something, layer the coals with fresh green leaves still damp with morning dew so they'll smoke, and then you can climb up there and retrieve your treasure. What do you think?"

Allsup looked up at the barely visible beehive.

"We need smoke?"

"Yes, it pacifies the insects, so they'll not be overly aggressive."

"You want me to climb that tree with a container of hot coals and smoking leaves and knock down that beehive?"

"No, no, you don't want to knock it down! That'll just rile them up. You want to bring it down gently."

"Oh—and we're doing this at sunrise?"

"Yes, the workers leave at sun up. We'll give them a chance to be on their way and then we'll strike…Tomorrow we're going to have us some honey!" Andrews announced, rising. "I'm un-harnessing the horse and turning in. You too, Little Tammy. Let me see if we have a blanket in the buggy—though I doubt we do."

Danny Allsup

Returning from tending to his horse, the elderly man said, "Just as I thought, no blanket in the buggy."

"You can use mine," offered Allsup. "It's a pleasant night. I won't be needing it."

"Really? That's kind of you." Andrews spread out the ground tarp they had been sitting upon and laid down next to his granddaughter; after ensuring she was adequately covered by the blanket, he snuggled under as much of it as he could. They watched as Allsup unbuckled his holster and placed it, along with the pistol, underneath his saddle and leaned his rifle against the same tree. With heavy eyes, they watched as he slid down, his duster draped over him, and stretch out on his back with his head propped against his saddle.

Allsup relaxed, looking up at the hive. Now that a plan was proposed, he pondered the possibilities of its success. The potential for failure seemed probable to him and achievement remote; still, his desire outweighed his concerns; he drifted off to sleep with thoughts of honey on his mind.

Once during the night, he rose to throw new logs on the fire. If smoke was necessary for the success of their endeavor, he wanted to make sure they would have plenty of it. Andrews must have had the same thought because later, he interrupted Allsup's sleep to feed the flames.

It was the morning sun's brightness, not the heat, which caused him to open his eyes; he lay his arm across to shield them. It was in the shade of his arm that his gaze rose to the beehive, and he remembered their quest. Sitting up quickly, he found Mr. Andrews and Little Tammy sitting opposite where he lay.

"I hope you don't mind," Andrews said. "I gave the child a chunk of jerky and hardtack; she was hungry."

The two were sitting across the smoldering fire, red coals still burning brightly. Tammy sat eating hardtack, watching Allsup rub the sleep from his eyes.

"Would you like coffee?" he asked.

"No, thank you," answered Andrews. "I do not indulge in the beverage, but certainly make some for yourself if you wish."

Rising and stretching, Allsup said, "No, I'll save the water for later."

Standing with hands on hips and looking up at the hive, he asked Andrews, "Well, what should we do?"

Andrews struggled to get up because of age and girth but eventually joined Allsup underneath the trees.

"Here's what I propose," proposed Andrews. "We pack up for departure because when we're done, we're going to want to skedaddle out of here. Then we throw hot coals into your coffee pot and add green vegetation and get it smoking real good. Then you climb the tree. Holding the smoking coffee pot under the hive will calm the remaining bees so that you can gently remove the hive from the tree and gently, I repeat, gently, climb down. As soon as you're down, we'll quickly bolt out of here and hopefully leave any emerging bees in the wind."

"Why does that sound painful for me?" asked Allsup, his hands still on his hips.

"Shouldn't be," assured Andrews. "We'll wrap your coat around you as best we can use your bandana to protect your face, and of course, you'll be wearing your hat and gloves."

"I have this image of myself in the middle of a swarm of angry bees."

"There are bees in the hive, make no mistake about that, but most have gone out to pollinate and gather. I don't see getting the hive as the major danger."

"Oh?"

"I fear getting up and down the tree will be our biggest obstacle."

The two men walked around the trees, searching for the best route to their grail. Each made comments and suggestions, but it soon became obvious this was going to be no easy task. With both hands free the climb would be challenging, but Allsup would be carrying something going up and down. Up, the hot smoldering coffee pot, and down, the hive alive with stinging bugs.

"Do you have a bucket?" Andrews inquired.

"I'm traveling on horseback. Where would I keep a bucket?"

"A little testy in the mornings, aren't we?" Noted the older man with a smile.

"Sorry, not usually, but I'm recovering from a back injury resulting from a fall, and here looks the possibility of it repeating."

"Well, Mr. Allsup, I'm afraid I'm too old to make it up that tree, and Tammy's too young, so if it's that honey up there you desire, you'll have to get it yourself."

"Right." Allsup clapped his hands together and prepared to begin. "Let's get a rope. I'll climb the tree with one end, and we'll tie the other end to the coffeepot handle. As soon as I'm in place, I'll pull the pot up, smoke the bees, and when you think enough time has passed, lower the pot and work on the hive."

"We can use my coat to wrap the hive in," suggested Andrews. "You can tie the rope around the bundle and lower it back down to me."

"Sounds like we have a plan; let's get everything packed up."

Tammy was out in a field playing around the grazing horses as the two men gathered their belongings. Allsup whistled and Chestnut looked in his direction before slowly ambling toward the campsite. Andrew's horse watched Chestnut's departure and decided to follow in turn. Several minutes passed before Tammy realized she was alone in the field, and she, too, began walking back.

With his horse saddled, loaded, minus a coffeepot, and ready to run, Allsup buttoned up his Duster coat to the neck, tied his neck scarf to easily pull up over his face, and grabbed his coiled rope from the saddle. Andrews approached with a smoking coffeepot in hand.

"So far, so good!" he declared, holding up the functioning coffeepot. "Little Tammy! Now you stay in that buggy! Do you hear me?" Tammy was in the process of returning to play in the field.

"Yes, Grandpa," came the little girl's voice. She climbed into the buggy and twisted around to watch the two men.

"When you've reached the point from which you'll work, pull up the coffeepot and hold it just below the hive, close enough to engulf it in smoke," Andrews instructed. "Hold it until you hear the activity inside subside, and then hold it just a little longer to be sure. Then, you quickly lower the coffeepot, and I'll exchange it for my jacket—"

"We can use my blanket," proposed Allsup. "No sense ruining a fine coat for honey."

"No, we'll use my coat because I plan on keeping the hive," explained Andrews. "How will you ride with it if you keep it? For how long? There's going to be a lot of honey in a hive that size. What will you do with the rest after you've satisfied your craving?"

"Yes, you're right. Those are good points," Allsup agreed. "I have no problem with you taking the hive; allow your people a chance to enjoy it."

"You're a good man, Danny Allsup," Andrews said, shaking his hand. "Now, let's get that honey."

Allsup loosely tied one end of the rope around his waist and after careful examination of the tree, began his ascent. He used the lowest hanging branch to pull himself up into the center of the tree. From there, he continued climbing from one branch to the next careful with his footing and dependent upon a firm grip on the branch above.

Soon, he found himself straddled on a young branch that ran directly above the beehive. If he advanced himself out mere feet from the trunk and lay on his chest, he'd have access to their prize. He merely had to reach down with outstretched arms and remove it from its fixed place from the branch below.

Slowly, with great care, he pulled the smoking coffeepot up, cringing every time it struck a limb.

He could hear Andrews below instructing, "Easy—easy—"

He glanced up from his reclined position and saw Tammy's face framed in the back window of the buggy's black curtain. Her expression caused him to pause as she appeared both concerned and confused.

The smoking coffeepot was almost within reach when he realized his approach had been wrong; he would not be able to hold the coffeepot below the hive from his position above. Already the rising smoke was burning his eyes.

"I have to stop!" he called out, his eyes watering from the smoke. "I have to change positions! I'm lowering the pot!"

"All right, all right," muttered Andrews as he watched the pot descend.

"Grandpa!" called out little Tammy.

"Not now, sweet pea. Grandpa's busy!"

"Grandpa!"

"Little Tammy, now you just be quiet while us grownups work!"

"Grandpa!"

"Confound it!" He turned his attention to his granddaughter sitting in the buggy. "What is it?"

"Climb that tree, Grandpa!" She pointed to the middle tree.

"What?"

"Climb that tree!"

"Sweet Pea, I'm not climbing any tree! I—"

"Wait!" shouted Allsup.

"What?" Andrews turned back, looking up at the man

straddling an upper branch.

"She's right!" Allsup declared. "Look at that limb growing out from the tree!"

An almost level branch grew out from the second tree mixed in with limbs from the first.

"I don't know why we didn't see it!" mused Andrews. "It's just so busy up there with all those branches and limbs. I'm surprised Tammy was able to note it. Thank you, Sweet Pea! That was very helpful!"

"Extra dip or two of honey for that girl!" announced Allsup as he gingerly climbed down, having difficulty with the rope tangling in little branches and offshoots. Muttering under his breath, he untied the rope and let it drop.

Tammy grinned proudly, standing next to the buggy.

"Get back into the buggy, Little Tammy!" Her grandfather ordered. "We're going to have to leave here quickly in just a few minutes, and I don't want you being left behind. Understand?"

"Yes, Grandpa." She climbed back into the buggy but quickly reappeared in the buggy's back window.

Andrews refilled the coffeepot with fresh smoldering coals before he searched for new vegetation to put on them. Allsup began his second ascent, up the middle tree this time, with the rope retied around his waist. Eventually, he found himself straddling a limb approximately five feet below the hive. By reaching up, he had easy access, working just a foot or so above his head.

He carefully pulled the smoking coffeepot up and held it directly under the hive that was soon engulfed in a cloud of smoke. The hum of activity within gradually diminished until it was almost silent. Several minutes passed with no additional changes.

"I'm sending the coffeepot down," he announced as quietly as possible and still be heard.

"Send it on," responded Andrews. "I'm ready."

Once Andrews had the pot, he tied his coat to the end of

the rope and told Allsup, "pull away!"

Up the coat went, snagging on branches here and there; at one point, the coat refused to free itself regardless of how hard Allsup pulled.

"Jerk on it!" shouted Andrews. "Don't worry about the coat; just get it up there!"

With an 'Oomph!' Allsup jerked on the rope, tearing the coat's pocket, and freeing it from impediment. Carefully, he wrapped the hive with the coat and gently wiggled it back and forth to break it from the limb.

"Gently, gently," Andrews softly coached as if anything louder would alert the occupants of the hive.

With a number of curious bees flying about his head, Allsup pulled it free and rested it between his straddled legs on the branch. He wound the rope around it several times, knotting the end, and prepared to lower it to the awaiting Andrews. As he finished securing the hive, he noticed the humming inside increasing; the effect of the smoke was wearing off.

Down the coat-wrapped hive went between branches and limbs. Occasionally, it would bump against a limb and another small flurry of bees would escape.

"Don't swat at them or make sudden moves," Andrews instructed as he reached up to take the descending hive. "If they don't feel threatened, they're less likely to become aggressive. Come down as quickly as you can!" he told Allsup. "We've got to leave this place, and the bees, behind!"

Allsup dropped to the ground from the tree's lowest branch and, while coiling his rope, joined his elderly accomplice.

"Use your gloved hand," Andrews told Allsup as he approached. "And see if you can reach inside and extract a chunk of honeycomb."

Allsup reluctantly pushed his hand slowly into the hive and pulled out a piece of honeycomb the size of a deck of playing cards and several active bees.

'Just set it there on the ground," Andrews instructed. "As they come out, they should go directly to it."

As they watched, many of the bees were already migrating to the comb on the ground clutched in Allsup's abandoned glove.

"I am reluctant to bring this hive into the buggy with Tammy. Can you carry it with you on your horse?"

"Yes, let me get mounted and you can hand it to me." Allsup retrieved his horse tied to the buggy and climbed onto the saddle.

With three or four bees flying around him, Andrews carefully handed the hive to Allsup, saying, "Careful—careful."

As Allsup gently took the offered hive, Andrews advised, "I suggest you take off and let that stallion run as fast as he can, leaving those emerging bees behind. Two or three miles ahead, there's an apple orchard on the right; wait for us there."

"Ow!" Andrews cried, slapping his neck.

"One get you?"

"Yes, by golly, one did!" He rubbed his neck. "Painful things, bee stings!"

"I'm surprised they haven't got—Ow!" A bee had crawled up Allsup's sleeve and stung him above his wrist.

"Ride on, man! Ride on!" cried Andrews.

"Hee-ah!" shouted Allsup and with a nudge of his heels. Chestnut surged ahead into a full gallop leaving the buggy and its occupants behind at the three trees. The pounding of the horse's hooves created a rhythmic pattern as they crossed unfenced fields, catching the attention of workers out tending crops. Allsup noted that, as predicted, the bees emerging from the hive were quickly left behind. As he approached the distant orchard, he slowed Chestnut to a canter and observed that they appeared to be bee-less.

Chestnut walked into the tall grass toward the orchard

Danny Allsup

casually, without haste. The hive, tucked beneath his left arm, wrapped in Andrew's coat was laden with dripping honey. That honey was a distraction to Allsup. He hardly noticed where they were headed, trusting in the common sense of his horse and turned the hive upside down so that the dripping bottom was now pointing up, just inches from his chin.

Before they reached the orchard, Chestnut gradually slowed to a walk stopping to munch on grass tops. Allsup could not take his eyes from the coat saturated with honey and had no idea they'd stopped. He looked back to see if there was any sign of the buggy, there was not. As if he were committing a crime, he checked his surroundings to confirm he was alone before reaching down and scraping off a large glob of honey with his finger. Quickly placing the finger deep within his mouth, he slowly withdrew it, savoring every drop.

Allsup's head dropped back and an audible 'Mmm' could be heard as he savored the sweet nectar. Glancing back over his shoulder again to check on his co-conspirator's progress, he repeated the action a second time while coaxing Chestnut on with his heels.

As they ambled towards the apple orchard, he noticed a man, probably a farmer, standing in a distant field, watching. Allsup raised his hand and waved. With little enthusiasm, the farmer returned his greeting before turning away, walking across the field.

When he reached the stand of fruit trees, Allsup dismounted, careful not to disturb any remaining occupants within the hive. He sat spread-legged with the hive sitting in between and wondered if he should wait for the Andrews arrival before opening the prize. It was while he was contemplating this that Chestnut nickered, breaking his concentration. Looking up, he saw the horse's head turned, watching the approaching buggy. It was traveling at a fast clip, the horse speeding along at a quick canter. Allsup quickly stood and waved his arms, announcing his location.

The three sat on the ground in a circle with the beehive in the middle. Fingers poked into the split-open hive where honey oozed around a thick block of comb. The motion was continuously rhythmic: first, Tammy's finger dipped into the gooey sweetness and was no sooner removed when her Grandfather Andrews' finger plunged in; by the time the grandfather's finger reached his lips, Allsup was twirling his finger in a little puddle of honey, and so the sequence continued in that order over and over again; all the while, moans of exquisite pleasure was expressed by all three.

"We should stop," Andrews suggested as he dipped his finger yet again. "Before we get sick."

"You can get sick from eating honey, Grandpa?" the little girl asked.

"Oh, yes, too much of anything can make you sick," he answered. "Always remember that, little Tammy. Live your life always in moderation."

The three continued to finger-dip, lapsing into silence once again.

After several minutes Allsup asked, "Do you know what moderation means, little Tammy?"

She shook her head, concentrating on her hand deep within the hive. Allsup looked at Andrews. Andrews looked up and looked down again before realizing Allsup's intent.

Her grandfather rested his arms on his knees, one finger wet with honey, and told her, "Moderation means never too much, sweetness, never do anything too much, because there are lots of things in life that can be harmful. Do you understand, now, what Grandpa's trying to tell you?"

She looked at the two men with a finger in her mouth. After removing and examining it to ensure she had captured it all, she answered, "That we have to stop?"

Both men chuckled and rose to their feet.

"Yes, sweetness, we have to stop."

"One last time, Grandpa?" She looked up with pleading

eyes.

"She did tell us about the branch in the other tree," Allsup reminded him.

"One last time." Grandpa relented.

Chapter 32

They parted ways upon reaching Versailles. The horse-drawn buggy turned north just before reaching the town with the hive wrapped tightly in a coat and lying at their feet. The rider on horseback watched them ride away. As Allsup watched the departing buggy, he knew he would be the subject of conversation for a few more days.

He stopped long enough in Versailles to get a new pair of leather gloves to replace the old honey-smeared ones and moved on as soon as he concluded his purchase. He traveled westward along roads when they suited, across fields and through forests when they did not. At least once each day, he would give Chestnut his rein and let the horse travel at its own pace, which was more often than not a full run.

He traveled west across the Indiana landscape, passing through farming villages and towns like Vernon and Freeport, Bedford and Scotland. He stopped when necessary to replenish his supplies, but his intention was to continue riding and put as many miles behind him as possible. He was growing impatient to see and cross the mighty Mississippi.

It was while he stopped in Bedford to have a cooked meal at the Plowman's Tavern that he learned of Vincennes. Evidently, it was on the Indiana side of the Wabash River with a relatively easy crossing into Illinois. Located there was what they called a Buffalo Trace, where bison crossed during migrations long ago; travelers used it to cross from one state to the other.

Over a beefsteak the size of a wagon wheel and boiled potatoes with onions, he was advised that to reach Illinois, Vincennes was the best route to take in this part of Indiana. He sat at a table, a solitary man, with a mug of warm beer to accompany his meal as he conversed with the waiter who also served as the bartender of the establishment. Allsup's intent was to sit at the bar with Al, the friendly, talkative bartender, but Al informed him no food was permitted at the bar—house policy, he pointed out.

They spoke from their own location, Allsup at the table closest to the bar and Al standing behind it.

"How's that beefsteak?" Al inquired.

"Good," Allsup answered while laboriously chewing a bite that was as tough as leather. "Good."

"Yeah, that Bette can cook a beefsteak. Ought to be able to, she's been cookin' so long, I swear she prepared Adam's first meal, and he refused to share! That's why hungry ol' Eve ended up with the apple."

"Not too busy today," Allsup observed.

"Stick around when those Cutters get off, those that'r single will be in here orderin' what you're eatin' now; that or the beef stew."

"Beef stew good, is it?"

"Shor' is! Same thing you're eatin' now 'cept its inna bowl and has carrots."

"Oh…What are Cutters?"

"Workers in the limestone quarry; spend their days cutting rock."

"Sounds hard."

"Won't catch me doin' it," Al said before asking, "ya stickin' round for a while?"

"No, no, I'll be moving on when I finish here."

"The bar or the town?"

"Both."

"So soon—and at this time'a day…" Al left the thought incomplete.

"I'm on a mission," confessed Allsup.

"What mission?"

"I'm determined to see the Pacific."

"What?"

"The Pacific Ocean; I want to see the Pacific Ocean."

"Oh, that—Well, okay, I wish ya luck then." Al's

manner indicated the conversation had run its course.

"Thank you, sir, and please give my compliments to Bette on the beefsteak; very good."

"She already knows, but I'll tell her all the same."

Chapter 33

Chestnut revealed a new aspect of his character that Allsup had not had the opportunity to discover until leaving Indiana to enter Illinois crossing the Wabash River—*trying* to enter Illinois. They were following the Buffalo Trace when the stallion stopped midway across the river, the water just up to its knees. Allsup thought the horse might be taking a moment to relieve himself, but that didn't appear to be the case.

So maybe he's thirsty, he thought, but no, the horse was not drinking.

"What's going on?" Allsup softly asked the horse while stroking its neck. He tried prompting the horse on by applying light nudges with his boot heels, but still, the horse would not move.

"Well, all right, I guess we're just going to sit here for a while; well, I'm going to sit. You're standing knee-deep in the river."

Chestnut snorted a reply and looked back at his rider.

"I'm sorry. Did I offend you?"

"Horse won't go?" A man called out from a passing wagon whose wheels were creating a small wake in the water.

"He's decided to cool off for a while, I guess," answered Allsup, using a gesture of 'what-can-you-do?' with his hands.

"Take a rein to him!" The man on the wagon called out as he passed on.

"He'll get bored and move on. I'll wait."

The man on the wagon waved as he emerged from the water on the slightly steep Illinois riverbank and continued until lost in the trees.

"Well, don't we look foolish," Allsup admonished.

D. Dean Carroll

"Standing here like a stump sticking out of the river. Well, you've got no more sense than a stump, I'll tell you that. Least the stump has an excuse: it's rooted in the river bottom. It can't move. But you, why you have four legs. You walked this far into this river and no further with about an equal distance still to go. Why'd you stop? I don't understand. Okay, well, whenever you're ready, I'm all for moving on."

The horse snorted, pawed at the water and looked back once again before abruptly sitting down.

"Whoa! What are you doing?" Allsup cried out while frantically reaching back to untie and remove his bedroll and saddlebags containing all his worldly possessions. "What are you doing?"

As the horse lay down on its side, Allsup stepped off, pulled his rifle from its scabbard and found himself standing knee-high in water, just high enough to pour into the top of his boots.

"What's wrong with you, horse?" Exasperated, he looked from one side of the river to the other. There was a small cluster of people on the eastern bank, the Indiana side, watching with attentive amusement. He decided against going back. Lugging his bedroll and rifle in one hand held high out of the water and his saddlebags in the other at equal elevation, he trudged against the river current to reach Illinois. At one point, he stepped into a hole and the water rose chest-high. The crossing became laborious and resulted in the contents of both hands dipping into the water more than once.

The water receded as he reached higher ground. Soon he was standing, dripping and soggy, on the dry banks of Illinois. He unrolled his bedroll and emptied his saddlebags to allow the contents to dry, then pulled off his boots and emptied them of water, next his socks, and finally, his shirt.

People on the east side began to hoot and holler with the removal of each article of clothing.

After his pants, Allsup found himself in only his red

long johns with a wet, droopy bottom flap and a gathering audience on both sides of the river. The weight of the water pulled the crotch of the garment down to his knees.

He sat down on the riverbank, letting the sun dry his clothing and watching his crazy stallion frolic in the water. Chestnut was rolling from one side to the other, the river washing over the animal, evidently enjoying the coolness of the stream.

"I'd guess that'd be your animal," a man standing beside him said.

Using his hand to shield his eyes from the sun, Allsup looked up. He was a short, portly man wearing buckskin chaps, rattlesnake skin boots, and a tan-colored hat. He looked like he had been squeezed together at head and foot, forming a bulge in the middle.

"What gave it away?" he asked the man as he noticed the small group formed on his side of the bank.

"Is he hurt?" The man took a step closer, watching the horse.

"No, just being playful."

"I can get him up here for ya if ya wish."

"No, I'll wait. He'll come along soon enough; give me time to dry off."

"Horse ought to be learnt."

"How would you do that?" Allsup asked, again shading his eyes with his hand.

"I'd do whatever it takes. More likely a whip or strap."

"You'd break the spirit of the horse to get him to comply?" Allsup was getting agitated.

"Gettin' 'em to comply don't necessarily break their spirit," the man argued with a smile. "That horse just let ya climb on his back, never havin' been rode before?"

"No, I'm sure he was broke—"

The man smiled.

"Just cause ya get the horse to obey don' mean ya broke its spirit. That there horse looks to have a lotta spirit to me.

Learnt is good for man and beast."

"Well, just in time." Allsup observed, standing up with a grin. "Here he comes now."

Chestnut came fording casually through the river, the saddle hanging cockeyed on its side, the reins floating on the water's surface, squiggling back and forth like snakes swimming upstream against the current. He walked up the bank to Allsup, stopped, and shook all over attempting to remove excess water. With a snort, he rubbed his nose against Allsup's arm.

"Often," Allsup said to the stranger while stroking Chestnut's forehead. "You can get the same results with patience as with force. Only with patience everybody's happy."

The man, who stood watching the two, shook his head before asking, "What if ya was in a hurry?"

"I'm not," Allsup answered as he removed the wet saddle from the animal. "Haven't been since I acquired him. He doesn't know hurry—unless it's just to run."

"Well, it's your horse," the man noted as he swung up onto the saddle of his own. "Hope he didn't give mine any ideas. Good day to ya." He nudged his horse on, and they waded into the river.

Allsup removed the bridle freeing the horse of the last of its gear, and the unencumbered animal walked to the top of the riverbank in search of grass. Allsup sat back down at the edge of the river, then reclined, basking in the warmth of the afternoon sun. As sleep began to overtake him, he thought, I'm in no hurry at all.

Chapter 34

Illinois, the land of Abe Lincoln, who was said to be buried somewhere in the state. Allsup had little opinion of politics. Except for the war, which took his two sons, politics had always avoided a direct impact on the Pennsylvania farmer's life. He was against owning slaves himself, but he was never a man to tell another how to live. However, splitting up families was wrong no matter how you viewed it, and if the war put an end to that, well, maybe it was worth the loss.

About a mile past Lawrenceville, he decided to stop. The ground, made up of small grass-covered rolling hills, seemed to go all the way to the horizon. It looked as good as any other place, and Allsup was tired. He chose a spot on a grassy knoll out in the open, thinking we'll be gazing at stars tonight.

After gathering broken sticks and branches deposited by forces of nature from distant trees, he fried bacon purchased while passing through Lawrenceville, along with a can of pre-cooked beans. He was looking forward to settling in with a good meal and a good night's rest under an unhindered sky. The coffee pot nestled deep in red coals began to boil rapidly announcing the fulfillment of its purpose. Allsup tossed hardtack into the bacon grease, hoping it would absorb the flavorful liquid and become softer and tastier. It did, and it didn't. It didn't absorb the grease which coated one side of the cracker similar to butter spread on bread, but it did improve the flavor. Unfortunately, it still broke apart with a snap.

The fire burned brightly as Allsup reclined on his ground tarp. Instantly his back felt better. As his head rested against his saddle, he gazed at the night sky, a midnight blue filled with bright shining stars and wisps of drifting clouds.

D. Dean Carroll

The occasional shooting star filled him with wonder: why did most stars stay put while others broke free and escaped streaking across the heavens?

Chestnut's silhouette was just a few feet away. He could hear the horse tearing the grass from the ground as it ate, chewing, taking a step, and repeating. There was no other sound except the popping of burning wood in the fire. No wildlife, no trickling brooks or creeks. He and the horse must be the only living beings where they now rested on this part of the Earth.

He found the North Star. His father had shown him how when he was a boy. Find the Big Dipper, follow it to the Little Dipper, and at its tail is the North Star. He had passed this on to his sons as well. He wondered if there was ever a time after they went to war when they had to use that knowledge.

"Everything circles around you," he whispered, staring up at the star. "Everything."

He heard it first, on the ground, big heavy drops. Then one hit him square on the forehead, a big wet splat! It was starting to rain. They fell like little bombs, exploding on impact and falling more frequently.

Allsup jumped up from his bedroll and began rolling it up. He looked around for Chestnut but did not see him, so he whistled loudly. While he was emptying the coffee pot and throwing as much of the grease out of the frying pan that he could, he realized Chestnut was still not there. He whistled again.

"Oh, no," he muttered as he stood waiting for the horse's return.

The rain was falling in smaller droplets but coming down hard, creating a patter so loud it obscured everything else. He stood next to the now extinguished fire, wearing his duster and hat, his saddle in one hand, his bags in the other. He whistled again.

"Come on horse," he muttered. "Come on."

Rainwater fell in mini streams from the rim of his hat, which was growing heavy with dampness. His tanned duster was almost black from wet in the rain-filled night; he whistled again.

"I'm not walking; confound it! You better get back here, horse."

Eventually, it reached the point when it became obvious the rain was not going to slacken. Allsup needed to decide to either start walking or sit down. He could not bring himself to take the first step to leave the horse behind but had no desire to sit on the rain-soaked ground either, so he remained standing.

His arms grew tired and so did his eyes. He released his grip on the saddle and bags yet continued standing, his arms grateful for the lightened load. Swaying caused him to jerk awake when his eyes didn't open after a blink, and he pulled off his hat to let the cool rain wash over his face.

"Chestnut!" He whistled before calling again, "Chestnut!"

In the distance, north of the campsite, through the curtain of falling rain, he thought he saw him. Something crested a hilltop and appeared to be running his way. He put his hat back on and leaned forward, straining to confirm his hope.

The image disappeared between hilltops and with the rain falling, it was hard to determine if his expectation would be fulfilled. Allsup remained standing; it seemed like hours. The rain continued to fall, his soggy hat rim drooped down over his ears, and he could feel a damp chill soaking through his coat, but none of that bothered him as he waited for his horse's return.

And there he was, running up the side of the hill. The horse whinnied as he saw the man waiting.

"You had me worried!" Allsup cried out over the rain as he affectionately stroked the horse's wet neck. "I will admit it! You had me worried!"

Chestnut returned the affection by nuzzling his nose into Allsup's shoulder.

"Well, we're up and soaked. What'd you say we just ride on, huh?"

He saddled the stallion, secured his bags, and swung himself onto the horse who, anxious to get started, pawed at the muddy ground.

"Don't fall down," Allsup told the horse as he prepared to depart, adjusting the reins in his hands and settling down onto the now familiar saddle. "All right, boy, let's go!"

It was a scary, thrilling feeling riding a horse at full gallop in the pouring rain in the dark. Allsup couldn't see a thing. The horse made the turns; his rider again did not guide him. There were several instances when the horse was spooked, causing it to skittishly lunge to the side, almost throwing his rider, but Allsup clung tight and rode low over the animal.

They'd been riding in this manner for a time when Allsup noticed the gradual lightening in the east—dawn approached. While it did begin to lighten, however, the morning sunlight couldn't pierce the heavy, gray clouds that covered the sky.

They rode in the rain through the morning and into the afternoon. Both man and horse thoroughly soaked to the bone. At one point, they stopped under a small cluster of trees that provided little shelter, and after a short period, they resumed walking across a flat field filled with new sprouts breaking through the wet soil, getting their first taste of precipitation.

Out of the corner of his eye, Allsup saw a man in the distance, standing in the same field, appearing to watch him pass. Allsup assumed he was the farmer; it was probably his field. He was standing, watching, as wet as the horse and rider.

Allsup doffed his hat to the man, who returned the gesture. The farmer began motioning Allsup to him, broadly beckoning with his arm. The rider turned the stallion, and they slowly made their way across the muddy field to its owner.

"Hello," Allsup greeted when within earshot.

"Howdy," replied the farmer.

"Nasty weather," Allsup observed.

"Has been for a while; could be good for the corn you're ridin' through."

"Too much can be harmful."

"Yep—I imagine you be wantin' to get out of it."

"I would, yes."

"Why don't ya give me a ride back to the house, and I'll set you up in the barn. What'd ya think about that?"

"That sounds inviting, but I have to tell you this horse has never been rode double. He's a young stallion, and like most young ones, he often acts before thinking and has a mind of his own. I'd hate for him to throw a man making such a generous offer."

"The ground's soft from rain, I'm wet, way I see it, I got nothin' to lose. If you're willing, I'm game to give it a try."

"Climb on up then and let's see how he likes it." Allsup extended a hand to help the farmer mount.

He swung up behind Allsup and once settled, Allsup gave the horse a gentle nudge. At first, Chestnut did not respond as if puzzled by the additional weight. The two men sat astride the horse, its ears drooping in the rain. It did not move, so neither did the riders. After a minute and a snort, Chestnut decided to continue, but sullenly: a casual stride, slowing to almost a stop at times.

"Can't get him to go any faster?" the farmer asked after they'd been riding in that manner for a while.

"How far is it to your farm?" Allsup inquired.

"Up a'ways. Should be in view shortly."

"He's quite independent—the horse," Allsup answered the previous question. "I tend to let him choose his own pace unless, you know, it's an emergency."

"How 'bout makin' it an emergency."
"You want to go faster?"
"Yes, please. I'm tired and wet."
"Well, let's see what he does."

Allsup gave Chestnut a stern nudge, and the horse broke into a trot.

"How 'bout that!" exclaimed the farmer as he rapidly bounced up and down on the horse's rump. "Maybe you could smooth out the ride by bringing him to a canter."

"All right, let's see." He gave the horse another prod.

The horse increased to a smooth three-beat lope that was comfortable to all.

"Now that's more like it!" shouted the farmer as the brim of his hat flew up flat against its crown, the rain stinging his face.

"You want to see something?" Allsup shouted over his shoulder.

"Yeah!"

"Watch this!" Allsup relaxed his grip on the reins and let them hang loose along the horse's neck; by experience, the indication the horse was free to choose his pace, always fast.

Chestnut stretched out in long, full-length strides, tearing across the field, hooves splashing mud, throwing it skyward.

"Holy—" the farmer clung tight to the back of Allsup's duster.

The horse picked up his pace as he worked to release pent-up energy. They traveled down a row in the field, a ragged straight valley between two miniature parallel mountain chains of raised dirt.

"Any chance he could slip and fall?" the farmer asked. "Travelin' at this rate?"

"I'm sure there is."

"Mayhap, you could slow him down back to that canter."

"Is that your farm up ahead?" Allsup pointed in the distance to their right.

"That'd be it, all right."

"The horse sees it too. It's not that far—I believe I'll let him have his run. Hang on!"

D. Dean Carroll

Chapter 35

"The barn won't do much for warmth, but it'll keep you dry," the farmer said as Danny Allsup removed the saddle from his drenched horse. "If ya wanna get outta those clothes, I'll get ya a pair of my pants and a shirt to wear until yours gets dry. Momma will hang 'em by the fire."

"Tell your mother I appreciate her efforts."

"No, she's not *my* mother." The farmer chuckled. "She's my wife, my children's momma."

"Oh!" Allsup laughed. "Well, tell your wife I appreciate her efforts."

"Cause the kids all call her Momma, ya see? I fell into callin' her that too."

"I understand. I'm going to get out of these clothes now and wrap up in the blanket to get warm. I got a chill in me that feels like it'll never go away."

"All right, I'll run the clothes to the house and come back with dry ones; maybe somethin' to eat as well."

"Thank you. I do appreciate your hospitality."

"It's the Christian way is all," he answered, smiling. "That's all, just the Christian way."

After the farmer took off running through the rain to the house with Allsup's clothes, Allsup wrapped himself in a blanket and began to brush down his horse, still dripping with water. Each brush stroke sent a slim clear wave of water across his back and down his sides. The horse stood without moving; both his head and his tail were still drooped low. Allsup didn't notice at first, but the lack of any movement gradually caught his attention. While brushing, he spoke softly to the animal.

"Long day, huh, boy? Plenty of water, no question about that. You did good today." Allsup chuckled as he realized the horse had fallen asleep.

"That's all right. You deserve a good rest." Like always, he gave the horse's rump a slap as he walked past. The horse gave a start, looked back, and snorted a reproach before returning to his slumber.

As Allsup walked to an empty stall in the barn where he planned to make his resting place for the evening, he heard what sounded like a giggle, a child's suppressed giggle. It sounded again, but fuller, as if a group was giggling. He looked quickly at the barn's entrance in time to see three little heads quickly disappear behind the barn door.

Making sure he was adequately covered by the blanket, he quietly raced to the entrance and waited for the faces to reappear. After a short wait they emerged one at a time, peeking inside the barn. Allsup was greatly surprised when after the first face came into view, the second one appeared looking identical to the first. When the third face inched into view, it was an exact replica of the previous two, and each conveyed the same cheerful childish mischievousness.

All boys, no more than four or five in age, their eyes looked eagerly around for the stranger staying in their barn not realizing he was standing next to them on the opposite side of the door. Little rivulets streamed down their faces and soaked hair was glued to their foreheads; they seemed not to notice.

"Do your parents know you're out here?" Allsup whispered.

"No," they whispered, shaking their heads. All three realized at the same moment that they were not only *talking* with the stranger in the barn, but they were standing next to him as well. They cried out in fear and turned to hightail it back to the house, only to run directly into the legs of their father.

"Pa! Pa!" they called out to him. "We saw him, Pa! We saw him!"

"All right, all right," their father responded. "Settle down. It ain't like ya saw the bogeyman. Now, get on inside that barn outta the rain. Lord gave at least one'a the three of ya better sense than that."

All three hung back behind their father, clutching a fist full of pant leg in their small hands, causing their father to walk clumsily into the barn and hand Allsup a stack of folded clothes.

"They might be a tad small, but they ought'a do 'til your's is dry."

"Thank you." Allsup gratefully took the clothing. "If you'll excuse me, I'll step into that stall there and dress."

"Sure. Boys, you get away from that horse!" the father ordered. His sons were quick to obey, knowing the possible consequences.

Allsup returned with a shirt and sweater that only reached the top of his wrists and pants that went down as far as his ankles. The socks, with one toe bare, covered his legs and shielded them from the cold.

The sight of the man looking like a farm boy who'd outgrown his clothing initiated laughter and pointing by the boys, which was so contagious that soon their father and then Allsup were compelled to joined in.

As the laughter subsided, the farmer turned to Allsup and said, "We never had a chance to introduce ourselves. I'm Ben Wheeler; these are my sons Matthew, Mark, and Luke over there that best get away from that darn horse!"

The boy immediately scurried back to his father.

"Danny Allsup, a Pennsylvania farmer now retired, I guess. I'm pleased and grateful to meet all of you."

"Calico had babies!" one youngster exclaimed.

"Six babies!" another added. "But one died."

"Calico?" Allsup looked questioningly at their father.

"It's their cat. She just had a litter yesterday; like Mark said, one didn't make it."

Allsup addressed the three boys, "They're cute when they're little like that, aren't they?"

All three enthusiastically agreed.

"I know it's not," Wheeler admitted. "But we're treating it kind'a like a miracle."

"A miracle?"

"Yes. We got the female from a farm down the road 'bout two miles. Calico's been with us for two year now, I believe. She's a good cat: loving and friendly, wouldn't hurt a fly, plus, she's a good mouser as well!"

"What's a mouser, Pa?" Either Matthew or Mark or Luke asked their father.

"Well, Matthew, what do you think it means?"

"I donno."

"Sure, you do! What's the word sound like?"

"Mouser...mouser..." Matthew studiously repeated the word. "Sounds like 'Mouse' to me, Pa."

"Yes, that's right! Now, how does 'Mouse' connect to Calico, Huh? What do mice have to do with cats?"

"Cats catch mice!"

"That's it, by golly! So, what'd ya call a cat that catches mice?"

"A Mouser?"

"Yes, that's it! A Mouser!" The farmer reached down and pulled the boy to him for a hug.

"That's how ya solve problems, Matthew, ya break everythin' ya know down and ask questions. Understand?"

"Yes, Pa."

"Okay, now you run over there with your brothers and watch those kittens don't try to run off."

"Okay!" He scampered off into an empty stall, which was serving temporarily as a temporary nursery.

Watching the father-son exchange brought up feelings in Allsup. He remembered his two sons at that age; it seemed, in some ways they were the same as Matthew— happy. That's what it was; they were happy.

"The miracle?" Allsup returned to their earlier discussion.

"Miracle...Oh, yeah! Calico! Well, like I said, she's a

good cat. She never leaves the farm that we know of, always on the porch or in the barn. My point being: she don't leave. So, who's the daddy of them kittens in there? None of us saw another cat around, and she don't leave—What happen?"

"Hence, the miracle," Allsup declared, grinning.

"Hence, the miracle."

"I imagine there's a few other options to consider in addition to the one you've chosen."

"Oh, probably a few, I'm sure, but…we like option one."

"Me, too." Allsup extended his hand, and they shook over their concurrence.

They discussed Allsup's farming experience and compared Illinois farming to that of Pennsylvania farming. Wheeler had much more land. "Twenty acres, give or take some," as he expressed it to Allsup's twelve. That led the conversation to why Allsup gave it up and what he was undertaking.

Finally, Wheeler said, "Well, I hate to leave ya out here, but it's time for the four of us to head in for dinner. I expect we'd dawdled too long already, and Beth is gonna remind me 'bout who's supposed to be the responsible one. I wish I could invite you in to join us, but we have this rule. Beth convinced me to be of the same mind before she would agree to move here: no strangers in the house."

"That's all right."

"She read once in a newspaper about a family that tried to be Christ-like and welcomed a traveling man into their home. Evidently, he killed the family, everybody: husband, wife, and children. Anyway, it put a fear in her that she can't shake, and I don't push it. It's not like there's a lot of strangers walkin' the roads or fields, so it's not an issue that arises often. But with you here, it does arise. I hope you understand."

"I do." Allsup sought to assure him. "I'm grateful for the shelter."

Danny Allsup

"We'll bring you out dinner; don't you worry about that," Wheeler informed him. "We may not be acting Christian-like in our hospitality, but that don't mean we ain't Christians."

"Of course, I understand. I'm warming up and dry; you've done enough already."

"Let's be going, boys, before your momma decides she needs to come get us. We don't want that to happen, do we?"

The three identical boys voiced their agreement that their mother coming out in the rain would not be a pleasant thing, and so all four Wheeler males dashed for the house. Allsup surveyed his surroundings. He was in an almost empty barn, stalls filled with clean straw awaiting their tenants.

Using a lantern, because along with the storm contributing to the current darkness, dusk had set in and the hour was growing late, he went into the cat's stall to check on the kittens. All five of the litter were sleeping, curled up into tiny balls of fur nuzzled against the stomach of their mother, lying serenely on her side enjoying the peace and quiet.

As promised, a good while later Wheeler and two of the three boys returned to the barn carrying a bowl of stew, a slice of bread, and a glass of milk. Farmer Wheeler carried the bowl and milk. One boy carried the bread wrapped in a towel, while the other carried a plate with a large slice of rhubarb pie.

"I'm sorry it took so long, but we have a brief Bible study each night after dinner…

"And Mark was bad!" interrupted one of the two boys.

"Yeah, he wouldn't stop playin' during prayer!" added the other.

When they noticed their father's stern look, they both apologized for interrupting.

"As I was sayin' before bein' rudely interrupted." Another firm glance at the boys. "We had Bible study and then I had to inflict the wrath of God on Mark. Here's the promised meal, though, hope you enjoy it. Momma can make a good stew, can't she, boys?"

They nodded in agreement.

"It's gettin' late," Wheeler continued. "So, we'll leave you to your meal and retrieve the dinner dishes tomorrow. Will you be here?"

"Probably," answered Allsup. "I'm not too eager to head back out in this rain, so if it's still coming down, I may linger a while to see if it lets up."

"Well, stay as long as you like. We start milkin' at sunup, so you'll probably hear us if you're not already awake."

"I start my days early; some farming habits are hard to break."

"I suspect we'll see you in the mornin', then. Tell Mr. Allsup goodnight, boys."

The boys said their goodnights, and Allsup wished them the same before thanking them once again for their hospitality.

He ate his meal by lantern light while sitting on the floor of the barn. He could faintly hear the kittens mewing for their dinner while Chestnut talked in his sleep, making grunting and snorting noises in the stall.

Calico came walking out of the nursery and brushed up against Allsup's leg. Purring, she passed back and forth several times before curiosity overcame her, and she investigated the residue of the remaining stew in the bowl. Allsup stretched out on the floor beside the cat and watched as she licked it clean. The calico cat sat up, licking her lips and looked around the barn with mild interest. She looked over at Allsup and caught him staring at her; they looked at one another, eye to eye, for almost a minute, waiting for the other to look away. The man relented. With a smile and a blink, he looked at the bowl and placed it, along with the plate and glass, in a stack on the floor.

Danny Allsup

Allsup grabbed the blanket he'd used earlier and made his way into his chosen stall where he lay down on a bed of straw, turned down the lantern, and sighed a long sigh, the kind of sigh that gently moves you closer to a deeper state. He listened to the rain falling on the barn roof, falling outside the open barn door, falling all around the barn, sounding like a million tiny hands clapping, creating a calming, soothing sound that lulled one into a peaceful slumber, and with a final sigh, he was asleep.

He didn't know how long he'd heard the rustling from the main part of the barn before it finally woke him. Through the stall entrance, he could see the silhouette of the cat once again at the stew bowl, but something about the black shadow alerted him to the fact that things were not quite right: the animal at the bowl had just a stump of a tail. Allsup slowly rose upon his hands and knees and crawled to the stall entrance. His eyes squinting to improve his vision, he saw that it was larger than the Wheeler's cat though not by much and this cat's ears grew up into fine points that Calico did not have.

It was a bobcat! He crawled closer to the stall entrance for a better look. His movement caused a frightened mouse hiding in the straw to panic and scurry out into the open barn, exposed. The bobcat, licking what it could from the empty bowl, saw the mouse and in an instant, pounced upon it. The feline sat up and looked around proudly with one paw holding the mouse in place. Lifting its paw, it allowed the small rodent about two seconds chance to escape. Realizing it was free, the mouse made a hasty dash back to the stall from which it came.

The bobcat sprung up into the air to recapture its toy, but upon landing at the entrance of the stall found itself staring face to face into the eyes of a man on hands and knees! For just a second, the shock of the one unexpectedly seeing the other froze them both in place. Before the man could do or say anything, the bobcat raced out of the barn and disappeared into the darkness and rain. Allsup, still on his hands and knees, looked across the barn into the opposite opened stall and saw Calico watching him.

"Sorry if I upset your plans," he told the cat. "But truth be told, he surprised me as much as I surprised him. I won't be here long; he'll be back."

Allsup returned to his straw bed, rolled up into his cozy blanket, and allowed the rain to lull him back to sleep.

Danny Allsup

Chapter 36

The ground was still sloshy from the rain that had finally stopped just before sunrise. Each step of the horse made a splatting sound like a hand smacking wet mud. The chestnut stallion was feeling frisky in the morning air that held a bite of chill, hinting at colder days to come.

Allsup had been up and saddling Chestnut earlier in the still-cloudy morning when Wheeler came into the barn carrying Allsup's clothes. Allsup dressed quickly, the air feeling icy on his bare skin.

"Again, I appreciate your hospitality," he told the farmer as he pulled on his socks. "From what I saw, you have a good family. Don't stop appreciating them."

"I am a lucky man, alright. I don't take my blessings for granted."

"Say, I may have another option for your miracle. Have you looked closely at those kittens?"

"No, they was born day before yesterday, and I never got around to it yet. Why?"

"Let's go take a look."

Allsup led the way to the cat nursery. He reached down and extracted one from its morning breakfast. It had no qualms about expressing its displeasure and mewed in protest. Allsup examined the kitten's hind end, specifically the tail: this cat's resembled Calico's, long and thin with orange and black markings. Returning one kitten, he removed another with the same response and the same result.

"What're we looking for?" The farmer watched over Allsup's shoulder.

"If I'm right, you'll know it." Checking kittens three and four, Allsup found only long calico tails.

The fifth and last kitten selected elicited an "Ah!" from the examiner.

"What?" asked the farmer.

"Look here." Allsup held up the kitten.

The final kitten had pointed ears and a little stub of a tail.

"Well, ain't that somethin'," declared the farmer.

"I met their daddy last night."

"What?"

"I did. A bobcat—he just walked into the barn like it was his own and commenced to finish off what was left of the stew in the bowl. There wasn't any stew left, by the way, and it was delicious. Anyway, I scared a mouse, which became a temporary plaything for the bobcat, and while it was trying to catch the mouse, we had an encounter."

"You don't say?"

"I do, and that made me suspect that perhaps I'd found the explanation for your miracle kittens. And this little kitten here validates my suspicion."

It was the look on Wheeler's face that lingered in Allsup's thoughts as he remembered the morning while riding his horse west on a muddy road: a look of disappointment. Allsup had robbed the man and his family of something special; something unusual had happened in their lives on the farm, and he took that away. He felt strong remorse for having done so. He regretted he could not give back what he had inadvertently taken.

The horse wanted to run, but Allsup was not in the mood. They were heading toward the town of Olney, where Allsup hoped to replenish supplies detrimentally affected by the wet. He was feeling melancholy about the whole cat incident and was in a foul mood.

They passed several other travelers. Allsup greeted each with a simple nod or tip of his hat. In the past, he would verbally address those encountered, but not on this day. There was no spoken "Hello" or "Good day;" a smile never crossed his face. A dark cloud seemed to be following him in addition to those in the sky overhead. Even Chestnut

Danny Allsup

sensed that this was not a day to test his patience and settled into a brisk walk.

It was late morning when they rode into Olney. He tied the horse to a hitch in front of a general store and walked inside. After ordering hardtack, coffee and sugar, and salt, plus more dried beef jerky and two cans of beans, he went about browsing through the store as the clerk filled his order.

He was deciding on a pair of new leather gloves, his were stiff from the rain when he heard a commotion outside. Both Allsup and the clerk walked to the front window to discover its source.

A white man holding what appeared to be an ax handle was striking a black man who had fallen in the road. A small crowd of people formed, joining two other white men who were shouting encouragement to the assailant. The black man attempted to escape, but a cohort pushed him back, and the ax handle knocked him to the ground once more.

The crowd watched silently; they neither cheered nor rebuked. The store clerk next to Allsup clucked his tongue several times and shook his head before returning to the task of filling the order. Allsup continued to watch.

"Why don't they do something?" he asked.

"What?" The store clerk looked up.

"Why don't they do something?"

"Who?"

"Those people out there."

"Why?"

"Why?" Allsup echoed incredulously. "Because it's not right to treat a man like that. It's wrong to treat *any* animal like that!"

"It's just a darky," the store clerk observed as he returned to his work. "It don't matter."

"It's not right...Why don't they do something?"

"Why don't *you* do something?" the store clerk inquired as if it suddenly occurred to him to ask.

Allsup wasn't prepared for that, and for a moment, he

was at a loss about how to respond. He continued to watch as the black man held up his hand to protect himself from a blow to his head. The ax handle broke his arm, as was evident by the bone pushing against the skin.

Allsup quickly looked away, embarrassed. He looked at the store clerk who was watching him.

"All right, I will."

Allsup stormed out of the store just as the white man holding the ax handle high over his right shoulder prepared to swing again. Coming from behind, Allsup quickly grabbed the handle from the man's hands. Surprised, he turned to find out who had interrupted his entertainment.

"That's enough," Allsup told him while holding the handle in both hands.

"Who the hell are you?" the man asked, winded from his exertions. "Mister, you're in a hell of fix…

"I got the ax handle now," Allsup interrupted. "I figure I can do about as much damage to you as you did to him." He gestured toward the black man still on the ground, propped up on his good elbow, holding his bad arm.

"Shoot this son-of-a-bitch!" The man ordered. His friends stood grinning foolishly but made no effort to comply.

"Darryl! Shoot 'im!"

"I'm sorry, JJ, but I ain't shooting a man just cause you wanna beat on a ni…

"Shoot him!"

Allsup swung the ax handle, landing it hard, with a 'thud' into the side of the man's ribcage.

'Oomph!" went the white man as he dropped to one knee, his elbow held in tight.

Allsup reared back and swung from the side, this time landing a blow to the man's stomach. He folded in half, his head resting on the ground in front of his knees, his rear end sticking up looking like an inchworm. Gasping for breath, he let out a moan.

Danny Allsup

Allsup brought the handle down once again, solid, against the man's back, flattening him on the road. Winded, Allsup looked down at the man, then at his two friends, who quickly backed away. Walking over to the black man, he offered him the ax handle.

"You want to take a swing or two?" Allsup asked.

"Nah," the man answered as he struggled to his feet. "I cain't." He held up his arm as evidence before admitting after a moment's reflection, "I doan wanna."

"Want me to find you a doctor?"

"Ain't no doctor gonna hep me. I'm goin' home."

Allsup watched the man walk down the street before turning to face the still-gathered group of people.

"There are no Christians in this town!" he loudly declared. "Not a soul here with a lick'a compassion."

He tossed the ax handle down in disgust beside the prostrate man and returned to the store to collect his purchases.

"What do I owe you?" he asked the clerk as he walked up to the counter.

"Not a thing, 'cause I ain't serving you," advised the clerk while backing away.

"What do you mean you're not serving me? When I left you were about done filling my order!"

"I put it all back. I ain't selling you nothin'!" Allsup stared at the man before asking, "You still got my list?"

"Yeah...Maybe...Why?"

Allsup stormed back outside and grabbed the ax handle. Carrying it with him, he returned to the store and marched up to the counter.

"Hey-hey-hey, take it easy," the clerk protested as he placed a full sack on the countertop. "I was only joking. See? I got all your stuff right here."

Allsup peeked into the sack before asking, "How much do I owe you?"

"That would be a dollar ten."

Allsup counted out the money and tossed it down on the counter.

"Throw in some bacon for the poor humor," he ordered, his nostrils still flaring with anger.

"I ain't got any bacon."

The ax handle slammed hard against the countertop.

"Throw in a ham, then!"

"I think I gotta pound of bacon here." The clerk found and wrapped the meat in paper and set it down next to the sack.

"You're a real piece of work, aren't you?" Allsup put the bacon in the sack and headed for the door. A large jar filled with balls of candy sat on a corner of the counter. As he passed, he bumped it with the ax handle sending it to the floor. With a crash, the candy scattered, rolling everywhere.

"Aw, gez…" whined the store clerk as the door closed.

Chapter 37

Leaving Olney behind, Allsup and horse continued west at a casual pace. They passed through Maysville, where only three residents of the town were visible, two women in plain cotton dresses and a man in a dark, worn-out suit. Allsup greeted them with a tip of his hat, but they declined to respond.

His plan was to make it to Salem, where he hoped to find a bath and lodging for the night and get a good meal, but Salem was still a day's ride away.

About an hour out of Maysville, he decided to stop where a stack of straw in a field was piled high into an impressive mound just off the road. The top of the straw was dry, so he spread it out on the ground to ward off the wetness. It was while he was lying on his back on his tarped-covered straw mattress that he realized the sky had cleared and every star in the universe was visible. They appeared so close that he felt he could reach out and run his hand through them like flower petals floating on a still pond.

The town of Cato proved interesting as they rode through the next morning. The local law enforcement came out to greet him personally. Wearing torn leather chaps over pants held up by suspenders and a shirt that may or may not have been washed within the last two years, the sheriff strode up and walked alongside horse and rider.

The holstered pistol hanging from his hip was his only sign of business. He advised Allsup that he should not stop in Cato, not for a meal, a beer, or a piss. The people of Cato were not welcoming to strangers and preferred that they just pass on through, which was what was expected in this instance. The man on the chestnut should just pass on through.

Allsup expressed his appreciation for the people of

Cato's hospitality and informed the man they could rest easy knowing he had no intention of stopping for any reason that could come to mind.

"Just so long as you keep ridin'," the officer emphasized.

"Well, as I just stated, that is my intention."

"Fine, fine, as long as you keep ridin' we'll have no problem, you and I."

"Well, we have no problem then. As you can see, walking at my side as you are, I continue riding through your town. You can stop your exercise; I can find my way out."

"I'm good, I'm good. Just doin' my job. Makin' sure we're on the same page."

"You're referring to…

"You not stopping and ride on outta town."

"Yes, well, I think you can see I've grasped your meaning and, by my reckoning, I'm almost out of town. We can say goodbye here, then."

"Just makin' sure," the officer repeated as they continued walking together toward the town's building line.

"If I go faster, will you?" asked Allsup.

"Probably not."

"Good day to you, sir. Chestnut, let's go!" Using his heels, he nudged the horse and like a bullet, they were flying out of town. Looking back over his shoulder as they sped away, Allsup saw the officer, hat in raised hand, bidding them adieu.

Chapter 38

Salem, Illinois had the accommodations he sought for both himself and his horse. He found a room in a six-bedroom house run by Mrs Thomason, who also provided breakfast between eight and ten and dinner between five and seven. She was a widower who let out four of the bedrooms as a means of income. The fifth room was her own and the sixth she kept ready for her son, who'd gone off and joined the cause.

"21st Regiment - Company G." She liked to inform anyone and everyone who would listen. He went off to war and had yet to return. They never found his body after a skirmish in Tennessee, so they couldn't be certain he was dead. That was enough for her to build hopes on. She was sure that one day he'd walk back into the house, and when he did, his room would be ready.

Allsup had heard about the Thomason Boarding House when he stopped at the Half Way Tavern east of the city. Several men, including the bartender, were boasting to a group of travelers about how Lincoln, in his younger years practicing law, often stopped at this same establishment on many occasions—well, at least once.

Two men sitting with Allsup at the bar recommended the Thomason House. "It's clean, with good food and good beds," one of the two advised. "What else can ya ask for?"

The big benefit was that the lodging cost included a hot bath upon request.

"Mrs Thomason likes her place clean, so she wants her guests to be clean," the man explained. "Who's gonna complain, right?"

Allsup took advantage of that when checking in by asking that a bath be drawn. He'd like to be clean for dinner; Mrs Thomason was only too happy to oblige.

D. Dean Carroll

The tub was constructed from a hammered-copper sheet mounted on a wooden box frame. It had high sides and an even higher back. A pipe from a cork-plugged hole ran from the low end of the tub and through a hole in the wall; hence, they could quickly drain it if necessity warranted. A fireplace was always in use in the room, Allsup was told, and always with large containers of water sitting within the perimeter of the heat to assure a hot bath was readily available, no waiting.

They left him with the hot bath, a towel, and a used square of lye soap. To his surprise and disapproval, he discovered they had scented the tub water with a perfume of some fragrance; he felt that was a bit too much. Nevertheless, soaking in the tub of hot water was a completely pleasurable experience for him.

On the farm, his wife bathed first. Next, the boys climbed into the same wooden tub-water, first one then the other, and when they were through, Allsup would get his turn. The water was neither warm nor clean after three other people. That was how people bathed in rural Pennsylvania. He never gave it any thought.

This tub of hot, sweet-smelling water was his impression of heaven. After several deep sighs, he relaxed, closed his eyes and allowed himself to float lightly. Never had he felt so tranquil. As a result, he dozed several times before being awakened when he slipped down into the water.

He stayed two nights to spend one whole day in Salem. He could not recall another period in his life when he was so well-pampered. Mrs Thomason was a gracious host gushing over each of her boarders at mealtimes to ensure their satisfaction. The food was good and abundant; the bed was the softest he'd slept in, and there were the baths. Besides the one he took immediately after checking in, he took two the following day and was tempted to have one more the morning before checking out but decided against it. He was informed that St. Louis in Missouri was still two or three days away, depending on how hard and how long he chose to travel.

'The Gateway to the West wasn't going anywhere he decided, they could take their time, but he was anxious to be on his way. From Allsup's point of view, they were on the verge of leaving civilization and entering the wilderness, the West. The real adventure was two or three-day's ride away.

Chapter 39

He traveled through the day after leaving Salem, encountering little traffic on the road and few sightings of people working in fields. Allsup was a bit surprised, believing that the closer to St. Louis, the busier it would become. He reminded himself that Salem was a few days east of the city, so the expected traffic was still a day or two away.

He stopped at an inn a few miles from Carlyle. It was late in the day, and he was ready to stop. The proprietor of the inn informed Allsup that there was a room available upstairs, one of three. The other two were occupied, so Allsup rented the remaining room for the night. It was not the Thomason Boarding House, the bed sagged in the middle and there were no baths, yet the bed looked inviting, and Allsup looked forward to utilizing the room's purpose after a hot meal.

As he rode through Carlyle the next morning, he noticed, as he passed, the sign on the post office read, "Carlisle," with a line painted through the '*is*' and a '*y*' crudely painted above the crossed-out letters. Evidently, someone didn't approve of the spelling.

St. Louis was big. Danny Allsup thought Cincinnati was big, but he was wide-eyed and amazed when he first saw St. Louis. The approach was different. He descended into Cincinnati; you entered St. Louis on a level plain and from a good distance out. The surrounding land was flat farmland, the closer to the city, the more fenced-in it became. Farms miles apart gradually became located closer together. Eventually, neighborhoods formed into blocks of houses laid out along straight, maintained streets.

As he rode further west toward the city, the buildings began to grow taller; multi-stories became more frequent.

The streets and sidewalks were nearly vacant at this mid-afternoon time of day. The People he observed moved casually, unhurried, but gradually, the streets and sidewalks became more populated as he rode along; their pace increased as well.

He soon realized that he was not in St. Louis at all, but in an area referred to as *East* St. Louis as he was still in Illinois. Crossing the Mississippi would put him in Missouri and his destination city.

He continued west into the swell of East St. Louis. Ahead between buildings, he saw the pilothouse and smokestacks of a riverboat pass and knew the river was before him. He'd been so preoccupied with the street level of the city; he hadn't noticed until now the large gray cloud hanging ahead over the river. Just as in Cincinnati, the steamboat traffic on the river was a constant source of smoke. On calm days like this day, the haze didn't drift away but remained suspended over the city and river, accumulated gray cotton against a blue sky.

The riverfront was a flurry of activity, but at street level, having no higher source of perspective, it was impossible to tell what was going on anywhere but before you, like a small child behind a row of adults at a parade. River vessels were coming and going, loading and unloading horse-drawn wagons and men pushing carts burdened with goods. It was a continuous cycle where no wagon came in empty, and no wagon left without a load. Commerce was active all around him. It made him smile.

He stopped a man having just set a barrel down and asked about crossing the river. The man advised him of a "bunch'a ferries all along the front. Keep goin' you'll see."

So, he did. He dismounted and led Chestnut through the throng of people, wagons, animals and goods, concerned the horse might be sensitive to it all, but the horse just appeared as curious as Allsup, looking left and right but always alert to what's ahead.

D. Dean Carroll

He decided to take the first ferry service they encountered.

When Allsup inquired of the ferry pilot about the fee for crossing, the pilot asked, between matches trying to light a pipe, "How many?"

"Just my horse and me."

As he got the pipe going, puffing hard and quick, he looked past Allsup and asked, "That it? That's all your belongings?"

Allsup nodded the affirmative.

"Go on board," the pilot instructed. "Laymen's Livery is payin' good for crossin' those four over," he nodded towards the four wagons waiting on the ferry. "Plus four more after. They won't know someone's hitchin' a ride."

It wasn't long after they'd boarded that the steam whistle blew, the small engine revved up, and the two paddlewheels, one on each side, started turning and churning water. Chestnut acted skittish at first as they pulled away from shore but soon settled down.

"Been to the other side before?" a younger man asked, standing beside Allsup.

"No, I've never been here before."

"I been over," he said proudly.

"You have?"

"Yeah, I go over a couple'a times a day carrying messages, urgent 'That needs an answer right now!' kind'a messages."

"That must be interesting."

"Yeah, ya meet people. I got friends over in the city, I do. From time to time, Mike there." He pointed at the pilot. "Will run me over and back for nothin'. I go over and have a few with my friends in the city, then go home. So, ya never been before."

"No."

"I go all the time; know St. Louis like the back'a my hand. Say, maybe I can show ya round, help ya get settled."

"I wouldn't want to bother…

"No-no-no, it ain't no bother! Ya pay my way back, and I'm yours for as long as ya need me."

Allsup studied his fellow passenger. He was a large man, muscular, with a round head and brown hair that looked as if it had never been combed. He was dirty; his boots scuffed with worn heels, his pants stained, the shirt and vest he was wearing needed cleaning, and he held the stub of a cigar in the right corner of his mouth. It was obvious he was a working man. In Allsup's opinion, there was nothing nobler than a hard-working man.

"All right," Allsup agreed, extending his hand to seal the deal. "I'm Danny Allsup."

"Paul O'Neil, at your service." He shook the proffered hand.

"What're they building there?" Allsup inquired as they passed a massive stone piling in the river.

"A bridge, a very big bridge."

"It looks like it. I crossed a big bridge in Cincinnati. It was impressive."

"Cincinnati, huh? Where ya from Mr. Allsup?"

"I'm from Pennsylvania."

"Pennsylvania! You're a long way from home."

"No, not anymore; I sold my home, my farm and decided to head west. I'm homeless. I guess you could say."

"That's a sad thing to say," O'Neil observed.

"No, it's not, not anymore anyway. It's God's will."

O'Neil stood watching his new acquaintance. He smiled and, chewing on his cigar, asked, "You really believe that?"

Allsup answered, "I have to."

"Yeah, I see. I understand."

The ferry's whistle announced their approach to the western shore of the Mississippi River and the city of St. Louis. People became alert as the ferry drew near and began preparing for their departure.

"Here's the thing, Mr Allsup…

"Danny."

"Here's the thing, Danny, ya want to stick to me like skin on a pig when we get off. It's really busy over here; it is, after all, St. Louie. If we get separated, we may not be able to find each other again, so stay close."

As they drew nearer, O'Neil reconfirmed the arrangement.

"You are gonna pay my way back, right?" he asked.

"I am."

"Could ya do so now, in case we get separated?"

"Sure."

"Hey, Mike!" O'Neil called out to the pilot who was guiding the ferry to its ramp among many ferries. "Mike!"

"Damn it, Paulie! Can't ya see I'm busy here?" The ferry gently bumped against a piling embedded in the river levy before they lowered the massive ramp to the shore. Workers on and off the commuter boat began to secure it in place and remove the chain that closed off its exit.

"Now, what is it, Paulie?" Mike asked, his task completed.

"This man is paying my fare back, aren't ya, Mr All...uh, Danny?"

"I am."

"Then settle up, and I'll let Lonnie know to bring ya back if you're comin' after I'm through."

While securing the ferry to shore two other large paddleboats loaded with goods pulled up. The first docked along the levy while the other tied off against the riverside of the first boat.

Allsup watched as large boarding planks on the sides of the paddleboats lowered. Immediately, like a swarm of ants, workers from the boats and the dockyards were scrambling up and down the planks to move the goods. Pallets of freshly sawed lumber and large bales of cotton, along with bags of grain and various other products to meet the demands of trade. All were offloaded while previously-stored goods on shore were taken aboard for export elsewhere.

The beehive of dockside activity contributed to their separation.

"Stay close, now," reminded O'Neil as the first of the four horse-drawn wagons prepared to disembark.

"I'm right behind you," Allsup responded right behind him. He was leading Chestnut, who was acting testy and skittish. Allsup tried to steady the horse by talking softly as they made their descent onto the dock.

"We'll head to Fourth Street," O'Neill advised, glancing back over his shoulder to make sure they were still together. "That's where all the good hotels and restaurants are; lotta shops and offices too. Anyway, we'll head to Fourth."

"Right behind you," assured Allsup. He kept his eyes on the dirty brown vest and shirt, not wanting to forge his way through this throng by himself. They seemed to pass through waves of dockworkers. Occasionally, they would thin out only to be replenished by another influx of laborers.

Chestnut frantically jerked back suddenly, spooked by something and tried to pull away, backing up, his head held high and wide-eyed. The horse almost pulled the reins from Allsup's hands; they zipped through his fingers before he was finally able to regain his grip.

Workers shouted profanities as the horse backed into them, their carts and wagons. All the while, Allsup continued to talk tenderly while stroking its neck. Eventually, the horse calmed and stopped its resistance.

Once the animal was manageable, Allsup turned to apologize to O'Neil, but he was nowhere to be seen.

"Where did he go?" Allsup muttered.

He stood holding Chestnut's reins, searching for his guide. He climbed up onto the saddle, hoping the elevation would give him an advantage, but it did not. Now, all that could be seen were the tops of men's heads, and since most wore hats, and the hats seemed remarkably similar, it proved pointless. It occurred to Allsup, though, that O'Neil might possibly see him sitting atop Chestnut, so he remained for a while, waiting and looking. After several minutes, he decided it was time to move on and gently prompted the horse slowly through the mass of workers.

Allsup tried to remember where they were headed. He recalled it was a numbered street.

Gradually, they emerged from the crowded, frenzied docks and entered the organized chaos of the civilized streets and buildings of St. Louis. Horse and rider found themselves at the corner of First Street and Olive, and Allsup remembered that Fourth was the street O'Neil had referred to. They rode down Olive past Second and Third streets and stopped again at the corner of Fourth.

Buildings several stories tall lined both sides of the street running east and west of Olive. As O'Neil had indicated, there were hotels, restaurants and saloons, along with offices and storefronts.

Allsup rode east on Fourth until he saw Maxwell's Saloon and decided to stop for a drink and get his bearings. He tied Chestnut to an already crowded hitching post and strode into the tavern. There were men lined up along the bar and most tables were occupied, the site of card games and dominos. Allsup squeezed his way in between two men at the bar and ordered a beer. While he was drinking his warm, frothy beverage, he overheard two men to his right talking.

"Paddleboat's the only way to travel west'a here," one declared.

"I gotta disagree," responded the other. "Railroad is the safest. Ya got the comfort of those railcar seats, and ya don't have'ta worry none about obstacles in your path or boilers blowin'."

"Yeah, but ya got that jarrin' and jerkin' back'n forth on a train. I was on one once, was shakin' and jerkin' so damn bad made me drop my bottle. Bottle broke and the rest'a the way smelt like a brewery."

"What was in the bottle?"

"Why whiskey, as I recall."

"That'd be a distillery."

"What?"

"They make whiskey in a distillery and beer in a brewery."

Allsup watched as the two men stared at one another, the one man looking as if he'd taken offence at the correction.

"Excuse me, gentlemen," Allsup interrupted, breaking the tension. The two turned to acknowledge his intrusion. "I couldn't help overhearing your conversation about travel westward from here. I am in the process of doing just that, traveling westward, and was curious about just when I would enter the—west, I guess, for lack of a better term."

"I don't get your question, sir," one responded. He was a big round man with long thick black hair and beard. He was dressed in dark wool pants hitched high over his protruding stomach, held in place by a large black leather belt with a hefty silver buckle. The shirt he wore may have been white at one time but was now a stained yellow with several of the buttons missing down the front.

"What I meant was, how far a ride is it from here before I might enter the wilderness and hostiles?"

"Sir, ya have pretty much the entire state!" answered the other, who was thin in shape, his hairline almost nonexistent from his forehead to his crown.

"I'm sorry?"

"He means ya gotta get outta Missouri before ya get into that territory," the large man explained.

"Missouri's a civilized state, sir," added the thin man. "It's the last vestige of civilization before the—what you called wilderness."

"Oh." Allsup sounded disappointed. He was excited about entering the part of the country where white men were regarded as unwelcomed intruders.

"Be glad, sir," the thin man continued. "Because once

you cross into Indian Territory, you leave behind all the comforts and safety that we, here, take for granted. Many go in, but few make it out."

"I see. I was under the impression that after St. Louis, you were in the wilds."

"Was like that once," the large man said. "But that all change even b'fore the war. Now, there's all sorts a people livin' throughout the state; all farmland 'tween here and Jefferson City, I 'spect."

The thin man nodded in agreement before asking, "If I may pry, why do ya want to go west? Got gold fever?"

"No. Gold fever, just decided to see the west."

"Where ya from?" the large man inquired.

"Pennsylvania."

"Where's that?"

"East, quite a ways east from the Mississippi."

The thin man gave his friend a nudge and said, "Ollie! You never heard'a Pennsylvania?"

"No, why should I have?"

"A number of important men who founded this here United States were from Pennsylvania. Ever hear of Ben Franklin?"

"No, why should I have?"

"If that don't Beat the Dutch." The thin man shook his head in disbelief. "Never heard a Ben Franklin. Why—oh, never mind. How far do you intend to go?" he asked Allsup.

"All the way to the Pacific."

"Well, now, don't that beat all," declared Stan. "I ain't even been that far. When ya leavin'?"

"Tomorrow, I hope."

"Well, Ollie, what say you and me take this gentlemen, what's your name?"

"Danny Allsup."

"Danny Allsup to Faust's for oysters and dinner. We'll give'im a real St. Louis send-off."

Ollie agreed and the three walked down Fourth Street,

turned north on Elm and walked to Fifth, where a good-sized building on the corner with a large black sign announced *Tony Faust's Oyster House & Saloon* in white lettering. Chestnut would be safe tethered at Maxwell's Saloon. Both men assured Allsup, and they would not be gone long.

"Oysters!" exclaimed Ollie as they each took a chair at a white, cloth-covered table. A man with a white apron tied around his waist came over and took their order for three beers and three dozen shucked oysters.

"Have ya had oysters before?" The thin man Stan, inquired.

"No, never," he answered.

"They don't have oysters back in Pennsylvania?" Ollie asked.

"Not where I come from. We lived on a farm out in the country near a small town called Lebanon."

"Lebanon, huh? Never heard of it," Ollie admitted.

"Bah, that don't mean nothin', Ollie; you never heard of Pennsylvania!" Stan retorted.

"Here's the thing about oysters, Danny," Stan explained. "They look terrible, like hog boogers or somethin', but they taste like the ocean 'cause that's where they come from."

"Hog boogers," Ollie repeated, chuckling.

The waiter arrived with a tray held shoulder high carrying their three beers and another tray with three platters of opened oysters sitting on their half shells. He first placed a beer before each man and followed with a platter each of the oysters. After asking if all was well and correct, he left them to their indulgences.

Stan and Ollie raised their mugs of beer; Allsup quickly followed suit as Stan recited:

"Here's to the man that ate the first one,
"Pried it open and slurped it down.
"I wonder if his face expressed that of pleasure,
"Or did it contort into a disgusted frown."

They clinked their mugs together and each took a long swallow.

"That was pretty good," Allsup observed, wiping the remnants of the beer's foam from his upper lip. "Who wrote it? Do you know?"

"I did," Stan proudly answered.

"Well, I must say that was pretty good. Is there more to it?"

"Nope, that's all I got."

"Here's what ya do," instructed Ollie, holding a half shell. "Ya tip it up and let it slide into your mouth." He proceeded to demonstrate and the first of his twelve disappeared.

Allsup stared down at the plate of bivalves before him.

"They don't look edible right now," Stan explained. "But once ya start eatin' 'em, that platter will be like candy to a baby to ya."

"Really?" Allsup sounded skeptical.

"Squeeze a little lemon on 'em," suggested Ollie pointing to the lemon wedges on his plate. "Some people like to eat 'em that way."

Allsup picked one shell up and brought it to his nose. After sniffing it several times, he grimaced and set it back down.

"What's wrong?" asked Ollie. "You're not going to try one?"

"I am."

"Just pick it up and slurp it down!" urged Stan. "It's like eating the ocean."

"Okay." Allsup picked up the half shell again and immediately let its contents slide into his mouth.

"Oo, I hew it?" he asked, still holding the oyster in his mouth.

"Yeah! Chew it!" responded Stan with a laugh, slapping Allsup on the back.

Allsup chewed and swallowed the shellfish quickly

before shaking his head, taking a long swallow of beer and exclaiming, "Nope!"

"What's a matter?" asked Ollie, grinning. "Don't ya like it?"

"Have either of you ever been to the ocean?" Allsup asked, wiping his mouth with his napkin. Both admitted they had not. "Then how do you know it tastes like the ocean?"

"Cause that's what they told us," Ollie confessed.

"Well, I sure hope the ocean is a far sight better tasting than this—stuff!"

"Maybe he got a bad one," Ollie suggested.

"A bad one?" Allsup sounded aghast.

"Could be, I guess. How's yours?" Stan asked his large friend.

"Mine is fine," Ollie replied and to demonstrate, he consumed another.

Stan upended another oyster and, smacking his lips, declared, "By golly, these are about as good as they get!"

"How do you tell if they're bad?" asked Allsup.

"They taste nasty," Stan replied.

"You jest with me, sir!"

"No, sir, we do not!" countered Stan.

"They taste wretched when they're bad," added Ollie. "You ain't retchin' are ya?"

"No," conceded Allsup. "No, I'm not retching."

"Let me try one'a yourn," Ollie suggested. "Jest to make sure."

He took a half shell from Allsup's plate and let it slide into his mouth. After sloshing it around from one side of his mouth to the other, he chewed and swallowed the mollusk.

"Dee-vine!" he proclaimed, smacking his lips. "Excellent!"

"Well, I leave you both my remaining 10. I believe I will retrieve my horse and continue on my way." Allsup rose from the table.

"Wait! Wait!" Stan protested, also rising. "You can't

leave with this bad impression. Let us make it up to you."

"That's not necessary," Allsup assured them.

"Yeah, there be, don't ya see?" Ollie jumped in. "It's the way ya said it that betrays your feelin's."

"Sit down, Mr Allsup—Danny," Stan hopefully suggested. "Let us make it up to ya. How 'bout a nice big, thick steak?"

"Well," Allsup returned to his seat. "A steak does sound good, and I am hungry."

"Waiter!" Stan called out, his hand raised, fingers snapping. "Cut my friend here a nice piece'a beef, 'bout two inches thick. Throw it in the pan 'n brown it on both sides, then bring it to him bloody."

The waiter nodded and was about to turn away when Allsup stopped him.

"Excuse me, but I prefer my steak cut thin, maybe about half an inch or less, and cook it well done, almost to burnt."

The two men sitting at the table with Allsup sat frozen; the waiter stood with his mouth agape.

"You be funnin' us now, ain't ya?" Ollie suggested, breaking into a grin.

"No, that's how I like my steak."

"Ya ever try it, ya know, thick and bloody?" inquired Stan.

"No, I prefer my steak absent of any animal characteristics that would remind me that I am made the same."

"Really?" muttered Stan as if presented with a bit of enlightenment.

"What?" Ollie asked, confused.

"Just get him his steak," Stan told the waiter, who left to place the order.

"I don't get it," Ollie announced. "What just happened here? Is he gettin' a steak or not?"

"He's gettin' a steak, Ollie."

"Thick'n bloody?"

"Thin and crispy."

"Really?"

The three sat at the table quietly. Each man lost in thought before Allsup said, "Gentlemen, finish your oysters and mine as well, by all means. Enjoy them while they're fresh."

Ollie and Stan expressed their appreciation and continued consuming their gifts from the ocean.

"You traveling by horse?" Stan inquired after a drink of beer.

"I am."

"Where ya goin'?" asked Ollie.

"Jefferson City next, but the Pacific is my goal."

"Why don't ya take a steamer up to Jefferson City," Stan suggested. "Relax and travel in comfort for a spell."

"I hadn't thought of that."

"Yeah, it's just a day or so ride up river from here. Give your horse a break."

"I might look into that," Allsup mused.

"My friend George Ashbee." Stan turned to Ollie. "You know, works on the docks?"

Ollie nodded his recollection, so Stan continued, "He's been loading the Gold Dust all day. Says she's leavin' this evenin', heading for Jefferson City."

"The Gold Dust is a sweet steamer, it bein' new and all," Ollie said. "I know Gould McCord. He's one'a the pilots. I rode up and back with him a couple'a times."

As they were talking, the waiter timidly approached their table. Stan noticed his hovering and asked his purpose.

"I don't know how to tell you this," he said, head down and staring at his shoes.

"Well? What is it?" Ollie asked.

"Well, it's the cook, sir."

"What about the cook?" Stan jumped in.

"Well, sir, he won't...he won't..."

"What will he won't?" demanded Stan.

"He won't cook the gentlemen's beef as requested."

"What?" the three said in unison.

"He, by which when I say 'He' I mean the cook, refuses to cook the beef in that manner; said he'd quit before he burnt steak intentionally."

"By, golly, I never..." Stan was completely flustered.

"Go get that gul'darn cook and bring him out here!" ordered Ollie to the trembling waiter.

"Gentlemen, no," Allsup interrupted, rising once more. He motioned the waiter away before continuing, "I appreciate your friendship and good intentions, but this was not to be. I am leaving with a light heart and that's because you desired that I stay."

"But we didn't get to buy ya that meal!" Stan pointed out.

"I'm fine, I assure you. Gentlemen, it's been a pleasure making your acquaintance." The two men rose and shook his hand. "And now I'm off to get my horse and find the Gold Dust."

Chapter 40

He sat at a table on the second floor of the paddleboat, Gold Dust. This part of the deck was opened and available to all passengers, all ten, including Allsup. The entire main deck area was reserved for cargo and freight, as was its purpose. Carrying goods from Cincinnati, New Orleans and Memphis as well as from St. Louis, passengers were not considered necessary or required and were confined to the second deck, which had the appearance of a moderately priced hotel lobby with a few available rooms.

Several woven carpets covered its floor, the chairs were cushioned, and the surrounding windows gave an excellent view of the passing landscape. There were finer paddleboats traveling on the Missouri River, but the Gold Dust was currently the newest. The pilot master, as well as the five-man crew were proud of its cleanliness and maneuverability.

It was nine o'clock in the evening, and at present, no countryside was visible. The moon was new, and the sky was cloudy. Allsup had found the paddleboat ready for departure. Only the last few barrels remained to be loaded. He was welcomed and paid a fare for himself and Chestnut. The horse was led to a stable-like area and fed sweetened oats and hay while Allsup was directed upstairs, where he sat at a table by an open window allowing the cool night air to enter the room.

Across from him, on the opposite side of the cabin, sat a young family of six, a husband and wife sitting at a table, and two boys and two girls sitting at the table next to them. The youngest was a boy of about two who was actively climbing on top of everything. The oldest, a proper-appearing daughter, sat reading while correcting her siblings when they became too loud or rambunctious. The delegation for parenting had obviously been passed on to her, as the two parents tended to themselves and ignored their children regardless of how much noise they made or how high they might unsafely climb.

Allsup glanced at his timepiece more than once, wondering why at least the younger children had not been sent to bed. He reasoned that the excitement of traveling on a riverboat might discourage efforts of slumber, not to mention the many oil-burning lamps mounted on the walls around the room and dangling by chains from the ceiling that gave the interior the appearance of daylight.

Two men at the back of the cabin were sitting at a table playing a card game. The active children were getting on the nerves of one player because he began to make loud comments about parenting skills at every disturbance. Allsup considered a correlation between the player's patience thinning with the increase in his losses.

The tenth passenger was a man in a dark suit slouched down in a chair along the same wall as Allsup, with his legs stretched out and a black derby hat pulled down over his eyes. Every once in a while, he would jump when one of the children would let out a shriek or scream, but then he'd adjust his hat and doze off again.

"Are you a cowboy?" a young boy of about five asked Allsup. A sister of about the same age accompanied him; they were both studying him earnestly.

"No, I'm not," Allsup responded, smiling. "Do I look like a cowboy?"

"Yep," the boy answered.

"You do," confirmed his sister nodding her head.

"What do cowboys look like?" Allsup asked.

"Well..." the boy was giving his response serious thought.

"They got boots!" blurted the young girl.

"Yeah!" The boy jumped in. "They do got boots!"

"You got boots." The girl pointed out.

"I do. You're right, but a lot of men wear boots. That

doesn't make them all cowboys, does it?"

"No," they both agreed.

"You got a cowboy hat." The boy pointed out.

"Yeah!" agreed his sister.

"I do have a hat, but a lot of men wear hats."

"That's a cowboy hat, though," argued the girl.

Allsup removed his hat and examined it closely.

"You got me there. It's definitely a cowboy hat, but..."

"You got a gun!" the boy announced, his eyes wide with wonder. The little girl gasped loudly.

"Jenny! Robert!" called out their older sister. "Get over here and leave that man alone!"

The two looked at Allsup for a minute before saying goodbye, each leaving with a wave. They ran back to their sister excitedly, telling her about their first cowboy.

"Marie," said the mother sounding annoyed. "Why don't you get them into bed? It's getting late; you should all be in bed."

"Yes, Mama," answered Marie, who proceeded to direct her siblings down the room to the doorway leading to the overnight berths. The mother and father then returned to their conversation without regard for their parental duties or affections. Evidently, their oldest had become the nanny they could never afford. This was a circumstance Allsup highly disapproved of; they were denying the young lady the chance to live her own life.

The couple caught Allsup staring; both nodded and smiled; he merely looked away.

"Would you object to company, sir?" The man in the dark suit who'd previously been sleeping was standing at Allsup's side.

Allsup looked up and rose, extending his hand.

"No, sir, I would not. Join me, please. Danny Allsup."

"Glenn Perkins, at your service," responded the man as he took the chair across from Allsup. Now that those children are silenced, I can't seem to get a wink of sleep."

Allsup smiled and nodded.

"Bound for Jefferson City?" Perkins asked.

"A stopping point."

"On your way to somewhere else?"

"Indeed, the Pacific."

"Ah, the 'Peaceful Sea.' I've seen it many times."

"You have?" Allsup leaned forward.

"Yes, I've traveled west on many occasions."

"What is your occupation, sir?"

"I am a wagon master. I lead wagon trains westward, usually to Oregon."

"You don't say?"

"I do," Perkins answered, smiling.

"Why are you on the Gold Dust?"

"On my way back to lead another train. I come back by ship around the strait, usually to Boston, occasionally New York—this time to New York, then travel overland to Independence. I pick up another train and—repeat."

"Well, that's interesting," Allsup commented.

"You're heading west, you say?"

"I am."

"Do you have a horse?"

"I do."

"Can you shoot?"

"Tolerably."

"Why don't you join me?"

"I will consider it," answered Allsup.

"Would you oppose a spot of brandy?" Perkins raised a silver flask.

Allsup gestured the negative with a slight shake of his head.

"Perhaps you'll join me?" The flask was extended and as Allsup reached for it, Perkins toasted, "Here's how!"

For the remainder of the evening until the early morning hours, the flask passed from one to the other, stopping only for necessities and refills.

Danny Allsup

Along the way, the Gold Dust made brief stops at towns along the river, such as Franklin and Herman, before reaching Jefferson City in the early afternoon. They moored parallel to the shore along with other boats, dropping their plank down from the side of the vessel. Allsup was waiting with Chestnut and at the first opportunity, disembarked.

His newly acquainted friend, Glenn Perkins, had advised that he get a room at the Schmidt Hotel. "A fine establishment," Perkins had declared. "With a fine bar and restaurant on the first floor. First rate, being the state capital, all the important people meet there."

Allsup was determined to do just that. He was not used to the early morning hours accompanied by an unending supply of brandy. His brain was telling his body that it needed rest and very, very soon. He moved with determination to find the hotel and a room. After several inquiries regarding directions, he located the Schmidt and marched into its lobby.

"I'd like a room," he informed the desk clerk.

Standing straight as a board and as somber as a Calvinist minister, he added, "And someone to tend to my horse." He gestured over his shoulder before correcting himself, "Outside, the horse is outside—I would seriously like a room."

Chapter 41

Coming down the stairs of the Schmidt Hotel, he felt considerably better than when he had made the ascent several hours earlier, at which time, he immediately fell upon the hotel bed and remained there until early evening.

With a change of clothes and attitude, he walked into the hotel's parlor where many had gathered to drink and converse. Allsup made his way up to the bar and stood next to three other gentlemen, businessmen by their suits and manner. They were engaged in a lively conversation resulting in frequent bursts of laughter. At one point, the man beside Allsup backed into him, causing Allsup's glass to slip from his hand, spill and shatter.

"My God, I'm sorry!" exclaimed the man as he realized what had occurred.

"Good work, Gruelle, you made the man spill his drink!" commented another.

"I'm sorry," Gruelle said again. "Let me buy you another. Come join us, if you will."

The circle of three expanded to include a fourth as fresh drinks were distributed.

"I'm Wallace Gruelle. Sorry, again, about the drink."

"Daniel Allsup." Shook hands all around.

"That man is T.D. Rapp and this young man here is the infamous Joe Pulitzer."

"Infamous? Should I know of you?" Allsup asked.

"You're not from around here, are you?" T.D. Rapp stated more than inquired.

"No, just passing through."

"Well, we're all newsmen, reporters," Rapp advised.

"Except for Pulitzer here," Gruelle added. "He's also the state rep. for this district."

"A state representative, well, that's impressive."

"I was shanghaied into the job," said Pulitzer, grinning. "Wasn't even in the room when they confirmed my nomination."

"That way he couldn't protest!" Rapp added, laughing.

"But, by golly, once he accepted," Gruelle noted. "He threw himself into the election and won the damn seat."

"A Republican in a Democratic district," Rapp shook his head in disbelief. "Only Pulitzer could have pulled that off."

"To Representative Pulitzer, then!" Allsup toasted, his glass held high; all glasses were raised and emptied.

"You said you were passing through," Pulitzer addressed Allsup. "From where to where?"

"Here we go," Rapp protested. "Always asking questions. Joe, we're having drinks! Let's just talk."

"I am talking," counter Pulitzer. "I'm trying to engage in conversation with Mr Allsup here by inquiring about his travels."

"I'm coming from Pennsylvania and heading to the west coast, to the Pacific specifically."

"That's quite a task you've set for yourself."

"Going alone?" Rapp asked.

"Yes, I am—well, I have a horse."

"This is very interesting," Pulitzer observed. "I'm curious about what could have been the impetus for your journey."

"Joe, please!" Rapp pleaded laughingly. "Let the man be. That's personal and not to be shared over drinks in the parlor of the Schmidt Hotel with three drunken reporters he's never met before!"

"Yes, yes, yes, you're right," Pulitzer admitted. "I'm sorry, I get curious is all. But one last thing: can you read and write?"

"I can," acknowledged Allsup.

"Well, how about keeping a journal of your travels? Send them back to me, and we'll publish them in the Post.

We'll pay you for each one we print. What do you think?"

"I don't know. I'd never thought about writing other than making a list or writing a letter."

"Well, why don't you swing by tomorrow and we'll work out a contract."

"I don't think so," Allsup advised. "If I write, I'll send it back; if you print it, you can pay me. But I probably won't be writing."

"No?"

"No, I should be too busy living it to write about it."

"Here! Here!" shouted Gruelle and Rapp. "Well said! Well said!"

As they ordered another round, Allsup pointed out it would be his last, and Pulitzer prepared to take his leave.

"I'm off to the telegraph," he announced. "A good evening to all; safe travels, Mr. Allsup."

"An interesting man," Allsup observed as he watched Pulitzer leave.

"He really is," agreed Rapp. "He shot a man for calling him a liar right on this very spot."

"Right here?" Allsup looked down at the floor.

"Yes, sir, Edward Augustine called him a liar to his face. Joe went home, got his pistol, came back, and shot him."

"Well, he shot Augustine in the leg as they scuffled over the gun," Gruelle corrected the narrative.

"That was right before Augustine clipped Joe across the forehead with his derringer."

"And he's a state representative?" Allsup shook his head.

"Yes, sir, a very respected one at that," said Gruelle. "He's made quite an impact on the region as a reporter."

"He's well known and highly regarded," Rapp added.

"Well, gentlemen," Allsup finished his drink, "if I don't get beef and potatoes in me very shortly, I fear what I have been drinking will have an adverse effect, and I don't want that to happen. Would you care to join me for a meal?"

Both reporters declined. After recommending several local restaurants, they said their goodbyes over handshakes and best wishes.

It was over a large beefsteak cooked well done that draped over the edges of the plate like a cloth, juices formed a ring on the table around it, and a bowl of boiled potatoes. Allsup decided two things: he was leaving tomorrow, and he was going alone.

Chapter 42

By nine o'clock that morning he was an hour out of Jefferson City. En route, he passed the West End Saloon on the city's outskirts advertising it was "the last Watering Hole going west." Allsup had decided to travel as he had before; using roads when they coincided with his intention and cross-country when they did not.

He passed through the little town St. Martins where all he heard spoken was what he supposed was German. His familiarity with the language was small. He heard it spoken at the Cincinnati Exposition. Also, there was a German family back in Lebanon that lived on the eastern side of town; so Allsup's contact with the family was limited. He and his family had participated in the barn raising on their farm. He found their food unusual but enjoyed the ale they served at the end of the day when the completed two-story structure loomed large behind them.

The road he currently followed was busy with traffic flowing to and from Jefferson City. Most were friendly calling out a greeting and exchanging a word or two as they passed. Chestnut seemed content to amble along with the current not displaying any of his usual friskiness.

They came upon a creek off the road, and Allsup stopped to allow his horse refreshment; concerned about its demeanor. Chestnut took a small sip from the stream, but then backed away, his head hanging low looking miserable.

"What's the matter, boy? You're not getting sick, are you?"

As he continued to pet the animal, another rider approached the stream. He nodded a greeting, dismounted, and allowed his horse water.

"Gonna be warm today," the man observed.

"I'm sure." Allsup focused on Chestnut.

Danny Allsup

"Somethin' wrong with your horse?"

"I think so. He appears to be in discomfort, but I can't figure out where or what."

The man, wearing pants and red long johns, came around from the side of his mount and gave Chestnut a look over.

"He appears bloated," he observed.

"Bloated? Really?" Allsup stepped back for a better view.

"Yes, sir. See how big and round his belly is?" He thumped the horse's drum-tight stomach with his finger. "Like he was eatin' oats and allowed to eat too much. Maybe he got into the feed. Anyways, when they drink after somethin' like that, the oats swell and cause the animal's stomach to bloat up; there's been times, I heard, their stomachs *did* blow up and kill the animal!"

"Well, that's something I didn't need to hear," a worried Allsup said as he watched his horse. "I'd heard that in my youth but have no experience with it."

"Funny," the man continued, "horses will eat themselves sick like that, but a dumb ol' cow won't."

"What should I do?"

"I donno, seems like a good fart would help, but if all that's oats," he indicated the horse's stomach, "he's gonna need to take a couple of shits, too. The sooner, the better. I'd keep him walkin'."

Allsup led the horse back to the road and they continued westward, walking side by side. They followed the road as it rose and fell with the countryside. They passed through Centertown on their way to California, Missouri.

After a while, Allsup became conscious that the road was taking an undesired northern turn. He did not, and they began their first cross-country journey in quite some time.

As they walked over a grassy plain, Chestnut moaned softly and stopped.

"What's the matter, partner?" Allsup asked, scratching

behind the horse's ears.

The horse groaned again, dropping his head.

"Come on, Chestnut, you have to get better," Allsup whispered. "You can't die on me now, not you too. We're in this together, you and me. We're going to the Pacific."

The horse's stomach rumbled loudly, and it moaned again.

"No, no, no, you can't," pleaded Allsup, his heart breaking. "You can't die."

With his head hanging low, the horse looked sorry and mournful as it groaned loudly and appeared defeated. It looked up at Allsup. As he stood rubbing Chestnut's neck soothingly, the horse arched its tail and released an incredible amount of gas followed by the plop, plop, plop, of excrement adding to an expanding pile on the ground. On and on it continued, the pile growing in height and diameter accompanied by flatulence the likes Allsup had not heard before nor smelled. He was not aware that a horse, or any animal, could emit such quantity, volume, and stench.

The horse seemed finished; its tail dropped, and it took several steps forward.

"You feel better now, I'll bet," Allsup said, elated that the horse was going to survive. "Huh? You feel…

Interrupted by more flatulence, the tail rose again and the whole process began anew. After a period, the tail dropped and with a snort, Chestnut raised his head and gave it a shake before proceeding casually onward without waiting for his rider.

They passed through the towns of California and Harrisonville, spending their nights out in the open country. Allsup became more comfortable and confident about sleeping in the wild. They developed a routine in which at some point during the late afternoon they'd stop near water, usually a creek or stream. While Allsup would gather firewood, Chestnut drank his fill or searched for vegetation. By dusk, a fire would be burning and something heating up beside it, coffee if nothing else. After dinner, Allsup would stretch out with his head resting against his saddle and gaze up at the stars.

One night he found himself thinking about how far he had come: the incidents that had transpired, and the people who had come and gone in his travels. As he stared up at the stars he accepted, finally accepted, that he truly was going to the Pacific. He had long ago stopped considering the option of changing his mind, and while he must have known it all this time, it was the first that he had openly acknowledged it to himself. As he stretched and crossed his arms behind his head, he smiled; he was excited again.

It was after Chestnut had completed a burst of speed and ran several miles over the countryside the following day, they happened upon a farmer herding three cows. He carried a long branch cut from a Weeping Willow with all the leaves removed except at its tip. Whenever a cow would begin to wander, the farmer would swish the branch, like a whip, by its ear bringing it back.

"Hello!" Allsup called out as they trotted up to join him.

"Hello," answered the farmer with tip of his straw hat. "Git back there Jessie!" Swish wentthe branch.

"Can you tell me where we are?" Allsup asked.

"Well, I should hope so!" the farmer chuckled. "Billy, where ya goin'?" Swish! The leaves at the tip fluttering like a bird taking flight.

"Well?"

"Well, what?" the farmer looked up at Allsup.

"Sir, can you tell me where we are?"

"Why didn't ya ask me that in the first place? Gretchen! Git back there!" Swish!

"You are playing with me, sir, and I find no humor in it."

"Billy! Back!" Swish! "You're right, I was, but I'll stop, didn't mean to upset ya."

"That's quite alright, just tell me."

D. Dean Carroll

"What?"

"Sir!"

"All right, all right," he chuckled. "You're in Lykins County, Kansas. Damn ya, Billy, behave!" Swish!

"Kansas!" Allsup stopped and pondered the information for a moment.

"If ya ain't comin' along I'll say fare-thee-well!" the farmer called back as he kept pace with the cattle. "They're easy to get started together, but hard to stop. Gretchen!" Swish!

Kansas. There was no question they were on the verge of entering the wilderness and all the dangers that dwelt there. Allsup wondered if it might not be wiser to head north and catch the wagon train. What did he know about surviving in the wild where your gun might be used for a purpose other than hunting? There was safety in numbers, they say; that's why people joined wagon trains. That and you're traveling with someone who knows what they're doing.

The sun was setting in the west as he sat astride his stallion; the sky was blotted with clouds that occasionally blocked it from view. Sunlight radiated from around a cloud illuminating the Earth with visible rays. It reminded Allsup of illustrated pictures in the Bible where the light represented God's presence.

Allsup turned in his saddle facing north; he turned back facing west. He knew the smart thing to do was join the wagon train and travel with them. His chances of success were greater, and it would be less frightening, but there was a strong tug within him to go on, just Chestnut and himself.

"Chestnut, I'm going to let you decide. You're in this, too." He stroked the horse's neck. "Whenever you're ready, you just go and that's the direction we'll travel."

The horse remained standing.

"I was under the impression that eventually, you'd

move. I don't want to coax you; you might interpret it as a suggestion. So, how 'bout you just move on."

Chestnut pawed at the ground and snorted, but made no effort to move.

"He-yaw!" shouted Allsup making every effort not to nudge the horse. "Chestnut, let's go!"

The horse gazed over the rolling countryside but remained stationary.

"All right, I'll give you a nudge, but you don't have to go straight. Any direction you want to go, we'll go. You choose."

Allsup gave Chestnut's ribs a slight prod with his heels. The horse turned and headed south.

"Okay," Allsup reined him to a stop. "Not that way. I should'a said, not south or east. I don't know if you'd understand me even if I did say it, but I should'a told you: north or west."

Chestnut looked back. Allsup wasn't sure if he was considering the direction or his rider. The horse turned west and began walking.

"That was my choice, too," Allsup admitted as they rode into the setting sun. "Let's look for water."

D. Dean Carroll

Chapter 43

Kansas was the confluence where civilization diminished and the wilderness expanded. Allsup and Chestnut traveled days without passing through a town or meeting another traveler; they left the road in Lykins County and had not crossed another since. The silhouettes of farms were occasionally visible in the far distance with hair-thick smoke rising from tiny chimneys. They were too far away, and Allsup never felt the urge to visit. The countryside was green and lush. The rolling hills expanded; their inclines became more gradual. He could see greater distances, but there was nothing to see other than more grass-covered hills and the occasional cluster of trees.

Living on the go and in the wild began to suit him. He became accustomed to the seclusion of his existence; often his own voice was the only human sound he would hear. He traveled for as long as he wanted before stopping for the night. From time to time, they would stop at dusk after journeying the entire day; on other occasions, they would find a desirable spot in the early afternoon and decide to suspend travel for the remainder of the day.

Allsup was slowly improving his marksmanship. It was taking him fewer shots to hit a moving target that had not been moving until after his first miss. Before he would fire five or six times before he hit the intended target or it safely escaped. Now, it required two or three shots, and he was hitting the game more frequently his first effort. Roasted rabbigroundhoghog, or pheasant had become a regular staple of his diet. He also followed creeks and streams to their shallows where schools of Bluegill could be found. When a fishing pole made from a tree branch failed, and his efforts to create a makeshift net with a shirt produced no better results, he resorted to his rifle. When the fish was close enough to the surface he would fire. It took adjustments, but he became quite proficient in obtaining dinner in this manner.

One day they stopped early having come to a stream with thick shade trees on one side and a stretch of tall grass swaying back and forth like ocean waves on the other. Their location promised food for dinner while the shade and breeze offered comfort from the day's heat. After Allsup had removed the gear leaving the horse in its natural state, Chestnut waded into the stream and began to slurp water loudly quenching its thirst.

Allsup organized their campsite laying out his ground tarp and blanket with his saddle at the end; getting out the coffee pot and cast-iron skillet, and resting the saddlebag containing his provisions by the saddle. He collected firewood from the surrounding stand of trees and soon had a fire blazing. His camping skills were improving each day with their overland progress.

Loading his rifle and adding a couple of extra shells to his coat pocket, he waded across the stream and ventured into the tall grass. It was his hope that he would find this night's dinner. He didn't desire to wade up or down the stream looking for fish in the shallows, for it seemed that he'd been eating a lot of fish over the last few days, so it was his hope that tonight's dinner would be something obtained from above the water.

The grass varied in height, ranging from knee-high to waist; it was impossible to see the ground. He couldn't see where he was stepping and worried about snakes. Something, probably a rabbit, went running away to his left. He couldn't see it but heard it and saw the tops of the grass flutter and part as it ran. That was not good. If he couldn't see the game, he couldn't very well shoot it.

He continued hoping his approach might stir a pheasant to wing, *that* he could see and shoot. No sooner had the thought crossed his mind when a nest of pheasants quickly flew up into the air. Five of the birds with their wide wingspans and long tails flew skyward and for a second, Allsup was distracted by their elegance. Suddenly, he regained his wits and raised his rifle to fire. He fired three times in succession before one of the bird's wings stopped and it plummeted to the Earth. Delight over his success was short-lived, however, immediately after he had fired his last shot, two others echoed across the countryside and two more birds fell from the sky.

"Hello?" When there was no response, he called out again, "Hello?"

He looked around, searching for the source of gun fire, but saw no one. He had not realized he had set up camp at the bottom of a hill until two ragged hats came into view on the horizon of the hilltop followed by the heads beneath. Allsup became apprehensive. Their clothing looked as raggedy as their hats, made mostly of hide crudely stitched together. They crested the hill, each with a rifle in one hand and reins in the other, and each leading a pack animal laden with buffalo hides. They stopped at the top and looked down at Allsup and Chestnut still standing in the stream. Allsup stood with rifle in hand prepared for whatever may come.

"We ain't lookin' fer trouble," one man growled slowly, barely audible, his voice as raspy as sandpaper. He had long gray hair well past his shoulders and a matching beard hanging down to his belt. His companion looked much the same, except his hair was bright red.

"What?" Allsup called back.

"We ain't lookin' fer trouble!"

"We come in peace!" shouted his red-haired partner.

"Come join me, then." Allsup waved them down.

As the two men descended the hill, Allsup asked, "Did you get your birds?"

"Not yit," growled the gray-haired man as he climbed down from his mount.

"Saw the smoke," explained the other as he rode up

beside his associate.

"You got fire. We cook our meat?" gray hair pointedly asked.

"Yes, certainly." Allsup motioned to the fire, still apprehensive.

They tied their pack animals to nearby trees before remounting their horses.

"We git da birds," the gray-haired man announced. "Ya git yorn bird?"

"I did." Allsup held up his pheasant by its legs.

"We git da birds!" the man shouted and the two dashed across the stream on their mounts into the tall grass.

Allsup believed plucking feathers from a chicken, or any fowl, the most tedious of jobs. That task fell to his wife when they were all back on the farm; she became quite apt at the process. What would take him an hour or more, she could accomplish in thirty minutes, less if she was pressed for time.

He thought of his wife, her long brown hair hanging down her back almost to her waist; her nimble fingers pulling the feathers from the hen and putting them in an empty flour sack to save for later uses. Nimble, that word described Nancy. Everything she did was done with agility and grace. His memory of her in the kitchen was almost like a dance, the way she moved from counter to stove to table. If he was sitting there watching, which he did at every chance, she would have a smile on her freckled face that would every so often break into a grin. Occasionally, she would purposely swirl causing her dress to twirl out and up. He would reach for her, but she would slip away, laughing. The boys would come in and she'd become a mother again.

They had always been playful throughout their marriage; up until the boys didn't come home. The playfulness slipped away with their boys. His thoughts were interrupted by a strange cry.

"Ooo-Eee!" shrilled the red-haired man, announcing

their return as the two men came riding out of the grass at a gallop. "Ooo-Eee!"

"Alright! Dat be 'nough wit dat!" scolded the older gray-haired man. They rode across the stream tossing their two birds down beside Allsup before lashing their horses to trees alongside their pack animals.

"I be Julie McNutt," the gray-haired man announced extending his hand in greeting. "That be Red Johnson." He gestured to his partner who waved to Allsup. "We fetch hides together."

As Allsup introduced himself, Julie McNutt pulled out a pipe and loaded it with tobacco from a small leather pouch. He used a stick from the fire to get it burning to his satisfaction. The three men knelt by the stream and finished plucking and disemboweling their pheasants.

With their birds impaled on a common stick and placed over the campfire, each man put in his time turning the spit. They pooled their rations to round out their meal. Allsup brought his skillet filled with water to a boil and cooked dry beans. Julie produced six biscuits left over from breakfast that morning obtained from a restaurant in Council Grove, with Red giggling that two were from a table nearby.

"I got somethin' you doan know!" Red mischievously exclaimed as he picked up a bag; his grin revealed blackened teeth, many rotted to the gum.

"What you got?" Julie inquired.

"You doan know!" Red repeated, excitedly. "You got to wait till after wes eat. It be for after wes eat."

"Oh." Julie was disappointed.

The three sat around the fire as Allsup slowly turned the stick-impaled pheasants. Red fell asleep lying on his side on the bare ground while Julie watched the stream water pass, throwing a pebble into it upon occasion.

Allsup thought the two men must be used to silence together. Spending all their time in each other's company for months at a time, over many years, they probably knew the ways of the other.

"You eats fish?" Julie asked.

"Yes, I like fish," Allsup answered. "Been eating more lately than in the past."

"I doan eats it—fish." The gray hair man admitted. "It look bad."

"It's good we have the pheasant then, isn't it."

"Yeah, I doan eats fish."

While Julie started his pipe again, Allsup asked where they were headed.

"We go Jeff City." An ember fell onto his beard, which began smoldering. He beat it out by rapidly pounding the beard against his chest until extinguished. Leaning back against his saddle he continued, "We sell dem pelts, git fair trade, buy goods, go back."

"How long have you and Red been riding together?"

After a pause and smile, Julie answered, "Year—many, many year."

"Where do you go?"

Through puffs of smoke, Julie looked at Allsup suspiciously.

"Jeff…City." He said the name slowly.

"No, no, I mean when you leave Jeff City, where do you go?"

"Oh," Julie responded laughing. "Just now I think you dumb in da head! We go way out, out more den others. Place no white man see."

"To the mountains?"

"To da last mountains."

"To the Pacific?"

"What?"

"The Pacific Ocean, beyond the mountains."

"No, doan know ocean."

"That's where I'm going," Allsup informed the gray-haired man. "Beyond the last mountains to the ocean."

"Who wit?"

"Just me and that stallion there."

"No one?" Red asked, sitting up.

"He wake!" Julie announced, surprised.

"Just me."

"You go b'fore dis, no?" Julie looked at Allsup hopefully.

"No, dis, *this* is my first time."

Julie and Red looked at each other a bit puzzled.

"Dat, I think no good," Red informed him while getting up and walking to the stream to relieve himself.

"You git dead," Julie said bluntly nodding his head. "Go like dat, you git dead."

"Well, you may be right," Allsup admitted. "But I've made it this far, I'm determined to finish it."

"Why nobody but you?" asked Red sitting back down by the fire and taking his turn rotating the birds. "Go wagon train, or…Eh, I got idea! Allsup ride wit us!"

"By, criminy, but dat's a good idea!" responded Julie. "Allsup? You wait 'n ride wit us!"

"Hmm, I'm tempted, but I have my mind set on moving on tomorrow. I do appreciate the offer though. I'll bet there's nothing like traveling with you two."

"I be sorry to hear dat," Julie said shaking his head, disappointed.

"Deez birds cooked, I be thinking," Red said lifting the spit from the fire.

"I think the beans are done too." Allsup stirred the boiling beans in the cast iron skillet. "If the birds are done, I'm declaring the beans done too just because I'm hungry!"

"I like hear you talk," Red told Allsup good-naturedly. "Sounds funny."

"I like to hear you talk, too," Allsup replied. "Sounds funny."

"No, it doan!" Red protested. Turning to Julie, "Do it?"

"Criminy, yeah, it do," Julie conceded before declaring, "We eat!"

Danny Allsup

They each had their own tin plates on which they poured beans. Ollie distributed a biscuit each, and upon each plate of beans, a charred black bird. Allsup poured himself a cup of coffee, but the two hunters preferred to share a jug. They offered it to Allsup, but he'd had enough of what he suspected its contents.

Over the meal, they offered Allsup tips and suggestions. He should stop in Council Grove because that was the last town for quite a while, and he could get supplies. They told him to take as much water as he could carry; water they emphasized was more important than coffee pots and coffee beans. Hard tack, jerky, oats, and water should be all he carries. Shoot game when he can and trade with others when possible.

"What will I have to trade if I only have hard tack, jerky, oats, and water?" Allsup asked.

"All," Julie answered. "But doan trade water, no time water."

After they had finished their meal and the tin plates were empty of all contents except for the remains of the birds, Red got up slowly, grinning.

"Eh?" he said as he moved to his saddlebags. "You men, who want somethin'?"

The jug's content was having a definite effect.

"Ahh, yes!" exclaimed Julie holding out his hands like a child awaiting a surprise.

"Yes, yes!" Red excitedly agreed as he approached the two men, his hand in a bag.

He stood before Julie and said, "Julie, my friend. Da biggest."

Red pulled out a peach the size of a large man's fist. He handed it to his friend who accepted it with a look of wonder.

Red, with his hand in the bag, stepped before Allsup.

"Allsup, new friend, I doan know you much, you git small." He handed Allsup a peach not much bigger than a snowball.

"Thank you, Red," Allsup said, taking the fruit. It was mushy and bruised, and his finger easily slipped into an over-ripe spot, but he hadn't tasted a peach since Pennsylvania, and he was grateful. "Where did you get this?"

"Council Grove."

Red took the last for himself and sat back down by the fire.

The three sat admiring their peaches savoring the moment. Turning the fruit this way and that; smelling the distinct sweetness. They looked at each other happily like children on Christmas morning. They longed to bite into it, to feel the juice explode, their mouths salivating from the thought of it. But to begin would be one bite closer to the end, and they couldn't bear the thought of it ending; of not having their peach.

"Eat! Eat!" Red instructed, happily, watching the two men.

"What you say, eat," Julie replied. "Red eat!"

"No! Julie eat! I give!"

"Allsup," Julie turned to their new acquaintance. "Allsup, you eat!"

"All right, I will." Allsup took a large bite of the over-ripe peach, his teeth passing through it like a warm knife through butter, juice dripped with each bite down onto his pants.

"Good?" Red anxiously asked.

Allsup nodded his head as he continued to eat, moaning with satisfaction.

Both Red and Julie began eating. Lips smacking and slurping erupted around the campfire along with moans expressing immense enjoyment and delight. Allsup who finished first sat contentedly sucking the pit secured within his left cheek like a chipmunk pouch. It wasn't long before each man was settled back against their saddles, each savoring their pits.

Danny Allsup

Soon, darkness fell completely; the night sky was filled with sporadic clouds that often obscured the moon casting the land in complete darkness. With only the diminishing campfire for illumination, the three men were content to remain as they were, relaxing, listening to the song of the nearby stream that was no longer visible.

Before long, Red or Ollie, Allsup could not tell which, began to snore, and before too long the other joined in. A sort of duet commenced that can only be described as two grizzly bears attempting to intimidate the other by the ferociousness of their growls.

Danny Allsup, ignoring the noise, smiled. His past had trained him to do so. His wife had snored to such an extent that he was convinced that were it a contest, and they issued medals for snoring; she frequently would be the winner. Late on their wedding night, he was alarmed to discover this characteristic. She prevented him from sleeping and could not understand why he was so tired and lethargic the next day. He loved his wife deeply and so trained himself to block it during the hours of darkness.

When his sons grew older, they demonstrated their inheritance of that particular trait. When the combined clamor of the three became too great, Allsup often took refuge in the barn. Even there, the din could be heard and seemed to unsettle the animals. He often took refuge in the barn.

The sound of movement caused Allsup to open his eyes; Red and Ollie were packing up. Dawn was breaking; everything appeared gray. Allsup glanced over to where the two had been sleeping. Their bedrolls were gone as were all the cooking utensils and everything else that had previously been on display. The only remaining thing from the night before was Allsup himself still lying on his bedroll, his head resting against his saddle. He discretely glanced over to where their horses were tethered, and there they were; their pack animals packed and ready. Julie sat on his horse while

Red adjusted the saddle on his own, and Chestnut, wearing a halter, was tied to the last pack animal.

"Red be going!" Julie whispered harshly.

"Yeah, yeah," Red responded without much concern.

"Allsup wake up!" Julie pointed out. "Be goin' now."

"Yeah, okay, we go." Red dropped the saddle stirrup and prepared to mount. Just as he was swinging himself onto the saddle, they heard a click. Neither had noticed Allsup rise and remove his pistol from its holster.

"Good morning," greeted Allsup, his gun held steady.

"Yeah, yeah," Julie sheepishly chuckled. "Good mornin' to you, Allsup."

"We see," Red added with a shrug of his shoulders. "Mayhap good, mayhap not so good."

"I don't want trouble," Allsup told them. "I just want my horse and other goods returned to me. Then you two can go on your way."

"We have no goods 'a yourn," replied Red.

"The horse then, we'll start with him."

"Not Allsup's horse," Julie advised. "Julie's horse."

"Yourn?" Surprised, Red turned to his partner. "Yourn?"

"Yeah, yeah, Julie's horse."

"Why no Red's horse?" Red countered.

"Julie's horse, and dat's dat!" he answered threateningly.

"Gentlemen," Allsup interrupted. "The horse is mine and stays with me."

"No, I doan…" Red had no sooner started to respond when Allsup cut in.

"I am not a very good shot," he admitted. Both men looked at him waiting.

"What I mean by that is, if one of you do not dismount, now, and untie my horse and return my goods, I am going to shoot you in the leg."

"Ha! Allsup no good shot," Red pointed out, laughing.

Danny Allsup

"Allsup miss."

"I wager I can get pretty darn close!"

"Close, but no hit!" Red could not believe this stupid man.

Julie was not laughing.

"Red," he called out before calling out again, "Red! Where bullet go?"

"Huh?" Red looked questioningly at his friend.

"Where bullet go, Red?"

Red looked down at his leg straddling his horse.

"I don't want to shoot your horse." Allsup still held the gun steady, pointed toward the two. "I will seriously, I promise, aim for your leg, but I cannot make promises I'll hit it."

"Allsup no shoot," Julie smugly said. "You no shoot."

"Well, we'll test it on you, Julie. Untie my horse and return him to me."

"Allsup no shoot." Julie remained staring him down.

"Seriously? You're going to let me shoot you in the leg just to keep my horse?"

No one answered. Red and Julie sat atop their mounts, waiting, watching Allsup. Birds could be heard singing in nearby branches. Bees hummed loudly as they flew from one flower to another. Something, probably a deer or a fox, could be heard splashing through the water up stream. The loudness of the gunshot silenced it all.

With a moan, the horse fell onto its side with Julie's leg trapped beneath.

Another gunshot sounded and woodchips fell upon Allsup's hat and shoulders. Red had drawn his revolver and returned fire striking the tree directly behind Allsup. Allsup quickly ducked behind it as Red fired another shot.

"Hey! Hold it!" Allsup called out. "I don't want to shoot anybody, and I don't want to be shot myself!"

"You shoot Julie!" Red answered, firing again.

"Whoa! Whoa!" Julie cried. "Move dis horse!"

"All I want is my horse back!" shouted Allsup.

"Move dis horse!"

"We stop to move Julie's horse," Red proposed.

"What? You want to stop and move the horse so he can get up and assist you?"

"Huh?" responded Red.

"My leg!"

"We help Julie, so Julie help Red?" Allsup rephrased his question.

"Yeah, yeah!" Red was so happy that Allsup understood he stepped out from behind the tree from which he'd sought protection while re-loading his pistol. Before he could respond, Allsup was upon him and knocking the pistol and bullets from his hands. Red found himself with Allsup's gun barrel shoved under his chin.

"Give me my things back!" Allsup ordered. "You already know I'll shoot."

"Yeah, yeah," Red replied as Allsup slowly lowered his pistol. "I get gun?" he asked hopefully, gesturing down at his weapon lying in the dirt surrounded by scattered bullets.

"No, I get gun." Allsup picked up the weapon before telling Red, "Get my things."

"My leg!" cried Julie. "Move dis damn horse!"

"Soon," Allsup answered, leading Chestnut to be saddled.

"Des Allsup things." Red was carrying the cast iron skillet, coffee pot, a cup and plate, and a fork.

"Put them in that bag, there." He pointed to a potato-sack bag with a drawstring top. "Bring it to me." Allsup tied the bag to the saddlebags beneath the bedroll and mounted Chestnut.

"You boys should stick to the fur trade because you're certainly not cut out to be thieves." Allsup nudged Chestnut and they scaled the hill back towards their original route.

"But Julie! We move da horse!" Red reminded him.

"You'll figure it out," replied Allsup as he neared the

crest of the hill.

"Red's gun!"

Allsup pulled the horse to a stop and turned around.

"Oh, yeah, I forgot." Allsup pulled the gun out of his holster belt and held it momentarily in his hand as if pondering its fate. "Here you go." He threw the gun high overhead, and it landed in the stream with a splash.

"Sorry."

D. Dean Carroll

Chapter 44

Council Grove was a miniature version of St. Louis. Located on the Neosho River, there were fewer buildings and people, but the activity was just as intense as clusters of covered wagons awaited their opportunity to depart and head west towards hope, opportunity, and a new life. With wood buildings lining a wide dirt street that served as the main route through the town, people scurried everywhere in anxious anticipation of departure.

"Excuse me," Allsup called out to a man walking along the building fronts. "Can you suggest an inn or tavern where I can get something to eat?"

"The Hays House up ahead." The man pointed down the street. "They got food'n such."

"Much obliged," Allsup said with a tip of his hat before horse and rider sauntered down the street. He stopped at a water trough along the way where Chestnut took the opportunity to drink.

He continued until he came upon a wide, two-storied building with a large flat-roofed porch. A sign on the wall of the second story above the porch, announced *Hays House est. 1857*. Allsup was eager for a good cooked meal; he tied Chestnut's reins to the hitching post in front of the restaurant and ventured inside.

Scattered tables with occupants at most filled the large dining room. Off to the far side, between two windows, a man was playing a song that no one was listening to on an upright piano. Waiters moved between the tables taking orders, replenishing drinks, and cleaning off tables for the next customer: in this case, Allsup.

He ordered that day's special: pan fried chicken with potatoes, spinach, and bread along with coffee. As he ate a man approached wearing a worn, brown frock coat, a frayed wide brimmed hat from which hung small beads dangling around his head, and a full brown beard covering his face from his nose down to his chest.

"How's the meal, friend?" the man asked.

Allsup set his fork upon his plate and wiped his mouth before answering, "Good, very good."

"That's what I like to hear. Name's Seth Hays, I am the proprietor of this establishment. Don't get up. Continue with your meal. Mind if I sit?" he asked as he pulled out a chair on the opposite side of the table.

Allsup wiped his mouth again while gesturing with his hand to the chair before replying, "Please do. I am Danny Allsup."

"That's damn good chicken, ain't it?" Hays inquired as he sat down heavily with a sigh.

"It is," Allsup agreed. "About the best I've had."

"Aunt Sally, back there," he motioned to the back of the room. "She's about the best cook this side of Ol' Man River. It's said her cooking has caused many a man with the intention of heading west to stay on, and I believe it too."

"Is that why you stayed?" Allsup asked.

"No, I came to these parts in '47 with the intention of staying. Started a trading post and over the years found myself engaged in all types of enterprises. In fact, just this year I started a newspaper, the *Council Grove Democrat*."

"Is that a fact?"

"Yes. There's money to be made in these parts, you just have to take the initiative to get it."

"Really?"

"Yes, sir. As a matter of fact, the money's becoming so plentiful I'm working on opening a bank within the next month or so." Hays was openly excited about his new ventures, his eyes sparkling as he talked. "The *Council Grove Savings Bank*, where people can secure their money, knowing it's safely there when they need it."

"I can tell you've put a good deal of thought into all

this," Allsup observed before taking a sip of cup.

"Yes, sir, Council Grove is going to grow into a major city someday; I aim to help it grow—and grow with it."

"I'm sure you and Council Grove will be quite prosperous."

"Already are, my friend, already are," he replied with a gleam in his eye as he leaned in resting his forearms on the table. "You'd be wise to stick around and grab the ring yourself."

Smiling, Allsup declined relating, once again, his quest and determination to fulfill it.

When Allsup had finished, Hays, stroking his beard, asked, "Who are you traveling with?"

"No one, just my horse and myself."

Hays' eyes took on a look of seriousness when he said, "You'll never make it. It's impossible for a first timer, an Easterner at that, to successfully cross the mountains alone."

"Mr. Hays, I must tell you that at the start of this endeavor, I had serious doubts about my successfully seeing the Mississippi River. I did, and I crossed it and now here I am sitting with you in Council Grove, Kansas. I am safe, secure, and healthy. I made it this far; I believe I can make it to the Pacific."

"There's a vast difference between that side of Ol' Muddy and this. Let me ask, through all your travels here, did you ever feel really alone? That you'd never encounter another?"

"No, I can't say that I did," Allsup admitted. "I usually traveled alone, but there were always people along the way."

"Where you're headed there's no one. There are Indians, and there's you. Just last year Indians raided the state northwest of here. Do you know that there's a desert so vast that you can find your way across following the trail of bones? That's if you don't contribute to the trail. There are mountains to cross that are so high winter covers their tops year-round. Water becomes less available the farther west you go until there ain't no more. Often, you can go days and days without seeing it. Would you like to know the secret for those who have successfully crossed?"

"I would, of course."

"They didn't travel alone. If you'll excuse me," Hays said rising. "I'll leave you to your meal. I must check on the other diners and see how Aunt Sally's faring in the kitchen. I hope to see you again, Mr. Allsup. If not, success and safe travels on your journey."

"It was a pleasure meeting you, Mr. Hays." Allsup rose from his chair and shook the extended hand. "I wish you great success with your different enterprises."

Allsup returned to his meal as Seth Hays approached the next occupied table and took a seat joining two diners.

D. Dean Carroll

Chapter 45

"Hey, Tom! When ya gonna get in more cloth?" shouted the man from the back of the store. "This is the second week I been in and the shelf's still empty! Wife's gettin irritable."

"Should be in today!" Tom, behind the counter, responded. He was a middle-aged, heavy-set man with a full head of graying hair growing exclusively from the sides, the top was bare. "Freight s'pose to be in this afternoon; cloth should be with the freight."

"I ain't waiting." Annoyed, the man walked past Tom towards the door. "Best be some cloth when I come here next week."

Smiling, Tom answered, "You ain't the only customer, Wiley. If it comes in and no one buys it all, it'll be here next week for ya."

"Goddamn it," Wiley muttered before stopping in the store's doorway and turning to Tom. "You ain't gonna be so smug when another store opens here someday."

"Wiley, I am certain you're right, but today, right now, I'm all there is. I will enjoy my time of smugness while it lasts." To Allsup he asked, "Can I help you, sir?"

Wiley remained standing in the store's doorway watching the exchange. A small man in weight and stature, Wiley liked to dress when going to town and at present, wore a coat intended for a man several size larger. The shirt beneath the coat was collarless and stretched emphasizing the skinny neck it encircled.

"Yes, I'm about to embark westward and want to store up on supplies and goods. I'm hoping you can assist me with this." The hawk-nosed man wearing the dirty tan duster waited expectantly for a response.

"I'm just the man!" answered Tom. "Here at the Last Chance store people like yourself are our biggest customers.

Danny Allsup

I'm Tom Hill, and I ain't bragging when I say I have knowledge in this matter based upon years of experience."

"That's fortunate for me. I'm Danny Allsup."

"Well, Mr. Allsup, let's get you started; first thing, how many in your party?"

"Just one...myself...me." He was becoming self-conscious about that point since it seemed to be an issue for everyone else.

Tom Hill stopped in his tracks and turned back to face Allsup.

"You're goin' alone and you're asking me what you'll need?"

"Yes, that's right. I want to be confident I'm prepared."

Hill looked at Wiley still in the doorway and then back at Allsup.

"The best suggestion I can offer is get another plan. Don't do it."

With a slightly impatient chuckle, Allsup said, "With all respect, Mr. Hill, you are far from the first to offer the same advice. From Pennsylvania to Kansas, many have wondered if my mind is right and in truth, there have been nights when I wondered the same, but here I am. I'm on the cusp of leaving all that I know and stepping into a world completely different. I am aware of the dangers and the risks and the odds that I most likely will not make it at all but think if I do! By golly, think if I do. Imagine how I'll feel then."

Tom Hill looked at Allsup with a changed expression. He nodded his head in understanding and said, "Then let's get you fixed for the best chances of success."

Hill walked Allsup through the store suggesting this or that. Wiley slowly returned within the store and followed them as they shopped. Occasionally, he'd offer his opinion and advice and before long the three men went through the entire store resulting in a small pile on the countertop.

When they finished and Allsup had paid his bill, Hill asked, "When do you plan to go?"

"As soon as I get these goods secure on my horse, I will be on my way."

"Won't wait till morning?" Wiley asked.

"No, I am ready to move on, anxious, really."

"Well, we'll go out and help you figure how to load all this," Hill said as he gathered from the pile on the counter, "and see you on your way. Come on, Wiley, grab some of that."

Three new canteens plus his original, two weeks of feed for Chestnut to be used only when nothing else is available—and sparingly, jerky, hardtack, dried beans, ammunition for the pistol and rifle, a pot, plate, fork, spoon, and cup, spare clothes, and bedroll with ground tarp left Allsup barely enough room to sit astride his saddle.

"I hope you make it, Mr. Allsup," Hill told him reaching up to shake his hand. "If you happen to come back this way, stop by and let me know."

"I will."

"Watch for snakes," Wiley advised, shaking his hand. "They don't tell ya that, but they's dangerous in that tall grass."

"I will. Good health and prosperity to you both."

As if on cue, Chestnut began walking west leaving the Last Chance Store, and civilization behind.

Chapter 46

The prairie grass was tall, brushing beneath Chestnut's chest and stomach along with Allsup's boots. The wind blew waves across the grass causing it to make a rustling, almost hissing sound. Allsup imagined that snakes would be dangerous since they would be nearly impossible to see. Other than the insects annoying his ears and face, most other lifeforms seemed non-existent. Trees on the prairie were scarce; so, few birds flew overhead. The occasional frightened quail and pheasant would fly off to escape, and a rabbit or fox might dash through the grass, but for all purposes Allsup felt very much alone.

As the afternoon sun began its descent, he worried about finding a suitable place to camp. If he couldn't find a clearing along a stream or on a hilltop soon, he'd have to clear an area by hand to avoid starting a grass fire.

They crested a knoll and down below a stream meandered through the rolling hills. In a bend below, a sandy clearing deposited along the inward side of the stream gave promise of a stopping point for the night. The stream was about five feet across, but signs along its banks indicated times when it rose higher.

Chestnut stopped to drink before wading across upon the sandy shore. Allsup dismounted and examined the beach on which he stood. It was wet. The narrow heel and pointed toe of his boots left temporary imprints wherever he stepped. He scanned the surroundings and noted the absence of trees, no wood for a fire.

His plan was to unpack Chestnut in the reverse order that they'd packed the animal with the intention of performing the opposite task the next morning in the same order. Night was falling quicker than expected and before long, without a fire, visibility in the dark would be limited.

D. Dean Carroll

Eventually, dusk became dark, and his unpacking efforts became futile; everything was sliding around and off what he tried to stack. It reached the point where he revised his efforts to sorting based upon which side of the horse it came from.

The night sky was moonless so that the plethora of stars were the sole source of illumination; so many stars that they seemed to merge into one giant cloudy belt overhead. While the heavens were beautiful to observe, they did little to help him see the hardtack clutched in his hand Stretched out on his ground tarp, his head on his saddle, he amused himself by trying to make images out of the twinkling lights above. In one cluster, he envisioned the outline of a rooster. As he bit off a strip of jerky, he chuckled as another cluster resembled a buggy. Far to the left and high in the sky was a ladle, the Little Dipper, and near it was another but larger.

To the sounds of wind in the grass, Chestnut resting nearby, and the stream rushing to somewhere else, Allsup fell into a deep peaceful sleep.

For the next two days they traveled in this manner. The streams and creeks became scarce, so Allsup and horse became dependent on canteen water. Game made its presence known, but without the ability to build a fire there was no point in hunting. A re-occurring question that pestered Allsup was how did people cook food on these grass-covered prairies? How did they build fires? What did they use for fuel? He was becoming weary of hardtack and jerky. He'd started on his second canteen, Chestnut was two-thirds through his first bag of feed, and they had yet to encounter the deserts and mountains. The vastness of the land and the isolation created a sense of loneliness that Allsup found disconcerting. They had yet to meet another human being since leaving Council Grove. It made him wonder; how could anyone survive.

Later, on his third day on the plains, with the sun still prominent in the late afternoon sky, Chestnut began to act skittish. He repeatedly tried to turn southward and resisted Allsup's efforts to correct their course. The grass swished around them as they continued downward along the side of a hill.

It was during this descent that Allsup detected a low rumbling to the north. At first, he thought it thunder and cursed the possibility of rain. Chestnut tried to veer south again, but Allsup turned him back.

"Criminy, Chestnut!" Allsup declared as he struggled to bring the horse under control. "You've never been frightened by thunder before! Settle down!"

He noticed the rumbling grow louder and seemed to get closer as well, and it stopped sounding like thunder but something else—Allsup couldn't quite put his finger on it, but it sounded familiar.

Chestnut became more and more agitated, turning in circles as Allsup tried to direct him westward once again. The horse began vocalizing his protests by whinnying and making guttural sounds. Concerned, Allsup jumped down from his mount and attempted to calm the animal as he had in the crowd on the St. Louis docks. Chestnut tried to pull away as Allsup noticed the ground shaking.

"What in the world?" He had never experienced anything like it before. He thought if a glass were sitting on a stump, it would shake to the edge and fall off! He had to decide if he should mount Chestnut and let him have his way or continue to stand and try to calm him down.

The rumbled turned into a roar, that mixed with the sound of animals bleating, adding to his confusion, and he wondered if it could be cattle. Suddenly, over the hilltop came a flood of dark mass, like a wave stretched as far as he could see, approaching like a landslide It swarmed over the top and down the side so fast that Allsup barely had time to remount Chestnut and give him his rein.

"My, God!" shouted Allsup over the din as Chestnut bolted away just before the first of the buffalo reached them.

D. Dean Carroll

There was nothing to do but try to stay ahead because the front line of buffalo stretched as far as the eye could see in either direction. The horse ran with all that he had and was maintaining a lead despite the bags of feed, food, water and utensils bouncing against him. Twice they were on the verge of tumbling forward because of depressions in the ground hidden by the tall grass, almost somersaulting the second time. The latter stumble found the herd swarming around them like a creek-bed filling after a hard rain flowing around a dry rock. Chestnut continued at a full gallop but no longer tried to stay ahead just avoid going down. They were like an island in the center of an angry black sea; carried along by a force beyond their control.

The buffalo were so close that Allsup worried they might gorge the horse or knock them both over. The large animals bumped against them repeatedly, cutting before them back and forth. The heat from the running animals was almost unbearable; the musky smell overwhelming. He could hear bleating and grunting and wondered when it would ever end? How could they escape?

The herd answered those questions for him. Gradually, they began to slow, many stopped completely and began grazing creating gaps through which horse and rider could pass. Eventually, the entire herd stopped and were grazing as peacefully as milk cows on a Pennsylvania hillside.

Chestnut slowed to a trot, breathing heavily, as Allsup looked for a way through the mass. Buffalo were everywhere. There was no reason to try to go back to where they had been scooped along, he knew he wouldn't recognize the place if he saw it.

He did know two things, however: they couldn't spend the night amongst these enormous creatures, and he did, in fact, know which way to go.

They headed west, slowly passing through the herd like a boat gliding through water lilies.

Chapter 47

It was the light from the rising sun that woke him, but he became conscious of being awake from the chill. He was rolled up in his blanket and ground tarp shivering. It occurred to him that he awoke at the same time the day before. Was it that late in the year, he wondered, or were they traveling on higher ground? It amused him that he had no idea of the month after spending so much of his farming life ruled by the months of the year. There were certain tasks on the land for each month, while working on one you prepared for the next.

He sat up and noticed his visible breath, like steam emitted from a boiling teakettle, and looked around expecting to see frost on the ground, but there was none.

There was, however, someone approaching from the east on a buckboard wagon pulled by a team of beige horses; he was dressed darkly but wore a white, wide-brimmed hat. His approach was casual, unhurried. Allsup continued watching still seated, wrapped in his bedroll.

As the wagon drew nearer, Allsup saw that the rider's gun was drawn and hung loosely in his hand between his legs. The horses stopped about twenty feet away.

"Good morning," he called out.

"Good morning," replied the driver.

They remained thusly for what seemed a long time before Allsup asked, "Why the gun?"

The driver looked briefly at the gun in his hand but did not put it away.

"I mean no harm by it," he answered. "But I don't know you. I don't know your intentions."

"As you can see, I'm still bedded. Until minutes ago, I didn't know of your approach or existence. I have no ill intentions towards you, sir, and as you can see, I am unarmed."

"I can't see that. I have no idea what might be with you beneath those covers, a six-shooter aimed at my belly for all I know."

"Let me assure you by getting up that I'm the only thing in this bedroll." Allsup stood dropping his bedding. "In truth, I'm far too chilled to be able to hold a weapon steady if the necessity arose."

The driver laughed and coaxed the horses forward.

"Hot coffee will help alleviate those shivers," he said before climbing down from the wagon and extending his hand. "John Thompson. Sorry about the poor first impression."

Allsup introduced himself and apologized for not having coffee or a fire.

"You sacrificed the coffee for food and water, I imagine. I can understand that," Thompson observed. "But why no fire?"

"Look around, there's nothing for fuel but grass, and I don't know how to use it properly. I worried I might end up with a fire bigger than intended."

"You don't use the grass for fuel, Mr. Allsup. You use buffalo shit."

"Excuse me?"

"Buffalo shit, turds, patties, many call them buffalo chips. You use dried buffalo pies."

"Wait." Thompson went searching in the grass around the campsite.

"Ah-ha" he exclaimed and picked up a large round, brown disk. As he returned, he asked, "You haven't seen these around on your travels?"

"Yes, of course I have."

"Do you know what it is?"

"Yes, of course! It's dried buffalo manure."

"I suppose that's what it is. We call it buffalo shit. When it dries up like this, we call them chips or patties. They burn real good."

"You make humor at my expense," accused Allsup.

"No, sir, I do not!" countered Thompson. "I'll show you! Look around and gather more. Once we get this burning, we'll want to keep it going for a while."

By the time Allsup returned with several dried buffalo chips Thompson had the patty he'd picked up burning with a low flame. He added two from Allsup's harvest and soon they had a nice fire burning.

"Have any water?" Thompson asked.

"I do." answered Allsup.

"Well, I have a pot and coffee, what say we brew us a pot?"

"I would like nothing better."

Over coffee they discussed many things. Thompson revealed he was on his way to Fort Lyon in the Colorado Territory with a wagonload of goods. He made the trip from Council Grove about twelve times a year carrying goods of sorts to sell and trade. He always returned with a pocket full of cash and a wagonload of hides. Outlaws had stopped him twice; one time he went home with just hides, the second time he sent them scurrying off with extra lead weighing them down. That was the reason for his approach with the pistol.

"As a matter of fact, the coffee we're drinking is from a ten-pound sack in the wagon that sits with nine more," Thompson informed Allsup. "That pot is from one of five. I'll clean it out when I reach the fort and sell it as new. They'll never know."

Allsup retold his story for the umpteenth time and added a few of the escapades he'd encounter along his way.

"What hubris led you to believe you could make the crossing alone?"

Allsup laughed, "Et tu, John Thompson?"

"What? What do you mean by that?"

"It's Shakespeare, from his…

"I know it's Shakespeare," Thompson curtly countered. "From Julius Caesar. I'm an educated man. What I meant was, why say that?"

"Because almost every person I have encountered since I embarked upon this journey has wondered the same."

"It's not an unfair question." The wagon driver pointed out.

"You're right. Chestnut and I have made it this far healthy and with all our body parts intact. I have faith we can finish the journey the same. Anyway, all life's in God's hands."

"Amen."

"Do you have anything to eat on that wagon?" Allsup inquired. "I've been living off of hardtack and jerky for the last week."

"I have flour, sugar, and unfortunately, beef jerky and hardtack."

"We'll share mine then," Allsup said reaching into his saddlebags for the dried nourishment.

"You know what?" Thompson suddenly sounded excited. "I have flour, salt, and lard in the wagon. We could whip up tortillas!"

"Tortillas?"

"Yeah, tortillas. Mexican pancakes. They're used for bread."

"Before we do that, let's spread out and see if we can obtain meat," Allsup suggested.

Thompson agreed and while he walked north through the grass, which had been diminishing in height with the rising elevation, Allsup set out south. Neither man was aware of it, but each said little prayers along with words of encouragement that one or the other, or both, would have the opportunity of a rabbit or quail. Thompson walked alert, eyes ahead, waiting for a sudden burst for safety, while Allsup walked eyes to the ground watchingfor snakes.

Dusk was beginning to overcome day, and the cool wind

whipped across the grass tops creating a sound similar to tree leaves blowing in the breeze. Visibility was still good, but the shade of gray from the sun lost behind the horizon made objects softer, less pronounced and focused.

Allsup was caught completely by surprise at the sound of a rattler at his feet! He pulled his revolver and fired all six rounds at the coiled mass to the right of his foot. He was shaking so much that he fumbled his efforts to quickly reload as he realized the head of the snake rested upon the toe of his boot.

"Did you get it?" Thompson called from a distance.

"Think I did!" Allsup watched the head expecting it to move.

"What'd you get?"

"A snake!"

"What kind of snake?"

"Rattler!"

"Good! How big?"

"It looks very big to me!"

"How long is it?"

"I don't know!"

"Is it dead?"

"Possibly!"

"Well, pick it up and see!"

Silence.

A gunshot sounded and was quickly absorbed in the silence.

"What was that?" called Thompson.

"I wanted to make sure it was dead!" Allsup answered and after a pause, "It's about six feet in length!"

"That's dinner!" shouted Thompson. "Come on back!"

In a pot from the wagon, they cooked the rattlesnake meat along with wild onions Thompson had picked while hunting, and ate it rolled up in flour tortillas baked on the bottom of a skillet. Both men claimed, while resting against their saddles and drinking after-dinner coffee, that it was a

D. Dean Carroll

fine meal.

Chapter 48

Allsup rode Chestnut alongside Thompson sitting on the buckboard, as they set out westward in the cool early morning. Over coffee the previous night, they decided that Allsup would accompany Thompson to Fort Lyon since they would both be heading in the same general direction. For that reason, they traveled side by side, conversing at times but not all the time.

"How long till we reach the fort?" Allsup asked.

"Very late tonight or early tomorrow morning; depending on when you want to stop."

There were times as they traveled, that they climbed steep inclines which were usually followed by an equally steep descent, but more and more often, they continued on an upward grade.

Later in the day during a quiet period of travel, Allsup happened to glance over his shoulder and stopped Chestnut.

"My God," he uttered as he dismounted.

Spread out lay what appeared to be all the lands to the Mississippi. Hills he'd crossed days past could be seen in the distance. The tall brown grass extended on forever before disappearing far, far away. Rays of sunshine broke through dark clouds to the south forming bright circles illuminating vast areas of land. To the north, a dark rain cloud had just reached its capacity and dropped its contents on the rugged terrain below.

"I've never seen so much land," said Allsup, amazed.

"It's funny," Thompson responded. "I seen it so many times I don't notice it anymore, but as you have brought it to my attention once again, you're right. It is a very impressive sight."

"Should we camp here tonight?" Allsup suggested. "Or move on?"

"Well, I like the view," Thompson admitted. "But see that rain to the north there? It's heading this way and may very well hit us before morning. Still want to stay?"

"If we were a day back and you saw this rain coming, what would you do?"

"I'd look for high ground and sleep under the wagon."

"Let's do that."

Thompson chuckled as he asked, "Does that sound like fun to you?"

"Well…" Allsup did not want to admit that he found the idea exciting.

"All right, let's look for suitable high ground." Thompson glanced around at their surroundings, muttering, "He puts the green in greenhorn, by golly."

"What?" Allsup asked.

"I said I think we may already be in the most ideal spot we could hope for; we're on a hilltop, the rain that falls will flow downhill away from us, no puddling."

They began gathering their belongings and supplies just as the first of many large drops fell from the sky.

"Help me cover the wagon!" Thompson requested as he unfolded a large canvas tarp. Together the two men secured the tarp over the wagon keeping the goods within dry as well as those beneath. They tethered Thompson's two horses; Allsup did not bother with Chestnut.

The rain began to fall in greater quantity. The extinguished fire left them in darkness.

"Throw your bedding under the wagon!" Thompson shouted, as the sound of falling rain grew louder, and he did the same. Soon the two men were reclining under the wagon partially protected from the downpour. Allsup had spread his ground tarp, so they were relatively dry above as well as below, and before long Thompson was snoring. Allsup wondered which was worse, the din of falling rain or his companion's snoring?

As he waited for sleep to take him, Allsup reached a

decision, he would no longer re-tell the reason for his journey. That seemed like the distant past now, and he was tired of repeating it. From now on, he was just a traveler, an adventurer wandering his way west for no reason other than curiosity.

He smiled as he considered his decision. It felt like the right thing to do. Chestnut walked up beside the wagon; the covering tarp concealed all from Allsup's view but the knees of the horse down. His eyes grew heavy as he lay upon his side watching the horse's four limbs within arm's reach, and as he wondered what the horse might do if he suddenly reached out and grabbed one, he fell into a deep, restful sleep.

Chapter 49

Danny Allsup woke early that morning shivering with cold; his blanket was stiff as hard cowhide on a winter's morning. He rose up on is elbows and saw Thompson rolled up in a ball still sleeping. He attempted to lift the tarp hanging down from the wagon, but it was too stiff, so he lay back down and looked out from under it. Everything was wrapped in ice appearing as if covered in glass. He scooted out from under the wagon and stood, looking for his horse. The stallion was nowhere to be seen, neither were Thompson's two wagon pullers. Allsup's first inclination was to whistle, but he remembered his tent companion still asleep and decided consideration was in order.

He retrieved his blanket, still frozen in the shape of a 'U' and wrapped himself as best he could. He decided to go in search of the animals but found upon taking his first step, walking on ice would be difficult as it resulted in his landing flat on his back; a sharp, electric pain ran down his right shoulder to hip, a reminder of a previous mishap.

He rolled over onto his hands and knees and attempted to stand, but was no sooner standing, crouched low, when both feet went flying out ; with an "Oomph!" he landed hard on his backside—and there he remained for several minutes.

Gradually the cold began to seep through his clothing chilling that part of his anatomy in contact with the ice, motivating him to try to stand again. Onto his hands and knees once more. He discovered his boots provided no traction on the glass-like surface; their smooth leather soles were like ice on ice.

Slowly, Allsup regained his balance, standing, though it was unsteady more often than not, and as long as he made no attempt to move, he thought he would be all right. He looked around at his icy surroundings and observing it with the absence of panic found the view quite impressive. Everything unsheltered was covered and stiff with ice. The wind was blowing gently, but the tall grass did not stir, as each blade was a miniature stalagmite. Where they were, on their hilltop, a giant ice sheet spread out in all directions. It was on that giant ice sheet that he felt himself slowly sliding away from the wagon.

He attempted to take a step upward but found himself frantically running in place, arms flailing in an effort to regain his balance. With that accomplished he stood steady and helpless as he continued to slowly slide He dropped to his hands and knees to stem his descent but found the hill's incline now steep enough that he continued to slide. Out of desperation, he dropped flat upon his belly and lay spread out, arms and legs extended in their own directions, and gradually he came to a stop.

The ridiculousness of his situation caused him to laugh. Two years ago, if someone had suggested he would now find himself lying prone on an ice-covered hill he would have thought them crazy. Yet here he was, and he laughed again.

"John!" Allsup called loudly. "John Thompson!"

Surely, he reasoned while prostrate, the sun should be rising soon; its heat will melt the ice.

"John! John Thompson! Wake up!"

He heard a whinny at the bottom of the hill and saw Chestnut and one of Thompson's tethered horses watching him. He realized that the ice sheet that held him prisoner also prevented the horses from making their ascent. Now that he knew Chestnut was safe, he could focus on his own personal dilemma: returning to the wagon.

From his position, he tried to push himself up onto his feet, but his boots only served as ice skates, and he slid farther down the hillside.

"John Thompson! For the love of God, man, wake up!"

"What the hell!" a groggy Thompson stuck his head out from under the wagon. "Can't a man have a little peace and quiet?"

He climbed out from under the wagon and stood, stretching, before his feet flew out from under landing him squarely on his bottom.

Danny Allsup, lying prone on his stomach, burst into laughter.

"What the hell?" Thompson asked again as he took in their situation for the first time. "What happened?"

"Last night's rain turned to ice," answered Allsup below.

"What are you doing down there?" inquired Thompson, squinting because of the morning sun's glare off the ice.

"That's the problem, Mr. Thompson. Every time I attempt to climb back up, I slide further down! If you don't find a way for me to get back up there, I'll have to wait until the sun melts this ghastly cold ground."

"I have rope in the wagon. Let me get it."

Thompson rolled over to the wagon and grabbed the rear wheel. He used the same to help him stand. As he leaned into the back of the wagon searching for the rope, his feet gradually began to slide back away from him. With his legs stretched out on the side of the hill, Thompson hung at arm's length from the wagon's hatch, resembling a man stretched on the Rack in medieval times.

Allsup could not contain himself, he was laughing so hard that it caused him to slide an inch or two more, which quickly sobered him so that he lay as still as possible.

Pulling himself to a standing position, Thompson clung tightly to the wagon as he continued his search of its contents for a rope; it wasn't long before he found a coil. He tied one end to a wagon wheel and tossed the other down to Allsup, landing on his backside in the process.

"Sun's heat is having its effect," Allsup announced as he carefully pulled himself up to the hilltop. "The ice's surface is melting, making it twice a slick."

"Those our horses down there?" Thompson asked.

"Yes."

"I only see two. Have you seen three yet?"

"No."

"Damn, that don't sound good." Thompson solemnly shook his head as he watched the horses at the bottom of the hill. The two animals pawed the icy surface in search of something to eat.

"No, it doesn't," Allsup conceded. "But what can we do? Frankly, I'm surprised any of them made it. I mean, look around; everything is covered in ice. How did those horses survive? If you ask me, I say Divine Intervention. Anyway, there's nothing we can do about most anything right now. I suggest we stay off the ice, maybe go back under the wagon until the ground is once again passable."

"Yeah, all right, maybe I can go back to sleep."

The two men cautiously worked their way around the sides of the wagon never relinquishing a strong grip on its wooden panels. Allsup climbed under and wrapped himself in his blanket, but Thompson remained standing. Slowly, Thompson made his way back to the roped wheel.

"What are you doing?" a bewildered Allsup asked.

"Nothing—maybe—I don't know."

"What? What are you thinking of?"

"Come here," Thompson requested. "I may need ya."

Allsup climbed out from under the wagon and stood next to the trader.

Thompson reached down and picked up the rope laying it loosely over his shoulder while still holding it limply in his left hand.

"Watch this," he said as he let go of the wagon and attempted to walk. With a cry of pain he found his feet flying before him almost head high as he landed on his back!

He used the rope to pull himself upright and tried to go down the hill again, this time in a crouched position. After a shaky start, he found himself gliding downward over the ice, picking up speed. He mustered the courage to rise slowly to an almost upright stance, keeping a slight bend at the knees.

"Woo-hoo!" He was now sliding confidently over the ice and descending quickly to the watching horses below. "Woo-hoo!"

Allsup was excited, watching the trader's escapade; a smile on his face so big it was easy to read the mood of the man. He clung to the side of the wagon, the cold weakening his grip.

"Try it!" shouted Thompson from the bottom.

"Right!" answered a grinning Allsup, eager for his turn.

"Drape the rope over your shoulder and hold it loose in your hand so it will slide through easily," Thompson instructed. "If you fall, you'll still have hold of the rope and can pull yourself up again."

Allsup crouched low as he gradually began sliding down the hillside. As he proceeded to pick up speed, he stood at an almost upright and made it to the bottom without falling.

"Good job, Danny!" Thompson told him with a slap on the back.

"That was fun!" Allsup declared, laughing. "Let's do it again!"

For the next hour, the two men reverted to their adolescence, a time when it was so easy to laugh and have fun. Up and down they went, up much slower than down. They yelled and laughed, tried tricks, and for the first time in a long, long time, they abandoned maturity for foolishness and fun and played.

Allsup was the first to discover the sun was finally having its effect on their ice sheet. He was sliding down the hill when the heel of his boot broke through and snagged a clump of grass sending him flying down headfirst.

"It's melting!" he called out from the bottom.

"Well, we knew it would eventually," answered a disappointed Thompson. "Come on back up and we'll get our gear together. Then we'll go look for that lost horse."

Danny Allsup

It didn't take long to find it. When the two men went down the hill to retrieve the two horses, they found the third, on its side, lifeless in a small gully.

"Guess he couldn't take the cold," Thompson said, shaking his head.

"I'm surprised any of them did, exposed to that kind of weather." Allsup responded before asking, "What do you want to do with it?"

"Huh?" Thompson looked bewildered.

"The horse—what do you want to do with it?"

"Leave it. It's no good to us now."

As the two men began leading their horses to the top of the hill Allsup commented, "I didn't know if you were, you know, attached to the animal or not."

"Just a horse," Thompson replied as he led his sole survivor by its halter. "It's just a horse."

Allsup said nothing; he turned and looked with appreciation at Chestnut who followed along without guidance.

D. Dean Carroll

Chapter 50

They agreed that since both were headed in the same direction, and Thompson was shy one horse, Chestnut would be recruited to fill the vacancy. The horse did not particularly object to the harness or pulling the wagon, but did have trouble adjusting to the pace; he was always pulling ahead of his companion, which required Thompson continuously reining him in.

It was near noon by the time they departed their campsite. The ice was mostly memory, but the air was still cold as was evident by the clouds of their exhaled breath.

"When should we reach the fort?" Allsup asked Thompson as they sat side by side on the wagon's bench seat.

"I would guess early evening. Of course, if we give your stallion his rein," Thompson chuckled, "we'll be there in an hour or two."

The countryside was now a constant gradual incline. A few of the hills had outcroppings of rock and the grass grew shorter and shorter. No longer tall blades swaying as one with the breeze, this grass was greener and only boot-heel high.

After riding in silence with only Thompson breaking it to chastise the horses, mainly Chestnut, he spoke to Allsup.

"You ever kill a man?" he asked.

"No."

"Not even during the war?"

"I didn't go," Allsup told him. "I didn't enlist. After my two boys went, I decided to stay at home and tend the farm—and my wife."

Thompson seemed lost in thought before he said, "I did."

"Did what?"

"I killed a man...back in Saint Joe."

"I'm sure you had good reason."

"He was trying to steal my wagon. I was eating in Sammy's, a bar I go to whenever I'm in Saint Joe, and a guy came in and announced someone was driving off with a team and wagon. Said the way the guy was acting he must have been up to no good."

Thompson paused to collect his thoughts.

"Obviously, he was taking your team and wagon," Allsup observed.

"He was. I ran outside just as he was getting the horses to pull away. I shouted for him to stop, but he ignored me. So, I drew my pistol and told him again to stop. I figured I'd fire off a shot and maybe he'd realize I was serious."

"Did he stop?" Allsup asked.

"Well, yes and no. He stopped but the horses did not. To my complete surprise, when I fired the shot, I hit him in the back of the head. He slumped down on the seat; the reins fell from his hands. The horses continued running through town pulling the wagon with the dead man on it."

"My God," said Allsup somberly.

"It torments me now. Is a man's life worth less than two horses and a wagon? Seems I could have gotten a ride and gone after him; forced him to give them back. How hard would that have been? I acted in haste without much thought to alternative possibilities when I fired that gun. Now a man, a son, maybe a brother and husband and father is in the ground in an unmarked hole. No one knew who he was. If anyone comes looking for him, he'll never be found. In a month, the grass will be grown and there will be no trace of him having ever been here...It torments me."

"I can appreciate that, but it was unintentional," consoled Allsup.

"Makes no difference, the result's still the same."

They rode on, each absorbed in their own thoughts. Allsup broke the silence by asking, "What about you, did you heed the call?"

"I did."

"I assume you were able to avoid taking lives during your enlistment?"

"I was a quartermaster; first in Pennsylvania and then the Ohio, down in Cincinnati."

"How did you like Cincinnati?" Allsup asked.

"Too many people; there are too many people everywhere east of the Mississippi," Thompson observed. "They said I was out in the country in Pennsylvania, a scattered population they called it, but in my opinion, if you can see the smoke from your neighbor's chimney, then you're too close. After leaving Saint Joe this trip, other than Diamond City, I've seen few people."

"I passed through Cincinnati. I liked it. They have a big bridge there crossing the Ohio River. I had to muster my courage to cross that thing. I must admit I found it intimidating. They also had a fair on technology, the arts and the like. It was interesting."

"I imagine you've passed through quite a few towns in your travels."

"I have."

"None where you wanted to stay? None you were reluctant to leave?"

"There were nice places, I admit, and I've met good people along the way like yourself, but I'm not stopping until I can travel west no more. I aim to see the Pacific."

"I admire your determination," Thompson admitted. "But aren't you worried about dying alone? Who will note your passing? Like that guy back in Saint Joe, who will know you were ever here?"

Allsup contemplated Thompson's remarks. After a period, he said, "Well, *you* will know."

Thompson studied his seat-companion before replying, "That's true."

"I've met people along the way that might recall our

encounters now and then during the course of their day, surely that should count."

"Yes, yes, you're right."

Something hit the side wagon directly behind Allsup; it hit with a solid "Thud." Allsup looked to the side and saw an arrow protruding from it. He stared at the arrow in disbelief, as another whizzed past him inches from his head. Transfixed by the sight of the arrow in the wagon, he observed a second one strike the side of the seat he currently occupied.

"John, I think we're under an Indian attack!" he exclaimed turning to his partner, but John could not reply. An arrow pinned his hat to his head directly above his right ear, blood flowed from the wound and streamed down upon his shoulder. His eyes were still open, but he did not see.

From a hilltop not far away, Allsup saw four Indians mounted on horses, two held bows notched and ready.

"My God!" muttered Allsup as he frantically grabbed the reins still held in Thompson's hands.

Standing, he yelled, "Hee-Yah!" to encourage the horses to make posthaste away from their current location and dilemma. Motivated by Chestnut's eagerness to run, Thompson's horse lunged forward, too, sending Allsup back onto his seat. Both horses were running full speed in synchronous stride while Thompson's lifeless body bobbed and wobbled back and forth still sitting on the bench-seat. Flying across the prairie the team of horses gave it all they could muster as the wagon threw up plumbs of dust into the faces of the Indians pursuing their prize.

Allsup looked over his shoulder and saw the four at a full gallop; one was firing arrows that either fell short or missed completely. He abruptly steered the horses to the right. Thompson would have slid off the wagon had Allsup not grabbed his blood-covered shirt and held him in place.

"Don't slide off, John Thompson, because it doesn't look like I'll be able to come back and get you!"

D. Dean Carroll

On they went, followed at a distance by the Indians. Soon the two wagon horses' sweat begin to lather and the un-named horse was wearing down, stumbling too often in its effort to keep up. Allsup began to think about a plan for when they stopped which by all accounts would have to be soon. There was nothing from which to take shelter, no trees or boulders, so he began a mental debate about the advantages of a hilltop over a valley.

Military strategists would argue the high ground held the advantage, but he would most likely be taking cover under the wagon, so it seemed to him they'd have greater access to him as they reached the top of the hill; an arrow from cresting a hilltop would have greater opportunity hitting the target.

In a valley the wagon would provide better coverage, he reasoned, as the Indians would be firing from above while he was hiding beneath, but the width of the valley was important because if it were too wide, once the Indians reached it, they would all be on level ground.

There was a tall, narrow hill ahead that was considerably higher than the surrounding landforms. Its steep sides would make it difficult for them to ride up un-noticed. Allsup headed for it with the Indians in pursuit.

The high grade of the hill's incline made it difficult for Allsup's team to pull the wagon. Chestnut pulled with determination, but the second contributed little. Chestnut's neck, chest, and foreleg muscles bulged as he struggled to ascend the hillside. The burden was entirely his, the other horse had given up completely and now directed its efforts to staying alongside Chestnut. Breathless, gasping loudly, Chestnut had slowed to almost a crawl, yet still he forced himself to take another step, followed with great effort by another. The entire weight of the wagon, including Allsup and the deceased Thompson, rest solely on the stallion.

Allsup was almost in tears as he witnessed his traveling companion bear the burden and refuse to give up.

Danny Allsup

The Indians had stopped at the bottom of the hill, contenting themselves with watching the horse's struggle. At one point, Chestnut stopped but found the effort to keep the wagon from rolling backwards as great as continuing, so he continued, and the Indians below let out cheers of admiration!

Huffing and puffing, Chestnut reached the hilltop, and once they had, Allsup had him stop; both horses were heaving and soaked as if walking in rain.

Allsup pushed Thompson from his seat; the body landed solidly with a thud on the ground. Then he jumped from the wagon and quickly un-hitched both animals taking a moment to rub Chestnut's neck expressing his appreciation for the gallant effort. Still wearing their harnesses but free of the wagon, Allsup sent them on their way to safety he hoped.

When he glanced down the hill to check on the whereabouts of the Indians, he found only one, who was allowing his horse to walk casually up. Allsup dashed under the wagon and, with great difficulty, managed to pull Thompson under. Once he had the body safely stowed beneath the wagon, Allsup went back to check on the advancing Indian who had halfway completed his ascent. He ran around the hilltop's perimeter checking the other sides and found the other three Indians, at different cardinal directions, also climbing.

He realized he had to stop at least two of them before they reached the top, or he would be overwhelmed. Carrying his rifle, he pulled out his revolver and decided it was time to prove his metal. Walking over to the west side, he found the first Indian within talking distance with an arrow nocked, ready to release. The flying arrow missed its target and sailed high, skyward.

Allsup heard it pass before he started firing. His fifth or sixth shot, he couldn't tell which because once he started, he fired continuously until all six chambers were empty, but it was his fifth or sixth shot that felled the horse. Rider and mount tumbled downward; Allsup mentally noted one down.

With a sense of euphoria from that success and fueled by adrenalin, Allsup ran to the north side of the hill, but found it absent of an approaching Indian. He took a moment to reload his weapon before running to the east side. As he neared the shoulder, an Indian on horse leaped onto the top, heading directly towards him. Allsup was so surprised he failed to respond as the Indian, who spang from his horse, and attacked with frightening cries and a knife in hand. The sight of the knife along with the whooping, rapidly approaching Indian prompted Allsup to fire quickly once more, emptying his gun into his assailant when just a wagon's length away. The body laid motionless, the knife intended for Allsup buried to the hilt in the dirt at his feet. The dead man wore only a buckskin loincloth, his long black hair was tied in a single braid that now concealed his face, and white and black stripes were painted on his back as well as rings circling his arms.

Allsup stared down at the corpse, pondering the thought that he'd killed another man. In Pennsylvania, he killed livestock and fowl to place on the table so his family would not go hungry, self-preservation. He did it without a second thought; it was necessary. Now he did the same and thought the same about killing his own species; that did not feel Christian, he did not feel exalted.

A shriek snapped him from his reflection returning him to the here and now as another Indian reached the hill's summit and charged toward him from the far side of the wagon. Allsup raised his pistol and pulled the trigger, but it only clicked; the cylinder was empty. He raised his rifle as the Indian jumped up onto the top of the wagon and leaped, with a knife in each hand. The rifle would not fire; it was unloaded.

The impact of the Indian hitting him and landing on top as Allsup hit the ground knocked the breath from him. Holding one of the Indian's knife-held hands by the wrist an arm's length away, Allsup struggled for air as he felt a sharp pain shoot through the top of his right shoulder followed by another just below the collarbone.

The third Indian reached the hilltop and was busy cutting away the canvas tarp covering the wagon's goods. With the certainty that his raiding companion had everything under control, he pulled away the remaining rope that bound the tarp to the wagon. A final pull freed it of its restriction, and he discarded it off to the side. The Indian gave a cry of celebration as he viewed his treasure and immediately began rummaging through the contents.

Allsup frantically searched for anything to help him remove the Indian busy trying to extract the knife from his chest. While his hand flailed around, slapping against the ground, desperately hunting for anything of assistance, he looked up into the Indian's dark frightening eyes; briefly, the two men looked at the other.

Allsup's hand bumped against his rifle stock, his fingertips brushing against its butt. The knife had lodged into Allsup's chest, and the Indian was having difficulty removing it. The knife held in the other hand, the one Allsup still held by the wrist managed to swoop down in an arch just missing his face before Allsup pushed it back to an arm's length distance.

Suddenly, the knife pulled free from his chest, and the Indian raised it again when he let out a cry of agony! With his face in a painful grimace, the Indian fell back off his intended victim. Panting and in extreme pain, Allsup was surprised to see Chestnut holding the Indian's shoulder in his mouth. As the Indian struggled and thrashed to free himself from the horse's bite, Chestnut shook his head violently and dragged him further away.

His shoulder throbbing with pain and his right side covered in blood, Allsup picked up his pistol and with shaking hands attempted to reload it.

The Indian swung a knife-held-hand upward trying to

obtain his release by stabbing the horse in the forehead, but the hard skull-bone deflected the strike and the Indian lost his grip on his weapon.

The gun now loaded, Allsup began running towards the Indian for a closer shot not wanting to risk shooting the horse. As he ran, something heavy struck his back knocking him to the ground. Wincing from pain, he looked over his shoulder to see the Indian from the supply wagon jumping down and running towards him howling to elicit fear. Allsup also saw a hatchet lying beside him and surmised that must have been what struck him.

Still on his stomach, Allsup turned back to the horse and Indian who was now free of the animal's grip, his shoulder bleeding profusely from the bite. The Indian examined his shoulder before directing his attention to the white man on the ground pointing a six-shooter directly at him. He laughed aloud as he proceeded to walk toward Allsup, still holding a knife; his painted face displaying serious intent.

Allsup was aware he was out of time with one Indian approaching from behind and another from the front. Trying to control his shaking hands, Allsup took careful aim and fired a shot striking the Indian in the same shoulder as the bite. The Indian let out a howl as he took a step back before laughing again and continuing his approach. Allsup fired again making what appeared to be a third eye in the Indian's forehead causing him to stop in mid-step, sway slightly and crumble to the ground.

Allsup let out a painful cry as he rolled onto his back to find the fourth Indian standing over him with the hatchet raised high. Without thought or consideration, Allsup fired the remaining four shells into the man's torso. With a surprised expression, the Indian dropped the hatchet and turned to walk away before his legs buckled and he too went down.

Breathing heavily and in pain, Allsup remained on his back not sure if he could rise or if he should attempt to do so. Hearing movement, he looked up over his head to see Chestnut ambling toward him with three small bloody streams running down from his forehead. The horse nudged the man with his muzzle. Still on the ground, Allsup reached up and pulled the horse's head down to him to express his appreciation hugging and petting the animal.

"My God, Chestnut, but you must be a divine gift," he whispered, his labored breathing easing. "I'd be dead right now if it wasn't for you."

With great difficulty, Allsup used the horse's wagon harness to pull himself to his feet using his non-wounded arm. He draped that arm around the horse's neck for both support and gratitude. Chestnut stared intently to their left across the hilltop, captivated by something; Allsup followed his gaze.

On the opposite side of the wagon, watching, was the fourth Indian on horseback.

Allsup reasoned he must be the first he encountered who tumbled down the hillside.

They continued to watch each other, Allsup and the Indian, each waiting for the other to decide their fate by what they did next. Blood dripped down Allsup's arm and flowed across his chest, obviously wounded and susceptible to defeat. He looked a defeated man, but he was the one still standing. By ascan across the hilltop to an unbiased eye, he was currently the victor.

The wind from the west held a tinge of cool, a bite of briskness that shivered a man. It blew the Indian's fine black hair from his face presenting, in contrast to the setting sun, a distinguished profile, noble. His horse snorted and pawed the ground. Holding by his side a hatchet from the supply wagon, he raised it high overhead as if preparing to throw. Instead, he casually tossed it to the ground landing with a bounce a few feet away. He turned his horse and disappeared down the hill.

It was deep into dusk. Horse and man stood on the quiet

hilltop, bodies and debris scattered everywhere. Orange sunlight, almost extinguished in the west, cast long eerie shadows of the wagon, the wheel spokes stretching toward them like fingers. The wind, growing in strength, sharpened the western coolness; Allsup shivered. Examining his surroundings, he quietly exclaimed, "My God."

Chapter 51

As soon as he had regained his senses, when the adrenaline had subsided and the fear and excitement diminished, he climbed into the back of the wagon searching for anything to stitch his wounds leaving red handprints on all he touched. He found a crate box labeled, *"Fort Lyon - Medical"* tucked safely beneath the wagon seat. He removed it from its secured location and pulled open the top.

The box contained bandages and wraps, needles and thread along with various pills, ointments, and liquid remedies. A large glass jar containing a clear liquid was labeled, *"Alcohol - Antiseptic"*. Allsup recalled Doc Russell used something like that on Curly Baumgardner when he accidently miss-struck a tree limb with an axe while helping clear a field for Max Lunsford and bounced the axe head into his shin just missing the bone. Doc said antiseptics killed germs and prevented infections.

That sounded good, so he poured the liquid over the top of his wounded shoulder allowing it to flow down over the knife wound below his collarbone.

Chestnut raised his head; feed from the wagon fell in little granules from the sides of his mouth as he looked to see what caused the man to make such a commotion. Gradually, the din lessened, and the man began to search through the box again as the horse returned to his meal of oats mixed with maple.

He was able to stitch the lesions with the assistance of an oval-shaped, hand-held mirror framed in ivory. He felt pain as he sutured the wounds, but not so much. When the needle point first pushed against the skin before piercing and passing through, it hurt, and pulling the thread tight to close the wound was painful often enough that he wanted to cry out but didn't.

D. Dean Carroll

What did it matter? He chuckled between gasps and grimaces. There is no one around to hear me scream.

Content with the bandaging of his shoulder, his next task was removing Thompson's body from beneath the wagon. Allsup began tugging and pulling on the body, which was already displaying the effects of rigor mortis. The corpse was stiff enough that Allsup had to pull it out from the back of the wagon, as it would not bend to slip between the two side wheels. He pulled Thompson to the far side of the hilltop away from the wagon as much as possible.

He was exhausted; his left shoulder and arm throbbed with pain. He wanted to lay down where he stood and sleep, but he looked at the Indians' remains and knew he wasn't finished.

It was night by the time the last body was placed alongside the other four, including the white trader, on the far side of the hilltop away from the wagon. He silently prayed they remained downwind for the next few days.

Weary and worn out, Allsup could barely move. He stood swaying slightly looking at the wagon on the other side of the hilltop and thought it so far away. His injured arm had long since become numb and, because of fatigue and the desire for rest, no longer bothered him.

He chanced to look up and then looked up again at the star filled sky. Only the light wind rustling the discarded trap broke the silence that surrounded him.

With great determination, he set himself in motion trudging back to the wagon; it was a slow, arduous task.

He climbed back beneath the wagon, covered himself with a blanket and tarp, and slept for the next two days.

He awoke with a start feeling stiff and sore. There was dried blood on the top of his shoulder and below his collarbone but nothing fresh; he felt surprisingly good.

Chestnut was grazing down the hillside, a gentle, unpredictable breeze made clear why.

Allsup rested and ate from the goods in the wagon to

regain his strength. When he reached the point where he could tolerate the pain but no longer the stench, he began digging in the hilltop. Progress was slow; he used his good arm and both feet to bury the shovel blade into the soil then holding the shaft in his armpit and over his forearm managed to toss the dirt off to the side. He dug between intervals of rest; it took almost two days. The burial place, hollowed out head to the north, was about two feet deep. It took him another full day to drag Thompson's body over to his final resting place, lay him in properly, and refill the grave.

He felt bad about Thompson's death, but felt no sense of loss and sympathy, or remorse over his haste to get the man planted in the ground as quickly as possible. The body had begun to decompose, and the smell was unbearable. He cast aside any thoughts about saying a few words prior to returning the soil to its hole. Allsup had not seen a human body in such a state of decay. Every time he attempted to move the rotting corpse, he became nauseous requiring him to cover the body with a blanket making it abstract and no longer the maggot-filled remains of a recent acquaintance.

As he shoveled dirt while holding his breath, he did say a brief prayer. "Lord, I pray you accept the soul of the recently departed; far as I could tell he was a good man to ride with, and I regret his passing. Amen."

He wanted to be respectful towards the remains of the three Indians but didn't think he had the strength to dig individual graves, nor one big enough to accommodate all three, so while riding Chestnut in search of Thompson's missing horse, he gathered enough wood and buffalo chips to build a funeral pyre. Two nights after the Thompson's burial, the night sky was lit by a billowing fire, with flames and glowing embers dancing skyward as the spirits of the cremated rose up to join their ancestors.

Allsup continued to rest and eat what was available from the wagon; he felt better with each passing day and continued his search for the lost horse. He eventually ended that endeavor reasoning that the horse was probably now the property of some lucky Indian.

He cleaned the wagon of his bloody handprints during this period of recovery and re-organized its contents in the anticipation of their eventual departure. He tried to configure a better way to attach a single horse to a two-horse wagon, but in the end gave up, deciding to hitch the horse as it had been to the right side of the wagon tongue and adapt to the reduction in horsepower.

On a sunny, brisk morning, Allsup took a deep breath of the fresh cool air. He was ready to move on. His shoulder was still stiff, but there was little pain, so it was time to continue.

He climbed onto the wagon and sat down on its bench seat. As he picked up the reins, he noticed for the first time the damage done to his coat. Darkened slits in the material, stained and made stiff by blood, appeared like oddly placed eyes without pupils, watching.

"Let's get going, Chestnut." As the creaking, rattling wagon moved on, the sun crested the eastern horizon, and shone brightly on Allsup's back sending a long shadow before him pointing like a compass the direction to go.

Chapter 52

He sympathized for Chestnut pulling the loaded wagon alone without assistance. Allsup had greater respect for the animal's intelligence after the Hilltop Battle, as he referred to it. The horse returned to save him. Allsup never fathomed a horse could think like that, but Chestnut did. He returned on his own volition to save him.

Allsup's intention was to stop at Fort Lyon, if he could, and leave the wagon and its contents with the commanding officer. If he missed the fort he would continue west until he met someone to take the wagon off his hands allowing him to resume his travels as before. In the event neither prospect panned out, he would abandon the wagon and carry on.

He was one and a half days out from the site of the Hilltop Battle when a man on horseback leading two pack animals appeared in the distance. Three black specks ambling toward them without haste before a bank of white clouds hanging low on the western horizon. As the proximity between the two grew smaller, they made no effort to acknowledge the other. Eventually, the train of three horses came to a stop allowing Allsup the option of moving forward or stopping as well. Allsup moved forward stopping when they reached an easy speaking distance, almost side by side.

"You look like you've done well," observed Allsup good-naturedly with a nod towards the two fur-laden packhorses.

The fur trader nodded a reply, a hand-carved pipe with unusual designs held in his mouth.

"I'm heading towards Fort Lyon, myself," Allsup informed him. "Delivering this wagon of goods."

The trader looked as wild as the animals he encountered working deep in the forests on the low side of the mountains. His gray hair was full, un-kept and un-combed; it surrounded his face and fell down upon his shoulders. A full, matching beard covered most of his face with the exception of his dark eyes, which were currently staring intently at Allsup.

"Do you have any knowledge about the fort?" Allsup asked. "Where it is? How far away?"

The trapper removed the pipe and answered in a soft raspy voice, "Close."

"Really? How far would you say?"

"Hmm…'bout half'a day's ride."

"Well, that's good news!" Allsup sounded cheerful. "Can you give me a direction?"

"Half'a day forward fer me." In the midst of all his hairy madness, one exposed eye appeared to be twinkling. "Half'a day back fer you."

"A half'a day back!" Allsup turned on the bench seat looking back over his shoulder. The idea of going back had never been an option. He'd not done it yet on his travels, never had the occasion to do so, and the idea of doing it now, it just didn't set well.

"About a half'a day," he repeated facing ahead. "Backwards…"

"I be hazardin' the time some, no doubt," the trader conceded. "But I got the direction true."

Allsup sat thinking, trying to wisely consider all the options, the pros and cons.

"Will you take the wagon to the fort?" Allsup asked the trader. "You can load most of the skins on the back, and with two horses pulling, you'll travel twice as fast, and may be able to sit with your legs together for a time" He chuckled.

"Huh?" the trader seemed un-amused and possibly offended by the comment.

"I'm sorry, I'm sorry, let me try again. You can have the wagon and its contents; *Have* being the key word. I don't want it, so you can have it. Take it to the fort, sell off all the goods, sell the wagon, along with your skins you could become a wealthy man."

Danny Allsup

The trader took the opportunity of Allsup's explanation to load his unusual looking pipe, which, in Allsup's opinion, was beginning to resemble a bear or lion, or maybe a dragon's head with a ferocious mouth opened wide carved into bone. After packing a ball of dried tobacco leaf in its bowl, he used his knife, a flint, and a very small pinch of black powder sprinkled on the tobacco, to get it started. In less than a minute, the fragrance of burning powder and tobacco drifted across the span between the two.

"Do I look like a man that ever sat his ass on one'a those?" He gestured with his hand towards the wagon. His soft, raspy voice sounded indignant.

"No, sir, you do not."

"No…Don't git how'a man can choose to sit on'a board, when he can sit on'a horse."

"I can appreciate that," Allsup said. "I feel the same way."

The trader sat astride his horse, staring with dark, fanatical eyes at Allsup sitting on the bench seat of a buckboard.

Feeling foolish at his hypocrisy Allsup added, "Perhaps not as strongly though."

"Ya ain't goin' back?" asked the trader, puffing small clouds of smoke, working to keep the tobacco-filled bowl smoldering. He cleared his throat, hawked up a glob of phlegm and sent it sailing where it landed a few feet from the wagon.

"No, I'm heading west; I'm going to keep going."

"You could leave it," suggested the trader referring to the wagon with a nod of his head.

"I know, I've thought of that, but then it would all go to waste if never found. Forgotten pans left to rust; food and other things left to spoil, mold and rot; senseless waste. I want to make sure it goes where it can help. Abandoning it would have to be a last resort. No, I'll ride it west as far as I can, or until I meet someone who can use it. It'll work out.

Let me ask, how long does that unusual cloud range ahead stay so low on the horizon like that? I've been watching it all day. Do you know what causes it?"

The trader twisted with difficulty in his saddle to glance back at Allsup's reference. He looked for a minute before asking, "Huh?"

"I'm asking about those clouds there." Allsup pointed west along the horizon. "How long do they hang low like that? What causes them to do so?"

Chuckling, the trader turned back to Allsup.

"Ya ain't been out here b'fore, have ya?"

"No, this is my first time west."

The trader, shook his head and smiling, said, "Those be the Rockies."

"Rockies?"

"Yeah, mountains."

"Mountains? Those are the Rocky Mountains?" Allsup looked to the horizon with newfound amazement.

"That be 'em."

"There are no trees!" Allsup pointed out. "I've crossed mountains before, they were covered with trees! Those look like they're covered in clouds!"

"That be snow."

"Snow? But it's only...what?...September, October?"

"Always snow up them mountains."

"Are the trees covered in snow? Is that it?"

"No trees up there, too cold."

"So, that's just the ground covered with snow then?"

"Rocks, all rocks up there."

"Just rocks...So those are the Rockies." Allsup had never seen anything like it; mountains of rock so high they were covered with snow all year long. The idea of having to cross a mountain range that appeared so daunting had never crossed his mind.

The trader's "clicking" to get his team moving distracted Allsup from his thoughts; he turned to watch them go, each packhorse passing by.

Curious, Allsup called out, "Do you know the date?"

After the fur trader failed to reply, Allsup asked, "What about the month? What month is it?"

Still, the trader gave no response as the team rode east over land Allsup had previously traveled.

He sat watching them ride off before turning back to the west, the mountains, and their future.

With a soft whistle, he let Chestnut know it was time to move on; with head thrust foreword and chest and leg muscles straining at the leather harness, the horse began doing just that. The wagon rolled on.

Allsup continued to stare at the mountains before shaking his head slowly and exclaiming, "My Gosh."

D. Dean Carroll

Chapter 53

The seemingly level grass-covered land continued to increase in elevation, an unending subtle incline, leveling out often before inching upward again. The landscape appeared to be as vast as the ocean; hilltops, valleys, and plains as far as the eye could see. Storms, many miles off could be seen; sheets of rain falling like curtains from dark clouds with flashes of lightning on the horizon while he currently experienced blue skies overhead and sunshine.

One day while sitting on a hilltop looking down over a vast valley, he saw a train passing through its length from the east. It was so far down and away that it looked like a toy. He could not hear the train's engine, but a tiny flow of smoke was visibly billowing from its stack; faintly, he could hear its whistle clearing a small herd of buffalo from the tracks. He watched its progress, fascinated.

What an immense country this is, Allsup pondered sitting on the wagon appreciating the panoramic scenery. He felt alone and small, and at this particular time, at this particular place, as if he was the only person on Earth.

Until on another hilltop on the opposite side of the valley, he saw a rider on horseback also watching the train. From the distance, Allsup could not tell if the individual was Indian or white but appeared to be as mesmerized by the locomotive as he was.

The train was about midway through the valley and still had a distance to go when Allsup decided to move on. On the happenchance the rider in the distance was watching him as well, Allsup raised his arm and broadly waved goodbye. The individual across the expanse returned the valediction before turning away.

Chapter 54

The days were getting colder; his breath was now visible throughout most of the day and frost covered the ground most mornings. The mountains were drawing nearer, no longer looking like a cloudbank but like jagged teeth; they were becoming more distinct and defined. The white covered peaks gave way to different shades of granite gray before a timberline, dark green like a painter's brush stroke, grounded it to the Earth. Green trees clothed the foothills and spilled out onto the plain upon which Allsup rode.

Even with the sun shining brightly in a cloudless blue sky the cold lingered. It wasn't unbearable, but it left a chill in Allsup that he could not escape. He normally wrapped himself in a blanket while riding the buckboard, but several times during the day, he'd toss it aside and jump down to walk alongside Chestnut. He could talk to the horse without interruption expressing thoughts and sentiments, and the vigorous physical exertion helped alleviate the chill. It was on one such walk that he saw the smoke rising from the chimney of a cabin.

It was a distance away, maybe a mile, and were it not for the smoke he probably would have missed it. He doubted they'd see him unless they were looking. Therefore, he had the advantage of deciding how to proceed.

He could skirt the cabin maintaining the current distance and ride on without an encounter, or he could ride in, introduce himself, and hope they'd be gracious and allow him entry to cast off the chill for at least one night. He decided to try latter.

He believed he'd been lucky with the people he'd encountered on his travels; most had been good people. That must be what life is like in general, he considered, most people are good. A few are not, and that, he reasoned, was what was used to measure true character, how you dealt with the people who were not good.

Allsup acknowledged that how one dealt with such people, all people really, was determined by how each of those people wanted to be dealt with; but it was his belief that everyone wanted to be treated the same in one regard: with respect.

It was his intention to drive the wagon up to the cabin, introduce himself, and inquire about one or two nights lodging. If he could rid himself of the chill and even warm up a bit, he felthe'd be ready to take on the ragged geographic features that lay ahead and whatever obstacles Mother Nature might throw his way.

He crossed the prairie towards the cabin without haste; a wagon with a man sitting on the bench seat pulled by a single horse ambling along without hurry. Chestnut had become accustomed to pulling the wagon. Allsup rarely had to correct the horse's inclination towards changing direction; it appeared that it had finally grasped the man's intent.

The cabin was close enough to make out the door and the windows on either side, all closed. A small, crude, rail-fence corral was built off the side of the cabin with a lean-to covering a portion, from his distance all appeared to be empty.

When he was within shouting distance, the door opened, and a black man came out carrying a rifle. The cabin door quickly closed.

The man was dressed in buckskin pants and a blanket with a hole cut in its center to allow his head to poke through. There were no sleeves, his hands came up from beneath the blanket to hold the gun. He wore a woven hat made from dried grass whose brim flopped almost down to his shoulders.

"That's good," a woman's voice called out as she aimed the rifle towards the man sitting on the wagon. Allsup brought the wagon to a stop.

"You're a woman."

"What want?" The voice did not match the body; high-pitched and soft, almost musical, it contained no hint of threat or danger.

"Warmth," Allsup replied, with a smile. "I would like to feel warm for just a little while."

"Think git here?" She sounded irritated. "Why?"

"No, I...Hold on, this isn't going right." Allsup stood in the wagon and removed his hat. "First of all, my name is Danny Allsup, and I mean you no harm. I can't emphasize that strong enough, I have no plan or intention of robbing you of your property or causing you harm."

"Why, Danny Allsup? Why I give two shits?" She adjusted her stance and brought the barrel of the rifle more in line with the man. "B'fore ya do that, I kill."

"I believe you would."

After a drawn-out minute, she said, "So?"

"May I get down?"

"No."

"Okay." Allsup sat back down. "I've been riding across this prairie for a while now, and for the last couple of days it's been cold, as you well know. I can't seem to warm up, and...well, it's getting the better of me. I don't want anything from you. I won't eat your food. As a matter of fact, I have a whole wagon full of food and goods that I'll be happy to share with you! I assure you I will be no imposition. I just want to feel heat again and get warm."

"Huh?"

"I said I've been...

"Where go?" she interrupted.

"To the Pacific, the Pacific Ocean."

"Huh?"

"The Pacific Ocean." He pointed toward the mountains.

"West?"

Allsup nodded.

"Cross mountains?"

"Yes."

"Bitch 'bout cold now..." Her voice expressed disbelief mix with annoyance.

"To be honest, I don't know what to expect. I'm determined to see the Pacific, and if I have to cross the mountains to do so, then I will. I deal with things as they arise."

She lowered the rifle, shook her head and declared, "Dead man. I talk to dead man."

"I hope not," Allsup meekly responded.

"Come." She turned back toward the cabin. "Stow horse in stockade. I clear corner by fire."

"I appreciate your hospitality."

"What?"

"Your hospitality. Your generosity. Your kindness."

"Oh. Don' turn away can help." She stopped walking towards the cabin and turned back to address him. "Gimme weapons or stow in wagon. No in home."

"I'll leave them in the wagon under the seat. There's no one around to make off with them."

She disappeared within the cabin as he busied himself unhitching Chestnut. Allsup released the horse with a couple of handfuls of feed before securing a tarp over the contents of the wagon to protect it from the elements. Satisfied that all was as it should be, he made his way to the cabin door and knocked gently three times.

The door opened to reveal a tall very dark complected woman who had suffered a harsh life. She was very slim, almost frail in appearance, with coarse black hair pulled back and held together by a buckskin string before exploding into a burst of free hair. Her face looked tired and weathered making her appear older than she probably was; dust and grime had settled into the creases around her eyes and mouth. Her eyes betrayed she'd long since given up hope for better; they looked dull and empty.

Her blanket-coat now discarded, she wore a nicely

ornamented skin top with fur lining, painted with different child-like designs and animals.

"There." She pointed to the corner to the right of fireplace. "There. Don' move without my say, yes? We eat, you eat, yes? Ya git warm. Yes?"

"Yes, thank you very much." Allsup tossed his blanket and tarp into the corner along with a saddlebag containing salt, beans, and preserved fruit in a jar, all taken from the wagon. "And I'll stay right here. Yes?"

"Yes."

The woman turned her attention to making corn tortillas on the table and was in the process of kneading the dough. She lunged into it aggressively, pushing with straight arms before pulling the dough back, forming it into a ball and slapping it down on the table to repeat the process over again.

Allsup stood close to the side of the fireplace basking in its warmth. He faced the flames until his face could no longer stand the heat then turned around exposing his back. When it became unbearable he turned around again, like a piece of meat on a vertical spit.

It was very quiet in the room with only the crackling of the fire and the thumping of the dough disturbing the silence. Allsup straighten his night gear in the corner and sitting on the floor, made himself comfortable leaning back against the wall.

As his eyes adjusted to the darkness of the cabin, he took inventory of the room's interior. Before the fireplace, a sturdy table, currently in use, with four chairs. A cabinet stood at the side of the room to the left of the fireplace. A heavy, woodblock counter was beside it. At the other end of the cabin was a store-bought bed running parallel to the back wall. On the floor at the foot of the bed sat a person watching him.

"I thought you were alone." Allsup spoke softly to the woman currently shaping the dough into flat disks.

"No say." She didn't allow the comment to interrupt her work.

"No, no you didn't. I was just under the impression you were."

"Huh?"

"Who is that?" Allsup asked, watching the figure by the bed.

"She my."

"Your daughter? Really? Can you tell her I'm not going to hurt her or you? I'm really just a traveler who's grateful for your hospitality. I would never betray your trust and kindness."

"She don' like men too good, me too. If ya weren't cold 'n whining 'bout needin' warm, well, differen' weather call for differen'…"

"Please tell her she needn't be afraid. I don't want her afraid in her own home."

The woman stopped her tortilla making, a small stack sitting on the table and looked at him, sizing him up.

"Baby, come," the mother said standing at the table with cornmeal-dough stuck to her fingers. "Come now. Don' make Momma make bread my own! Come now!"

Slowly the figure rose, unfolded herself to a standing position looking as thin and fragile as her mother who she cautiously joined.

"Make bread on stone," the mother instructed pointing to a flat stone at the hearth before the fireplace.

"Do you like to help your mother make bread?" Allsup asked the girl who appeared to be about ten.

She looked at Allsup, then to her mother, before turning to her task without response.

"When I was a boy, I'd steal a bit of the dough to eat before they cooked it," Allsup confessed, smiling. "Do you ever do that?"

"No, don' waste; be foolish," the woman scolded, her soft, high-pitched voice making it sound comical.

Allsup acknowledged his rebuke with a nod of his head. He glanced over at the daughter who was smiling with delight, sneaking a pinch of dough.

"Oh! Excuse me!" Allsup quickly stood; his abruptness had both mother and daughter's attention.

"I have stuff here." He held up his saddlebag. "I thought you might be able to use."

Both mother and daughter approached warily, stopping at a safe distance.

"Let's see...What have we got...Ah! Beans! Can you use beans?"

The mother eagerly nodded they could. He handed her a sack of dried beans.

"Here's some salt! What about salt?"

Again, she happily acknowledged they could use the salt, so he passed on another bag.

"And what do we have here? What's this? A jar of peaches! Dessert!"

The daughter clapped her hands excitedly, frequently clutching her mother's arm. She looked like a child on Christmas morning.

"Put salt 'n soup." The mother said and went to a cauldron hanging over the fire to sprinkle the spice into the pot.

"Time," she announced. "Let cook."

The young girl could not tear her eyes away from the peach jar. Her attention might get distracted, but it always returned to the preserves.

"Have you ever had a peach before?" Allsup asked her.

She nodded.

"So *that's* why you can't take your eyes off the jar." Allsup smiled.

She smiled too.

"Excuse me," Allsup called out to the woman who seemed to have disappeared. "Hello?"

"Huh?" She was sitting on the side of the bed, outside

the perimeter of the firelight.

"I am Danny Allsup, of course you already know that. I told you earlier. Anyway, I didn't catch your name." He pointed out extending his hand.

The woman looked hesitantly at him, unsure. Finally, she rose and took his hand. "Millie."

"Millie," repeated Allsup. "Nice to meet you, Millie."

The two looked at her daughter who was staring at her mother wide-eyed.

"My don' know," Millie said, smiling, embracing her daughter. "Been long, long since I say, Millie—Millie."

"She can't talk?" Allsup softly asked.

"No."

"That's too bad. Was she born that way?"

"No."

"Oh."

"Bread!" Millie called out, and to her daughter, "Turn!"

The daughter rushed to the fireplace to attend the tortillas.

"She happy baby." Millie watched her daughter. "She happy, laugh, sing! She talk, she talk, she talk. Happy." She paused as her daughter returned and clutched her mother around her waist. Looking lovingly down at her daughter, she repeated, "Happy."

"Borg, my man, her daddy, mean, like to hurt. Like to hit. Talk make Borg mad. Happy make Borg mad. He hurt her bad, ropes, sticks…she happy make Borg mad."

"Borg make mash; drink mash, drink mash. Git mean. Say words, hurt me, her." Millie brushed her daughter's hair with her hand.

"Time back, she five summers, she run in house talk, talk, talk."

"Borg drink mash, drink mash. Mean. Mad. Sleep in chair but no, her talk he say. Tell me 'Shut her damn mouth!' he say." She said this in a loud gruff manner leading Allsup to think she was imitating her husband.

Millie looked fondly down at her daughter before continuing.

"Don' know," she whispered. "Stop talk, don' know. I shh, put bed, sing, but—but she happy, talk."

A tear dropped onto her buckskin top, above her right breast leaving a dark spot.

"Borg say, 'Nough! Cain't quiet her, I do.' Borg grab knife." She pointed to a knife on the table. "No sharp. Borg grab her! Borg put her down! Borg sit on! Big self! She scream. She scream. Borg grab…Borg grab…"

Millie was crying, her chest rising and falling rapidly. The daughter continued to hug her mother, resting her head against her and rubbing her back soothingly, but she didn't shed a tear.

"Sorry," she whispered to her daughter. "Momma sorry."

Allsup couldn't recall when he had felt so awkward. This woman was opening herself up to a stranger, someone she was reluctant to allow into her home earlier, and now she was revealing what is surely to be horrible.

"Maybe I should…" he started.

"Borg git tongue," she interrupted. "He cut wit knife, n' cut, n' cut tongue off in his hand. Baby scream then sleep. I happy she sleep, quiet like now."

"How long have you lived here?" Allsup asked.

"All time." She motioned to the tortillas, and her daughter went over to replace the cooked with new. The lovely aroma of baking corn flour filled the cabin. It reminded Allsup of home many years ago.

"Borg sleep chair," she continued. "Wake, drink mash, sleep. Borg fall, he fall, he fall. I help to water. I help Borg out to water. Stand like tree in wind. Let go, fall in snow. Stay. Face in snow, make water in snow. Stay like dead. Go cabin git knife." She again pointed to the knife on the table. "Back, git Borg up. Grab Borg n' cut n' cut n' cut. Borg don' know. He scream like baby. I git on Borg, cut Borg tongue.

He bite first. Tongue come off in my hand. He scream. He scream. He scream. I tired scream. I stab knife hard in Borg eye, deep. Borg stop scream like her." A nod to her daughter. "Borg no wake." She smiled at the thought.

Allsup looked compassionately at the woman who seemed off in a world of her own. He looked over at her daughter, standing by a table chair watching her mother.

"Miss Millie," Allsup called softly. When he received no response, he tried again, "Miss Millie."

She blinked her eyes, looked at him confused, then smiled when she saw her daughter.

"Miss. Millie, I know what will make your daughter happy, very happy!"

The tall, buckskin-clad woman looked at him questioningly. Allsup pointed to the jar of peaches.

"Let's eat those while we wait for the soup," he suggested.

"Eat?"

Her daughter's eyes widen with anticipation, and she eagerly jumped up and down clapping.

"Yes. Look at her, she wants them so bad she can almost taste them."

The mother saw the hopeful look in her daughter's eyes; just the thought of her happiness made the mother smile.

"Yeah."

The girl, jumping up and down, screamed with delight, covering her mouth with the palm of her hand, before running over to her mother to reward her with a hug.

"Git jar. Git knife. One'n one'n one." She pointed to each including herself.

"One'n one'n one," She repeated.

"Okay, just one!" Allsup was enjoying himself. While the daughter gathered the jar of peaches and the knife, Allsup wondered if he really wanted to use *that* knife to retrieve his peach. But the thought was quickly replaced by another.

"What's her name?" He asked while they watched the

girl struggle with the jar lid.
   "Gabby."

Chapter 55

Danny Allsup stayed with Millie and Gabby for almost a week. The days passed quickly as both mother and daughter were pleased to have a guest, and their guest was pleased to be staying with them.

Early, he became aware that although Gabby couldn't speak words, she had developed a method of communication that her mother understood with little difficulty. She did this by using her voice to sound the words without using her mouth.

Allsup never saw her opened mouth. When eating or laughing, she used a hand to conceal whatever difficulties she preferred unseen.

It wasn't just the sound and similarity of the word she used to communicate, but her facial expressions and gestures mimicking that idea or word, made her very capable of expressing herself—and she would express herself all day. It wasn't long before he could catch the gist of her conversation without the necessity of seeing her expressions. He learned the little nuances and inflections to the sounds she used regularly.

Her common sound was, "Mmm," like a hum. This she used with all her other communication skills to convey a wide range of thoughts and opinions. Through most of each day, similar to the buzzing of a bee, Gabby's "Mmm" could be heard at different pitches and tempos, volume and intensity, depending on the subjects she chose to discuss or respond.

Allsup was amused and inspired by the young girl who retained her happiness despite having endured such extreme pain and horror.

Allsup and Chestnut roamed the countryside looking for livestock. By Millie's recollection, she had one mule, a milk cow that didn't produce enough to warrant being referred to as such, a bull that seemed to have no purpose in life, six pigs, a sheep, and a handful of chickens and roosters. She conveyed this in her stilted broken English, requiring a considerable amount of time, patience, and questions. Before winter hit, she had made an account of her animals. She had to decide which to keep on hand and which to send out to fend for themselves.

Allsup and Chestnut took the opportunity to wander the countryside, leisurely at times, other times at break-neck speeds; these excursions tickled the itch to continue their journey. They rounded up the mule and cow along with the sheep and three pigs. The chickens and roosters tended to stay around the cabin providing fresh eggs and new chicks.

He fixed the corral fence with Gabby's assistance. A new person to talk to resulted in her spending every possible moment by his side. Allsup didn't mind, particularly after he learned the nuances of her language. She wanted to know everything.

The cabin and the land surrounding it was her world. An illiterate mother her only source of information. Gabby knew there had to be more, but her inexperience led her to conclude that it was more of the same. She was mesmerized by the stories of his travels, and all that he had seen and experienced left her wanting more. Comprehending vastness and size was difficult for her; the idea of a body of water the size of the Pacific as he described it was impossible to conceive. The Rockies in the distance provided no basis for awe at their height and grandeur since they did not appear towering from her perspective. As they worked on the fence, she would pepper him with one question after another often sounding skeptical at his responses. Their conversations lit a fire in her imagination that he was sure could only be extinguished by experience.

One chilly morning he put on his Duster and discovered the knife holes from his altercation with the

Indians neatly sewn closed with fine, thin strands of buckskin. Over the next few days designs were painted around the coat's scars concealing the blemishes.

The day after his arrival, he gave them the wagon and its contents. Like excited children in a candy store, they went through it piece by piece. They found items that would be of use, but most of the contents were beyond their knowledge and were tossed aside. Anything related to food was taken inside to be scrutinized, categorized and discussed.

Millie and Gabby prepared a special dinner one night to show their gratitude. She made every effort to incorporate all consumable goods found in the wagon in one meal. She made a prairie dog stew supplemented with her own grown roots and salt and pepper found in the wagon. She found a bag marked "Rice" and asked Allsup about it. He had no knowledge of what it was or how to prepare it. She dropped two handfuls in the stew and stirred it regularly. It surprised Millie to see the grain became puffed and full and that it complemented the stew.

Allsup declared it the best meal he'd ever had which made mother and daughter smile proudly. Millie was especially pleased with her discovery of the rice. Often, she would walk over and pick up its bag. She would stare at it, thinking, then set it down and go on.

The three were walking down from the cabin to a nearby stream that fed into the Arkansas River. It was a pleasant evening, the horizon glowed hot orange from the setting sun with the silhouette of the mountains, their different shapes and peaks, in the foreground. Overhead and to the east the sky turned a dark midnight blue illuminated by planets and a vast array of stars lighting up the galaxy. It all seemed magical. Gabby alternated between holding her mother's hand before switching to Allsup's then back to her mother's.

"I think I'll be leaving tomorrow," Allsup informed them. Surprised by his announcement, the two females stopped.

"Go?" Millie asked. "Go?" She made a leap motion with both hands as if jumping from one side to the other.

"Yes, tomorrow."

A rapid tapping on his elbow caused him to turn and face Gabby, shaking her head saying, "Hm-mm."

"I must say that I have truly enjoyed my stay with you." He placed a hand gently upon the young girl's shoulder while looking at her mother. "But, but the Pacific calls. I've told you about my aspiration to reach the ocean. It's time to begin again."

The mother took her daughter's hand and the two returned to their cabin leaving Allsup standing alone by the stream.

The morning ground, crusted with frost, caused a crunch with each step. Allsup hoped to head out early steering clear of emotional farewells, but both were up and busy as he gathered his possessions. No one spoke. Mother and daughter avoided his look.

He saddled Chestnut in the dark; the horse pawing the ground as if eager to be on its way. Both man and horse's breath were visible in the early morning moonlight. He heard the cabin door open and close and turned to see the two approaching.

Gabby carried a slice of buttered bread and her mother, a cup of coffee brewed in a coffeepot from the wagon. Allsup smiled as he watched them draw near. Gabby handed him the slice of bread, which he took, expressing his thanks. He ate while they both patiently watched. When finished, Millie handed him the coffee. It was a bit strong, but he wasn't going to be around to drink it again, so he smiled and conveyed his gratitude. After the third sip, he handed the cup back to her.

"Well..." he said reluctantly.

Gabby hugged his waist and said, "Mm Mm Mmm." Her eyes expressing more than her sounds. "Mm Mm Mmm."

D. Dean Carroll

"I love you too, Gabby." He looked fondly down at her. "Go out and see the world. You'll be so glad you did."

She nodded and gave him one last hug.

Allsup turned to her mother, Millie. They embraced and she whispered, "Good man. Good man."

When they stepped apart, she told him, "Follow water. El Pueblo. Find Anta Katete. Say 'Millie say take cross mountains.' Anta Katete take Danny Allsup cross mountains."

"How will I find him?" Allsup asked.

"Anta Katete big Indian. You find."

"Okay, well, thank you Millie, I have enjoyed being your guest. I wish you and Gabby good health and happiness. May God always smile upon you both."

Danny Allsup climbed up onto the saddle and after one final glance, said, "Let's go Chestnut before I change my mind." The horse began an immediate canter westward past the empty buckboard and corral.

"Say 'Millie, Anta Katete, man-wife Anta Katete take Danny Allsup cross mountains!'" Millie called out as she and Gabby watched him ride away. In her normal voice she commented, "Anta Katete take Danny Allsup cross mountains." To her daughter she said with a wink, "Gabby see."

Chapter 56

The El Pueblo settlement spread across the junction where Fountain Creek emptied into the Arkansas River with the Rocky Mountains sitting in its backyard; it was an ideal location for trade and commerce. Allsup, atop Chestnut, ambled down Santa Fe Avenue noting the different enterprises the street had to offer.

He passed a butcher shop guaranteeing fresh meat. A sign advised the proprietor, John Wheelock, owned a slaughterhouse outside Pueblo. There were two grocery stores, one not far from the other resulting in a rivalry in which one incorporated a fruit stand selling mostly citrus, along with apples and grapes to lure the customer.

Allsup stopped in front of Bartels' General Merchandise and decided to start there. He picked out a heavy full-length coat, a fur-lined cap that had flaps to cover his ears, and a pair of sealskin boots, also lined, that Mr. Bartels assured him would keep his feet warm *and* dry.

While he was paying for his new apparel, he inquired about Anta Katete.

"He's a big Indian I'm told," Allsup explained to the clerk. "Big enough to stand out."

"I don't know him," answered the clerk, "but I've only been here 'bout two weeks goin' on three."

He next ventured to the grocery with the fruitstand where he replenished his supplies for the next leg of his journey. He was advised to avoid foods that would require cooking; a waste of time and energy, he was told.

"You want to take foods that will give you energy boosts so you can keep going," the store's proprietor advised. "Foods like bananas and oranges, which we currently have, are good. You slice them up and allow them to freeze, then as you travel you pop one in your mouth, let it thaw and chew it up.

"Nuts are also a good source of energy," he continued. "I currently have walnuts and almonds. You chew on a couple throughout the day, and they'll help keep you moving. I recommend the almonds, but the walnuts are easier to open."

"Of course, I have honey. Honey's good for a lot of different things, but it'll also give you the oomph you need when you need it. Don't eat big, eat small and frequently. Mark my words, sir, only two things will kill you crossing those mountains: cold and starvation. You get the right gear and eat the right foods; you'll get over those mountains. Mark my words, I got that straight from a fellow from some university back east."

"Give me all of that, what you just said," Allsup ordered. "Plus whatever else you think I may need. Bear in mind it's just me and my horse."

As the clerk helped Allsup pack his purchases in old flour sacks, Allsup inquired about Anta Katete, providing the brief, limited description: he was a big Indian.

"I seen someone who meets that description," the clerk advised. "At the X-10-U-8 Saloon on Santa Fe out on the edge of town. Big Indian, I seen him there a couple of times."

Allsup paid his bill and expressed his appreciation for the advice and information and quickly departed the store. Before heading to the saloon, he wanted to find lodging for the night, a place to safely secure his possessions when he went out in search of Millie's Indian.

A passerby informed him that a small hotel could be found on Lou Ann Street just off Santa Fe. Called the Hotel Lou Ann, it was really a good size home converted into a boarding house, but it was clean and warm, and for a nickel more, he could order up a hot bath. Allsup signed the Guest Registry.

The evening was getting cold; the sun, long since passed the mountaintops in its descent, still cast off a pinkish-orange illumination on the rippling clouds overhead. Allsup was trying out his new fur-lined long coat and was glad to have it, though it felt cozy and warm, its lining made it difficult to put his arms down or reach into its pockets.

The X-10-U-8 Saloon was busy, most of the tables were taken, and the bar was crowded with men talking and laughing over their drinks. Oil burning lamps cast a yellowish hue to the room as well as dark shadows moving about the walls. An unoccupied upright piano stood at the back of the room. A black, cast-iron stove near the far wall gave off so much heat that tables around it were pulled back in search of relief.

"Evening," greeted the bartender. "What'll it be?"

"Good evening. Can I get a coffee?" asked Allsup.

The bartender looked at him in disbelief before replying, "This is the X-10-U-8 Saloon, friend, we have beer, whiskey, and beer. What'll it be?"

"A beer, please."

As Allsup sipped his beer, he leaned back against the bar and took in the room. It was filled with what appeared happy men of good nature. Many had suffered some form of disappointment, but the ambiance of the bar and the influence of the alcohol alleviated much of their despondency. Laughter and good cheer was the predominate mood.

When the bartender returned to refill the mug of another at the bar, Allsup inquired about Anta Katete.

"Anta Katete?" the bartender repeated the name reflectively. "Never heard of him. Must be an Indian with a name like that."

"He is," answered Allsup. "A big one I'm told."

"Oh, wait! You must be talking about Lone Mountain! A big ol' Indian comes in most evenings around this time."

"Yeah? Is he here now?" asked Allsup as he looked around the saloon again.

"No, he ain't here yet, but you'll know when he arrives.

He's a big man. You can't miss him. Set you up with another?" the bartender asked referring to Allsup's beer.

"No, thanks, still have this one."

"'Bout do for a fresh one then."

"No, thanks," replied Allsup. "This one's good."

The bartender moved on as Allsup leaned back against the bar to watch and wait for Anta Katete, or Lone Mountain.

The evening was growing long, and Allsup could no longer suppress his yawns, one coming after another. The clouds of smoke hanging over the room caused his already tired eyes to burn and tear. The Regulator clock mounted on the wall over the piano, its pendulum click-clocking back and forth, indicated it was almost eleven-thirty. He decided that he would leave at twelve if Anta Katete failed to make his appearance by that time.

By eleven-fifty, the crowd in the bar was beginning to thin out. It became much quieter as patrons departed and those remaining, like Allsup, nodded off or were lost in reflections of another time; perhaps a sweetheart left behind. Allsup had taken a chair at a table facing the door, his chin resting in the palm of his hand. More than once the pillar supporting him gave way causing his head to jerk awake before hitting the table.

"There's a man been here looking for you."

Allsup heard the words but associated no meaning.

"Where?"

"He's over there, at that table there."

The "Hmm" sounded like a deep solid punch and suddenly the Earth moved.

The table went flying out from under and he found himself falling with his chin still resting in his hand. He scrambled too late to catch himself for his elbow hit the floor driving his hand into his jaw driving his jaw into his upper teeth chipping several. He was surprised, injured, and half-awake; he jumped to his feet angry.

With clenched fists and a sore mouth, he shouted, "Who

did that?"

"Me."

As Allsup regained his senses, he focused on the man standing before him, slowly looking up at his face.

Lone Mountain was an appropriate moniker for the man standing there calmly. He was the tallest man Allsup had ever seen, with a large head and dark, deep-set eyes. His straight black hair, cut short, revealed a neck almost as big as his head. A large, round body, not muscular nor fat, but large, was followed in structure by his remaining torso; his arms looked like large branches of an elderly Oak and his legs resembled its trunk.

"Why'd you do that?" Allsup rubbed his chin.

"Heard you been looking for me?" the deep voice rumbled like thunder.

"Anta Katete?"

With a chuckle that seemed to growl from his chest, the tall Indian answered, "Haven't been called that in a while, but that's me."

"What would you rather I call you, Lone Mountain?"

"That's what your people call me. I don't care I guess; it doesn't matter."

"Somebody gonna straighten my table and chairs?" asked the bartender; the table was still resting on its side and three of the chairs remained scattered.

"Pick up the table and chairs before Johnny gets upset," directed Anta Katete. Allsup did as instructed, and as he placed the final chair at the table the Indian sat down. Allsup was about to sit at the opposite side of the table when the Indian said, "Get us something to drink."

"What?"

"I'll have two shots of whiskey and a beer."

He looked at the seated Indian who returned his gaze. Allsup's head had cleared enough for him to resent the Indian's orders.

"What's the matter?" asked Anta Katete. "You're not

going to get us something to drink?"

When Allsup failed to respond, the Indian scooted his chair back causing it to make an unpleasant scraping sound and rose to his full height.

"All right," the man said. "I'll get'em. What do you want?"

Allsup was confused. Different questions popped into his head. Was the Indian still a threat? Was he mad about something? Was he mad at Allsup? Or did he want to sit and talk over beers? And why did he talk like that? He spoke better than most people.

Allsup wanted his help getting over the mountains, and he always maintained there was no excuse for rudeness, so he said, "No, I'll get them." And, to feel like he was on equal footing brazenly added, "Sit down."

They sat at the table together drinking. Anta Katete was on his fourth shot of whiskey and his second beer; Allsup was still nursing his first. It was quiet because the bar was empty except for the bartender, a man asleep in the back by the piano, and two men sitting together at a table.

"Why are you looking for me?" asked Anta Katete.

"Where'd you learn to talk like that?"

"I was taken in by an old couple from Iowa. They wanted to convert me to Jesus and save my soul."

"How'd that come about?"

"My family was killed during a raid by the army. I'm told everyone was killed but me. Hal Alexander was with the army; he discovered me watching from the hills. Wouldn't let them kill me. He took me home to his wife."

"That was fortunate for you."

"Maybe, maybe not. Momma wanted a pet, something she could baby and cuddle. I guess I was it. That's what she called me, her pet."

"So, you have a Chris—a white name?"

"Yeah, Kenneth Alexander. They called me Kenny."

"How long did you live with them?"

"I stayed until I was about twelve. I was big then, not so cuddly. I became an Indian as far as Momma was concerned. Her affection disappeared, replaced with anger and resentment. She took me out of school, said it was a waste of time on an Indian even though when she originally enrolled me, she thought it was important for me to be able to read and write; to know things.

"Hal, Daddy began to drink to get away from her anger. That only made things worse, so I left."

"You made it back to your people?" Allsup pretended to drink from his now bubble-less beer.

"I have no people," the Indian answered staring into his glass.

"Who gave you the name Anta Katete?"

"The people. I was up north in the Colorado Territory when a raiding party found me and took me back to their camp. I was big and alone, so they called me Anta Katete."

"Were they from your, uh, I don't know what you'd call it, your tribe?"

"I have no tribe. I have no one."

Anta Katete went to the bar and returned sloshing the contents of two mugs of beer in one hand and two more shots in the other.

"Here," he said sliding one mug across the table towards Allsup. "You been playing with that beer so long it's not even fit for piss."

They sat quietly for a spell. Allsup considered the fresh beer quite an improvement. A man walked in through the open bar doors, looked around, then walked back out.

"I'm heading west towards the Pacific," Allsup stated. "I have to cross the mountains to do that. I need your help getting across."

Anta Katete sat staring at Allsup with his dark eyes. After a time with no change of expression or utterance, Allsup thought he must have fallen into a trance. Were his eyes not open, he could reasonably be assumed asleep.

"Millie said you'd take me." The trance was broken, the eyes shifted just a bit.

"Millie?"

"Yes, Millie. I spent a week with her and Gabby before coming here."

"You saw Gabby?"

"I did," answered Allsup.

"Gabby," Anta Katete repeated softly and looked down at his hands. "How are they?"

"They're both good, doing very well. That Gabby is a very curious girl."

"She's the sweetest thing in this world," the large Indian declared looking up at Allsup with tears in his eyes. "The sweetest thing."

"She is," Allsup concurred.

"Millie's a good woman."

"She is. She said I should find you. She said you'd take me over the mountains."

After a moment, Lone Mountain said, "Sorry, but I have plans. Going over the mountains aren't in them."

"Maybe you'd consider guiding me after you've finished with your plans," Allsup suggested.

"No, I got other plans."

"I'll be glad to help you with your plans if you'd agree to take me."

"No. Plans have already been made."

"So that's it?" Allsup sat back, defeated. "There's nothing I can do or say to get you to change your mind and help me?"

"No, sorry, like I said, plans have been made."

"Millie said if you got me safely over the mountains, you and she could be, uh, man and woman."

"You mean man and wife?"

"That's what I take it to mean."

"She said that?"

"Yes." Allsup was amused. "And she was smiling when

Danny Allsup

she said it."
"I'll take you cross the mountains."

Chapter 57

"This isn't the best time of year to start crossing, but then, there are worse times." The big native appeared even bigger bundled in a makeshift winter coat made of different skins crudely tied together, the fur providing the inner lining. He wore pants made in similar fashion that extended down over his boot tops. "To keep the toes warm," he commented,

On his head was a leather, fur-lined hood that tied under his chin covering everything but his face creating an unusual looking sight. It was impossible to tell what direction he was looking because the hood didn't move when his head did. "We'll get through," he added.

Fall was growing closer to winter and their elevation contributed to the bitter cold they now experienced. The wind blowing between the mountains felt like a current of ice freezing any exposed flesh, so cold it felt like a burn.

The two men were almost completely concealed, their faces wrapped by hat and scarf, their hands encased in thick fur mittens. Lone Mountain had his horse draped in a large skin-made blanket to protect it from the cold. Chestnut did not have that good fortune, and it bothered Allsup. He stopped shortly after starting and made a covering for his horse using his ground tarp and bedroll. The difficulty was finding a way to secure them together to prevent flapping and escaping body heat.

Anta Katete solved that problem with a sharpened piece of wood a hand's length long, and made a hole in its opposite, wider end; a long leather strip ran through the hole, like a needle and thread. He pushed Allsup aside and began stitching together the flaps by forcing the wooden needle's point through the materials and pulling the leather thread taut securing the flaps together. In this manner, he sewed Chestnut into his winter protection.

Danny Allsup

The incline of their climb had reached the degree they now had to serpentine their ascent up the mountainside. They continued as the weather became increasingly harsher and colder. The clouds hung low concealing the tops of the surrounding peaks, and often they found themselves passing through the clouds.

As the sunset earlier and earlier each day with it came darkness making it difficult to judge their progress. Crossing one mountain range only revealed another and so much of their travel was going up and down, scaling steep inclines and carefully descending sharp slopes.

On their third morning, the sky was clear, and the temperature felt almost moderate. Allsup had his first clear view of the mammoths surrounding them.

"My Gosh, look at that mountain!" he pointed north to a towering mountain standing high above the rest.

Anta Katete looked north and smiled.

"The Arapaho people call it Heey-ootoyo," he explained. "Long Mountain."

"I've never seen anything so high before."

"People have been up on it."

"To the top?" Allsup asked in disbelief.

"Yeah, to the top."

"My Gosh. You?"

"No, no, no." Anta Katete laughed. "I go no higher than I have to."

"The weather has become compliant and agreeable," Allsup observed. It was still cold but not as much, the wind seemed to get lost in the mountain passes, only light breezes slipped through, and the sun was bright and warming.

"Yeah, it always is along here." Anta Katete nodded. "Wish it was like this all the way."

They continued riding, banishing their heavy winter wear for more moderate clothes: Allsup in his duster and Anta Katete in his deerskin shirt and vest. Allsup pulled Chestnut's head out through the opening of his cover and allowed him the luxury of experiencing the pleasant weather.

"Cañon City's ahead," Anta Katete told him. "We'll stop there."

It was an unusual place to say the least: sunny, cool but not cold, and the wind when there was one, was never harsh. Cañon City was in an ideal location for a mountain city. Nestled in and surrounded by mountains that blocked the worst elements of the region but high enough in elevation to allow sunshine throughout most of the year keeping the climate moderate and dry. The Arkansas River flowed directly to its south, making the city a popular stopping point for travelers and traders alike.

On the corner of Third and Main, they found the Strathmore Hotel, a large three-story, red-bricked building, and while Anta Katete tended to the horses, Allsup went in and booked two rooms.

He was talking with the hotel bellhop when Anta Katete came in to join him.

"What's he doing here?" asked the bellhop.

"What do you mean?" asked Allsup.

"I know what he means," Anta Katete interjected flatly.

"What do you mean?" Allsup asked again.

"We don't allow Indians in here," explained the bellhop. "He can't be in here."

"But he's with me. I've already paid for our rooms."

"You need to talk to Mr. Eddy, the manager. But I wouldn't get your hopes up. We lose our standing as a quality place we start letting Indians in."

"I want to speak with Mr. Eddy," Allsup stated.

Mr. Eddy provided no support or assistance, maintaining the hotel's strict policy of no Mexicans, Blacks, or Indians. He further suggested that they consider finding suitable lodgings elsewhere.

Allsup agreed but was surprised to be told at the hotel desk that since he'd already checked in there would be no refund for the reserved rooms as they were now considered used.

"But we haven't been up to our rooms!" protested Allsup angrily.

"We have no way of knowing that sir," the desk clerk smugly replied.

"You can ask Mr. Eddy, or the bellhop over there, I've been with them since checking in."

"Can you say the same for your friend?" Indicating Anta Katete with a nod of his head. "Has he been with you this whole time?"

"No, but he hasn't been up to his room, I have the key."

"Sir, it is hotel policy not to issue refunds on rooms that have already been checked in. Now, if you'd like—"

"What's the problem?" Anta Katete asked Allsup.

"They don't want to give us our money back because they say we've already checked in and could have used the rooms."

"But we haven't been up to our rooms yet."

"I know that, and he knows that but…"

Anta Katete addressed the desk clerk. "We haven't been to our rooms. Give him his money back."

"Sir, hotel policy states that—"

"Do you want to see why they don't let Indians stay in this shit-hole of a hotel?" Anta Katete rose to his full height.

"Excuse me?" asked the startled desk clerk.

"I asked, do you want to see why they don't allow Indians here?"

"No, no, I don't think I do," stammered the clerk.

"Then give him his money."

"We did not use the rooms," argued Allsup. "We did not go to the rooms. We did not use the services you are providing; therefore, we are due a full refund."

"Give him his money." Anta Katete's dark eyes stared intently at the desk clerk.

"Oh, all right," the clerk relented and opened a drawer from which he took out a stack of paper money. "Not worth the trouble, really. Don't know why I was making such a noise about it."

He counted the money out in two piles, combined the piles, and handed the fresh, smaller stack to Allsup saying, "Here you go, two rooms for one night. Sorry, again, about the fuss."

"Not a problem," replied Allsup before turning to Anta Katete. "Let's go."

"You might try Tarboton's Boarding House," the desk clerk called out. "It's just down Seventh Street. They don't maintain such policies."

Tarboton's Boarding House eagerly took advanced payment for two rooms over one night. For that payment, they would also receive an early breakfast and a corral for their horses.

Their beds were stuffed feather mattresses, packed full and tight; and when Allsup lay upon his he felt as if he were adrift on a cloud. He sunk into the mattress several inches creating the sensation of weightlessness yet being cradled.

Anta Katete was having a similar experience in his own room despite the fact that his feet extended past the mattress by several inches; from the ankles down hung unsupported and exposed.

The thought of the man in each room was the same: their departure tomorrow. Allsup had been warned by more than two that traversing the Royal Gorge was difficult and dangerous, especially this time of the year with the snow. He was told the ledge they would travel on was barely wide enough for a horse and in places not wide enough for a horse with a rider. It sounded frightening.

Anta Katete was frightened at the thought of walking the gorge. He'd traveled it twice before almost falling each time. Yet here he was, lying on a mattress that seemed to caress him differently each time he moved. He'd survived. It had been scary, but he made it through that gorge four times, there was no reason to think he couldn't do it two more; but still…

At about the same time, both men settled into their mattresses and sighed, and drifted into a deep restful sleep.

D. Dean Carroll

Chapter 58

"Unprecedented!" declared the banker at the breakfast table in Tarboton's Boarding House. They had a snowfall the previous night and now much of Cañon City was snowed in, and in the process of clearing it away. "Hasn't been a snow like this in the past twenty years," he continued while spreading strawberry preserve on his still-warm biscuit. "I can tell you that."

"It'll be gone by mid-day," added a scruffy-looking man dressed in several plaid shirts and wornout dark pants covered by chaps. "That noon sun hits it and it'll be gone by two—mark my words."

Anta Katete had elected to remain in his room rather than attend breakfast for reasons unexplained. Danny Allsup's hunger dictated his morning agenda. He sat at one end of a table occupied by four other guests enjoying the delicious breakfast cooked by Mrs. Tarboton.

"Do you think that's likely?" he asked his dining companions. "That the sun will melt it all away?"

"It's possible," softly answered an elderly man wearing a yellowish shirt under a brown button-down knit sweater covered by black suspender straps. "This time'a year ya can't tell. In a hurry, are ya?"

"I am anxious to be on my way," answered Allsup.

"Where're ya headed?" asked the fourth man at the table. A redheaded man wearing gold-rim glasses, a green and blue-checkered suit, and sporting evidence of facial hair. He held his coffee cup in mid-air awaiting a response.

"West, to the Pacific."

"You're crossing the mountains this time'a year?" the banker asked in disbelief.

"Yes, that's my plan."

"Well, I hope ya got yourself a good guide!" stated the

old man.

"I believe I do."

"Who?" pursued the banker. "If I may ask?"

"An Indian by the name of Anta Katete; he's very competent."

"Anta Katete? Never heard of him."

"Yes, ya have," corrected the scruffy-looking man in multiple plaid shirts. "Lone Mountain. You know, the guy that brought that group back 'bout two years ago? Big Indian. Everyone else wanted to leave them for dead, but Lone Mountain went out by his own self and brought them all back alive."

"Yes, yes, I have him now," The banker acknowledged. "Competent, yes, yes, very competent if you ask me. Bringing those people back like that. A hero. A real hero!"

"Yeah, well, no one else called him that, 'cept a'course, those he returned," added the scruffy man. He had a droplet of egg yolk snagged on the stubble of his chin. The elderly man tried to discreetly advise him of it by brushing his own chin but without success.

Mrs. Tarboton returned with a pot of fresh hot coffee, which she set on the table. Before returning to the kitchen, she remarked, "Mr. Carrington, you have egg on your chin." He wiped it away with the top shirtsleeve.

"Use your napkin, Mr. Carrington, use your napkin," she scolded. "This isn't a flophouse, ya know."

"When did you plan to depart?" asked the quiet old gentleman.

"My hope was for this morning," answered Allsup. "But I will have to see what Anta Katete thinks. He's my guide, so I'll listen to his advice."

"I wouldn't attempt it in this weather," the banker stated.

"Nor I," added the red-haired man. "It's much too unpredictable."

"Well, like I said, I'll see what Anta Katete has to say."

D. Dean Carroll

Allsup scooted his chair from the table and folded his napkin placing it beside his plate before rising.

"I have enjoyed the breakfast and the company. I bid you all a good day. Delicious breakfast, Mrs. Tarboton!" he called out to the kitchen; receiving no response, he returned to his room.

Chapter 59

The snow fell in light flurries between the gorge's walls dusting everything in white including the two men on horseback traveling along the banks of the Arkansas River. The day never warmed enough to melt the accumulation, so the ground now experienced a continuous coat of several inches. Little pools that formed in nooks and crannies, between rocks and crevices along the riverbanks were covered with thin sheets of ice. Allsup looked back to see that their trail was slowly being erased, so the snow behind them looked as new and pristine as that ahead.

When Allsup had sought the advice of Anta Katete regarding the snow and proceeded onward, the tall man responded, "The only better time will be summer. Do you want to wait?" That determined his decision to press on.

The mountains in this part of the country were massive hills with rounded tops showing their age. The ragged, pointed structures of snow-covered rock jutting skyward were still a distance away, so their travels were not difficult but tiring.

The two men became better acquainted as they traveled. Allsup was surprised to learn Anta Katete was literate, having advanced to the fifth grade in school before being withdrawn by his adoptive mother. Anta Katete told Allsup that he enjoyed reading, but other than the occasional newspaper, he no longer had access to books; being an Indian the libraries denied him admittance; just as when he was younger and the schools denied him admission. He was one of the few people on Allsup's journey, including whites, that knew of Pennsylvania. When he learned of Allsup's quest, the Indian looked at him with astonishment.

"You're a farmer who just decided to give up farming and go on an adventure," Anta Katete observed. "That's unwise; you have no experience. How do you expect to survive?"

Allsup looked upon the Indian with amusement, saying, "I've made it this far."

"I know," acknowledged Anta Katete. "But still—it's dangerous."

"I've been blessed with meeting good people, such as yourself who have been helpful."

"That's hard for me to understand. When I was young, my people died because they wouldn't leave their homes. How could you choose to leave your home? It's your *home*!"

"Bad memories," Allsup explained. "It didn't feel like home anymore."

They were quiet for a time, watching the campfire burning wood to glowing embers before Allsup asked, "How old are you, Anta Katete?"

"Twenty-seven, I think."

"You are fond of Millie, I know."

"She is the only woman for me. She knows this. That's why she told you to tell me she'd be my woman if I took you over the mountains. She knows I would walk through fire for her."

"That's called love," Allsup said, smiling.

"That's a white man's word; I have no word for it."

"Doesn't change anything," countered Allsup. "Call it whatever you wish or call it nothing at all, the way you feel for Millie is what we call love—plain and simple."

Anta Katete looked up at Allsup across the fire, his dark eyes staring intently.

"Is something wrong?" Allsup asked.

"No, nothing is wrong. I don't like losing arguments," explained the Indian. "Especially, to you people. White people feel so superior. It puts you at a disadvantage. You think you're so much smarter than everyone else and when you're not, well, like everyone else, you end up looking foolish."

"I believe what you say is true," agreed Allsup. "But we're not all like that. At least I hope I'm not."

"No," Anta Katete replied stretching out under his bedroll by the fire. "You are probably the exception. I like you, Danny Allsup. Except for leaving your home and land, I'd say you're no fool. Better rest, the mountains ahead won't be this comfortable."

The Indian rolled over onto his side with his back to the fire and the white man, and within seconds, he was breathing the deep heavy rhythm of sleep.

Allsup looked at the back of the large man through the campfire. "I like you too, Anta Katete."

Chapter 60

He had not anticipated the conditions could be so bad. They were on a high mountain path so narrow a misplaced step would result in falling several thousand feet into the invisible; obscured by the heavily falling snow pushed this way and that by the wind. The mountain wall they walked beside, the ground on which they walked, and the tremendous expanse to their left was nothing but white, all white. Allsup clung tightly to the tail of Anta Katete's horse not from fear of getting lost, but to reassure himself that he was not alone; he walked gingerly not knowing if the next step he took would be on solid ground or into air plunging him to the depths below.

Their clothing did little to protect them; the cold wind penetrated as if they wore netting. Using linen strips provided by Anta Katete, wrapped like a scarf around his face leaving only his eyes exposed, his eyelashes and eyebrows caked with ice. Allsup wondered if he'd ever be warm again.

They crossed the eastern range of the Rockies coming down into a basin that greatly contrasted with the cold, snow-covered rocks stretching skywards. There, the land was more level, with gentle rolling hills and stands of trees, a frozen small lake formed at its center, and tall, dry grasses protruded up through the snow around it. Even with an inch of snow on the ground, the basin still felt like a respite from their crossing.

They spent three days resting at a campsite they'd cleared of snow by the lake. Anta Katete killed a rabbit the first night, cooked over a fire of dry kindling; the second night he broke a hole in the ice on the lake and fish was their main course. Anta Katete told him to eat and rest as much as possible because the next range would be more difficult.

The winter months had set in over the Rockies, wind and blizzards were to be expected, and now they found themselves high on a mountain range with no visibility and very little footing.

Allsup's hands were numb; he wasn't sure if Anta Katete's horse's tail was still in his grasp. He tugged and felt resistance, so he wrapped it several times around his hand; only when the tail would pull would he venture forward slowly checking his footing. He held Chestnut's bridle in his other hand with a firm grip, keeping the horse's head as close to him as possible to shield the animal from the freezing winds.

It was their second day crossing the western range seldom taking breaks; there was nowhere to take one. They had continued through the previous night, the darkness of night no more impeded their visibility than the flurrying snow that day, so Anta Katete encouraged him to continue.

Now, on their second night on the range darkness was falling and there seemed little chance of stopping since conditions had not improved. Allsup longed for a cave or deep crevice in the mountain's side where they could escape the elements and rest but that didn't seem likely. The weather had failed to improve and seemed to be deteriorating. He had never felt so helpless and prayed that relief would come soon for his legs were tired, the cold air seemed to burn his throat with each breath, and his whole body felt numb. He was not sure he could continue much longer.

He felt a slight tug and heard, "Damn!"

"What? What is it?" he shouted over the wind. There was no response.

"Anta Katete! What is it?"

He pulled on the horse's tail only to discover that he no longer held it in his hand.

"Anta Katete!" he frantically shouted. "Anta Katete!"

The native did not answer, only the sound of the wind

whistling and howling responded.

He swung his arm back and forth searching for the backside of the horse, but it was not there. In his desperation, he carelessly stepped forward and found no footing. His grip on Chestnut's bridle was all that prevented him from falling. He swung back onto the ledge and clutched Chestnut's head against his chest.

"My God!" he cried out. "My God!"

Checking with his foot, he found that the ledge had narrowed to half its previous size; now there was little more than two feet on which they could travel. He had no inkling how far it continued or how he would safely lead Chestnut along it.

But he knew he had to do something. To do nothing meant certain death.

Pressing his back tight against the mountain wall, he proceeded; one hand stretched out before him feeling along the wall for guidance like a blind man, the other leading his horse who reluctantly but obediently followed.

Allsup grew weary, and along with his weariness, he became despondent. His hands and feet hurt from the cold. No longer able to feel with his hands, his arms were his unit of measure on how round the mountain wall felt in a turn or how straight. His feet now provided nothing but support having long ago lost the ability to measure the terrain; that he had not fallen to his death was the only testimony they were still working.

As they moved along the narrow trail Allsup's arm lost contact with the side of the mountain. He stopped immediately, breathing frantically, wheezing with each breath.

"What happened?"

He swung his arm back and forth but encountered nothing; the mountain was gone. He was reluctant to step forward, he wouldn't know if the path continued until he remained standing after the next step. Clutching Chestnut's bridle, he lifted his leg and set it gingerly down a step ahead. He did not fall.

Where was the side of the mountain? He swung his arm again searching for direction and realized his prayers had been answered: he'd come upon a cave. He took the ends of Chestnut's reins in his left hand and raised the other. The cave roof was a full arm's length above; neither he nor Chestnut would have trouble going through its entrance. He clumsily removed his pistol with his numb right hand, prepared for the unexpected; anything could be seeking shelter.

They ventured deeper; down a long corridor until a sharp left turn removed them from the weather. Though the wind could still be heard, there was nary a breeze that far into the cave. It was still cold, but the cold was not punctuated by the wind; it was a deep cold that settled in and it was dark.

They ventured further into the cave until the sound of the winter storm subsided into a constant drone and the clop, clop, clop of Chestnut's hooves became the dominant sound within. They reached the point where Allsup decided there would be no purpose continuing, it would not get warmer no matter how deep within the Earth they traveled, at least they were out of the wind and snow.

In complete darkness, Allsup unburdened his horse of its cargo allowing the saddle to remain in hopes it would help retain body heat. He rewrapped the ground tarp around Chestnut, and prayed, giving thanks for such a remarkable animal. He bundled the bags containing food together to make a pillow and lay down, huddled into a tight ball along the cave wall. His bedroll provided little warmth, but that was all he had.

He sighed several times as he tried to relax but continued to suffer from the angst of his recent experiences. The memory of nature's wrath beyond the cave caused him to shiver. Recalling Anta Katete's fate resulted in his lamenting occurrences over which he had no control. What is more, the fear that possessed him then possessed him now: What was he to do? How would he find his way?

What if he froze to death while asleep? This thought caused him great concern. Where before he felt so tired, he could barely keep his eyes open and yearned for sleep; now he could not calm his troubled mind to allow it.

To appease himself he decided to force himself to think positively and that led to the conclusion they would resume their journey at first light. The focus on this thought gave him comfort allowing him to slowly succumb to slumber.

Chestnut's slow rhythmic respiration revealed the animal had given in to sleep and Allsup measured the interval between each breath by counting. His eyes grew too heavy to open and he soon ceased trying.

The horse breathed in, it exhaled; it inhaled, it exhaled. Allsup was near to the depth of slumber, lost to this world when in the back of his mind he detected something, something intruding on the rhythmic breathing. He tried to ignore it, casting it out of his mind as he adjusted his blanket on his shoulder, but it would not stay gone; its returning gave him the opinion it must be of importance, so without opening an eye, he gave it his attention and listened.

Snoring! Something or someone was snoring in the cave!

Allsup lay shivering under his blanket wondering what he should do and conceived options for the different scenarios that raced through his mind. If it was another man, there were a couple of ways it could play out: they could partner up and cross the remaining mountain ranges together; or nothing would happen and they'd continue on their separate ways, (for all Allsup knew the stranger maybe traveling east not west); or it could result in violence, not something he wanted to consider.

An animal would result in entirely different scenarios. It could be a hibernating bear, in which case he reasoned, if they remained quiet, they would never know; or perhaps a mountain lion or bobcat was sleeping in their shared cave, which could be dangerous. The animal might awaken hungry, which could result in violence, again not something he wanted to consider.

Allsup yawned as he thought about, and re-thought about, what could be resting in the deep recesses of the cave. He was tired yet could not sleep because of worry and cold.

He became acutely aware of something pushing against his shoulder.

"Aaaugh!" he shouted, jumping to his feet only to discover Chestnut. It took just a moment for Allsup to realize that he could see his horse. He dashed to the turn in the cave and looked down its length to its opening, to daylight. The storm had passed; all was quiet.

He turned back to his horse and excitedly exclaimed, "We've got to get moving while we have the weather!"

Allsup re-loaded Chestnut and was in the process of securing a bag when Chestnut whinnied and nervously took a step back.

"What's wrong? What is it, boy?" Chestnut continued his attempts to pull away, jerking his head and snorting, as Allsup continued his efforts to calm the horse. "Easy, Chestnut, Easy. What's…"

Out of the corner of his eye, Allsup saw movement and became speechless from fear. A large, male mountain lion was ambling toward them and then stopped. His beige coat thick with winter hair appeared spotless and groomed as if recently washed and brushed. The upper portion of his right ear was missing, torn away by a past skirmish. The handsome animal sat and began grooming itself, licking his front paw and rubbing it several times over its good ear, repeating the activity for what seemed a very long time. Eventually, it rose and continued walking, without haste or aggression, toward Allsup and the horse.

Allsup slowly drew his revolver and cocked the hammer

to be ready as the lion continued its advance. Chestnut whinnied again and pulled against his reins.

"No, no, I've got this," Allsup informed the skittish horse, gently rubbing his muzzle. "Shhh, easy Chestnut, I've got this."

The lion came upon them and continued to pass glancing at the two standing nervously along the wall. It stopped at the turn in the cave and looked down the shaft at daylight. The large cat glanced back at its fellow occupants before making the turn and disappeared.

"My God, Chestnut, if this keeps happening, I'll have to join the ministry!" Allsup joked as he quickly completed preparing Chestnut. "I say we move and move fast so we get out of these mountains as soon as possible!"

He led his horse from the cave, and they gazed at the surrounding snow-covered mountain peaks, the bright morning sun sharpened their appearance. The day was crisp and clear, and Allsup felt it only appropriate that they pause and appreciate a view that few have a chance to see. Carefully, and slowly, they followed the narrow trail down the side of the mountain.

Chapter 61

The first running mountain stream not completely iced over quenched their thirst. He took his time to refill his canteens and have a bite to eat. He continued traveling through the mountains following trails made by man or animal, Allsup could not tell. Many led them through the range opening into small canyons where they could find shelter and game. In these instances, they would spend two or three days to rest and recuperate. Other paths ended abruptly at a wall of stone or open air; these obstacles required they return and try a different route.

At the base of one mountain, he entered a large bowl created by a ring of surrounding ranges.

The walls of the monoliths shielded the deep bowl from the snow-peaked blizzards and powerful winds, creating an almost temperate, pleasant climate within. The sun's warmth was a welcome relief from the freezing cold. Tall, brownish-green grass grew in abundance with patches of snow still lingering here and there, remnants from a recent snowfall.

Streams and creeks filled with clear, icy water from melted mountain snow rippled into small ponds that littered the basin. Gently rolling hills and level land dotted with scattered stands of Cottonwood, Birch, and Aspen along with a variety of pines enhanced the beauty of the area and made Allsup wonder if it wasn't Eden.

His favorite times of the day were sunrise and sunset. He was impressed by the way the sunlight played upon the snow-covered mountain peaks, their growing and receding shadows, and the various colors of orange, pink and yellow. Each time of day was different; the only similarity being each was spectacular.

He was no longer in a hurry. He forged for firewood at the stands of trees, hunted on the foothills of the mountains, or fished in the streams and ponds. He would walk through the tall grasses, Chestnut following as he had since their arrival, and would discover he was smiling for no apparent reason.

One early afternoon while heating coffee by the fire as he whittled a point at the end of a long pole, he wanted to try his hand at spearfishing, he heard a whistle. At first, he ignored it thinking the wind in the mountains was playing tricks, but when he heard it a second time, he noted it sounded more human-made. Standing, he surveyed his surroundings and saw a man in the distance waving a hat.

"Well, I'll be," Allsup muttered as he buckled on his holster. "Chestnut looks like we have company."

The horse looked up, saw the man approaching, and returned uninterested to his meal.

"Hey-Oh!" the approaching man called out, laughing. "Hey-Oh!"

His horse was moving at a canter, so they advanced quickly. He was wearing store-bought clothes, some time from new; his thick, worn winter coat, faded red and black checked, was held closed around him by a wide leather belt on which a sheathed knife hung on one side balanced by a holstered gun on the other. A fur hat covered his head, and his boots appeared to have reached the point of comfort. His brown hair was long but did not meet his collar, and his matching beard was neatly trimmed. The mountains and weather made him appear tough and rugged.

Allsup stood, hand resting on the butt of his revolver, watching. He didn't wish to appear unfriendly; however, he did want to project the image of a self-confident man; one not to be trifled with.

"Hey-Oh!" the man cried out again, a grin on his face the size of a mountain range. As he pulled his horse to a stop at the campsite he declared, "Didn't suppose I'd be seeing a man in this canyon, ha-ha-ha! Especially a white one! Ha-ha-ha!"

Danny Allsup

"Same here, I assure you," Allsup replied, grinning. The man's good humor was contagious. "I was making some coffee. Would you like a cup?"

"Coffee? This time'a day?" the man sounded incredulous as he dismounted from his horse. "Don't have anythin' stronger? Somethin' to burn your throat and punch your belly?"

"No, I'm afraid not; just the coffee."

"Well, then coffee will have to do," he responded boisterously as he walked forward extending his hand. "Jack Hamilton. Friends call me Jacky."

"Danny Allsup." He shook the man's hand before offering him coffee in his only cup.

"You ain't having any?" asked Jacky.

"I will shortly, just finished a cup before your arrival.".

"Ain't got another cup, huh?"

"No," Allsup admitted with a laugh. "But go ahead and have it. There's plenty still in the pot. I'll have some after."

"I'm 'bout a mile north'a here," the man explained. "Saw your smoke and wondered if the grass was aflame or if I had company. If it was company, I wanted to know if I should be on guard or sit for a spell."

"How long have you been in the canyon?"

"I don't know, a month or two I 'spect." The guest blew on his coffee to cool it down.

"You're a hunter?" Allsup asked.

"I do hunt."

"Is trapping your trade?"

"I been known to trap."

"Why do you linger here?" This question elicited a belly laugh from the man.

"Look around!" exclaimed Jacky with his arms extended indicating the view. "What man could come to such a place and desire to be somewhere else?"

"I've been having the same thoughts," Allsup admitted.

"How long you been here?"

"Three days. I cannot motivate myself to move on."

"Where you bound?" Jacky asked, handing back the empty cup.

"The Pacific Ocean; I am determined to see it." Allsup refilled the cup, offered it back, and took a sip when the offer was declined.

"That's quite an enterprise; for what purpose?"

"I am determined to see it."

"Well, if you're in no hurry, perhaps you'd care to stay a day or two with me in my cabin; well, you can barely call it a cabin, but it keeps me dry when the rains come and warm when it's cold enough to snow. What'd ya say?"

"I think I will!" Allsup agreed. "We can use a break, can't we Chestnut?" he turned to the horse currently preoccupied. The stallion was poking around the backside of Hamilton's horse. The mare whinnied in half-hearted protest offering little resistance to Chestnut's advances.

"I believe that's a vote for staying on my stud's behalf." The two men laughed as they watched the courtship before turning their backs to the enamored couple.

Allsup stayed three more days with Jacky Hamilton in his makeshift cabin. It was more of a lean-to built against the side of a steep hill put together with random-sized branches and limbs.

At one end a crudely constructed fireplace made from the inside of a hollowed spruce's trunk that stood about seven feet in height, It provided heat and a source for cooking. Along the hillside wall was a firepit dug out in the dirt with a small opening in the thatched-style roof for ventilation.

"What do you do when it rains?" Allsup asked.

"That can be a problem," answered Hamilton. "I've dug a deep, wide trough in the hill above the roof as a runoff for the rain. It works for the most part."

"And when it doesn't?"

"I lose my fire and walk on muddy floors for the rest of

the week!"

The two men spent most of their days riding around the basin exploring and hunting game and vegetation. One afternoon while hunting pheasant Hamilton revealed he was a "cracker jack" shot. He explained that when he was very young, an Indian raiding party killed his father and since he was the oldest of three children, tending the livestock and providing meat on the table became his responsibility.

There were many nights, he added, they went without meat. A farm hand by the name of Lucas O'Reilly taught him the intricacies of first a rifle and then a pistol. While O'Reilly was only at the farm through one summer and early fall, it was time enough to teach young Jacky how to shoot what he was aiming at.

Jacky was self-taught at speed shooting, and after O'Reilly left, the family rarely went without meat with their meals. To prove his point, Hamilton brought down the first pheasant taken to flight flushed from the tall grass using his quickly drawn pistol. Hamilton beamed with pride when the bird hit the ground with a "thud."

"Cracker-jack shot," he repeated as they rode to retrieve the bird.

Allsup, for his part, explained the reason for his journey and the events that occurred along its course over coffee the first evening.

Jacky asked no questions stating, "A man has to do what he has to do." They left it at that.

They chased a herd of antelope over the countryside one afternoon. Coming over a hilltop at a canter, they chanced upon twelve grazing innocently, a mix of bucks with their proud black prong antlers and does. Allsup was the first to pull his rifle and took aim, but Chestnut stumbled causing a misfire. That set the group on the run with the two riders in hot pursuit.

Hamilton fired and missed.

"Damn!" he shouted as they flew over the countryside.

D. Dean Carroll

Allsup took aim as best he could on the back of a galloping horse and fired again. He was sure he hit the ear of a doe, but it did not impede her speed. Jacky Hamilton, the crack shot, fired off three more in rapid succession resulting in a division of the herd, like the parting of the Red Sea, creating a clear, empty path through the middle. The chase passed around a small stand of trees and merged together into a single herd, like water in a creek flowing around a stone.

The antelopes headed down a steep hill in graceful leaps and bounds, their feet barely touching the ground. The horses descended at a full-out gallop, never slacking their stretched-out strides. Both riders were aware that one misstep would send them head-over-heels and most likely break their necks; still, they allowed their horses free rein and held on for dear life.

They reached a stretch of level plain, ideal for picking off the herd, but neither man made the effort; they were too engrossed in the thrill of the chase. The gap between the antelope and the chase grew as the herd gradually pulled away. It seemed as if the antelope had grown tired of the game and decided to leave harm behind. The sweating, panting horses began to slow, so the two men began firing in earnest in hopes of securing dinner for the evening. A doe fell, their efforts rewarded.

The meat popped as it cooked over the open fire. They had it impaled on a large branch stuck in the ground at an angle, the top resting securely against a boulder next to their cabin. The cooking fire cast a yellow illumination around a small area before it gradually gave way to darkness.

The two men sat listening to the meat cooking, the wood in the fire popping, crickets chirping along with other insects of the night providing a fine accompaniment to the occasional owl hoot; both men felt content.

The night sky was filled with stars. The half-moon had reached a third of its ascent while shooting stars streaked across the heavens. The two were in the midst of a contest to see who could spot them first as they passed overhead with Jacky in the lead by two, seven to five. He'd just chalked up number eight when the horses sounded unsettled.

"Sounds like that stud of yours is going to have another go of it," Jacky remarked before adding, "lucky bastard."

"He's unusually active," Allsup observed. "She must be a fine filly."

Their laughter slowly diminished and ended completely when four men with pistols drawn emerged from the darkness.

"Which one'a y'all is Jacky Hamilton?" a short, stocky man asked. He looked tired and ill-humored.

Jacky Hamilton and Danny Allsup both remained seated; neither answered.

"Come on," pleaded another, his gun hanging limply down by his side. "Ya know it's gonna end the same whether ya say or not. Why not save us time and speak up!"

Jacky looked at Danny, but both maintained their silence.

"Ya know," resumed the short, stocky man. "Y'all don't speak up we gotta take both'a y'all in."

"Someone not deserving the bein' taken in," added another wearing a black, round-top derby. "Mayhap won't like bein' taken in."

After the silence continued, the short, stocky man spoke loud and authoritatively, "All right! Both'a y'all git up!" He waved his gun as if meaning to use it. "Git up! Both y'all!"

Allsup jumped to his feet, but Jacky Hamilton remained reclined against his saddle.

"Wait a minute! Wait a minute!" Hamilton protested, using his hands to suggest calming down. "What's the hurry?"

"What?" the short, stocky man was caught off guard by the calm inquiry.

"What?" asked the man in the derby.

"What's the hurry?" Hamilton repeated. "You men are obviously tired, right?"

All four agreed, nodding their heads and mumbling affirmations.

"You've probably been out posseing for a time I'd wager."

Again, they agreed.

"Chasing all over for that damn bank robber."

Shaking heads.

"Probably for days and days."

"How'd ya know he robbed a bank?" Derby asked adjusting his hat.

"Well, I—I think that man there," Hamilton pointed to the short, stocky man, "mentioned…"

"No, I didn't! That's a lie!" The man pointed his pistol at Hamilton.

"All right! All right! You got me," confessed Hamilton, smiling. "I don't want anyone to die over a bank robbery!"

"Too late!" shouted a man standing in the darkness outside the firelight's perimeter. "Ya already killed a man!"

"No, no, I didn't." Still smiling, Hamilton appeared undaunted by this new allegation.

"Yes, ya did, goddamn it!" the man in the shadows sounded emotional. "Joe Crebb! He was'a good man! Just standin' on the sidewalk talkin' to the banker one minute, and the next, lying on the ground stone dead! Ya killed him, and you're gonna answer for it, too!"

"If that's true, I'm very sorry for it." Hamilton was no longer smiling and sounded sincere. "I'll go back; to clear this up one way or the other."

"Alright then git up." The short, stocky man repeated yet again.

"But my question remains the same," Hamilton continued. "What's the hurry? There's an antelope cooking over the fire. I bet you're all hungry, too! Why not rest a spell? Going back in two days isn't going to result any differently than if we go back in one."

"He's gotta point there, Levi," said the as-of-yet unheard from fourth member of the posse. "That meat does smell good. We ain't been eating nothin' but hardtack and jerk these last few weeks and ridin' hard," he explained.

"There, ya see?" Hamilton asked Levi. "You're all tired and hungry; rest and eat! We'll all feel better tomorrow."

"You ain't gonna run off if we do, are ya?" asked Derby.

"What?" Hamilton sounded offended by the question. "If I've killed a man, it's only right that I answer for it. That's *if* I killed the man."

"Oh, it was you what killed him alright." A tall, lanky man joined the circle around the fire and used his hunting knife to cut off a piece of meat from the antelope. Before taking a bite, he added, "There ain't no doubt."

"All right, that's 'nough talk 'bout what happened in Denver City," Levi jumped in. "Right now, let's enjoy this meat and have a little relaxing conversation; or better yet, no conversation would be good."

They talked very little as they consumed the antelope. They left the skeletal carcass on the spit over the fire rather than tossing it aside where it might attract other carnivores. It wasn't long before all six men had reached the point of being sated and were yawning.

"All right, we gonna have to sleep in shifts," the short, stocky Levi announced. "Aaron, you take the first…"

"Why do I have to be first?" Aaron protested. "I need me some sleep! 'Cain't hardly keep my eyes open as it were!"

"Somebody has to be first," Levi patiently explained. "And I choose you. Now, ya give me a spell, Aaron, then I'll relieve ya. Gerald, you be next and then Paul."

The other men nodded while Aaron continued to complain, "I cain't hardly keep my eyes open, I tell ya."

"Should we tether them two?" Paul, wearing the Derby, asked, indicating the two with a nod of his head.

"Tether us?" exclaimed Hamilton. "Why? First off, this man here doesn't have anything to do with what happened in Denver City. He didn't know anything about it till you gentlemen happened along. He wasn't there! We just met up a few days ago as he was crossing the canyon on his way west. Up till now, he probably thought me a decent man."

He turned to Allsup and said, "I'm sorry about all this, Danny, I am. We was having a good time, weren't we?"

"It was a grand time, Jacky," Allsup agreed. "I'll never forget chasing those antelopes."

"Maybe you'll remember me, too," Hamilton added. "I didn't mean to kill that man if I am the one that did it. Let justice be served."

"Well, what 'bout it, Levi?" Paul asked.

"Just Hamilton," Levi answered as he slid down by the fire resting his head on his saddle. "I don't reckon the other was there. Nobody said anything 'bout a second man."

Paul grabbed a coil of rope and headed toward Hamilton to do his duty.

"Wait'a minute! Wait'a minute now," objected Hamilton again. "That's not necessary. Think about it. Where am I going to go? I won't be able to take my supplies, not without alerting you of my intentions. There is no way I could survive out here just as I am! Even if I could sneak off with my horse, I couldn't cross the mountains without freezing to death. You got me, men. I'm ready to go back and take what's coming if I am the one that killed that man."

"Don't forget ya robbed the bank, too," reminded Levi as he pulled his hat down over his eyes. "Let 'im be. Just make sure who's ever takin' watch that ya sit right by him so he cain't pull any funny business, and that be startin' with you, Aaron."

"Aw, gez," he whined as he went over and sat by Hamilton.

"I got that hut there if you want to sleep in there for the night," Hamilton pointed out. "Keep you out of the elements."

"That your place?" Paul asked, looking at the crude structure.

"It is. I built it myself."

"It looks like it," Paul observed with a chuckle. "No, we'll sleep 'round the fire tonight. No tellin' what kind'a traps and such ya got set up in there."

"My word," Hamilton sighed, shaking his head as he reclined on the ground near the fire resting his head on his arm.

The rest of the men settled in for the night, talking quietly. Paul said something that made Gerald, the tall, lanky man, laugh aloud causing Levi to raise his hat and give them a look.

Allsup moved his bedding near Hamilton, and as he prepared to stretch out upon it, Hamilton extended his hand saying, "It's been a pleasure making your acquaintance, Danny." His handshake was firm and sincere. "Good luck with your travels west."

"I have enjoyed our time here, Jacky. I wish you the best of luck."

"Luck. I believe I've used up my allotment of that attribute, at least the good kind."

"Quiet, damn it!" Levi had his hat raised again.

The camp went silent. Soon, various pitches and resonances of snoring joined the sounds of the surrounding night symphony.

Chapter 62

"He's gone!" Gerald, the tall lanky man sounded the alarm. "The scoundrel!"

The five men in the camp were quickly up and racing about in response to their sudden awakening.

"His horse is gone!" Paul announced, disgusted.

"So's his stuff it would appear." Levi calmly stood and observed their surroundings.

All four men turned and looked at Aaron, still rubbing the sleep from his eyes.

"I'm sorry! I told y'all I was too tired!"

"It's too late for that!" shouted Gerald. "That's like 'pologizin' to Joe Crebb for him gettin' killed!"

"Well, I'm tired," Paul, with the black derby, stated. "We been runnin' round the countryside for more than a month. I got a family. I got things to tend to; I got responsibilities. I didn't sign on for this to be a never-endin' endeavor."

"I got things I…" Aaron attempted to contribute.

"Shut up, Aaron," Gerald said bitterly. "We cain't stop now. He cain't be far."

"'Bout a six-hour head start, I figure," said Levi.

"What'd you think, Levi?" Paul asked.

"Well, I didn't know Joe Crebb like Gerald," Levi answered. "He seemed a good man. Everybody that know'd 'im liked 'im, I know that."

"That's right," confirmed Gerald, nodding his head in agreement.

"But ya gotta ask," Levi continued. "How long are we gonna try to track this man down? When do we decide to accept the loss and move on? That's what we gotta ask."

"I say we done our best," Paul proposed. "I say we admit the guy got away and go home. I'm sorry Gerald, but enough is enough."

"I 'gree with Paul," added Aaron.

"What 'bout you, Levi?" asked Gerald with despairing eyes. "You gonna let 'ol Joe Crebb jist be killed like that?"

"I'm sorry Gerald, but I am," conceded Levi. "Let's go home."

The four men began gathering their few belongings, saddled their horses, and mounted to leave without acknowledging Danny Allsup's presence.

"I'm tellin' everybody when we get back that y'all gave up!" Gerald angrily announced as they prepared to depart. Levi walked over to Gerald's horse and grabbed the horse's bridle.

"You tell 'em we gave up if ya wanna but listen to me good." The short, stocky man was looking intently up at Gerald. "You don't say nothin' 'bout us havin' 'im and he gettin' away. It's embarrassin' enough we failed to catch 'im, no need to compound the failure. Everyone hear that? We don't mention he slipped through our fingers."

The other three men nodded in agreement.

Levi was the last to mount his horse. Turning to the others, he said, "Let's go home, men."

The four headed east across the canyon, the rising sun had just peaked the mountain ridges. Aaron looked back at Allsup still standing by the fire and waved.

Smiling, Allsup watched them ride away.

D. Dean Carroll

Chapter 63

He resumed his solitary journey across the canyon, half expecting, half hoping that Jacky Hamilton would appear on the horizon and join his adventure. That did not occur, so he traveled on continually gaining altitude.

Looming before him was another snow-covered range. The timberline that grew from the base of the mountains to the semi-grass-covered canyon upon which he now traveled looked dense and daunting. The dark green pines ribboned along mid-mountain like a belt, in contrast to the white snow above and the yellowish-brown grass below.

As the elevation increased so did the amount of snow-covered ground, the grasses grew sparse as patches of exposed rock became more prominent. It was not unusual for Allsup to awaken in the morning covered in dry powdered snow. He simply tossed aside his cover and the snow would fall.

He found to his good fortune the canyons had an abundance of streams and creeks that crisscrossed the landscape. He was never without fresh, cold water, or fish to eat if he could muster the patience and determination. Though it was becoming increasingly colder, and he was perpetually aware of his isolated existence, he found himself smiling more often than not and generally felt good.

It is as it should be, he thought riding his chestnut stallion. Just the two of us traveling west as we started.

He entered the timberline to the loud "swishing" wind passing through the upper swaying branches of the trees. At ground level, amongst the trees, it darkened as if dusk beneath the canopy above. Looking up he could see occasional glimpses of the sky through the gracefully waving greenery.

When he finally rode clear of the timberline high above

the foothills, he saw a gap in the mountain that he thought could be a pass. That became his destination, his focus as he rode increasingly higher.

Once again, the air grew thin and sharply cold. Allsup's beard, decorated with sprinkles of ice and snow, protruded between the folds of the scarf wrapped around his face. It had been some time since he last shaved. He vowed that would be his top priority upon reaching civilization again, to lose the beard.

The streams and creeks began to freeze over, often covered by thick sheets of ice; in several, the water was completely solidified. They camped by one that had the potential to still provide water but didn't. Having cleared an area of snow, he settled for hardtack and jerky for the evening meal and gave his horse several handfuls of grain.

Dusk turned into night as he lay atop his ground tarp, rolled up in two heavy blankets. He settled in a fetal position with a water jug under his shirt pressed tight against his bare belly and waited for sleep. The mountain gap stayed in his thoughts. He hoped it would be the pass that would get him through. He listened to Chestnut sleeping and longed for morning; he was eager to be on his way.

… D. Dean Carroll

Chapter 64

The gap in the mountain range was just what he had hoped for; though covered in snow, Allsup and Chestnut made it through in a single day's time. From high on the western side, he could see the land spread out for miles and miles with several small communities not far from the base with a large lake to the north. Beyond that, to the west, the land appeared to be dry, arid, and foreboding.

He spent one night halfway down the mountainside next to a creek that provided water, its ice covering thin enough to break under the heel of his boot. He followed the creek winding its way down until he reached the mountain's base then headed due west across terrain that gradually turned from green to brown and barren.

The second day down from the mountain, he entered Fillmore City late in the morning. A sign announced its name and boasted a population of 2,748. The city spread out between the Pioneer and Chalk creeks with mountains rising on every side in the distance.

Danny Allsup entered the town happily. He was glad to be out of the mountains and with people again. He took a room at the Fillmore City Hotel and Restaurant on Main Street and after getting Chestnut settled in a nearby stable, he stretched out and relaxed in the hotel's fine lobby.

Four large chairs, a classic round-armed sofa, and a chaise lounge, all upholstered in bright red velvet with embellished brass tacks, were thoughtfully placed throughout the lobby on worn carpets. The couch faced two of the high-backed chairs, while the chaise lounge was isolated along one wall and two other chairs were independently located in the back to ensure those wishing solitude could find it. Allsup selected one such chair, in the rear of the lobby, facing the front affording a view of all activity.

The proprietors of the hotel were Mr. Hawkins and his wife, who also managed the restaurant. They were an older couple with graying hair and widening waistlines who seemed born in good spirits with a desire to please. Mr. Hawkins, it was implied, managed the hotel and, indeed, could always be found behind the reception counter monitoring the comings and goings of those who entered and departed. Many who entered were town regulars stopping by for meals, coffee and conversation.

"Morning, Mr. Hawkins," one greeted upon entering the establishment's lobby before passing through the French doors that opened to the restaurant.

"Good morning, Mr. Beasley," the proprietor replied before addressing another. "Having your coffee in the lobby, I see, Mr. Johnson. Good!"

"I hear Fort Union is getting a new battalion, Major Barnett." Hawkins rested his arms intently on the counter. "Will they be passing through Fillmore City?"

"Did the freight arrive yet, Mr. Hawkins?" inquired a farmer who made no attempt to step past the entranceway.

"About an hour ago, Thomas; best hurry if you're wanting some of those chicks that survived the passage."

"I'm on my way!" called out the departing Thomas. "My best to Mrs. Hawkins!"

In this manner, Mr. Hawkins would address all who passed. The true manager of the whole enterprise, however, was Mrs. Hawkins.

At no specific time during any part of each day, she'd appear at the counter and inquire about the day's activities. How many checked in? How many checked out? Was he going to have Margie dust the lobby today, or did Mr. Hawkins feel it could be put off another month or two? And the Mexican in 2-A had to go; the señor had only paid for his first night's lodging, and he'd been with them for almost ten days! Mr. Hawkins was to talk to him today and that was that!

"That's the problem, Mrs. Hawkins," her husband meekly explained. "Señor Santiago doesn't speak a word of English, and I don't speak Spanish. The last time I tried to converse with the man he got the impression his meals are now free, and I can't convince him otherwise."

"He's been eating free all this time?" asked an astounded Mrs. Hawkins, her face reddening while her throat, which bulged out like a bullfrog's, jiggled from suppressed anger.

"Well, for the better part of the week, I'd suggest."

"Well, Mr. Hawkins, why wasn't I told?"

"Because of this."

"Because of what exactly?".

"This conversation."

"You didn't inform me earlier because you didn't want to discuss it?"

"I put it off as long as I could," a sheepish Mr. Hawkins replied glancing around the lobby to see who might be overhearing the exchange. There was only the new guest who had signed in earlier.

"For as long as you could?" she sputtered. "Mr. Hawkins, you do this frequently. Why put off having a conversation that you know to be inevitable?"

"I've had the conversation, Mrs. Hawkins, just…not with you."

"You've discussed this with others?"

"Sure."

"Like…who?" exasperated, she clutched the countertop for support.

"Well, most everybody, I guess. Frankly, I'm surprised you haven't got wind of it before now."

"Everybody!" Mrs. Hawkins appeared astounded. "You sir!" she called out to Allsup sitting in the back. "Did you know of this?"

"Ma'am?" Allsup leaned forward in his chair.

"Oh, never mind!" With a huff, she turned to leave but before she disappeared within the restaurant she added, "Señor Santiago goes today!"

Mr. Hawkins stared at the empty doorway before glancing back toward Allsup. With a what-can-you-do smile, he shrugged his shoulders and returned to looking over the guest registry appearing managerial.

Two little blond-haired girls came running into the lobby from the restaurant laughing as they jumped from one chair to another. Mr. Hawkins quickly scurried them back through the door, like chickens into a pen, before smiling apologetically to the man in the back.

Chapter 65

The next morning found the weather disagreeable; it was attempting to snow, but the current conditions hadn't yet been decided. There was a fusion of the stuff, heavy and wet, mixed intermittently with rain, rain so cold it often morphed into sleet. The new wet snow was settling nicely upon the previously fallen; if the temperature did drop, it would most certainly freeze glass-like and dangerous.

Allsup decided while lying in bed to remain where he was and forgo his intention of departing Fillmore City one more day. With a heavy quilt spread over the bed and soft cotton sheets hugging his body, one more day seemed exactly the correct decision to make. He happily drifted in and out of sleep, snuggled warm in his bed. It was during one such period when sleep had overtaken him that a knock sounded abruptly upon the door.

"Mr. Allsup? Mr. Hawkins here. Sir, may I inquire if you'll be leaving us this morning?"

"What?" asked Allsup, his mind still groggy from sleep.

"My wife, Mrs. Hawkins and I wanted a word with you before you leave as we are of the opinion you intend to depart this morning."

"That was my intention," Allsup responded, yawning. "But the weather has changed my mind."

"Oh! Oh, I see. Well, then we'll have a chance to speak later, as I understand it."

"Yes, yes, later."

"Rest well, Mr. Allsup."

It was late morning when Allsup entered the restaurant and found it deserted except for a young woman sweeping the floors around the tables. She glanced up, noticing the customer, smiled and said, "Wherever ya like, sir." And resumed her task.

He selected a table where he believed the floors had already been swept and sat down.

He sat waiting for several minutes before the young floor sweeper glanced up and noticed.

"Mrs. Hawkins!" she called out. "Ya got a customer!"

"Well, Lucy," came a scolding voice from the back. "See to him!"

"Sorry, mister, I thought Mrs. Hawkins was comin' to wait on ya, but she ain't after all," Lucy explained as she approached his table while wiping her hands on her apron. "It was a busy morning."

"That's all right," he replied with a wave of his hand. "Not a concern."

"What can I get ya?"

"May I still get breakfast?"

"You can get whatever ya want."

"Good! I'll have fried ham, three eggs with a soft yoke, and biscuits and gravy, please."

"Fried ham, three eggs soft, and biscuits," she repeated. "Only got beef gravy this time'a day just before lunch and all. Still want it?"

"No, just the biscuits, thank you."

"Sir, ya stayin' at the hotel here or just come in for the food?"

"No, I'm a guest here."

"Well, could I have your name? Mrs. Hawkins is on the lookout for one'a her guests."

"Allsup."

"Thank ya, Mr. Allsup. I'll get this goin' for ya."

She had just disappeared through a door in the back when another door not six feet away on the same back wall swung open and out came Mrs. Hawkins, followed by the two little blond-haired girls teasing one another.

"Mr. Allsup, good morning, sir!" she cheerfully greeted as she hastily dashed past him to the entrance of the hotel. "Please give me one minute."

"Come along, girls," the woman chastised. "Keep up!"

From the back of the restaurant, Lucy called out, "Would ya like some coffee, Mr. Allsup?"

"Yes, please, that would be good."

Mrs. Hawkins returned, along with the two little blond-haired girls and Mr. Hawkins.

"Ah, Mr. Allsup," Mr. Hawkins greeted him, eagerly shaking his hand. "No, no, don't get up. May we join you?"

He pulled out a chair for his wife.

"Yes, certainly."

"How is your stay?" Mrs. Hawkins pleasantly asked. "The room is to your liking? The bed?"

"I am enjoying my stay. With the weather outside such as it is, the bed was too inviting and held me captive longer than usual."

"Good, good." Mrs. Hawkins smiled while nodding her head.

"Good, good," Mr. Hawkins did the same.

"Good," added Mrs. Hawkins one more time.

"Do you have something you want to tell me?" Allsup asked.

"What? Tell you? No!" Mr. Hawkins laughed in response, along with his wife.

"A question then, do you want to ask me something?" The laughter stopped though the smiles remained frozen in place.

After a period of discomfort for all, Allsup asked, "Well?"

"We do have a favor to ask of you," conceded Mr. Hawkins.

"A Christian request," hastily added his wife.

"You have my attention.

To Lucy as she delivered his coffee, "Thank you."

After the pause of another minute, Mrs. Hawkins jerked her head towards her husband, encouraging him to continue.

"We are under the impression you're heading west,"

Mr. Hawkins began. "I overheard you speaking with another gentleman in the lounge."

"That's correct."

"How far west, if I may ask?" Mr. Hawkins inquired.

"To the Pacific Ocean."

The husband and wife looked at each other approvingly.

"You appear to be a Christian man, Mr. Allsup. Are you?" Mrs. Hawkins was quite earnest in her question.

"I am, yes," he answered.

"Oh, I like that!" exclaimed Mr. Hawkins. "No hesitation!"

"Oh, Mr. Allsup, you have been sent to us by Divine Providence!" Mrs. Hawkins excitedly declared. "The hand of God led you to us! Yes sir! Amen!"

"Amen!" repeated Mr. Hawkins, his eyes closed tightly.

"Amen," Lucy's light voice sounded in the back.

"I'm not sure I understand." Allsup looked from one to the other.

"We are in need of a shepherd, Mr. Allsup," Mr. Hawkins explained. "Someone to watch over our dear lambs and guide them safely home to their loved ones."

"Again, I'm still not sure what you're talking about."

"Cindy!" called out Mrs. Hawkins. "Sandy! Come here girls." The two blond-haired girls shyly approached the table.

"These two sweet things are our lambs." Mrs. Hawkins had an arm wrapped around each. "Not really ours, of course, but left in our care. You see, their mother, Mrs. Clipper, was a California Widow. The family was separated because of work, you know. She was taking their daughters to Sacramento to rejoin their father. They were traveling along with another family when she took sick and, well..." she covered one ear of each girl with a hand while pressing the other ear against her breasts. "She didn't recover. Before she passed, Mr. Hawkins and I promised to watch over these two until transport to Sacramento could be arranged."

"I am sorry to hear of their misfortune," Allsup consoled. "I don't know which is hardest, losing a parent or losing a child."

"It's a heartbreak both ways," said Mr. Hawkins, solemnly nodding his head.

"So, we call these two our little lambs," a more upbeat-sounding Mrs. Hawkins advised. "This is Cindy. She's the oldest. Tell the nice man how old you are, Cindy."

"I don't remember," the young girl answered.

"Yes, you do. Remember what comes after four? What comes after four, Cindy?"

"I don't remember." The girl stared down at the floor.

"How many fingers are on your hand, Cindy?" Smiling to Allsup, Mrs. Hawkins tried a different approach. "Count your fingers, Cindy."

"Five!" called out the other little girl.

"Yes, it's five, Sandy, but I wanted Cindy to tell us," the woman scolded as she squeezed the little girl affectionately. "We *know you* know the answer. It was Cindy's turn."

"But she didn't know, Grandma Hawkins. She kept telling you so."

"This little know-it-all is Sandy. Tell the nice man how old *you* are, Sandy."

"I'm three, but I'm gonna be four real soon," she proudly advised.

"Really?" an impressed Allsup asked. "When?"

"In twenty-three days. In twenty-three days, I'm gonna be four."

"Well, I'll be! And you're only three! And when is your birthdate?"

"December fifth, I'm gonna be four."

"December fifth—that means today is November—November thirteenth!"

"It is," confirmed Mr. Hawkins.

"And what day is it?"

"It's a Sunday, Mr. Allsup," answered Mr. Hawkins. "That's why the place is so empty. Come dinner, though, we'll be hopping."

"I'll be, Sunday, November thirteenth. It's been a long time since I knew that." Allsup thought for a minute before adding. "You know, I can't even remember the day I left."

"Mr. Allsup, back to the children." Mrs. Hawkins embraced the two girls again. "Knowing you're a Christian, God-fearing man, surely you'll not turn away from this mission He has placed before you?"

"Mission? I'm still confused."

"The children, Mr. Allsup," Mr. Hawkins broke in. "Will you take them?"

"Take them? Take them where?"

"Why, west, of course, with you!" Mrs. Hawkins answered, smiling.

Lucy laughed in the back, drawing a quick look of rebuke from the restaurant's manager.

"What? Wait!" Allsup was finally getting the picture. "You want me to take these two girls with me on horseback across the mountains?"

"Oh, heavens no!" replied Mrs. Hawkins with a laugh.

"Heavens no!" echoed her husband.

"You'll take them by train!" Mrs. Hawkins explained. "You'll take the Central Pacific out of Ogden. It will take you directly to Sacramento; you'll arrive in two or three days, I'm told."

"By train! I was not planning to travel by train!" Allsup sounded a bit frantic. "It was my intention from the very start to travel the distance by horse, on Chestnut."

"Oh, so you've used no other means of transportation?" asked Mr. Hawkins.

"Well. I did travel by flatboat down the Ohio," Allsup admitted.

"What's a flatboat?" asked Cindy.

"It's a boat that's flat!" an exasperated Sandy explained.

"Shh!" Mrs. Hawkins shot a glance at the two.

"I've traveled by paddleboat."

"Uh-huh?" Mr. and Mrs. Hawkins waited.

"I guess I'd have to add by wagon."

"So, you're not adverse to other means then?" Mr. Hawkins asked.

"I guess not, but..."

"Excellent!" Mr. Hawkins exclaimed as he rose from the table. "It's settled then!"

"Girls! This nice man is going to take you to your father!" Mrs. Hawkins announced. "Isn't that wonderful? And you're going to get to ride on a train!"

The two girls excitedly jumped up and down, singing, "We're going to ride on a tra-ain! We're going to ride on a tra-ain!"

"We'll work out the arrangements later," Mr. Hawkins informed the stunned man sitting at the table. Joining his wife, they escorted the girls out of the restaurant and into the lobby, leaving Allsup alone.

"Still gotta appetite?" asked Lucy, grinning. She was holding a plate in one hand and a pot of coffee in the other. "Ya haven't touched your coffee much neither. Want it warmed up?" Allsup sat staring as if in a trance; his brain seemed to have shut down.

When he failed to respond, she set the plate down gingerly so as not to disturb and picked up his cup, saying, "I'll just fresh this up."

Chapter 66

They traveled by covered wagon whose bent metal hoops formed a canopy over the back with a canvass cover. Once again, Chestnut was harnessed, pulling this time alongside a pretty black and white pinto mare that caused Allsup to worry. Should she go into heat during their trip, there'd be no controlling Chestnut and would require an explanation to the children. Neither of which he wanted to deal with.

Mrs. Clipper and the two girls had arrived with a wagon full of personal belongings and two horses. Except for the pinto mare and wagon, everything else had been sold, according to Mr. Hawkins, to pay for the children's expenses.

The wagon now contained very little. Allsup's saddle, bridle, and saddlebags containing his personal belongings rested in the corner behind the wagon's front bench seat. A large wooden traveler's chest located across from Allsup's gear held the girls' neatly folded clothes and other personal items. Quilts and pallets donated by several of the fine people of Fillmore City were carefully stacked in the gap between their personal possessions. There were also several small boxes of food and containers of water, Allsup's cooking utensils, and two cloth-made dolls with embroidered facial features, one missing an arm.

With so much vacancy in the back of the wagon, the girls had ample room to play. Before their departure Allsup purchased two Dixon graphite pencils, with the newly designed eraser attached on one end. Now images of animals and people, mountains, horses, and flowers decorated the wagon's floor and side panels.

They rode past Fort Union at a considerable distance, whose adobe structures were busy with activity. The girls stood on the bench seat for better viewing as they passed but soon lost interest and resumed playing.

They stopped two times in the morning: once for the girls, the second time for Allsup *and* the girls. Sandy and Cindy took care of their necessities back behind the wagon while Allsup remained seated in the front; Allsup would use the side of the wagon while the girls remained enclosed within.

They had a lunch prepared by Mrs. Hawkins consisting of thin slices of ham between two thick slices of buttered bread. They agreed it was an easy way to eat their food, and the jar of pickled eggs could wait until dinner.

Shortly after lunch, Allsup and the two girls climbed down from the wagon to walk. Allsup thought it would be good for all to walk, having been confined to the wagon for the better part of the day. He descended first from the moving wagon and prompted each girl to jump and keep pace with the wagon pulled by the two strong horses. The girls eagerly welcomed the opportunity to walk and run. Allsup would often join in and give chase around the always advancing wagon. He tried to teach them Duck, Duck, Goose in the snow, but it took too long, and they were constantly stopping to catch up with the wagon.

Eventually, they climbed back on board, where the girls spread out their night pallets, rolled up in their blankets, and napped stretched out in the back. Allsup was tired from the activity and crisp fresh air and could easily have dozed off himself, but he didn't want the horses to lose direction.

It occurred to him as he held the limp reins in both hands that this was the first time on his trip that he intentionally diverted from his original direction. Not only was he not traveling west but traveling north…to ride a train. It could be because he was tired, but he found this to be an irritable situation. As he remembered it, he'd been manipulated into this task, and he was mad at himself for having allowed it. He and Chestnut, riding due west, overcome what may, completing their quest as originally planned. That is what he should be doing.

Perhaps, he considered, he could find a couple in Ogden, traveling west, that would agree to take them along, or if necessary, someone that would be willing to take them for a fee.

His responsibility was to get them to their father, he reasoned. He didn't necessarily have to do it personally as long as the task was completed.

A small blond head popped through the cloth flaps that separated the front of the wagon from the back.

"I had a bad dream," Cindy said as she rubbed her eyes. "It was about Momma."

"Well, it was only a dream."

"Yeah, but it was about *Momma!*" she stressed and began to cry.

"Well..." Allsup was at a loss and busied himself with minding the horses.

"She was supposed to take us to daddy," the little girl continued between sobs. "Now she's gone. What if we can't get to daddy?"

"Oh, now don't worry about that," he consoled. "You'll be with your daddy again in no time."

"What if something happens?"

"Nothing is going to happen."

"How do you know?"

"Well, because...because..." he looked down at her teary blue eyes waiting for assurance. "Because I'm going to make sure nothing bad happens. I'm going to make sure you and Cindy...

"I'm Cindy."

"You and *Sandy* reach your father, and you'll all be together again."

"You're going to take us?"

"Yes, I am." She was kneeling in the back with her head thrust through the curtain flap, considering this information.

"Can I sit with you?" she asked.

"Yes, come on." She climbed through the curtain onto the buckboard seat still wrapped in her blanket and sat straight and rigid, curiously glancing up at him from time to time.

"Why's your nose like that?" she asked, referring to his hawkish-shaped nose.

"It's always been like that," he answered, glancing at her.

"It looks funny."

"Some might say it looks noble."

"I don't know what that means, but I think it's funny."

"Thank you."

"Are you cold?" Allsup asked.

She shook her head no.

As they rode on, her head slowly came to rest against his shoulder. He put his arm around her and pulled her over to him where she could snuggle between his arm and chest for warmth.

"Are you tired?" he asked.

"No."

On they rode, occasionally talking but mostly quiet.

By late afternoon, both girls were up and playing in the back of the wagon when the small town of Holden appeared on the horizon; Allsup decided to stop there for the night.

The town was located at the base of the mountains, surrounded by scrub trees and sagebrush; to the west was mostly arid. A cluster of buildings formed the town's center, with blocks of adobe houses spreading out in different directions. As they rode into Holden, they became objects of curiosity. People stepped out of doorways, houses, the general store, and a saloon to watch them ride through their town. When they pulled up to a saloon, several people gathered on the building's covered porch to watch them descend from the wagon.

"Good day to you all," Allsup spoke rather loudly to the

small crowd. "Do they serve food here?" he gestured toward the saloon.

"They serve food, all right," answered an older man. "It ain't good food. I'll tell ya that." A ripple of laughter ran through the group. "But to answer your question, yeah, they serve food."

"Good! Let's go eat, girls." He jumped to the ground and helped each of the girls down before taking their hands and heading toward the saloon's entrance.

"What are you doing, sir?" demanded a frumpish-looking woman stepping before them.

Caught by surprise, Allsup stammered for a response, "Getting dinner for the girls and myself, ma'am."

"Not in there!" shouted another woman joining the first. They both wore calico dresses, one in a faded green check pattern, the other a faded gray.

"What?" Allsup, confused, finally spoke.

"You'll not take those sweet young angels into a saloon!" declared the first lady. "Not in Holden!" Many in the crowd murmured their assent.

"Do you have another eating establishment in this town?" Allsup inquired.

"We do not," answered the second woman in the green-checkered dress with her hands defiantly on her hips.

"Well, ladies, these two girls have been entrusted in my care," Allsup patiently explained. "It is my intention to feed them. Unless you have another suggestion, I ask that you step aside so that we might enter this establishment to fulfill that task."

"Little girls and proper young ladies do not cater to bars and saloons, my good man!" the second lady adamantly declared.

It was a standoff as old as the Bible itself: a woman with a made-up mind and a man determined to change it. The two women stood blocking their passage, one with arms crossed and the other with fists firmly upon her hips. Allsup remained by the wagon with a young girl standing on either side, each holding his hand.

"Can anyone suggest a resolve to this predicament?" he beseeched the crowd.

"You can send 'em home with me," a younger woman proposed. She was slim, with brown hair pulled back into a bun. "I'll feed 'em, and they can spend the night too if you've a mind to stay that long."

"That's very kind of you, ma'am, but the girls have been entrusted to me. I've vowed not to leave them until they're reunited with their father."

"Well, come yourself, then," responded the woman. "I'll find someplace to put ya."

"Gertie, no!" objected the older woman dressed in calico, blocking his passage. "You can't have a man stayin' in your home without someone else bein' there! It ain't proper."

"I have no concern about what others might think of what goes on in my home," countered Gertie. "It's my home. I do as I best see fit. If Charlie's ain't good enough for those two children, then they're welcome to my home. It ain't Christian to do otherwise. They need to eat. I'll feed 'em; him too, if that's what it takes."

"It ain't proper," repeated the older woman, "You bein' a widow and all."

"I'll go with you, Gertie," volunteered another young woman, fair of complexion with dark blond hair. "That way, you'll be chaperoned, and it'll all be right and proper. Is that all right, Momma?"

A woman standing next to her nodded her consent along with the few others that remained at the saloon's entrance. Many had lost interest and dispersed, those that remained were losing attention once it became obvious there would be nothing more.

"Thank you, Rebecca," Gertie responded, and to Allsup, "If ya want to leave your rig with Smitty next door, he'll tend to your horses and your wagon will be safe."

Allsup thanked the two young women, and after depositing the horses and rig with Smitty, he and the two girls followed the women to Gertie's home, an adobe-built structure, much like most of the others, with smoke rising from its chimney.

It was dark when they finished their meal of boiled chicken and dumplings. Soon after, Allsup announced it was time they went to bed, for it was his hope to get an early start the next day.

Gertie instructed the girls to lay out their pallets at the foot of her bed in an area closed off from the rest of the room by a drawn curtain. She explained that she and Rebecca would be sleeping in the bed while Allsup could choose a spot on the floor. It wasn't long before the house was dark and quiet, the only light provided by the fireplace and the only sound was the cracking and popping of burning wood.

Allsup, stretched out on the floor wrapped in his blanket to ward off evening chills, sighed heavily and was soon breathing deeply. He dreamt of home, a real dream as if he was still there with them: he unknowingly smiled as he fished with his two sons; they argued over fishing poles, whose was whose.

In his dream, he was out in that intense thunderstorm when Betty, one of their milking cows, was having a difficult birth and refused to move from the hillside. He and Nancy delivered the calf in the pouring rain, standing ankle-deep in water as it rushed down the hill. He smiled again as his wife laughed that delicate laugh she had, like glasses bumping as they stood with his arms wrapped around her on the porch of their farmhouse watching the sunset; she seductively began to nibble on his neck. He smiled more as she began to rub her hand across that area that only a wife should and felt little kisses splash across his face. Her hand became more familiar and soon, he moaned softly in his sleep. It felt so real he never wanted to wake up, but he did so with the gradual realization that it *was* real, that there was someone's hand underneath his blanket!

"Whoa! Whoa! Whoa!" he exclaimed as he jumped to his feet.

Both women "Shhh'd!" simultaneously.

Recovering from his shock, he realized he was standing uncovered and exposed with his pants open. He quickly grabbed the blanket from the floor, covering himself, and, in doing so, exposed the two females who emitted muffled cries of alarm.

Gertie and Rebecca, giggling, pulled at the blanket to cover themselves while Allsup refused to relinquish any of his concealment.

"Now, now, stop!" he whispered sternly; they did. He turned his back to them while dropping the blanket and corrected his clothing, allowing them the use of the covering in its entirety.

"Are you covered?" he whispered. After they replied in the affirmative, he turned to address them properly.

"What are you doing?"

"We thought that maybe you would welcome some company," answered Rebecca, smiling coyly.

"What with you just passin' through, it seemed the perfect opportunity to indulge ourselves," Gertie added. "I been alone for a good long while now."

"Least ways you had a man," Rebecca pointed out. "I'm still waitin'."

"It's worse to already experience a man and lose 'im," argued Gertie. "Because then ya…ya know what you're missin'."

"I think not knowin' and wantin' is worse," countered Rebecca forlornly.

"Excuse me, ladies." Allsup stood over them with his hands on his hips. "What's going on here?"

"We thought you'd like it," Gertie explained. "Plain and simple. I thought most men would; I thought most men didn't care who they was with, they just liked it."

"We was hopin' you would," added Rebecca holding the blanket under her chin before allowing it to slide down to the top of her shoulders.

"We was hopin' it would be mutually beneficial," continued Gertie. The blanket slowly dropped to her lap. "That we would all be happy."

"You don't understand," Allsup protested. "I'm a Christian man!"

"We're both Christian women!" Gertie retorted.

"Yeah." giggled Rebecca. "You could look at it as we're God's gift to each other!"

"God led you to us," Gertie said mischievously, as she rose to her knees, allowing the blanket to slide to the floor. "It's what they call dee…dee…"

"Divine Intervention," Allsup completed her thought.

"Yeah, it's Divine Intervention that brought you to us… 'n us to you."

Rebecca rose to her knees, letting the blanket fall so that the two young women were kneeling before him without any manner of apparel like the sirens from Homer.

"Divine Intervention…" Allsup contemplated.

"Divine Intervention," the two women repeated.

"Right."

Chapter 67

Allsup and the two little girls rode out of Holden, Utah, just after sunrise. They had breakfast of biscuits and honey, and Gertie packed lunch from the previous night's boiled chicken and the remaining biscuits from breakfast.

They had not been traveling long before the girls realized that there had been a major change in Allsup's disposition. They were riding on the bench seat of the covered wagon, a girl sitting on each side of the man.

"What's wrong?" asked the eldest, Cindy.

"What do you mean?" Allsup responded. "Nothing's wrong."

"You're smiling," Sandy pointed out.

"No, I'm not…Am I?"

"Yesterday, you looked mad all day," Cindy noted. "Now you're smiling all the time."

"I wasn't aware of it."

"That you're smiling?" Cindy asked in disbelief.

"Yes, and that I appeared mad yesterday. I wasn't, by the way."

"Well, you're smiling a lot today!" Sandy exclaimed.

"That's a good thing, though, right?"

"Yeah," Cindy agreed. "But it makes your nose look bigger."

They rode in silence with only the sound of horse hooves striking the ground like the clapping of a big-handed man.

Sandy, the youngest, noticed his holstered pistol at his side. She reached down and rubbed her finger over the smooth leather before sliding it up over the metal hammer. Allsup noticed her curiosity.

"What do you think?" he asked.

"It looks big," she answered. "Is it heavy?"

"It has some weight to it, but I wouldn't call it heavy."

"Can I hold it?" She asked as she reached down to remove the gun.

"No." She withdrew her hand and let it rest in her lap, but her eyes wandered back to the revolver.

"Have you shot it before?" Sandy inquired.

"I have, yes."

"Have you shot anything with it?"

"Yes."

"What?" she asked.

"What?"

"What have you shot with it?"

"Many things."

"People?"

"What?"

"Have you ever shot a person before?" He didn't respond immediately, not being totally sure how he should continue. Should a young child be told the truth about such things, he wondered? Perhaps it's better to be evasive on such topics rather than risk upsetting the child with the truth. He was a staunch believer in honesty, though, and often told his sons the truth may hurt, but people will never doubt what you say if you're known for it. Honesty, he would say, garners respect.

"I regret to say I have."

"Really?" she sounded surprised.

"Really, what?" asked her sister Cindy.

"Mr. Allsup shoots people!" exclaimed Sandy.

"Wait! Now, wait!" Allsup jumped in quickly. "I don't shoot people! You asked if I've ever shot someone, and I honestly told you I have. But…"

"How many people have you shot, Mr. Allsup?" Cindy asked.

"Oh, I don't know."

"More than one?" screamed Sandy, rather shocked by the prospect.

"Well…"

"How many?" Cindy asked again.

"Well, there were these Indians, and…"

"Oh, Indians." The enthusiasm of both waned sharply upon this revelation, their disappointment obvious.

"What does that mean?" questioned Allsup.

"We thought you meant you killed *people*," Sandy explained.

"Indians *are* people."

"No, they're not," Cindy argued. "Momma said Indians ain't people. So did Uncle Sy and a bunch of people on our way here. They all say Indians ain't people. They're savages."

"Why do they say that?" Allsup asked.

"Look at them," Sandy explained. "They don't look like us!"

"Well." Allsup gave it thought before continuing. "They may not look like us, I admit; I mean, their skin is darker, and they all have dark eyes and hair, and they don't dress like we do, but what about everything else?"

"What do you mean?" asked Sandy; both girls were listening attentively.

"Well, we have two eyes, they have two eyes; we have a nose and a mouth, so do they, in the same place we do. Arms and legs, fingers and toes, we have them, so do Indians. We're really just different versions of the same thing."

"I don't get it," Cindy complained.

"Me neither," admitted Sandy.

"Okay, look at the two horses there," Allsup indicated the two pulling the wagon. "Are they both horses?"

"Yes!" they both cried out, giggling.

"Why? One is brown and the other is black and white. How do you know they're both horses?"

"Because," Cindy began to answer. "Look at them! They both have four legs and…"

"Oh," Sandy interrupted. "I know what you mean now."

"What?" asked Cindy.

"He's saying if the horses look different but the same and we call both horses, then people can look different but the same and we call them people. Right, Mr. Allsup?"

"That's it!" he was surprised and happy that he was able to enlighten the two and believed confidently that he was right regardless of what others might say. "It's the same for the Negro."

"The what?" they both asked.

"Negro…black man."

"A black man!" Cindy repeated skeptically.

"Yes, there are black people in the world, living here in the United States."

"Are there black women?" Cindy asked.

"Yes, of course."

"And black children?"

"Yes. Surely you've seen them. There are different colored people living all around the world, but they're all people. They look different but the same."

"But what about…" Sandy started to ask when Allsup interrupted.

"Let's play the Quiet Game, want to?" he proposed. "The first one to speak loses. Okay? Okay. One, two, three start!"

While in Fillmore City, Allsup learned that Holden was the town south of Scipio, about fifteen miles away and generally took a full day by wagon to travel from one to the other because of the rough terrain. After Scipio, it was a two-day ride to Nephi with nothing in between. That would be their next test.

The people of Scipio were not as zealous in their moral beliefs as those in Holden; curiosity still drew a few to the street to view the newcomers. They stayed in Bill's Tavern, which offered a well-made beef stew for dinner and a room upstairs that could accommodate the three.

D. Dean Carroll

They stayed late down in the tavern because two other travelers, who happened to be musicians, were also spending the night and agreed to entertain for a reduction in their expenses. One played guitar and the other a violin. The guitarist was a heavyset man whose girth barely left enough knee to rest his instrument; the violinist was a tall skinny man with no shoulders requiring he constantly hold the neck of the fiddle, having no means to wedge the instrument beneath his chin.

Their music was hill music brought by the two all the way from Arkansas. Though the music sounded simple, they incorporated intricacies and harmonies that embellished the common melodies. Cindy and Sandy loved the music and singing, joining in after they'd heard the chorus a time or two.

Allsup enjoyed the performance, but often the songs would take him back to Pennsylvania and step on his pleasure. Fifteen others gathered in the tavern and joined in when they could, clapping along enhancing their participation. It was almost ten when Allsup declared the evening was over for the three of them, it was time for bed. The two performers, along with the rest of the audience, sang one last farewell as they climbed the stairs bidding all a good night.

They rode out of Scipio the next morning, assured by several that Nephi was, indeed, only a two-day trip away, but they shouldn't expect to find anything between the two locations; even homesteaders were not known to have settled by those who travel the route.

There had been a light snowfall through the night, and all was fresh, clean and white. The temperature felt freezing, so when they began, the girls lay on their pallets in the back of the wagon wrapped in their quilts. The fresh snow made traveling more difficult, concealing many obstacles and defects in their trail. Slow and cautious was the rule, but gradually the sun had its effect and by late morning, much of the new snow had melted and they were able to continue at their usual pace.

By early afternoon they were walking. Allsup reminded the two girls to stay out of the puddles created by melting snow. He also instructed the girls to keep an eye open for wood to gather for a fire that evening, wherever they should happen to stop. The girls would run toward stands of trees passed in their travels and pick up broken branches and sticks, bringing them back and tossing them inside the moving wagon. Allsup kept a watchful eye on both, often calling them back with. "That's too far! Come on back!" He walked in circles around the wagon so he could monitor the movement of the girls on each side. "That's too far, Cindy! Come on back!"

Young Sandy found a cluster of small flowers with thin purple petals growing out from a yellow interior blooming between the rocks and called Allsup over to see them. There were many tiny blooms growing in bunches and patches scattered across the terrain.

"Aren't they beautiful?" she passionately asked.

"They are."

"I've never seen anything so pretty."

"Really? I have."

"Where?" The little girl looked up, eager to know.

"When I first saw you and Cindy, I thought to myself, there are two pretty little girls."

Sandy giggled modestly before saying, "Not like these flowers, though."

"Exactly like these flowers."

Cindy screamed; it wasn't her playful or excited scream. She was afraid. Immediately, Allsup began running to the other side of the wagon too long neglected. Sandy was right at his heels.

"Sandy," he shouted as he ran. "Get in the wagon and cover up with a blanket. Hear me? Head and all! Stay there till I come get you!"

He reached the other side to find Cindy standing at the edge of a stand of trees surrounded by wolves, seven wolves. They formed a crude circle with their noses pointed toward her. So intent were they with their prize that they failed to notice the approaching man until he called out.

"Cindy! Don't move! You're going to be okay; I'm coming to get you."

The wolves' heads jerked towards him with the awareness that there was a challenge to their efforts and for a minute seemed uncertain about what to do. Allsup shared their uncertainty. He had no idea how to proceed: wait and see or charge in? A large grey wolf with a thick winter coat made the decision for him; it grabbed Cindy's coat and began pulling her, screaming, into the woods.

Allsup un-holstered his pistol as he charged into the throng, firing, sending one or two running away yapping in pain as the others scattered. He tried to run and reload his spent chambers but couldn't, so he stopped and accomplished the task dropping a few shells in the process. Into the woods he ran, not sure where to go, but hearing her screams bouncing under the leafless trees. During a break in his panic, he noticed their tracks in the snow and damp ground and off he ran. Her screams sounded closer, and it motivated him to push harder, certain that this would be his chance to save the girl.

A loud explosion of gun fire brought Allsup to an abrupt stop and seemed to bring silence to a world where there once was no sound but screaming, and that had stopped.

On dashed Allsup and coming over an embankment, found Cindy sitting on the ground, crying; the wolf lying dead five feet away, and a grizzly of a man standing opposite the two holding a still smoking musket in the crook of his arm.

"I got 'em," he stated bluntly in a deep, gruff voice.

"Yes, you did." Allsup slid down next to Cindy and wrapped her in his arms.

"Wow! That was scary!" he whispered, holding tightly. "Wasn't it? Weren't you scared? I was and the wolf didn't have me!" her crying began to slowly ebb, but he still held her close.

"You have got to be the bravest girl in the world!" he told her. "You survived that scary attack and look how brave you are."

"I don't feel brave," she whimpered. "I feel scared!"

"Scared? Scared of what?"

"The wolf."

"Cindy, the wolf won't bother you anymore. Look over there," he indicated the direction of the wolf with a nod. "There's the wolf that got you. It's dead. It's not going to bother you ever again. And over there is the man that killed it."

She looked up at the big man dressed in many furs of different shades and colors. At the front of his hat was the head of a fox with empty eye sockets. The only visible thing through the thick hair on his head and covering his face was his eyes; they held a look of compassion.

"Don't you think it's proper to thank a man for saving your life?" Allsup asked Cindy. "What's your name, sir?"

"Knute."

"Thank Mr. Knute, Cindy."

"Just Knute, no mister." The fur-covered man corrected.

"Thank you, sir," she said softly.

"You're welcome," his voice resonated as if in an empty barrel.

"Do ya want it?" he asked Allsup, indicating the dead wolf.

"No, no, it's yours; you killed it. You earned it."

"That's good pelt there. It'll trade good if'n I don' decide to keep it my own self."

He easily picked up the wolf by its legs, front paws in one hand and rear paws in the other, and slung it up over his head, draping it around his neck like a scarf.

"I'll be goin'," he announced, turning to leave.

"Thank you again, Knute," Allsup called out.

"Jist happen to be here," the man gruffly replied without looking back or breaking his stride. "The Lord's a mystery."

Allsup continued to hold Cindy until she calmed down and ceased crying.

"Are you alright?" he asked. She nodded her head.

"Ready to head back?"

Again, she noted her affirmation with a nod.

"Oh, my gosh!" he exclaimed, jumping to his feet. "We have to get Sandy! She's hiding in the wagon."

The two quickly made their way back through the woods to where they'd left the wagon, only to find that it was no longer there; the horses had continued as they had since the beginning of their trip north. The wagon tracks were obvious in the damp earth and old snow, so it was just a matter of the two catching up. They ran a short way and located it at the bottom of a small hill heading east. Allsup gave a short whistle and Chestnut came to a stop, as did the Pinto. They climbed in to discover Sandy asleep under a quilt; she quickly embraced her older sister.

"You were gone so long!" she exclaimed, her face buried in her sister's shoulder.

"I got attacked by wolves!"

"Wolves!" Sandy's eyes were wide with astonishment as she looked at her sister.

"Yeah, and this big scary man saved me!" She turned to Allsup. "What was his name?"

"Knute."

"Yeah, his name was Knute, and he shot this wolf that was gonna eat me! Didn't he?" she turned to Allsup again.

"Yes, he did."

"Was it scary?" Sandy asked.

"Oh, a little," answered her sister, glancing at Allsup for correction but satisfied none came.

That night, using the collected kindling, they dined on

sliced fried pork belly and boiled potatoes. As they sat around the fire eating, Cindy recounted her trauma of earlier in the day, each time embellishing it just a little more. Sandy eagerly listened to the repeated story marveling over her sister's bravery.

Allsup helped the girls spread their pallets on the wagon floor and tucked them beneath their quilts. Sandy was tired, even with her nap that afternoon, and yawned repeatedly; she was ready for sleep. However, Cindy was apprehensive, still shaken by her experience.

"Where are you sleeping?" she asked Allsup.

"The same place I always do, under the wagon," he answered. "I'll be right below you."

"What if the wolves come back?" she whispered, glancing at her now sleeping sibling.

"They won't, especially with the fire going."

"What if the fire goes out?"

"It won't. I'll keep feeding it until morning."

"What if you run out of wood?"

"We won't, at least not for a long, long time, and by that time it will probably be morning."

"But what if the wolves aren't afraid of fire?" she persisted.

"Cindy, they—Do you want me to sleep in here with you?" She rapidly nodded her head.

Allsup grabbed his bedroll, climbed into the back of the now crowded wagon between the two girls and covered all three with the heavy wool blanket.

"Good night, Cindy," he said as he settled in as best he could.

"Good night, Mr. Allsup."

A minute or two later, she whispered, " That was nice of that man today, wasn't it."

"Very nice." he agreed.

"What was his name again?"

"Knute."

D. Dean Carroll

"Yeah, that's it. That's a funny name—Knute."

"Good night, Cindy."

"Good night." She rolled over onto her side, her back facing Allsup and whispered, "Thank you."

Chapter 68

They breakfasted on pickled hardboiled eggs and biscuits turning hard from age, provided by the tavern owner in Scipio. It began to snow as they set out for Nephi; the sky was overcast and gray, with a breeze strong enough to intensify the cold. The girls remained in the back of the wagon; Cindy was still haunted by her experience with the wolf pack and Sandy was not willing to leave her older sister alone.

Danny Allsup kept the two horses pulling the wagon headed in the general direction north, correcting them from time to time. As they journeyed, they encountered a few other travelers and discovered a road partially concealed by snow. Regularly placed telegraph poles that followed made the road's presence known.

They passed through the settlements of Chicken Creek and Leven. They stopped at the latter and picked up supplies along with peppermint sticks for the girls. They continued until late in the afternoon when the town Nephi came into view, nestled in the foothills of a towering mountain, the first of a range running north. To the south, towering red cliffs formed a wall that ribboned as far as the eye could see; Nephi was neatly settled between the two.

They stayed over an extra night to rest and clean up. It was some time since the three had bathed or slept in a bed. Allsup thought they deserved that and a good meal as well.

He arranged with the hotel proprietor for a girl to accompany Cindy and Sandy to their bath and assist with the task of cleaning. After their bath and a change of clothes, they returned in appearance to the little girls of the Fillmore Hotel.

Allsup's clothes were dirty and smelled, so while the girls were busy in the tub, Allsup visited a barber for a cut and a shave, then a nearby general store and purchased new clothes for himself, from socks to a black ribbon tie. His hat, like his duster, represented too much to consider replacing as he remembered his reflection long ago in the mercantile window, but he would have them cleaned.

The next day after a fine breakfast at Laverne's Restaurant, they walked the main street of Nephi. Allsup became curious as he noted many of the store signs listed as Salt Creek Livery or Salt Creek Feed and Grain, not mentioning Nephi. He occasionally overheard people referencing Salt Creek.

As they passed a man sweeping the entranceway to the Salt Creek Tavern, Allsup asked about it, "Excuse me, sir."

"Yes, sir?" the man stopped sweeping.

"We're passing through, spending one more night at the Nephi Hotel, and I couldn't help but notice that many establishments, such as your own, are listed as Salt Creek. I'm curious as to why?"

"Well, sir, there is a creek by that name that runs through the north part of town, and for many years the town bore that name. Course, when the government stepped in and began doing government things, they changed the name to Nephi. Many, including me, were not happy with the change and chose to keep the original as a way of linking the past with the present."

"That makes perfectly good sense," noted Allsup. "I have always been a bit sentimental in that regard myself."

"And," the man added with a sly smile, "it irritates the local officials like all get out."

Allsup and the two girls decided that it would make a favorable impression on their father if they had new dresses to wear when they met him. Sandy was one and Cindy two years old when he left for Sacramento, so the two had little memory of the man; they were both apprehensive about meeting him again.

They stopped at a mercantile that advertised a new

shipment of women and young girls' apparel had recently arrived, so they stopped and purchased new garments, assisted by the proprietor's wife. Cindy chose a white dress that buttoned up the back with blue ribbons woven around its edges, while Sandy selected a yellow dress of a similar design covered in lace. It took very little persuasion on the girls' behalf to convince Allsup that new shoes were also necessary. The clerk wrapped the purchases in wax paper and bound them with string for protection from the weather during the remainder of their travels.

While walking, they came upon a schoolhouse, which was in session. The students were at recess and playing in the snow; Allsup and the two girls stopped to watch. Cindy and Sandy said nothing, but their smiles betrayed their envy.

"Do you want to go play?" he asked, knowing the answer.

"Can we?" Cindy was so excited she could barely contain herself.

"Oh, yes!" cried Sandy.

"Go on then."

They ran to the school play yard and blended in with the other children immediately; they were neither shy nor reserved. Allsup walked up to the edge of the playground and stood watching. He could not recall ever having taken the time to watch his sons play.

The kids were running, laughing, and talking loudly without a care or concern on their young minds; he envied that. It occurred to him that at this stage in his life, he was not so different than those young children; he was free of responsibility, and there were no concerns weighing heavily on his mind.

True, he did have Cindy and Sandy, but it was temporary; once delivered to their father he would be free once again. And they were no burden. He was enjoying the time spent with them. It seemed he never took the time to watch his children develop and grow, so he made every effort to be conscious of the girls' discoveries, take pleasure in their conversations, and respect their thoughts. They were no longer the two playful little girls running through the Fillmore Hotel and Restaurant. They had matured, especially after the encounter with the wolves.

The teacher emerged from the schoolhouse doorway with a heavy shawl clutched tight around her shoulders. She stood watching the kids. She noticed Allsup watching her and waved. He returned her greeting and casually made his way around the playground's perimeter to the steps of the building where she stood.

"It gets so hot in the building and they get bored—sitting," she said as the wind blew a strand of hair across her face; she tucked it securely behind an ear. "I like to let them burn off some of that energy before calling them back inside."

"They certainly look as if they're burning it off!" Allsup observed.

"I assume the two are with you."

"They are. Do you mind I let them play?"

"No, no. Will they be coming again?" she asked.

"No, I'm sorry to say." He looked up at the teacher. "We continue on tomorrow. I'm taking them to be rejoined with their father in Sacramento. We're taking the train."

"Oh, I see. Are you a member of the family?"

"No. You could say they were thrust into my care." He laughed, remembering the conversation with Mr. and Mrs. Hawkins around the restaurant table.

"It's a long story," he said, amused while shaking his head.

"Well, I hope you have a safe trip."

"Thank you, my best to you, ma'am." He tipped his hat.

She called the students in. Cindy and Sandy ran over and stood by Allsup, watching them disappear within the building, waving goodbye.

"Was it fun?" he asked as they stood observing the

empty yard.

"Yeah," they both agreed.

They continued standing without speaking; Allsup noted their solemnness.

"Do you wish you could be inside with them?" They acknowledged they did.

"When you're with your father, you will be," he informed them. "You'll be going to school with other kids and playing and learning just like those kids."

That brought them back from disappointment to the cheerful talkative two before.

"You can come see us at school, too!" Cindy stated as they retraced their steps.

"Yes, maybe, if I'm there."

"If you're there?" Sandy looked up at him, confused. "Where else would you be?"

"I wonder what kind of house you'll be living in?" he quickly changed the topic. "Think it will have an upstairs?"

Cindy jumped on the subject, expressing her desire to have her own bedroom and describing all that would go in it. Sandy quietly walked along, shooting curious glances up at the man holding her hand.

D. Dean Carroll

Chapter 69

An early departure allowed them to pass through the town of Mona mid-morning. They followed a creek through a canyon between high-colored cliffs before entering a valley vast in size and joined a small group of travelers heading toward Newton not far away.

It was early evening and dark when they entered the small town, hungry and tired from their long day's journey. To his dismay. Allsup discovered there were no lodgings in Newton and only a saloon remained open; the few other establishments had closed for the night; the street was dark.

There was no greeting party, no gathering of the curious. Those they rode in with went their own separate ways leaving him sitting on the bench seat of his wagon wondering what to do; the girls were in the back, having fallen asleep a short time before. He drove the team between two buildings and came to a stop about ten feet behind one.

'Without waking the girls, he unhitched the horses and gave them feed. He no longer concerned himself with tethering the animals; they had become adapted to remaining around the wagon a while ago.

Allsup quietly and carefully removed his bedroll and ground tarp from within the wagon and spread it out beneath. Sighing as he stretched and relaxed, he fell into a deep, tired sleep.

It took three days to cross the valley. They could see a large lake to the east as they traveled. The girls expressed their desire to see a lake that big, but Allsup denied their requests and pressed on.

Three days traveled without encountering another human being; one spent laboriously traversing through a mountain pass that led into another valley larger than the previous. They had depleted their previsions by the third day, except for hardtack and jerky, some of which Allsup thought was from his original supplies purchased in Pennsylvania.

Allsup ventured a short distance from the ever-advancing wagon in search of game without success, so they dined on what was available. Neither girl complained. They discussed in detail, as they aggressively pulled on the dried jerky, the meal they would have when they entered the next town, often changing their selections based on what the other would choose.

Fairfield was a small, pleasant-looking town. It was bustling with activity as they entered, busy people trying to get done or somewhere before the day ended. The Stagecoach Inn happened to be before them when they stopped. Allsup took that as a sign and booked a room. Once again, he arranged a bath for the girls, accompanied by a young girl not much older than Cindy, before they could have that desired meal. He took one himself prior to joining them in the dining hall.

They had a grand time sampling the different items from the menu. 'Each girl was allowed to order three different items, he settled on a steak along with boiled potatoes smothered in gravy. After dinner, they retired early, exhausted from their travels. The girls slept in the one bed while Allsup took the floor.

The next morning two men dining at the next table suggested that they follow the route running southwest through a canyon leading to Rush Valley. After that, they advised, it was north into Tooele Valley and the Great Salt Lake. They also advised Allsup take plenty of provisions because the area was uninhabited until they reached the town of Stockton, a midway point to the Great Salt Lake. Allsup took an extra day to secure their requirements before heading out.

Their journey through the Oquirrh Mountains Pass was uneventful. In fact, their travels through Rush Valley also went without incident. Allsup kept the horses on a quick pace stopping now and then to allow them to rest. They had supplies enough to last a week, but Allsup had no intention for that to become necessary, so he pressed on.

The landscape was dry and yellow, covered in areas with sagebrush and wheatgrass with no sign of water. Hills and steep red cliffs dominated the valley, with the mountains always visible before them and behind.

At night, they could hear coyotes howling as if singing Call and Response songs to one another. Allsup appeased the girls' fright by assuring them it was the animal's way of staying in touch with their families and nothing to be frightened of. Allsup was aware there was probably no truth in what he told them, but it alleviated their fears and that was his intent.

The sky was so dark that every star in the galaxy appeared on display. Cindy, Sandy, and Allsup often would lie on their backs on the ground tarp watching for shooting stars while identifying the shapes of animals in the constellations.

Stockton was a small town consisting of nine buildings: a general store, a livery stable, one saloon, one tavern that served food with three rooms upstairs to let, a sheriff's office and jail, and a church. There were also three houses, two located at one end of town, the third at the other. The remaining population of Stockton, which was very small, lived on farms scattered around the area.

Over dinner in the tavern of bacon, eggs, and biscuits, Allsup overheard a conversation regarding the town's future prospects. It seemed that the area was rich in minerals and the possibilities of mining those resources made the town's future growth very favorable.

Another man contended that it was all a ruse to increase the population of non-Mormons to counter the church's influence. Allsup had no knowledge of Mormons, of what or who they were, so he lost interest in the discussion and focused on the girls finishing their dinners.

They pouted when informed they would not be bathing at this stop. They'd grown fond of the hotel bath during their travels, and when they loudly began to fuss about it at the table, he didn't let them finish their meal but promptly took them to their room and sent them to bed.

The next morning, they were at the general store when it opened, where they purchased their supplies and refilled the water casks for their final journey by wagon. The sun had not been up two hours when Allsup and the two girls were back on the trail heading north into Tooele Valley towards the Great Salt Lake.

The valley consisted of grasslands spread across to the mountains on either side and seemed to go on indefinitely. Allsup remembered his previous experience with grassy areas and snakes, so he required the girls remain in the wagon. They soon grew bored playing in the back and sat up front chatting endlessly with Allsup.

"What do you think our daddy looks like?" Cindy asked, sitting to his right.

"Well, I don't know," he answered. "Like you, I'd wager."

"No, sir," she replied. "Momma said we look like her."

"Yeah," affirmed Sandy sitting on his left. "We look like her."

"Do you? I never saw your mother or father, so I don't know."

"Momma had blond hair like us and blue eyes like us," Sandy rubbed her head as she spoke. "She said we look just like her when she was a girl."

"What color hair does your father have?"

"Momma said dark," answered Sandy.

"Yeah, Momma said dark." Her older sister confirmed, nodding.

They rode in silence with Allsup encouraging the horses now and then.

Finally, Sandy asked, "How will we know him when we get there?"

"Yeah, what if there's lots of people?" Cindy asked, concerned. "How will we know which one is daddy?"

More silence as all three considered her question.

"What if we never find him?" Sandy appeared to be on the brink of tears as she looked up at Allsup.

"Oh, we'll find him all right."

"But what if we don't?" Cindy's eyes were welling up.

"Will you leave us, Mr. Allsup?" Sandy asked, frightened.

Allsup pulled the team to a stop and wrapped the reins around the brake lever. He took each girl and set them on the toe board across from the wagon seat, so they sat looking at him and he at them.

"Now, I'm only going to say this once to the two of you, so I want you to listen very carefully, okay?" He rested his arms on his knees. They nodded.

"I'm only going to leave you with your father and no one else. I know we're going to find him because he's going to be looking for you. Mrs. Hawkins said she'd wire him of our intentions, so he's going to be very excited to see you again and have you with him, of that, I am sure. So, no more worry or talk about this anymore. You two are stuck with me until your daddy un-sticks us, okay?" The relief on the two young faces was immediate as they began to smile at once.

"Besides," Allsup continued enthusiastically. "If you look like your mother, he'll recognize you! Right?"

"Right!" they excitedly agreed.

"Now, who wants to go on a horseback ride?" he asked. They both jumped to their feet, eagerly screaming, "I do! I do!"

He placed Sandy atop Chestnut and Cindy on the painted mare, picked up the reins, and with a click of his tongue and a gentle snap of the reins, the horses continued. At first, the girls were cautious, clinging tightly to the horses' harnesses or mane. Gradually, as they became more comfortable, they began to talk, comparing horses and arguing over which was better. They decided to switch horses while in transit and asked Allsup if that would be okay.

"It's fine with me," he answered. "But remember, one hand should always be gripping a horse. If you slip, you'll be able to catch yourself."

They would slide down onto the wagon tongue between the horses and stand on it as they switched, using the harnesses to pull up on their new mount. Allsup kept the horses at a slow, steady gait; if they did fall, they were not far from the ground and odds were they would roll between the wheels. In this way, they actively played throughout the late morning into the afternoon, climbing from one animal to the other.

They spent the night in the back of the wagon with Allsup squeezed between the two. Late the next morning, they met up with two other wagons also heading for Salt Lake City.

The first wagon, pulled by a single mule, was a buckboard carrying cages of chickens driven by two men: both middle-aged, looking rough and talking loudly. They waved and shouted greetings and requested permission to travel along. Allsup stopped and discovered they, too, were on their way to the city to sell their hens, either for the cooking pot or for their eggs. When they continued, the chicken-laden wagon fell behind the covered one and they traveled on in a single file. Whichever man was holding the reins on the chicken wagon loudly berated the lonely mule.

Later in the day, another wagon full of potatoes quickly advanced, passing the two men while leaving a cloud of red dust in its wake. A stern-faced elderly man and woman sat upon its bench seat and were in the process of passing the first wagon when it slowed to keep pace with Allsup and the girls currently astride the horses playing.

"They should not be doing that," the woman said sternly by way of greeting. Both she and her male companion looked as if they hadn't smiled since childhood. He was dressed in a black suit tainted red from dust and wearing a flat, wide-brimmed hat. The woman was wearing a full, black dress that puffed up around her as she sat holding a kerchief over her mouth to prevent inhaling dust.

Surprised by the abrupt comment, Allsup said, "Ma'am?"

"I said those children should not be playing on those horses!" repeated the woman loudly. "It's too dangerous!"

"Oh, I see." Allsup looked at the girls who held the appearance they were expecting to be chastised as they nervously looked from Allsup to the couple. Allsup smiled at the girls and said to the couple, "Safe travels to you both."

"Aren't you going to stop them?" demanded the woman as they continued traveling alongside the covered wagon.

"No." Allsup tipped his hat.

"Sir, those children can be harmed playing in such fashion!" she exclaimed as she turned in her seat facing Allsup.

"Yes, ma'am, there is that possibility."

This caught the woman un-expectantly. Flustered, she shrilled, "I demand you move those children back to the wagon for their safety!"

"Yes, ma'am." Allsup tipped his hat again before telling them, "Now move on."

The two wagons continued side by side, with the third close behind. Allsup attempted to ignore the wagon to his right by watching the girls still riding the horses but no longer playing.

"Git up, ya damn mule!" shouted one of the men on the chicken wagon.

"Did you not hear me, sir?" the woman called out.

Allsup brought the wagon to a stop, the couple brought their wagon to a stop, and the mule stopped.

"What hell's goin' on?" loudly inquired a man in the wagon pulled by the mule.

"Doan know," his partner replied.

The two girls began climbing off the horses when Allsup stopped them saying, "Stay right there."

"God's wrath will be thrust upon you for your negligence should harm come to either of those children if you allow them to continue playing in such a manner!" she declared.

Allsup stood and said, "My wrath will be thrust upon *you* if you don't move on and leave us be!"

The girls looked at him wide-eyed. They'd not heard adults talk to one another in that tone before.

"Seems them old folks doan like the little ones playin' on the horses," a man on the chicken wagon loudly told the other. The two men were dressed in similar fashion: worn, faded pants held in place by suspenders wrapped over the exposed tops of dirty-white long-sleeved underwear. Their age was undeterminable, at times seeming younger in manner than they appeared.

"Why not?" the other asked.

"'fraid they'll git hurt."

"What?"

"I said, the old folks 'r 'fraid the little ones'll git hurt!" he shouted back.

"Oh, I doan think they'll git hurt," said the other, shaking his head.

"Seemed like they was havin' fun, to me."

"What?"

"I said, seems they was havin' fun!"

"Fer sure, they seemed to be," concurred the other.

There was a standoff. The girls remained on the horses as Allsup stood with his hands on his hips waiting; the couple sat glaring back.

"What they have in that wagon?" the one hard-of-hearing inquired, standing to see better in the wagon ahead.

"Looks like tators."
"What?"
"Looks like tators!"
"Oh…"

Finally, Allsup was at the end of his rope. He stood looking at the man sitting in the potato-filled wagon. He climbed down from his wagon and stood with hands on hips, glaring.

"Sir, I mean you and your mother no ill will…

"I am his wife, sir!" loudly protested the woman. "I will not be disrespected."

"I mean you and your *wife*, no ill will," he continued. "But if you don't move that wagon on and leave us be, I'm going to climb up there and move it on myself, and I won't guarantee you'll both be on it."

"What?" exclaimed the woman. "Why, I—"

The old man sitting beside her snapped the reins and their two horses pulled the wagon on with the woman berating the man all the while.

"Well, now," Allsup said climbing back onto the covered wagon. "Guess we can continue ourselves. You girls go on and play."

"I don't want to anymore," Sandy said as she walked the length of the wagon tongue back to the wagon, a hand sliding along on the back of each horse.

"Me neither." Cindy followed her sister back in similar fashion and climbed up to sit beside Allsup.

"Why did they do that?" asked Sandy.

"They didn't want you to get hurt."

"Why did you talk to them like that?" she continued.

"This is America, people can't tell you what to do."

"You weren't worried we might get hurt?" Cindy asked.

"Sure, I was."

"Why'd you let us then?" Sandy looked up at him.

"You were having fun, weren't you?" Both nodded.

"Life comes with risks," he explained. "Sometimes you

have to accept that to have fun, otherwise you'll end up never having fun; or doing much of anything."

"Oh." Cindy looked back at the mule-pulling wagon. "Who are those men?"

"I don't know."

Late in the afternoon, as dusk was first settling in, the two wagons came upon the third whose two horses were tethered and searching for grass; a fire was burning several feet from their wagon, the man and woman were sitting by the fire. The man rose and walked quickly to greet them.

"Won't you stop and camp with us this night?" he asked intently. "We've potatoes roasting by the fire and smoked ham. We'd be pleased to have you join us. These roads are never safe for travelers…safety in numbers as they say."

"Thank you," answered Allsup, "but first I would like to ask if you know how far we are from Salt Lake City?"

"Oh, we'll be there tomorrow, probably late afternoon."

"Then, yes, we'll stop with you for the night."

As they spoke the second wagon with chickens and the two men pulled up and stopped.

"What is it?" asked the driver.

"We're stopping here for the night," Allsup informed him. "They've offered roasted potatoes and ham."

"Oh! Well, if they're offering that, we'll throw in a couple'a hens!" he exclaimed as he dismounted from the wagon.

"What's goin' on?" loudly asked the other man. "Why we stoppin'?"

"We're stayin' with these folks," he told him. "They got taters and ham."

"What?"

"We're stayin' here tonight!"

"Oh, well, all right." He climbed down from the wagon.

"I be Louis," said the one man from the chicken wagon, "and this be my brother Theodore. He cain't hear too good cause'a bomb went off during the war and took it."

"I am Ronald Apmeyer, and that unfriendly, busy-bodied, Christian woman over there," he pointed over towards the fire, "is my wife Bette. We travel to Salt Lake City several times a year to sell excess produce. That's where we're headed now."

"I am, in fact, heading there myself," Allsup confided.

"Taking your daughters along, I see," Apmeyer observed.

"No, no, they're not my daughters."

"Oh?" Apmeyer eyed him suspiciously.

"I'm taking them to Sacramento to join their father," Allsup explained. "We're probably going to catch the train in Salt Lake City. Come along, girls."

The five walked over to join Mrs. Apmeyer while brother Theodore tended to the mule.

"Sandy, Cindy, this is Mr. and Mrs. Apmeyer," Allsup made the introductions. "And that gentleman is Mr. Louis...I'm sorry," he said to the chicken farmer, "I didn't catch your last name."

"Tanner. I be Louis Tanner and this," his brother joined them at the fire, "is my brother Theodore. He cain't hear none too good cause'a an explosion went off next to his head during the war."

"Girls, what do you say when you meet someone new?" Allsup asked.

"Nice to meet you." Curtsied Cindy looking bashful.

"Nice to meet you," Sandy mimicked her sister.

They sat around the fire waiting for dinner, the girls on either side of Mrs. Apmeyer. The Tanner brothers killed and cleaned two chickens, impaling them on iron rods from their wagon and hung them over the fire. With the potatoes cooking on rocks just beyond the flames reach, and two impaled chickens roasting over the fire, the group sat talking about different things. The cooking chickens popped and spit into the fire while Allsup told stories about Pennsylvania and his trip westward, often repeating himself for Theodore's benefit.

The Apmeyer's told of their family, three girls and two sons, and how they had settled in the Mormon town of Tooele years ago. They too had lost a son in the war. Talk continued as day turned to night, darkness extinguished the sunlight, and fatigue overcame energy. Finally, with the food deemed sufficiently cooked, they fed the two girls before the adults shared the abundant remains of roasted potatoes, smoked ham, and charred chicken.

Full and content, the men reclined against blanket-covered boulders and rolled up bedrolls sipping coffee while Mrs. Apmeyer and the girls cleaned the tin dishes, cups, and spoons. When they re-joined the men, Cindy and Sandy settled in beside Allsup, and for a time, no one spoke, all basking in contentment under the stars, staring into the fire.

"Girls," Allsup broke the silence. "I think it's time for bed."

The two complained and were rescued when Louis Tanner said, "Would ya like to hear'a story first? Can they hear'a story first?" he asked Allsup.

The girls begged; Allsup relented.

"I'm 'a tellin' ya the story 'bout these two boar tusks," he began, tossing a leather necklace with two large ivory tusks grown in a circle attached for the girls to see. "Would ya like to hear it?"

The two girls, each sitting on Allsup's knees, nodded enthusiastically as they rubbed the smooth ivory tusks.

"All right, then, I'm gonna tell ya—"

"What?" asked hard-of-hearing Theodore.

"I'm tellin'em 'bout the boar story!" Louis loudly informed his brother.

"Oh, I know that one. I'm turnin' in. Night to y'all." He unrolled his blanket, stretched out upon the red dirt, and turned his back to the fire.

"Okay, now, this here story I'm 'bout to tell happened long ago when I was 'bout yorn age, back in Arkansas."

D. Dean Carroll

"We're from Arkansas!" Sandy excitedly blurted.

"Ya are? Well, me 'n Theodore is too! When we was mites like yornselves, we played in the woods every chance, free from elders to tell us no and don't. There was a bunch 'a us kids we knowd from school that played, climbin' trees, swingin' from branches, huntin' crawdaddies in the creeks, diggin' holes fer rabbit traps, playin' like kids do. Do y'all play like that?"

They both shook their heads, eyes glued on the man, waiting for the story to continue.

"It sounds like fun," Cindy softly noted.

"It were! It were! Theodore was the best catcher. He could catch anythin'! Anythin'! He'd come home with crawdads in his pockets or sometimes squirrels' or rabbits roped to sticks. There was times he provided the meal in our house. Momma and Daddy was always proud 'a Theodore; suppose it was only right, he bein' the oldest 'n all."

Louis stopped for a moment, lost in memories, gazing into the fire.

"Was that the story?" Sandy asked, looking up at Allsup.

"No, no, that ain't the story!" Tanner laughed, his thoughts once again back at the campsite. "We was all in the woods one day, this is the story, and was headin' down to a pool we made by damming Johnson's Creek."

"How did you do that?" asked Sandy.

"With rocks and branches, jist piled 'em up in the creek and the water backed up. So, we was headin' that 'a way and was scrambling down the side of a gulley when at the bottom we spied a sounder 'a wild swine, six or seven boars 'n sows and a drift 'a young-ins, I doan know how many. One 'a the boars had tusks so long they curled up'n round forming a circle on each side 'a its snout. Now I doan know if *you* know that wild swine are mean by nature, boars in 'ticular, and this one big 'ol boar, you could tell his mood was sour cause 'a those tusks made it hard fer 'im to eat!

Danny Allsup

"We all knowd to stop dead in our tracks, cause 'a they doan see us, they won't give us no, never mind. So, we stood still as trees watchin' those 'ol pigs, waiting fer'em to git tired 'n move on. But they must 'a rooted somethin' cause they weren't in no hurry. We listened to'em grunt 'n oink, they'd squeal now 'n then fightin' over somethin'; 'n we just stood there, waitin'.

"Johnny Charles was there with his little sister, her name...I cain't recall, but she was a wee little thing younger than yornself," he said to Sandy. "She whispers, 'I'm 'a scared.' We all shh'd her and told'er to be still. She fussed, 'I wanna go home,' 'n we shh'd her again and said be still! She started cryin', getting' louder 'n louder. Johnny said, 'Beth!' That was her name! Beth! He said, 'Beth! Be quiet!' but he said it too loud 'n all those pigs stopped 'a rootin' 'n looked over at us. They was starin' at us while we was starin' at them.

"Someone yelled, 'Run!' and we started lickity-split up the side 'a that gully, runnin' fer all we was worth! It took a moment for those pigs to decide to see what we was all bout, but they soon started up after. There was a big oak at the top of the gully, and the first one up climbed that tree 'n we followed suit. Theodore helped each of us up. Lil' Beth was the last to reach the top; he helped her up too before climbin' the tree jist as that ol' boar came up on 'im.

"We was all sittin' on branches up in that oak watching the pigs swarmin' 'round below us. Theodore said, 'Everybody sit easy. They'll move on shortly.' So, that's what we did. Jist like he said, and after a time, they began to mosey on, headin' back down the gully to whatever it was that'd caught their fancy b'fore. But that big ol' boar with those big ol' tusks hung 'round gruntin', circlin' that oak time 'n time again, lookin' up at us as if to be sayin', 'Y'all gotta come down sometime.' Theodore whispered, 'Jist sit tight. He'll go away shortly, too.'

"I be sure to this day he'd 'a been right had not Lil' Beth

D. Dean Carroll

fallen from that tree. With a 'Thud!' she hit the ground and scrambled to climb back up, but she was too small. The boar eyed her fer a spell, not sure if that little thing was real or jist a vision. 'Be still!' Theodore shouted, distractin' the pig, 'Git on the other side of the tree!' She looked at that boar 'n his big ol' tusks and froze. The boar took a step or two closer, examin' her for the best place to chomp down, I 'spect; Lil' Beth was scared stiff. She started cryin' 'n screamin' fer her Momma, 'n we couldn't quiet her down no how. The boar took a step closer, 'n Lil' Beth screamed more 'n louder, 'n started runnin' her legs' but not goin' no wheres.

"I was waitin' for Theodore to do somethin'. We all was. But he jist sat there on his branch watchin' Lil' Beth 'n that boar. After'a time..." Louis paused his story and looked over at his sleeping brother before continuing softly. "After a time, I seed he was as scared as she. I seed he weren't gonna help her. The boar took a practice lunge, like a bull gittin' ready to charge. Time was runnin' short 'fore that o' hog decided to git'er done.

"There was a branch above me I was hangin' on to, no more 'n thumbnail thick. I started workin' that branch back 'n forth real fast till it split 'n I pulled it from the tree. Some 'a the bark coiled up like'a ribbon from the split point; it didn't look like much and weren't nothin' close to sharp, but it was gonna have to do. My hands was all sweaty, and I worried the branch would slip 'fore I could use it, so I gripped it tighter till my knuckles turned white. I prayed that ugly pig would git bored 'n move on, but it seemed intent on Lil' Beth. With a loud whine it suddenly charged, 'n 'fore I knowd, I was fallin' from that oak 'n landed atop that wild boar! I was on his back like I was ridin' 'a horse, and with two hands, I brought that stick down hard into the back'a its head! With 'a 'Huff!' its legs went out in all directions and it landed on its belly still as can be! Lil' Beth was 'a cryin', I was 'a cryin', her brother, Johnny, climbed down from the tree cryin'. Everybody climbed down from that oak 'a cryin', 'cept Theodore. He was still too scared to move. He stayed in the tree until he heard the adults 'a comin''; one 'a the other kids went 'n fetched 'em.

"I was 'a hero. They gave Momma and Daddy the boar as a reward fer my bravery. Momma and Daddy both talked 'bout how brave I was, 'n how this pig would feed us fer months! Theodore followed not sayin' nothin'. After our Daddy butchered the animal, he gave me the two tusks on this piece 'a leather here to keep 'n wear 'round my neck as I do now." Louis held up the leather necklace with the two tusks.

"Well, that was my story," he sat back, smiling. "What'd ya think?"

Both girls declared it a good story and said he was a very brave man; the adults smiled and agreed.

Cindy told of her encounter with the wolves, with Allsup adding a detail or correction here and there.

"You poor child!" exclaimed Mrs. Apmeyer embracing Cindy while giving Allsup a stern look of disapproval.

"That's a good story!" declared Louis Tanner. "Did ya git his tail?"

When she responded that she did not, Tanner took the tusks from around his neck and offered them to the girl.

"I had these long 'a 'nough, don't need them no more to show my bravery. You take these, lil' girl, and keep them to remind yournself of your own bravery, remind yournself 'a me."

Cindy looked up at Allsup for permission which he granted with a nod.

"Thank you, Mr. Tanner." She hung them around her neck and showed them proudly to her younger sister.

"All right," said Allsup rising, "say goodnight to everyone. Tomorrow we'll be in Salt Lake City."

D. Dean Carroll

Chapter 70

The campfire had burned down to glowing embers; the Tanner brothers were sleeping at different compass points around it, Louis to the south and Theodore to the east. Mr. and Mrs. Apmeyer were spooning under their potato-filled wagon for warmth as the night was accompanied by cold; too warm for snow but frost settled where it could.

In the covered wagon, Allsup lay squeezed between the two girls, on his back, awake. His nights since traveling with Cindy and Sandy were never restful. He longed to roll over onto his side. It didn't matter which side because his back had borne the burden of rest too long, but if he rolled onto his side, he relinquished wagon space never to be regained, for as soon as he shifted on to his right or left, the girl on the opposite side expanded, stretched out into the previously occupied territory now vacated, never to be surrendered until morning. Thus, he would be forced to remain on that side, longing, for the rest of the night, to return to his back.

He lay staring at the canvas ceiling thinking about the day, about their meal, about Louis Tanner's story, and contemplated his first train ride with the girls. They'd been traveling together for a short time, but already he felt parental protection and thought they viewed him the same. It would be difficult to part when the time came and in his mind, he imagined different scenarios that could prevent it. Perhaps their father would not be waiting; perhaps they'd never find him at all. Or maybe he'd fallen to the evils of addiction over the time they were apart and was no longer fit to take on the responsibility of fatherhood. He knew it was wrong to consider such possibilities, but his attachment had grown to the point that he did.

And what if the father *didn't* show up or *was* unfit? Would he abandon his goal to see the Pacific? Would he take them along? Or, maybe they'd remain together in Sacramento, and he would find employment and enroll them in school. They could return by train to Lebanon, where he could farm again. He shook his head trying to drive the tormenting thoughts from his mind, but like water returning to the lowest point, so returned his thoughts.

As he lay on his back staring up at the canvas covering, he heard Sandy sniff and then sniff again. He listened attentively and realized she was crying. She was lying on her side, her back to him.

"Sandy?" he whispered, placing a hand on her shoulder. "Sandy, what's wrong?"

She didn't respond but buried her face into her feather pillow.

"Why are you crying?"

She rolled onto her back, her eyes red with tears and told him, "I miss my Momma."

"Oh." He rubbed her shoulder comfortingly.

"I miss her," she said again. "I dreamed she was with me…and she's not."

"No, no, she's not." Allsup gently stroked her arm for lack of knowing what else to do.

"Do you think she misses me?"

After giving it thought, he answered, "No, I don't. Do you want to know why?"

She nodded her head, rubbing her nose on the back of her nightgown sleeve.

"Because I believe she's with you right now."

"She's a ghost?"

"No, no, she's not exactly a ghost, but you're her daughter, and she loves you very, very much. I believe when we die, we go to heaven, and I think heaven is whatever makes you happiest. I can't imagine anything making your mother happier than being with you and your sister."

"So, you think she's here right now?"

"I do."

"Where?" she looked around the covered wagon's interior.

"Everywhere you and your sister are."

"What if we're not together?"

"Who?"

"Cindy and me. What if Cindy goes somewhere and I don't? Who does Momma go with?"

"She goes with both of you."

"How?"

"She's in heaven. Remember, with God, all things are possible. Your Momma's heaven is being with you both, so she goes wherever you both go, even when you're not together."

"Oh." She lay silent, thinking.

"Okay?" he asked. "Think you'll be able to sleep now?"

Again, she nodded her head.

"Scoot over a bit so I can lay back again, please."

She made room for him to recline on his back. She yawned, so did he.

"When I couldn't sleep, Momma would put her arm around me and hold me." She looked over at Allsup resting beside her.

"That's nice." He yawned again.

"She'd put her arm around me, and I put my head on her shoulder till I fell asleep."

"That's nice." He looked at her, looking expectantly at him.

"Oh…Oh!..." He raised his arm and wrapped it around her as she quickly snuggled up against him.

"Good night, Mr. Allsup," she said, yawning.

"Good night, Sandy."

Danny Allsup

Chapter 71

The three wagons traveled in a single file: Mr. and Mrs. Apmeyer, with their potatoes, headed the small caravan, followed by Danny Allsup, Cindy, and Sandy in the covered wagon pulled by two horses, and bringing up the rear were the Tanner brothers sharing their wagon with two dozen chicken-filled cages pulled by a weary old mule.

The trail they followed was used and rutted; tall, dry grass yellowed by winter swayed gracefully along the trail's center as the wagons passed. Occasionally, a rabbit would flee through the grasses startling the horses. On two occasions, pheasants took flight; after the second bouquet took to wing Louis Tanner got out his rifle waiting for the next batch, but none came.

The girls were playing in the back of the wagon while Allsup sat lazily on the bench seat with his feet propped up on the wagon's toeboard when he noticed something peculiar, they were no longer on a crude trail made from use but were on a smooth wide road framed by straight edges that continued on before them merging and disappearing in a distant, common point.

Allsup pulled the wagon to a stop and stood, looking around at squared areas of land created by evenly placed roads; all north and south roads ran parallel as did all east and west, forming consciously created grids, vacant lots ready for occupation.

The Apmeyer wagon continued as the Tanner brothers rode by.

"Welcome to Salt Lake City!" shouted Louis, waving as they passed.

The girls climbed to the front to join Allsup and determine the cause of their stopping.

"What's wrong?" Cindy asked.

"Nothing," Allsup answered, smiling. Using his hands, he gestured outward, saying, "Just this!"

"Why did we stop?" asked Sandy.

"Cause 'a this." Cindy spread out her arms, mimicking Allsup.

"What?" Sandy asked, confused. "They're leaving us!" Alarmed, she pointed to the departing wagons.

"It's okay," Allsup calmly said, his hands resting on his hips as he continued surveying the area.

"I thought they were riding with us to the Salt City," said Sandy.

"We're here."

"This is Salt City?" she asked in disbelief.

"I don't see any buildings," Cindy added.

"It's Salt Lake City," corrected Allsup. "And evidently, this is where it starts."

The three stood at the front of the wagon, gazing at the repetitious patterns stretched out before them. The two accompanying wagons were now mere dots on the horizon.

"Who did this?" wondered Sandy.

"The Mormons," answered Allsup.

"Why?" Cindy asked.

"I guess they have big plans for the future. Let's see where this road takes us."

With a 'click' of his tongue, the wagon lurched forward.

Soon, trees began to line the roads, planted in neat rows. They continued along the perimeters of the blocks, turning down side streets at each passing intersection. The wagon eventually passed whole lots filled with rows of trees as neatly laid out as the roads. Gradually, small farms and houses appeared on the lots, never interrupting the pattern of the trees.

"Look up here," Allsup called out to the girls whose heads popped out from behind the canvass flap. "Are those steeples I see ahead?"

"That looks like a mighty big church!" Cindy declared.

"It's got three steeples!" announced Sandy, "one big one in the middle and two on the side."

The girls joined him.

"I see buildings now," Sandy advised.

"Yeah, lots of buildings," added Cindy.

A horse and rider galloped by while two other wagons fell in behind them from a side street. Soon, the traffic grew as other wagons, some carrying passengers, others carrying produce and goods, fell in line. Houses, shops and offices, side by side, appeared more frequently until they formed a wall of buildings behind the trees.

"There's a giant egg in front of the church!" exclaimed Cindy.

A large round topped structure stood before the three-spiraled building creating an image as much religious as mysterious.

"What could it be?" she asked.

"I don't know; maybe we'll find out," Allsup told her.

They rode into the heart of the bustling city, past the large shiny domed building and the massive church made from blocks of granite. They stopped at the busy intersection with the church to their left and remained there as traffic and pedestrians passed.

"Well, which way, girls," asked Allsup, "left or right?"

They were unanimous on right, so he turned the wagon in that direction and headed down the busy street. They were lucky to find suitable lodgings at the first hotel at which they stopped. The St. James Hotel, whose sign advertised 'A First-Class Family Hotel,' offered reasonable rates with rooms available with two beds, ideal for the three. The hotel clerk advised Allsup that many of their out-of-town guests stabled their horses at McKimmins' Livery and Seed just down the street.

A cleaning girl of thirteen by the name of Clare willingly agreed to watch the girls as they bathed and promised to have them dressed and ready for dinner.

D. Dean Carroll

Allsup drove the team down to McKimmins', where they agreed to stable the two animals and make it known that the painted mare and the wagon were for sale.

"What of the chestnut?" inquired Mark McKimmins, an unlit hand-rolled cigarette in the corner of his mouth. "The stallion, he for sale too?"

"No," answered Allsup. "He's with me."

They spent three days in Salt Lake City. The sale of the horse and wagon impeded their departure. A few inquiries had been made about the mare, but none whatsoever on the wagon. Their sale was necessary to offset the cost of their train fares. Allsup had enough to cover the cost of their transportation but didn't know if he'd be repaid at the end of their trip and with his own future ambiguous, he hoped to have funds remaining for uncertainty.

He decided that if they were going to be required to wait in Salt Lake City, they might just as well enjoy themselves while waiting. They went to the domed church, which they discovered is called a tabernacle, and marveled, upon being encouraged to enter, at the ornate design inside. An organist began practicing on its massive pipe organ, whose sound filled the nearly empty building giving it the aura of Holiness. Allsup and the two girls sat in a pew, appreciating the music and visual beauty within.

The building next to the tabernacle, which really looked like a big church reaching skyward, was still under construction. According to one of the workers, it was a temple being built for the glory of God. None of the three had observed a building so massive before. Allsup remembered the Cincinnati bridge and thought this similar—only reaching up.

"Okay," sighed Allsup looking around at the opposite three street corners. "I think we should have lunch and then try to find a school where maybe they'll have swings and a slide."

Over lunch their waitress spoke of a school just a couple

of blocks west of the restaurant that had swings; she wasn't sure about a slide. After their meal, they found the school; it had a slide.

Allsup leaned back against a tree, content to watch the girls play while sitting on a solid, non-moving surface. He watched as they slid down the slide together and separately, facing forward and back; they took turns pushing each other on the single swing. There was a small oval track off to the side of the school and they ran around it until they could run no more—two times.

When the girls grew tired, the three headed back to Main Street and the St. James. As they walked, they came upon the Wayside Store, where Cindy and Sandy begged Allsup to enter and look around. The girls, after looking at the different clothes available, deemed it necessary they have new everyday dresses to wear for the remainder of their trip.

"First impressions, you know," Sandy reminded him.

"How old are you?" asked Allsup.

It took little coaxing on their part before he relented and told them each to pick something out. Upon departing the Wayside, Allsup was carrying three bags, and the girls one each. They chatted all the way back to the hotel, never noticing the distance walked nor the lateness of the day.

They dined across the street at the Arcade Restaurant and Chop House on battered chicken and mashed potatoes. Allsup told their waiter the apple pie was the best on both sides of the Mississippi and took pride in being able to say so.

As soon as they returned to their hotel room, without any prompting from Allsup, both girls changed into their nightgowns and crawled into bed.

"Are you staying here with us?" Cindy asked as she pulled the covers up to her chin.

"Yes, I'm staying," he answered, sitting in a chair on the far side of the room next to a table with a burning oil lamp.

"Aren't you going to bed?" asked Sandy.

"No, not yet."

"What will you do?" she asked. Cindy was already drifting into a deep slumber.

"I don't know," he looked around and noticed a book sitting on the table. "Maybe I'll read for a while; someone left this book."

"Someone left a book?" Sandy asked as she settled in under the covers. "What's its name?"

"The Book of Mormon."

Danny Allsup

Chapter 72

The day was sunny; the air, supplemented by a gentle constant breeze, was cold. There was a group making the trip to see the Salt Lake, but Allsup decided against going. He was told that the train to Ogden passed close by the lake, allowing an excellent view. Also, he'd received a note from McKimmins that a man was giving serious consideration to the mare and insinuated he'd make his intentions known later that day. Allsup wanted to be available when called to finalize the sale, for he was certain this was going to be it.

The girls were disappointed but not extremely so; it was a big salty lake.

They breakfasted at the Arcade Restaurant before walking the streets of the city to enjoy the morning air and window shop, something of which the girls never seemed to tire. They strolled up and down the streets as if following spokes on a wheel with the livery stable as the hub. Never venturing too far, they walked up one street, crossed over and ambled back on the opposite side. Allsup was forced to divide his attention between conversations with the girls and keeping vigil on the stables.

The three were emerging from the Cohn Bros. Dry Goods store, where they were having a sale on many items, less now that Cindy and Sandy were able to convince Allsup of the many good deals when a rough-looking man walking briskly towards them called out.

"Allsup!" he shouted. "Allsup! Hold up!"

Allsup pushed the girls up onto the porch of a gunsmith shop and turned to face the approaching man.

"Allsup!" he repeated as he approached.

"I'm Danny Allsup. What need do you have to approach in such manner?" Allsup curtly inquired. "You appear threatening, sir; stop right there!" Allsup rested his hand on his holstered revolver.

The man stopped close enough to talk without being overheard.

"McKimmins says to find you, sir," the man stated. "And find you I have."

"For what purpose?" asked Allsup.

"Says there's a man there wants to buy your horse."

"Excellent! Excellent! Do you hear that, girls? We may be leaving tomorrow!" And to the stableman, "I'll be there directly. I'll stop by the St. James, leave the girls and join you at my quickest ability."

"McKimmins says come right away. The man grows impatient."

"I'll not drag these girls to the stables to observe a business transaction."

"I wanna go," Cindy said.

"Yeah, me, too!" Sandy seemed excited at the prospect.

Allsup abruptly turned to the girls and sternly said, "Quiet!"

They did immediately, not having heard him speak in that manner before.

"Go and tell Mr. McKimmins that I'm on my way," Allsup instructed the stable hand. "I will be there as quickly as I can. I can do no more. Come along, girls."

They dutifully came up, took his hand and quickly continued to the hotel.

"I'm sorry that I shouted earlier. I wasn't angry with you; I was angered by that man. I was wrong and I'm sorry."

Neither girl spoke as they struggled to keep pace with Allsup's long strides.

"I was wrong and I'm sorry."

Again, his apology elicited no response.

"Slow down!" Cindy said. "You're walking too fast. Sandy's going to fall down."

"I'm sorry." Allsup stopped, giving them time to catch their breath. "I'm just eager to get this sale over with so we can be on our way."

"I've never heard a grown-up apologize before," Sandy told him.

"What?"

"Yeah, and lots of times, too!" Cindy added.

"What?"

"Grownups don't ever say they're sorry to kids." Cindy said.

"Yeah, I never heard a grownup say I'm sorry ever in my whole life!" exclaimed Sandy.

"You're only four," Allsup pointed out.

"So? I never heard a grownup apologize to a kid that whole time!"

"Well, what do adults *do* when they're wrong about something?" Allsup asked, curious to know their response.

"They find a way to blame it on you...us!" Cindy answered.

"No, we don't."

"Yes, you do!" she continued. "One time Momma knocked a vase off this little round table and it broke. She said it was our fault because we had been playing around the table a couple of days before and must have knocked the vase too close to the edge. We didn't knock the table! Momma broke the vase!"

"Or sometimes they make it a learning lesson!" Sandy added.

"A learning lesson?"

"Yeah, they start by saying, 'Do you see what happens when...' you can finish it with anything *they* did wrong."

"Interesting. Come on." Allsup took each girl by the hand. "Just another block or two and we're there."

Allsup was happy with the sale of the mare. It more than covered the cost of their railroad tickets and nourishment along the way. He purchased tickets that very day on the Utah Central to Ogden, which left daily starting at six in the morning and arrived about an hour later. In Ogden, they would transfer to the Union Pacific, which would take them directly to their destination of Sacramento. After making arrangements with Utah Central for Chestnut's transportation, he returned to McKimmins to ensure the horse would be ready at five.

"What about the wagon?" Mark McKimmins asked.

"I tell you what, you keep it," Allsup told him. "Do with it what you will. The money from the mare is enough for our purposes. We need no more."

"Doubt anyone's interested in a covered wagon around these parts," McKimmins observed. "But the wood could be of value, cash-wise or other."

So, all was settled. For the remainder of the day, Allsup and the girls packed and prepared for their early morning departure. The girls were excited about riding a train, and truth be told, so was Allsup. Sandy and Cindy chatted away about it non-stop until, just to provide space between himself and the talking girls, Allsup suggested they return to the school playground one last time.

It was already late in the afternoon when they arrived and found it currently occupied by a girl and boy of about their age. It took a quick introduction before they were all playing together, laughing and talking. Allsup took a seat on a nearby bench and watched. The day had turned cloudy and gray; without the sun, the brisk breeze had turned bitingly cold.

"Daniel! Dorainne! Come along!" a man called from behind Allsup, who turned at the mention of his name. "It's time to head home for dinner!"

The man waved a greeting which Allsup answered in kind.

"Coming!" The sister and brother yelled goodbyes to Cindy and Sandy as they ran from the playground.

Allsup and the girls dined for the last time at the Arcade and, on this night, tried their famous pork chops. The three agreed they were excellent; Allsup proved it by consuming three.

They returned to their hotel room and the girls eagerly prepared for bed, for tomorrow they would ride a train, and the day after they would be with their father.

D. Dean Carroll

Chapter 73

It was a jolt! When the connections between the two railroad cars came to grips, as the engine began its departure, their car pulled forward with such a lurch that in any other circumstance would have been deemed dangerous. Allsup sat on a wooden bench seat similar in design to a church pew across from Sandy and Cindy, who sat facing him. They were wide-eyed, clutching their seats tightly, looking at Allsup for assurance as the train slowly pulled away from the station with much noise and fanfare, for the whistle sounded over and over announcing their departure and loud bursts of steam along with squeaking, grinding metal of spinning wheels made conversation impossible.

"Well, girls? What do you think?" asked Allsup when on their way, the train gaining speed as it wound through the countryside. "This is the future."

"It's too loud!" Sandy answered.

"Will it sway like this all the time?" Cindy asked.

"I certainly hope not," replied Allsup, who was at the moment feeling a bit squeamish. "It seems to be getting better!"

Indeed, it had; the train had gathered its momentum, moving as a single unit, proceeding along smoothly on the recently laid rails. It slowly chugged up a mountainside on meandering tracks, with many clutching their seats yet again.

Their car was full, filled with an assortment of people; most were individual men heading west for work and families. There were two women with children traveling without male accompaniment. With the families, the two women and their charges, along with Allsup and the girls, the car was full and loud. Kids ran up and down the center aisle and climbed over seats. They played games and used the girls' pencils to play tic-tac-toe and connect the dots on the car's floor.

At one point soon after the train's departure, the volume within the cabin rose, and people scurried to the left side of the car. Allsup strained to determine the cause of the commotion, which soon became apparent. The Great Salt Lake came into view. It stretched out like an ocean without sight of the opposite shore. The girls looked but were unimpressed, with Cindy observing, "It's just a big lake." Allsup attempted to explain that it was a big *salt* lake, very unusual, and the theories behind its creation when he noted that neither girl was listening, absorbed in a boy about their age across the aisle making faces.

It seemed no time had passed at all when they pulled into the Ogden Station. The kids shouted goodbyes to those not continuing, those that were, stayed close to their parents while they moved their belongings to the waiting Union Pacific train two tracks down. Allsup and the two girls monitored the transfer of Chestnut from one line to the other. After he confirmed the horse was settled, they went in search of their own car.

There were three passenger cars, two livery cars, and one freight followed by a caboose. The first of two locomotives puffed billows of black smoke skyward while occasionally relieving the steam pressure in loud bursts of industrial flatulence.

They were directed to the third car; the first two were filled to capacity. They climbed into a car paneled in stained wood with bench seats similar to their previous experience, but these were covered by cushions, both the back and the seat. There were stoves placed at the front and rear of the car for heating. As the morning had turned bitterly cold, both stoves were in use. When they walked into the car, they were hit with extreme heat from the forward stove. Allsup looked down the aisle to find the mid-section of the car, the area of the car with less heat, completely occupied while many vacancies were available the further away from the center one ventured.

He selected seats midway between the center of the car and the rear, and because of the stove, it was noticeably very warm. The girls complained as they removed their coats, wraps, and hats; Allsup slid open the window to vent out the heat and allow in cold, refreshing air.

A railway worker, referred to as a conductor, came through the car announcing their departure time would be in ten minutes. He stopped by Allsup and the girls and suggested Allsup close the window when the train pulls out.

"But it's so hot!" Allsup complained. "It feels like we're being cooked to death."

"Well, if ya leave that window open, you'll look dead with soot-covered faces," the blue-suited conductor advised, smiling. He had this conversation several times each trip; some listened, and some didn't.

"Once we get 'a goin' the smoke from that engine's gonna blow right back into this car. When we hit the steep slopes, and they fire up that second engine, everything a quarter mile from the tracks will be turned to black. You'll be surprised how dirty ya get even with the windows closed. Listen to a man of experience, close the window, and keep those little girls' pretty dresses nice. Five minutes, folks! We'll be on our way in five minutes!" He passed on to the next car.

For the first part of their trip, the train made several stops at other towns and villages, but later in the afternoon, their elevation began to increase, and the communities disappeared. An hour out of Ogden and all the kids in their car had become friends. When it became known that their car was less full, people from the first two came back to take advantage of the available space. Some just sent their kids to play so the parents could have a moment.

Passengers of the third car didn't mind the migration, except the more bodies, the more heat. A newer occupant to the car, one who missed the conductor's earlier informative explanation regarding closed windows, opened a window and, like a black ghost, the smoke swirled in and around the inner car, sprinkling all with ash and cinder. Admonished by all, he quickly closed the window.

The day drew late; a vendor pushed a cart filled with sandwiches and fruit to sell to those hungry and with money. Allsup purchased a sandwich and an apple for each. As the evening progressed and darkness covered the landscape, the train rose and fell on tracks forced upon the mountains, around and through them. The rocking of the car became soothing, along with the clickety-clack of the iron wheels rolling on iron tracks.

Sandy and Cindy were tired from their first day of train travel and all the excitement that went with it. They tried to pillow against each other, but it was too warm. They squirmed this way and that, whined about the heat or there wasn't enough room, they couldn't get comfortable.

Allsup was tired and trying to sleep with his hat pulled down over his eyes when he felt a light tap on his shoulder. Raising his hat, he saw a smiling young couple standing before him.

"Yes?"

"We're sorry to bother you," the young man said. "But I noticed your two girls are having trouble sleeping. My guess is because of the heat."

Allsup put his hat on and rubbed his eyes awake before repeating, "Yeah?"

"Well, we'll switch seats with them," he proposed. "They can sit where we were up ahead there four rows; it's much cooler, and we'll sit back here—with you if you don't mind."

"That's very generous of you," Allsup told them. "Are you sure?"

When they assured him that their intentions were sincere, Allsup relocated the girls to the cooler, central location in the car. Without the intense heat, the girls cuddled together, wrapped in their coats for blankets and quickly fell asleep.

Allsup wondered how anyone could sleep in this human furnace and was amazed that the young couple now sitting across from him were able to do so. Concealed by a blanket, ignoring the heat, they seemed completely comfortable and at rest. A soft female giggle from beneath the blanket revealed no sleep was going on underneath. The blanket began to move and bounce in different spots causing Allsup discomfort. He moved to a seat closer to the back, deciding things were going to heat up no matter where he sat; the move could be made without embarrassment for remaining would most certainly guarantee it.

The car was still and quiet. The hum of the wheels, along with the gentle swaying of the car, created a cradle-like environment that comforted all. A conductor came through and dimmed the oil-burning lamps intensifying the yellowishness of their illumination and softening the shadows.

Tomorrow will be an interesting day, Allsup thought, relaxing with his legs stretched out into the aisle, his shirt unbuttoned to help alleviate the heat. We'll reach Sacramento tomorrow. The girls will be reunited with their father. And Chestnut and I will be on our way, on our own once more.

Chapter 74

"We're on the west side of Nevada," the conductor told him in answer to his inquiry. "Where you headed?"

"Sacramento," Allsup replied.

"Oh, well, we should be there right around four o'clock, I would estimate. Still light out." The conductor smiled and adjusted a window curtain before moving on.

It was pleasant outside, not too cold, so the heating stoves were burning at minimum, making it pleasant inside as well.

Allsup sat with his eyes closed, his hat pulled down to conceal that point, and felt confident a nap would help catch up on what sleep he missed during the night.

The train slowed to a halt. Allsup sat up. Concerned passengers got up and talked about the possible reasons for stopping when a conductor entered, and the car became silent.

"Nothing to be alarmed about, folks. Got some deep snow up ahead, piled up in a narrow gorge we gotta pass through. The problem is, sometimes they have rock falls, avalanches they call them, and sometimes some mighty big rocks land on the tracks. We can push them off, but we sure don't want to crash into them. With the snow piled up as it is up ahead, we don't know if it's snow or snow-covered rocks. So, we sent a man ahead to check. It's slow but safer. Feel free to walk amongst the cars, stretch your legs, but please don't get off the train. We don't want to leave anyone behind; survival is near impossible. Thanks for your cooperation, and sorry again for the delay."

Allsup took that as all the more reason to take a nap; make the time pass.

He slid down in the corner of the seat, pulling his hat down over his eyes, balancing it on the bridge of his nose.

He sighed as he relaxed.

"Mr. Allsup." He felt a light tap on his shoulder. "Mr. Allsup."

He raised his hat and found Cindy and Sandy standing beside him, along with several other children.

"What? I thought you were playing. What do you want?" He sat upright and replaced his hat atop his head.

"We wanna know..." Cindy looked away shyly.

"We wanna know," Sandy jumped in, "if since the train stopped and it's not going to start going for a while, that's what that train man said anyway. We wanna know if we can go see the other cars and play with the kids there?"

"I guess it's all right." Allsup noticed the several other children accompanying the two.

"What did your parents say?" he asked one.

"I can go."

"What about your parents?" he looked at a brown-haired girl holding a doll.

"They said I can go."

Turning to Cindy and Sandy, he said, "Okay, you can go; but listen! When they announce the train is going to start, you come right back, okay? I don't want to worry about you, and I don't want to have to go looking for you, either. Okay?"

They agreed and dashed to the door to begin exploring. Allsup slid back down into his corner, adjusted his hat, and fell into a deep sleep.

He awoke with a start and wondered how long he had been sleeping. The train was traveling at a brisk pace; they were going down the side of a mountain and the brakes screamed their displeasure over the frequency of their use.

He cleared his throat and wished he had water, but his eyes were still heavy, so he let them close. At first, he thought of little except how nice it was in the swaying car; then he recalled that their train ride would end later in the day in Sacramento when he delivered Cindy and Sandy to their father. Cindy and Sandy—where were they?

He opened his eyes and noted how quiet it was compared to earlier when the children were all playing together. He glanced around the car; neither girl was there. He sat up and looked around again. Most of the adults, with their children at their sides, were watching him with looks of disapproval.

Allsup stood and headed toward the front of the car.

"Excuse me," he said to a couple whose children had been playing with the girls earlier. "Have you seen the two girls I'm traveling with? They were supposed to return when the train resumed, but I see that they did not."

Both adults shook their heads and answered, "No."

"What about you?" he addressed their children. "Do you know where Cindy and Sandy are?"

"They don't know!" the mother curtly informed him.

"Oh, okay, thanks." Allsup continued towards the car's front, asking several others. Each time he was rebuffed with a stern "No."

He entered the second car and when he could not see them, started walking forward again, making the same inquiry along the way. The responses and attitudes were similar to those in the previous car.

Allsup wasn't worried. He knew they couldn't have gotten off the train. They had to be in one of the cars, probably playing. He knew he shouldn't be mad, they were just little kids who probably hadn't noticed the train had resumed, but he couldn't help feeling annoyed that he had to go search for them and that the other passengers were being so rude and uncooperative.

When he entered the back of the first car, he found the girls standing at the front alongside an older couple who had a hand on the shoulder of each child. The couple were plainly dressed in gray and black, like so many of the people in that part of the world. The man wore a flat, broad-rimmed black hat, while the lady had her hair tucked under a faded white bonnet.

"There you are!" Allsup exclaimed, walking towards them. "You were supposed to come back when they announced the train was going to start, remember?"

Both girls nodded but said nothing, looking at him with frightened eyes.

"What's the matter? Are you alright?"

They looked at the older couple before nodding again.

"Okay, well, come, let's go. Say goodbye and let's go." To the couple, "Thank you for looking after them."

"They are staying with us," the man said bluntly.

"What?"

"They're staying with us," he repeated. "Until we reach the next stop where they'll be turned over to the authorities as you yourself will be."

"What's going on? Has something happened? Did they do something?"

"They have not!" the woman shouted. "It is you who have sinned!"

"What? Now, wait…"

"Abductor!" she shouted. "Abductor! Where are these girls' parents? Why are they with you?"

"Did you ask them?" Allsup was becoming irritated.

"They gave us a story that you must have put in their head about their mother dying and you're taking them to rejoin their father."

"I didn't put that story in their heads. It's a fact."

"Are you a relation to these girls?" asked the man.

"No, I'm not."

"Then why would the mother entrust their care with you?"

"She didn't. The owners of the Fillmore City Hotel, who had them in their care after their mother died, requested I deliver them to their father in Sacramento."

"Why would they allow the care of these sweet things to a stranger?"

"Because I'm going that way, I guess."

"I don't accept his story," the woman said to the man, who shook his head.

"Ask the girls!" Allsup suggested. "They'll tell you!"

"They'll say whatever you told them to say, I warrant," responded the man. "They're obviously terrified for their lives!"

"If they're terrified of anybody, it's you! They've been with me since Fillmore City; they're obviously unharmed and well-fed. If you'll remove your hands, I'll be taking them back to our car."

"They will stay with us until the next stop," the woman told him. "Where they'll be turned over to the authorities, and you can answer to them!"

Allsup looked at the elderly couple and sighed.

"Look, I know you mean well and have the best of intentions, but I have made a promise to these two that I will not leave them until they're with their father. I keep my promises."

"They will stay with us," the man forcefully replied, "where we can assure their safety."

"Come on, girls, let's go." Allsup turned to head back. The girls were held tightly by their shoulders and could not follow.

"They're staying right here," said the woman.

Allsup sighed again.

"I am normally a patient, reasonable man, but you are testing me on both accounts. I'll ask you again to release the children. If you have a mind to follow us back to monitor their welfare, you're welcome to. I won't try to stop you. But they will be coming with me."

"No, sir, they are not." The man stepped in front of the girls and woman.

Allsup stood thinking for a minute, considering his next step, while the other passengers in the car wondered the same. He sighed a third time and slowly pulled his revolver from its holster and held it at arm's length aiming it at the man. There were several screams as the other passengers made every effort to flee, moving quickly back to the second car. In just seconds, only the elderly couple restraining the two girls and Allsup remained.

"Sir, you do not know me. If you did, you would know how difficult it is for me to take the position I am taking now. I have never drawn a gun on another in my entire life until this trip, and I feel I've done more than a life's worth since I started. I am a man of my word. I make a promise. I keep it to adults, children, to all living things. Before the eyes of God, I promise you this, sir, that before this gun becomes too heavy in my hand, I will either have the children with me or I will fire it and have the children with me. I don't know where the charge will hit you, sir. I'm not that accurate but hit you, it will. I will have your response, sir. The gun grows heavy."

A conductor entered the car.

"Comin' out'a the Sierra Nevadas; Sacramento in two hours," he announced before observing the scene. "What's going on here?"

"We're having a dispute over who the custodian of these two girls will be," Allsup answered. "Sir, I remind you of the weight of a six-shooter such as I have in my hand. It grows greater by the minute."

"He claims he's taking these two girls to meet their father," the woman began to explain. "We suspect he's taken them, kidnapped if you will, with the purpose of bringing them west for God only knows what sinful purpose!"

"He *is* taking them to rejoin their father," the conductor advised. "In Sacramento, where in another two hours we will be arriving."

To Allsup, he said, "Put that away. You're scaring the dickin's outta those two girls."

To the elderly couple, "Release those girls and let them get back to their car. Your intentions are good, I'm sure, but your intrusion into another's business almost got you shot."

The conductor followed Allsup and the girls out of the first car as they headed back to their own. As he entered the second car, he announced, "Alright, everybody go back to their cars and seats. Just a misunderstanding. Sacramento in two hours. Let's make the rest of the trip uneventful. Sacramento in two hours."

When they were back in the third car, sitting in their seats, the two girls looked at Allsup in wonder.

"You were going to shoot that man!" Sandy quietly exclaimed.

"Would you?" Cindy asked. "Would you have shot that man?"

"Of course he would!" answered Sandy. "He would have shot him for us. Wouldn't you, Mr. Allsup?"

He looked at the two sitting across from him, waiting. He smiled and looked down at his hands clasped tightly in his lap to still their trembling.

"I'm glad I didn't have to find out," he answered in a whisper.

"You would have though," said Sandy. "You would have because you promised."

"Would you?" Cindy asked.

"For the two of you—yes."

D. Dean Carroll

Chapter 75

They had on their new dresses. A lady riding in the car with her family volunteered to fix their hair, so their hair was nicely brushed and braided on Sandy and ponytailed on Cindy. Everyone in the car declared the two pretty enough for a painting.

The girls were so excited as the train entered the Sacramento station. After the incident in the first car, there were few unaware of Allsup's purpose and many were curious to witness the father and daughter reunion.

The train platform was crowded with those waiting to board for parts farther west and those waiting to greet the arrivals: families, husbands, and hopefully, in at least one case, a father for his two daughters.

Allsup helped the two girls down from the car onto the platform. Taking two steps to the left to get out of the way of others wishing access to the car, they stood together, Allsup holding a hand of each, unsure of what to do or who they were awaiting. People milled around them, blocking the girls' view of everything from the waist up.

"Do you see him?" Cindy asked.

"How can he see him?" Sandy impatiently asked. "He doesn't know what he looks like!"

"Yeah, but maybe he'll see someone that looks the same as us," Cindy explained.

"The same as us?"

"Not the *same* as us, but *looking* for us. Looking, but they don't know who for."

"I think I've found him," Allsup announced, "Come on, girls."

He led them through the crowd to a man standing on a small box absorbed in scanning the faces of all who walked by. They approached unnoticed from his back right-side.

"Mr. Clipper?" Allsup stood with a girl on each side, looking up at the man.

He made no response, so Allsup spoke again.

"Mr. Clipper!"

Still no response from the man. Allsup reached up and tapped him on the shoulder.

"Mr. Clipper!"

Startled, the man turned and looked down at the three gathered before him.

"What?" he sounded agitated.

"Are you Mr. Clipper?"

"Clipper? No, I'm not Clipper!" He returned to his task of surveying the crowd.

"Well..." Allsup began.

"I'm Henry Clipper." A well-dressed man stepped through the crowd and approached. "I heard you calling my name."

At first, he focused only on Allsup and failed to notice the two girls who were lost in the forest of people. Then his eyes traveled downward and discovered his daughters. The girls smiled broadly but acted shy, each hiding behind one of Allsup's legs.

Henry Clipper kneeled and exclaimed, "My lovely daughters!"

When they continued to hang on to Allsup, Clipper looked up at him with despair and said, "They don't know me. Cindy was just little when I left, and Sandy was still a baby. I'm a stranger to them."

"Oh, well, I can fix that," Allsup said, kneeling as well. He brought each girl forward, with an arm draped around each slender waist. "Mr. Henry Clipper, may I present to you your eldest daughter..."

"What's that mean?" Cindy whispered.

"You're the oldest!" Sandy whispered back.

"Your eldest daughter," Allsup ignored the interruption and continued, "Cindy Clipper, and does she have some stories for you." He looked questioningly at Cindy, who nodded a bashful yes.

"Yes, she does!" Allsup gave Sandy a little nudge forward. "And this is your youngest, Sandy, who's as smart as a whip! I believe she's smarter than most adults, including myself, especially myself! Girls, this is your father, Mr. Henry Clipper."

"Oh, you need know me only as father, or papa, or daddy, or…I don't know! I don't care! Just call me something that means your mine!" With tears and open arms, he begged, "Won't you please give me a hug?"

Cindy ran to him and hugged his neck tightly, while Sandy remained shy and standoffish.

"My darling, Sandy, I fear if you don't hug me, my heart will explode!"

She walked to him, gave the hug he requested and endured his many kisses while her eyes repeatedly glanced back at Allsup.

"I have been waiting at this station for the last five days," Clipper said, rising. "When I received the wire from the Hawkins that you were en route, I could barely contain myself." He chuckled. "Kept amongst ourselves, I came to the station the day after I'd received the wire! While standing on the platform, I realized how foolish I was.

"Mr. Allsup, you'll stay with us, of course. Right girls?" They loudly voiced their agreement. Clipper continued, "I have a house. You're welcome to stay for as long as you like."

Chapter 76

Sacramento grew inside an elbow of land created by the river bearing the same name. The bend in the elbow created a wide 'V' shape producing the effect of a city surrounded by water on two of its three sides. It grew upon the land that fanned out between the banks of the river, spreading to fill the area in between. Though small segments of population settled across the river, lack of access kept it minimal. Danny Allsup spent two full days in Sacramento, leaving in the early morning hours of the third.

On the first day, Clipper took them on a tour of Sacramento. They visited the Capitol Building and walked along the riverfront. In the Pioneer Music Store, Henry Clipper displayed his musical talents by playing *Oh, Suzanna* on three different pianos. He played the same song on each and while it may have betrayed his limited repertoire, he played well and with much enthusiasm and successfully impressed his daughters.

The music store had many novelties: toys and games and other items to catch a child's eye. Cindy and Sandy were no different and they pulled their father, grinning broadly, through the store, begging for this and that.

"All right! Girls! Stop!" he commanded, standing in the middle of an aisle. The two obediently stopped and turned to their father.

"You must understand, young ladies, I am not a rich man. We are comfortable, yes." He boastfully looked around the store. "But by no means rich. I cannot afford to buy you whatever your lovely hearts' desire, would that I could, but I cannot. Tell me you understand, do you?"

They nodded.

"Ah, my sweet, beautiful girls!" He hugged each. "Now, go and pick out one thing and one thing only!"

D. Dean Carroll

They stopped at Malone Stables and Carriage, where Clipper shopped for a used buggy.

"My days of traveling by horseback are over," he proudly declared. "I have a family to transport now."

An employee of the stables presented two used carriages, both two-seaters, both equipped with a storage box on the back. One came with lanterns mounted on either side at the front of the buggy; Clipper liked that idea.

"Why don't you two girls take Mr. Allsup out to look at the horses while I conduct business with this man."

They left him in the stable and walked over to the corral containing several horses. As they were discussing which horse was prettiest or fastest looking, Henry Clipper rejoined them, and they continued strolling along the street.

"Were you successful?" Allsup inquired.

"No, not just yet," Clipper answered. "But I've planted a seed which I think will eventually bring him around to my way of thinking...unless someone else buys the carriage first."

"That is always a possibility."

"Yes, well, there are other buggies available, I'm sure. We'll continue looking." He shot a glance at Allsup before adding. "Another time."

The look of relief on Allsup's face caused the father to chuckle.

They visited Clipper's office in the heart of town. He worked for a railcar manufacturing company. Clipper's current job, along with four other engineers, was to design a refrigerated freight car. Fruits and vegetables from the western part of the country would sell well east, if delivered fresh. Clipper's department was to design the car.

They walked up the three flights to the floor of his office. The other four engineers were present and involved in a discussion they did not want interrupted, so they nodded or waved as they were introduced but never deviated from their conversation.

Danny Allsup

The girls took turns sitting at their father's desk in his woodened chair that happened to swivel nicely. With its gently rounded back made of wooden rungs that allowed one to comfortably settle in, and the chair's smooth flowing arms that were just the right height, it took little effort to stay seated during a spin. Round and round one would go, propelled by the other. They would abruptly stop, and the rider would get up to see how dizzy she might be; then change rolls and repeat.

After leaving the office, they continued their walk as the day grew later. They passed a storefront whose window contained photographs of different posed portraits. Clipper stopped and viewed the different pictures. He read the store's sign: 'Beal's Gallery.'

"I have a notion," he addressed the three. "I suggest we take an image of the four of us together to commemorate our reunion and the man who made it possible. What do you say, Mr. Allsup, shall we?"

He agreed and together they walked into the artist's studio. Mr. Beal was happy to be of service, as he explained, he had nothing pending for the day, no other customers scheduled or waiting.

Beal led them to a back room that served as his studio. Different colored drapes with different designs hung loosely along its walls. A variety of chairs and two couches were scattered about along with several pedestals, of which half were topped with ornamented vases and busts of historic men.

He pushed a plush upholstered chair with an intricately carved back that rose head-high in front of a dark green drape. He had Clipper take the seat and placed a daughter on either side, each with a hand resting on his shoulder and the other on his arm. Allsup was placed standing behind the three, his hands resting on the back of the chair. After making many adjustments, the girls were to look lovingly at their father, who should gaze somberly off to Beal's right, while Allsup looked into the camera, appearing protective of them all, Beal raced to his box camera and concealed his head under a black cloth attached to its back.

Under the cloth he directed, "You in the chair!" His voice muffled. "Chin up, sir, chin up! Yes, that's good."

"In the back! Eyes forward! Look directly at me!"

"But I can't see you!" Allsup protested.

"I am the camera, sir." He brought his head out from beneath the cloth. "When I am enshrouded in darkness with just your upside-down image in miniature my only light, I am the camera, sir, I am the camera."

"Yes, I see. I understand now. Please continue." Beal's head disappeared once again.

"Young lady on the left, *my* left, look at your father, little one, not at the man behind you. That's a good girl. I believe we're ready! One more check! Everybody hold completely still until I say we're done. Hold it…one, two, three!"

There was a flash of light from a small explosion atop a 'T' shaped devise held by Beal that left the smell of gunpowder in the room.

"Excellent!" exclaimed Beal. "I believe we have an excellent photograph. I should have it ready in three days' time. Feel free to drop by in two, if you wish, it's possible it might be ready early."

Back out walking, Sandy asked, "Mr. Allsup, will you be here in three days?"

"No, I intend to leave the day after tomorrow."

"But you won't get to see the photograph!" she protested.

"No, I won't."

"Maybe on your way back, you could stop by and visit," Henry Clipper suggested. "We could show it to you then."

"Yes!" Cindy clapped enthusiastically. "Say you'll stop on your way back!"

"I…" Allsup began before Clipper interrupted.

"Say you will," he suggested, smiling. "Just say you will."

"I will." Both girls cheered and took his hand, walking side-by-side down the street talking away as natural as can be.

They dined at the Central Restaurant and returned home in the early evening. Both girls were tired, so their father sent them off to bed. Complaining, they walked down the hall bidding Allsup a goodnight.

Allsup sat with his legs stretched out and his hands folded in his lap. It was a good day, he considered, though he regretted he would not get to see the photograph; it was his first. It would give them something to remember him by.

Clipper entered the room and said, "They want to see you."

Allsup followed their father into the bedroom the two girls shared.

"Well?" he asked.

"We can't sleep," Cindy complained.

"We hardly slept last night!" Sandy told him. "I don't think tonight's going to be any better."

"What's wrong?" he asked.

"What if a bad man tries to get us?" Cindy whispered.

"Nobody can harm you here."

"Yes, but what if…" Sandy quietly added. "What if something tries to get us?"

"Yes, like wolves!" whispered Cindy.

"That's enough, you two," Allsup playfully scolded. "What's going on here?"

"We're used to you sleeping with us," Sandy explained. "We don't have to worry when you're with us."

"Will you sleep here with us?" Cindy pleaded.

"No," answered Allsup. "And I'll tell you why."

He pulled a chair up between their two beds and sat with his arms resting on his knees.

"You've got your father now," he explained. "It's his

job to take care of you. And he wants to so bad. Can't you tell?"

Reluctantly, they agreed.

Their father stood just outside the bedroom doorway giving them the appearance of privacy.

"So, even if I wanted to, even if I *wanted* to, I have to let your father do it now."

"Does he have a gun?" Cindy asked.

"I don't know."

"Daddy, do you have a gun?" she called out.

"A gun? No, I don't."

"He doesn't even own a gun," Sandy bluntly pointed out.

"He probably doesn't need one living here in Sacramento," Allsup replied. "Maybe, since they have police officers all around the city, people don't need to carry guns."

"Do you think he's shot anybody?" Cindy further inquired.

"Probably not…"

"Daddy," she interrupted. "Have you ever shot anybody?"

"Have I—What? No, I haven't shot anybody! Why?"

"You need to stay," Sandy told Allsup.

"No, I don't. I'm going to call your father in and you're going tell him you want him to stay with you. He will. It'll make his day."

Allsup rose from his chair.

"Mr. Clipper! Your daughters have something they wish to discuss with you."

As their father walked into the room Allsup said, "I'll leave you three to talk. Goodnight, girls!"

Their response was expressed reluctantly, but they expressed it just the same.

He returned to his chair and stretched out once again, sighing with a smile. He wasn't there long when Clipper called from their bedroom, "Goodnight, Mr. Allsup, I'm staying with them tonight."

Allsup's second day in Sacramento was spent preparing for the next day's departure. He settled with Gillis and Company Livery for boarding Chestnut. He arranged to have him saddled and ready by seven the next morning; he planned for an early departure. Mr. Golden, co-proprietor of the business, assured him the horse would be ready as requested.

At the Capital Savings Bank he opened accounts with a deposit of fifty dollars for each of the girls. The bank official who provided the service assured him that the money would remain untouched until their fourteenth birthdays. They would have the option of leaving the money with the bank or withdraw the funds.

At Lindlay's Grocers, he replenished his supplies. He arranged to have them delivered to the Clipper house so he could continue with his preparations unburdened.

At the same time Clipper and his daughters were having a busy day as well. They visited the local schoolhouse and enrolled Sandy and Cindy. They would begin the following day.

He took them shopping for new clothes, suitable for school and church, and marveled over how mature they sounded when discussing their appearance and apparel. Their mother's influence was solidly instilled.

They rendezvoused with a colleague from Clipper's work and his daughter of thirteen who had agreed to watch the children after school. They met at a side-street restaurant for cake where Cindy and Sandy overcame their shyness and became fast friends with the older girl.

It took some time for Allsup to find the Central Restaurant later that afternoon; Clipper, Sandy and Cindy were waiting when he arrived. The Central was a favorite restaurant of Clipper's and he wanted to treat Allsup for their last dinner together.

"As a means of showing my appreciation for your care

and devotion to my daughters and delivering them safely to me," Clipper explained to the table in the form of a toast with his raised glass of ale. "And as a gesture cementing your place in our family and in our hearts, to Mr. Danny Allsup."

The girls raised their glasses of milk, Allsup his coffee cup, and the sound of celebration clinked forth from the table.

"Now you have to come back," Cindy told him.

"Yes," Sandy agreed. "We're family now. Right, Daddy?"

"That's right!" Clipper's face beamed happiness. "He'll be back. We're family now."

The sun was just emerging above the eastern horizon when he rode out of Sacramento. He'd returned to the Clipper house after leaving the stable on Chestnut to get his possessions. Sandy and Cindy, excited about their first day of school, were up and dressed. It was obvious they were saddened by Allsup's departure, but the excitement of school was stronger.

"Well, I don't want to stretch it out, so I'll say goodbye." Allsup extended his hand to Cindy. "I have enjoyed my time with you little one. When you think of—what was his name?"

"Knute," she reminded him proudly.

"Yes, when you hold that boar's tusk necklace, and think of Knute and Louis Tanner, maybe you'll think of me too." Cindy brushed passed his hand and hugged him tightly.

"I will think of you, Mr. Allsup," she told him. "I won't need the necklace to do it either!"

"That's my girl." He patted her back before turning to her sister.

"I'm expecting great things from you, little genius." He smiled as he extended his hand to her. "Don't let me down."

Sandy rushed to Allsup, like her sister, and embraced him tightly, her face pressed against his thigh.

"I know what you've done, Mr. Allsup." Her blue eyes

looked up at him. "We wouldn't be here if it wasn't for you."

"It was my pleasure," he replied. "I'm happy to have met you, all of you, and to have spent the time I did with you while staying in your home."

"Your home, too, Mr. Allsup," Henry Clipper reminded while shaking his hand. "Your home too. I count on your return in the future…the sooner the better.

Allsup mounted Chestnut and turned him towards the road.

"May God smile upon you always," he told the three with his hat removed. "And bless you with happiness all the days of your lives." And with a wink he said, "Watch this—Let's go, Chestnut!" The horse reared up on its hind legs and for a second seemed to pose to impress. As soon as his front legs hit the ground, he was running trying to beat the sunrise westward.

Chapter 77

"Less than a hundred miles, give or take a few," That's what the stable proprietor told Allsup when asked how far to the Pacific. The idea that it was so close excited him.

It felt good to be on his horse again, just the two of them. He enjoyed his travels with his young female companions, but this was better. Just the quiet made it better.

They were descending a steep hillside where the road could be viewed miles ahead. It appeared to be relatively straight with just a few soft curves. Though it appeared to be a well-traveled road, its surface packed and hard, there was no one else making use of it now.

He chuckled and rubbed Chestnut's neck, asking, "Do you even remember how to run, you old wagon pulling…"

Before he could finish, the horse dashed ahead into a full-out gallop, legs stretched out forward and back leaving a trail of dust rising slowly like smoke from a train. The horse raced along the road faster than Allsup could recall; pulling wagons obviously had its benefits.

They continued in that manner, a smooth, almost airborne ride for Allsup, who tried to keep himself as low to the horse as possible. A rabbit dashed out from the side of the road, but Chestnut never faltered, just sailed over its path before the hare reached the other side. A distance farther, displaced rubble appeared, evidence of a small landslide, and with it a small tree lying across the road. Allsup held his breath and Chestnut's mane as the horse leaped far too soon in Allsup's opinion and flew over the tree before landing without missing a step.

He spent the first night on a low, round-topped mountain covered with trees. Through the treetops, he could see the night sky; it seemed he had been gone too long. Under the stars around a campfire now felt like home to him;

Danny Allsup

a far difference from that first night in Pennsylvania. Though the night was cold, it frosted the ground, Allsup never felt it, even when the campfire burned low.

He was up at sunrise and headed down the side of the mountain without breakfast. He was anxious; the Pacific was a day closer. The sun warmed the mountain air enough that Allsup was compelled to remove his duster and drape it across the back of his saddle.

He reached the mountain's foothills, crossed a stream in a small valley, and began the ascent up the next round-top, as Allsup called them. Compared to the Rockies and the Sierra Nevada's, these were just big hills; much like the Appalachians back home but with not as many trees.

Shortly after high noon, he crested the mountain and saw at its base a large lake. By the time he reached its shore, Allsup reasoned, it will be time to stop for the day. Perhaps he would have fish for dinner tonight.

As soon as he reached the water's edge, Allsup bounded from his saddle and plunged his head into the ice-cold water; it felt refreshing and cool. Chestnut stood watching the man before shaking his head and began drinking.

Allsup raised his head from the water, shouting, "Woo-hoo! That's cold!"

He shook the water from his hair then drank several handfuls. Feeling extremely good, he donned his hat, rested his hands on his hips, and surveyed his surroundings. Five horse-lengths away stood an Indian with a bow and arrow.

He had long black hair streaked with gray tied behind his head; his stain-colored face was wrinkled and weathered; his eyes seemed to peek between folds. Wearing buckskin boots and pants, he was draped in an unusually designed blanket with crudely drawn animals placed randomly upon it, and a hole in its center in the manner of a poncho. He stood looking at Allsup with an arrow notched and partially drawn.

Allsup nervously smiled and raised his hand in greeting.

The Indian continued to study him.

"Stay?" the Indian asked.

After a moment, Allsup nodded, saying, "Yes, I hoped to."

The Indian nodded slowly before pointing to the water. "Fish?"

"Um, I like fish. I like to fish. I like to eat fish."

"Fish?" the Indian repeated, imitating eating with a hand to his mouth.

"Oh! Yes! I like to eat fish!"

"Hm...eat," the Indian contemplated. "Eat fish."

He turned to the water and pulled his bow taut. Allsup saw that there was a thin line attached to the arrow. The man waited patiently, scanning the water, his arrow ready. He loudly cleared his throat bringing phlegm to his mouth and spit the gob into the water. Within seconds, several fish were at the surface checking the floating glob for palatability. With a snap of the bowstring and a splash, the arrow was lost beneath the water's surface, seconds later it emerged bobbing on the water.

The man muttered something Allsup deemed Indian profanity.

Allsup began unpacking his gear to the sound of hacking as the fisherman continued his efforts. The white man released Chestnut to forage for food and noticed the Indian appeared to be traveling on foot. No other means of transportation was visible.

With a "Woo!" the Indian announced his success and proudly held up a flopping fish run through by the arrow.

"Eat fish!" he announced.

After the Indian cleaned his catch and skewered it to cook over the fire. Allsup stopped him before he could continue and brought out a small leather bag containing a mixture of salt and pepper he'd purchased while in Sacramento. He wet his finger and dipped it into the bag and removed it covered with the mix. He popped the finger into his mouth and savored the spices' flavor.

He offered the same opportunity to the Indian who took the bag and studied it intently. He sniffed the contents and must have pulled in a granule of pepper because he sneezed several times. Amused, he wet his finger and followed Allsup's example. When he placed his finger into his mouth, his eyes widened with delight! He pulled out his finger laughing and wanted to repeat the process, but Allsup stopped him.

He took a pinch from the bag and sprinkled it over the fish. The Indian understood at once and encouraged the white man to use more; Allsup relented and another pinch or two was added.

Over a dinner of fish cooked above an open fire, hardtack, jerky, and coffee, they attempted to converse. Allsup learned the Indian's name was Sem Yeto; he was of the Patwin people. When Allsup asked where the other Patwin were, Sem Yeto paused and considered for a moment.

"Gone," he said, gracefully spreading out his arms. He brought a hand slowly to his face, palm up, and blew gently across it.

"Gone," he repeated sounding tired.

"Where did they go?"

The Indian shook his head slowly. "Gone."

They sat solemnly by the fire staring at the dancing flames. After a time, Sem Yeto gently slapped Allsup's shoulder and motioned him to follow. They went to a clearing alongside the lake where the Indian broke a stick in two and drove one piece into the ground vertically a man's hand-length high. He pulled out a large white man's knife and flipped it, attempting to stick it into the ground as close to the peg as possible; it landed half-a-foot away. Sem Yeto stepped back and motioned for Allsup to take a turn. The white man realized the Indian's intent having played the game himself as a youth and removed his knife from its sheath.

The native and white man played well into the evening; each tried to put an extra flip or flare to their throw. They were like boys playing in the clearing by the lake with only the distant moon and campfire for illumination. There was much laughter and playful pushing and shoving, but neither talked; it was unnecessary.

The next morning as Allsup prepared to leave, he invited Sem Yeto to go with him, but the Indian declined, spreading out an arm gesturing to the lake, the rolling hills and mountains repeating a word that Allsup took to mean, "Home."

Smiling, Allsup touched his head and nodded and then touched his heart.

When he secured the last of his belongings to the horse, he turned to say goodbye.

"Sem Yeto," he said extending his hand. "I'm going." He tried to make his intention known through gestures.

The Indian watched, looked at the extended hand and then at Allsup.

"Where I come from," Allsup explained, knowing he would not be understood. "We shake hands as a gesture of goodwill when we say goodbye." He took the Indian's hand firmly in his own and shook it gently three times.

Sem Yeto abruptly pulled his hand back and looked at the white man curiously.

Danny Allsup shrugged his shoulders and mounted Chestnut.

"Well, it has been interesting, I'll give you that," Allsup stated.

The Indian stood looking up at the rider.

"Oh, I almost forgot." Allsup rummaged through a bag and, finding the little spice pouch, tossed it to the Indian, who smiled as he opened it and realized its contents.

"Well, I hope sunlight brings you good fortune," Allsup said. He gave Chestnut a nudge and the horse continued their journey westward.

As the white man rode away, the Indian raised the pouch and called out, "Eat fish!"

Chapter 78

He found a trail that led up into the mountains on the west side of the lake and followed it. The trail wound its way through mountain passes and over mountain tops, down through small valleys and through steep-sided canyons. They rode by a lake nestled in the hollow of a mountaintop with islands of thin sheets of ice floating on its surface. Allsup could see his reflection atop Chestnut as they passed and sat a little straighter.

Coming down the mountain, he entered a small-town bustling with activity. The sign on the mercantile identified the place as St. Helena, as in St. Helena Mercantile. Allsup had no intention of stopping, but his curiosity got the better of him. The street was filled with busy men and very few women. Most of the men were moving with determination and purpose.

"Excuse me!" Allsup called out to one of the few men not in motion, standing idly before a bank. He was middle age, graying at the temples, his paunch boasting prosperity and success. He wore a dusty grey pin-striped suit and a matching tie with a fancy pin holding it in place.

"Excuse me!" he tried again.

The man smoked a cigar while staring at Allsup; little clouds of smoke passed through his lips at regular intervals. He looked in both directions before stepping out onto the dirt street.

"What can I do for you, citizen?" he asked, the cigar gripped firmly in the side of his mouth.

"What goes on here? Why all the activity?"

"Ah," said the man, waving his hand in dismissal. "Another silver run. We get one every couple of months. Someone finds a nugget and before you know it, word's out it's a vein, then a mine. Before you know it, seems half the vagrants from each direction descend upon our town."

"I see," Allsup sat back in his saddle, satisfied.

"You here for the silver?" the man inquired.

"No, no, passing through. I was curious."

"Where you headed?"

"West."

"Citizen, where do you think you are?"

"The Pacific."

"Oh, the ocean. It's not far from what I hear. Strange, I've never seen it myself."

"Well, I won't keep you standing in the road," Allsup said, turning Chestnut west. "Good day to you, sir."

He stopped for the night a few miles outside of St. Helena. Many others were using the same road on the west side of the town requiring Allsup to ride a stretch inland to avoid the traffic. It was while he was resting, the campfire had all but burned itself out, that he heard the rain before feeling it, little plops hitting the hard-dry surface. He had just enough time to wrap himself in his ground tarp when the bottom dropped out and he was hit with a deluge.

There was no place for shelter; water was streaming down the mountainside, pouring in through little openings of the tarp, soaking him as if he were lying unprotected. It reached a point he could stand it no more. He stood and removed the tarp, whistled for Chestnut, and began packing his gear.

Chestnut walked through the trees to join him. His mane and tail hung wet, twisted together in thick clumps. The horse appeared as miserable as the man.

"Come on, Chestnut," Allsup shouted over the falling rain. "I know you're not resting any better than I am. I say if we're going to be awake and wet, we might as well be traveling and wet."

It took little time before they were descending the mountain. Allsup hadn't considered it at the time, but with the rain falling in sheets, visibility was limited. It soon became obvious to Allsup that they would not find the trail, so the direction they strived for was down.

Night gave way to dawn, which surrendered to daylight, but the sky remained overcast with dark clouds even as the rain lightened to a steady shower. He reached a clearing in his descent where he could see through the trees far into the distance to a valley below of rolling hills and plush vegetation.

He continued riding down the mountainside and noticed a change in the temperature; it was becoming increasingly warmer. The rain had stopped by the time he was riding through the valley filled with flowers, fruit trees, and meadow-covered hills gently rolling one into the next; the clouds dispersed, and the sun dried the wet.

This must be what Eden was like, Allsup thought again as Chestnut waded through a creek. He draped his duster over the back of the horse and basked in the pleasant weather; the cool air was warmed by the sun, and a breeze just strong enough to flutter leaves in the trees made him wonder why anyone passing through wouldn't decide to stay.

And stay is exactly what he decided to do, at least for the night. He made camp a few feet from a stream filled with ice-cold snowmelt seeking the lowest level. There was plenty of tall green grass for a change, so Allsup turned Chestnut loose to eat his fill while he went hunting for meat and scouring the area for firewood.

The hill he climbed with his rifle resting in the crook of his arm had a gradual incline and was covered with tall grass and wildflowers. He entered a stand of trees and found red, round-shaped bulbs scattered about; one was partially eaten by an animal and revealed hundreds of dark red berries within its interior. Poking a berry with his finger caused it to burst, squirting blood-red juice into the air. Without thinking, he licked the juice from his finger. He picked an undamaged fruit from the ground and used his knife to cut it

Danny Allsup

in half, each side filled with berries.

A single berry was sampled. Allsup waited for any unfavorable effects but only experienced the desire for more. The first fruit was completely consumed and half of the second before he stopped and leaned back against a tree with a sigh. He pocketed two for later and resumed the hunt.

The sun was dropping and with it, the temperature. The air was cooling, and he wanted to have the fire going, at least for coffee, before dark, so he headed back. He bagged a rabbit not thirty feet from the campsite.

As he sat licking the remnants of dinner from his fingers, Chestnut came up behind and nudged the man's shoulder with his nose. Allsup wiped his hands on his pantleg and rubbed the horse's muzzle, talking softly. Chestnut rested his head on Allsup's right shoulder and remained there for a time. While Allsup was scratching its forelock, Chestnut raised his head and moved back up the hillside.

"Guess we're done with that!" Allsup said as he watched the horse disappear into the darkness.

The next morning found Allsup reclined against his saddle drinking coffee; he was in no hurry to leave. In fact, the idea occurred to him that perhaps this might be a place he could come back to and settle down. He could not recall a prettier place, even that spot in Pennsylvania earlier in the trip.

But on he would ride. He saddled Chestnut and secured his belongings and motivated by the thought he could only be a day or two away, jumped up onto the saddle.

"Let's go, Chestnut," he said as they began to climb another mountain, "We're almost there."

Chapter 79

"It's snowing!" he said with annoyance. He was almost to the peak of another round top when it began to flurry. Allsup twisted and turned in his saddle, scanning the sky.

"There's not a cloud up there!" he exclaimed. "Where's it coming from? That's not possible, is it, Chestnut?" The horse plodded along, ignoring the man.

"I don't see how that's possible."

They traveled on with the snow settling where it landed. It wasn't wet snow, but a dry fluffy flake, light and landing gently, easy to brush away.

"And there are those who claim God doesn't have a sense of humor!" he said loudly with a laugh. "Don't tell me He doesn't have a sense of humor—He's laughing at me right now!"

He contemplated that thought before observing, "Snow on a cloudless day, a sunny day at that. It doesn't make sense."

Chestnut stopped.

"Come on, let's go." Allsup nudged the horse with his knees, but the horse refused to move.

"We're never going to make it if you don't move! Come on, let's go!"

Chestnut did not move on.

Exasperated, Allsup settled back in the saddle and let the reins drop across the horse's neck.

"All right," he conceded, his arms crossed. "You win. I'll wait."

For the first time, Allsup took in the surroundings. How pretty it was, all white, covered in fresh, clean snow. At their elevation, he could see distant mountaintops to the north and south; snow-covered. He wondered if there wasn't somebody on one of those other round-tops looking at him and wondering the same.

Ahead, he could see nothing…at first.

He *could* see something, but nothing like he'd ever seen before; no mountains, hills, or forests. Beyond the base of the mountain, beyond its foothills covered in a dense forest that spread in all directions, was a vast expanse of blue over the entire horizon! It was a color blue he'd not seen before, dark and bright at the same time.

As man and horse both stared off into the distance, reverently transfixed by the first sight of their destination, Allsup said, "And people say God doesn't have a sense of humor."

D. Dean Carroll

Chapter 80

It seemed the closer to sea level, the denser the forest and underbrush became. There were many times they had to backtrack and find a new route because of the thickness of the foliage. Re-routing was nothing new in their travels but being so close to their destination stirred impatience in the man. It finally reached the point where it became more practical for him to dismount and lead the horse rather than ducking and dodging tree limbs and branches while riding.

They were re-tracing their steps for the second time when Allsup stopped.

"What's that smell?" he said aloud, sniffing. There was no other there to respond but the horse, and he did not.

"Very unusual, isn't it?"

Again, he received no answer.

"Hm...Well, let's press on. It can't be far now."

He led the horse through thickets and bushes, many times forcing his way through.

"Do you hear that? Do you hear it? That's the ocean, Chestnut! That's called waves!"

He saw a clearing between two bushes grown together, a gap created when the breeze blew. He charged through it and almost fell down a sheer cliff that ended a considerable distance down on a beach running to the ocean. Were it not that he held Chestnut's reins, he would have fallen to his death, for it was from those very reins that he dangled beside the face of the bluff, struggling to hold on. He was in no condition to support his weight hanging freely as he was and well aware that in the units of time, he had mere seconds.

"Chestnut!" he wanted to call out but was too breathless; it sounded more of a whisper.

He tried to steady himself to limit swaying as his hands weakened and threatened to give out. He looked down and saw a jagged bottom made of eroded peaks that were soon to be his fate.

"Chestnut!" he managed to make that heard. It took a mere second or two, though to Allsup it seemed like hours before he was slowly being pulled upward.

"That's a good horse! That's a good horse!" he repeated during his ascent. Standing on hard Earth again, Allsup hugged his horse by the neck in gratitude.

Again, man and horse stood looking at their destination but were still unable to reach it.

"How do we find our way down there?" Allsup wondered. He decided to follow the embankment north with the reasoning that somewhere, there must be access to the beach.

They followed the embankment until he was offered the most beautiful sunset he could ever have imagined. The sun's reflection on the water made it questionable to one with an imagination: which was the sky, and which was the ocean?

A ravine cut them off. It ran like a knife slice from far inland before cutting deep down to the beach.

"This is a test," Allsup muttered as he looked down over the edge of the cliff; it was shaped smooth as if made by the backside of a shovel just having picked up a scoop. He looked at the gulley and saw only hopelessness. "This is a test."

He walked back and scratched the horse's ears, saying, "What do you think, Chestnut? We can follow this ravine inland and hope that it eventually narrows enough that we can cross or turn around and head south with the hopes of better results. What say you?"

The horse enjoyed the ear scratching without responding.

"All right, then, I'll decide. We camp here for tonight and tomorrow head up the ravine."

Allsup made no effort to start a fire; he wasn't hungry

and didn't want coffee. He laid his ground tarp and bedroll out perpendicular to the edge of the cliff, so his head faced west, faced the ocean.

Resting on his stomach, his chin on folded hands with the ocean wind blowing against his face, he listened to the waves and stared off at the horizon, wondering what might be on the other side. To the sound of crashing surf, he spent the night just feet from his final destination.

He was up at first light and prepared to head east following the ravine. Chestnut had not been unsaddled the past night; he stood ready, scratching at the ground, eager to go.

"All right, Chestnut, let's take a closer look at what we're dealing with."

Allsup walked to the ravine's edge and looked down over its side. He took a step closer and looked harder. He grabbed a branch hanging overhead and leaned out for a better view.

"Chestnut!" he excitedly called out. "I believe I see a trail running down the inside of this gully!"

He walked back, retrieved the reins, and led Chestnut a few feet inland along the side of the ravine.

"I believe we can make it down there." He was looking at the descending trail. "I bet it was made by goats or boars. Hogs, probably. It looks wide enough to accommodate a large animal. Now do not take offence," he said jovially to his horse. "You're a large animal because you're supposed to be large, and you are a fine specimen of your species if I do say so myself. I bet you're the smartest horse there ever was, and nobody knows it but me. Am I not a lucky man? Look there, my friend." He pointed to the ocean. "We have made it, you and me. We have crossed the entire country together to reach this point. Come on, let's go walk in the ocean."

It was rough going down the trail of the ravine. There were times it narrowed so much Allsup held his breath as

Danny Allsup

Chestnut slowly walked along it. He had to clear one area; a fallen tree blocked their path, but it had fallen so long ago that in its decomposed state, it was easy to break apart and push aside. Finally, they walked out upon sand.

Allsup turned to Chestnut and began removing his gear, the saddle, and blanket, making a pile to serve as a marker to the mouth of the ravine. He removed the bridle so that the horse was now in its complete and natural state.

"We are about to fulfill our purpose, old friend. Go ahead if you like, or wait."

Chestnut walked a few feet from the bluff, out into the sunlight, and at once galloped up the beach, kicking sand in the air.

Smiling, Allsup watched his horse race up the beach unencumbered, enjoying the spectacle of the animal running free. He removed all his clothing and stood without shame as the sun shone on him entirely with light and warmth, and a cool wind breezed around his naked body for the first time.

He walked down the beach, feeling the sand rise between his toes and laughed. The dry loose sand gave way to cool dampness that sucked at his feet, and he laughed even more. Intimidating waves broke a distance from shore, coming in tall and powerful, trying to reach his feet but failing.

He took several steps forward, assuring their success and when the cold water came rinsing his feet up to his ankles, he cried out in shock and delight. The receding water pulled at the sand beneath his feet, attempting to drag them out from under. He walked out until the water was knee-deep; he could feel the force of the waves pulling and pushing, breaking behind him as the water rose to his waist and fell.

Chestnut waded up beside him, the water lapping against his belly.

"Well, Chestnut, we did it. It's been quite an adventure, but we made it."

D. Dean Carroll

Allsup draped an arm across the horse's back, and they stood in the Pacific Ocean, man and horse together, looking at the horizon.

"What now?"

* * *

Made in the USA
Coppell, TX
28 March 2024